*Dearest Cynthia ♡*
*May your heart be filled with LOVE! xx*

# Roses

# in

# Winter

By

# Leslie D. Stuart

*Best Wishes Always ♡*

**World Castle Publishing**
http://www.worldcastlepublishing.com

*Leslie D. Stuart*

**World Castle Publishing**
Pensacola, Florida

Copyright © Leslie D. Stuart 2011
ISBN: 9781937593568
First Edition World Castle Publishing October 7, 2011
http://www.worldcastlepublishing.com

**Licensing Notes**

Cover Artist: Karen Fuller
Editor: Beth Price

# *Dedication*

**Family is forever, and forever isn't long enough for how much I love you.**

Thank you Mom and Dad. You taught me to say, "I Think I Can." Those words hold infinite power.

I'm grateful for my brother and sisters who will walk through life with me; especially Leah, who I see the most. You are a bright, happy, walking Thesaurus with just the right word on the tip of your tongue. You always know how to make me smile.

I am blessed to have Matthew, Tiffany, and now beautiful baby Scarlett to love. Family isn't just the ones you are born with, family is also the people you choose with your heart. I choose you.

I am proud of my son, Kyle. You listened, you encouraged, you inspired. You are valiant and strong. I'm honored to be your Mom.

But this book belongs to my loving, kind, husband, Matt. You are my world. You are my rock. Wherever I am, I want you to be right there too! We've made a thousand happy memories together. I look forward to a million more. You are my best friend and Forever really isn't long enough for how much I love you!!!

*Leslie D. Stuart*

# Chapter One

***Forever isn't long enough for how much I love you.***
*-- Ryan Patrick Rosemont-Graystone*

While driving down leaf cluttered country roads in upstate New York on a glorious coppery-gold September afternoon, her heart felt as light as angel kisses. It was a perfect day. For most, it might seem like an ordinary Saturday of riding horses in the meadow, but for no particular reason at all, today felt amazingly special.

Every moment left beautiful music playing inside her soul.

Glancing at her companion in the passenger seat, Arianna smiled. Earlier this morning at the stables, his sleepy face beamed with excitement. Warm breath made white puffs in the crisp autumn air while he brushed his trustworthy brown mare, Brandi. He loved that horse. He jabbered away to Brandi, telling her all about his busy week of music studies, explaining every song he had learned, as if the mare somehow understood the difficulties six-year-old fingers had with mastering the violin.

The sweet old girl nickered in sympathy.

Small hands stroked her velvety face.

Rewarding her gentle kindness, he offered Brandi crisp apple slices. She gratefully nuzzled the crunchy pieces from his outstretched palm, being careful not to nip tender fingers with big teeth.

They rode beneath tall crimson oaks and golden maples in the meadow. His auburn hair gleamed in the morning sun. She watched him sit tall in the saddle, noticing how his hair perfectly matched the red autumn leaves.

Ryan was the center of her world.

He was her music, her reason, her light.

So much like his father.

Yes, today was yet another priceless memory she would add to the collection of seemingly ordinary days she faithfully recorded for seven exhilarating years. His entire life, plus pregnancy. Why did she film Ryan's life? Because someday, to someone she dearly loved, witnessing this ordinary autumn day might feel extraordinarily special.

Ahh, there it was on the radio...her song.

The one she devoted her whole heart into writing.

"I'm turning it up." Ryan announced with a cherubic grin. Pride lit his sweet boyish face as those first romantic piano notes softly purred.

Their Mercedes became a concert hall.

Violins wistfully hummed of unspoken wishes. The piano sang of heartache and deep longing. Love was lost, the harp achingly implied.

Could it live again?

The notes were tender, like a woman standing alone in the moonlight, whispering her hearts desires to the stars.

Answering the woman's poignant question, synthesized electric guitars groaned to life. As if awakened from a deep sleep, they strummed an audibly male sounding timbre. The deeper sounds brought sensations of hope from the piano. Trilling with expectation, the womanly notes laughed with glee.

He heard her whisper in the dark!

Violins questioned. Can love live again? Drums struck a demanding tempo, transforming her polite plea into a purposeful emotional summons. *Please,* the notes distinctly begged, *open your heart to me. Let love live again.* The song climaxed into the powerful orchestrated chorus. The entire contemporary symphony joined in, echoing the piano's sweet warbling cadence with a magnificent surge of musical energy.

"Momma, do you think maybe," Ryan wistfully asked and glanced out his window as if the impending question held incredible importance to the six-year-old boy, "maybe, somehow...right now, he might be listening to 'Second Chances' too?"

"Anything is possible."

"I hope he is. It would almost be like we are together."

"In our hearts," she sagely replied, "he's with us every day."

Oh how she loved his radiant innocent smile!

Happy now, he passionately belted out the lyrics of "Second Chances, the wildly popular love song she recently composed. Recorded by a pop star diva with the voice of an angel, it topped the music charts. The woman's velvet soprano and thundering instruments blared inside her Mercedes. It made the small space seem like a grand music hall.

But another angelic voice sang every memorized word.

One far more innocent and pure.

As Ryan sang, her heart felt warm and tight. *This is better than Carnegie or Vienna... better than London Symphony Hall filled to the rafters with high society listening to me play.* How many other New Yorkers tuned into this radio station were hearing her special song too? Thousands? She smiled from the tips of her toes. Listening and driving, she basked in the absolute perfection of her musically magnificent life.

Arianna Hartwell never dreamed hell waited around the next curve. A single gasp of screeching panic was all it took. She made a split-second selfless decision that should have deflected hell's devastation, leaving her merely wide-eyed and gasping at the brush with danger.

It should have worked.

*Spare the innocent*, she thought, yanking hard on the wheel.

But hell kept coming. The evil beast was merciless.

Hell would not stop.

Next came an atrocious cruel eternity of helpless tumbling. Over and over, in agonizing mechanical slow motion. Seconds stretched on forever, distorted by the magnified nightmare horror of the churning mind.

Yet in those terrifying heartbeats, her beautiful song still warbled.

*"Second Chances…You were God's hand upon my heart…Forever Love deserves Second Chances…I was born to love only you…All my Life…"*

Almost mockingly sweet, the song sadistically competed against the brutal sounds of total destruction. The journey into Hell ended with a death-clutch of twisted metal wrapped so tight and viciously painful, it stole everything good.

Then she breathed, proving she survived.

But someone else was wheezing.

She knew in a heartbeat what it meant.

Hell had won.

Then amid men yelling and sirens blaring, her entire existence narrowed down into two precious minutes.

Two minutes. Unchangeable, yet changed everything.

She expected forever. At least seventy or eighty years.

She was given only two minutes.

In the aftermath of Hell's vengeful assault, after her anguished screams and hysterical cries of denial became desperate inconsolable whimpers, there came a silence to the world. Deafening silence. The dark curtain erased every note of music inside her soul.

Perfection was gone.

Hell had stolen everything good.

Now here she was on a frigid big-sky Montana morning in late October with her violet-blue eyes stinging again. Eyes that stung every god-forsaken day since that terrible instant perfection died.

Fifty-eight agonizing days.

She couldn't remember September. Or most of October. Yesterday she stared at the calendar, feeling utterly lost.

Today was October thirty-first. Halloween.

Ryan planned to be a pirate.

7

Tears silently fell. Arianna forlornly watched fat winter snowflakes stick to the windshield of her jeep as she drove through icy Harmony Hills, Montana.

Home.

The last place on earth she should be.

She didn't stop. Eyes focused upon the frosty highway, she drove straight through the familiar quaint tourist town nestled along a protective northern corridor on the outskirts of Glacier National Park.

Arianna's destiny was much higher in the cold wilderness and far more hostile. Mechanically, she drove. Silently. The only sounds were tires upon the road and the low mechanical rumble of the jeep engine.

No radio. Music belonged to another life, to another woman.

Twenty-three silent miles later, Arianna left the main highway. Turning north, the road the jeep now bounced over what used to be nicely paved and smooth. As she expected, it had become a neglected obstacle course of rutted potholes.

No one traveled this road. The mountain owned it now.

Twenty miles of slow bumpy climbing.

Six, she counted. Then five. Now only four miles remained.

High above Harmony Hills, the mountain reigned supreme here. In June or July, the lofty heights of Mt. Stimson and St. Nicholas that towered like angry untamable ice-gods would have been semi-hospitable, civil at least.

October? No way.

Those glacier-topped pinnacles soared above the valley, piercing the heavens in bitter white-blue contempt of fragile humanity, practically shouting for mankind to freeze in hell.

Winter was coming fast. The Montana wilderness gleefully welcomed the impending six months of deep freeze. Unforgiving, the mountains were so tall and mean the thick forests only dared blanket the lower half of their jagged peaks. Here, winter ended all life except for the extraordinarily strong. For trees and plants, bitter cold chilled the outer layer, but in springtime, life always sprang anew from the resilient core.

Only the valiant prevailed.

Life on the mountain was hard.

But Arianna's life ended here. Today.

No, life ended in two horrific minutes.

If only she could go back…change the past, never leave Montana…no, she knew that was a lie. She would have lived it exactly the same way, all over again.

All her life her heart overflowed with fabulously harmonious music. Angel songs, she called them, music given straight from heaven. She didn't write them. Nothing that pure and perfect could possibly be manmade! God himself whispered them to her. The inspiration came like shards of light, piercing her mind, filling her heart to overflowing until music poured from her fingertips.

But that sacred music wasn't meant for her heart alone.

Angel Songs were gifts for the entire world to embrace.

She was simply a tool.

Fulfilling her destiny, she left Montana at eighteen. According to His Great Plan, she played that glorious contemporary music and gave it to the world.

God blessed her.

But two minutes destroyed everything.

Two minutes: a theoretically lifetime in Einstein inspired time-is-irrelative ticking seconds. Now those minuscule instances were the only thing a desperate woman pathetically clung to, two minutes that still ticked second by second in her broken mind. Over and again the minutes replayed, leaving her wishing to change a single point in time that she just couldn't touch and aching with all her shattered existence for just one second more.

Two minutes, that was all she had to save him.

She couldn't.

She tried.

Ryan's innocent young life was far more valuable than her own. Seeing danger, she yanked the car sideways, making her door take the impact. But the big truck was screeching too! A professional moving van overloaded with furniture, heavy with someone's entire earthly possessions, it had been struggling for control long before her silver Mercedes appeared. Black tire smoke filled the air. Eyes wide in horror, the driver fought the enormous metal beast, begging it to stop, cursing. But the truck had a destructive will of its own.

It crushed into her.

The Mercedes careened wildly, jerking her body in nineteen different directions all at once. Bones screamed.

Or maybe that horrific noise was just her own terrified voice.

Then the rolling began.

Once, twice, three times…maybe another? She honestly couldn't remember. But she would never forget those two precious minutes.

Selflessness didn't save.

Now perfection was gone.

"I'm here."

Her own whispered announcement was jolting. Dark memories had crept without warning, threatening to steal her sanity.

She blinked again.

It was hard to tug her broken soul away from those final two minutes.

Back to the present.

The memories were so powerful. "I'm here." She repeated, feeling lost and hazy-gray inside. Turning off the jeep engine, both hands still tightly gripped the steering wheel.

She wasn't quite sure what else to do.

"Get out," she finally decided. "Get out of the jeep." Talking spurred her body into action. "Go inside."

Tumbling gamely out of the used blue Jeep Cherokee she hastily purchased this morning after her cross-country red eye flight landed in Kalispell, she clung to the open door with clenched fists and gingerly tested her left leg.

It was throbbing and feverishly hot.

Putting weight on it, she thought it might hold. Grimacing, she took that first excruciating step and wanted to scream. Instead, she stubbornly grunted. Fire shot through every mangled nerve as she tried not to fall flat on her face.

What had that damn doctor said? She hated him!

Cold, the proud surgeon touted as being a miracle worker heartlessly claimed she'd never walk again. He performed miracle surgeries anyway, taking his fat fee, loudly announcing her broken body was a complete waste of his precious time.

Weeks of unbearable pain had blurred into sad nothingness, but she clearly recalled the pious look on his self-righteous face the day she stood on both feet and defiantly proved him wrong. A triumphant moment. But taking that first shuffling step, she cried.

What had Dr. Evil said?

Oh…the pain meant she was still alive.

Yippee. What good was that when the one pure perfect thing God gave her was gone? Now living was hell.

She didn't want to play anymore.

She'd fix it. She still had that power.

The game ended today.

It was freezing cold outside the warm Jeep. Snow was sticking to the ground. Her breath made white puffs. Oddly, the icy air felt good. Throughout the fevered night of traveling her not-quite-healed body alternated between stifling hot sweats and chills so bone-deep it made her teeth chatter.

She was running a fever. A high one.

Her brain simmered. Thinking made her head wobble on its axis like a goofy bobble head doll. Tipping her face back to view ominous white clouds, frosty snowflakes landed on baking cheeks. They seemed to hiss and instantly melt.

It felt good. *So good.*

Frigid mountain air sliced through her thin pink tee shirt.

*Come on Winter, do your worst.*

It was trying. Droplets of sweat on her brow froze into tiny beads of ice. It was freezing here, so high on the mountain. She'd forgotten Montana's frigid bite. Her jeans and boots offered little protection from winter's icy hand permeating the air.

Almost mechanically, mostly from habit, Arianna reached inside the jeep and shrugged into her ridiculously heavy white parka.

Her fever might bake her brain, but she wasn't quite ready to become a frozen snowman…err, woman.

With long brown hair.

Did snowwomen have hair? Mops maybe. Definitely nothing like the thick sable sheet that fell clear to her hips, hair that never in her life was touched by scissors. No self-respecting snowwoman would have hair like that. It would freeze into slick chocolate icicles.

Her thoughts were tangled.

She knew it. But broken was broken.

*Good Lord, why am I here? Mom and Dad died years ago. I didn't come back then. Why am I standing here now?*

Staring up at the ancestral mountain chalet that in another lifetime was a thriving vacation resort bustling with visitors, she shuddered.

Graystone Heights Heritage Estates; Equestrian Stables and Wilderness Ski Resort. What a mouthful. Even its name felt grand and adventurous.

Quiet now. Empty.

Eighteen spacious bedroom suites. Year-round the sprawling mansion was booked months in advance. Graystone Heights was a celebratory place with a family feel. You arrived as a stranger, but left with twenty new friends. Adventure filled days of hiking, skiing, and riding horses, ended with dinner and wine in the common dining room where everyone enjoyed delicious family style meals and her parents entertained guests like lifelong friends.

People came to play hard, day and night.

Her parents played the hardest. Life was an endless party.

In her broken mind Arianna didn't see October snow falling, she clearly saw Yesterday. Ghostly memories of people long gone drank hot cocoa and gourmet coffee as they visited on the traditional wrap-around oak veranda and generous second story balconies. Ski equipment littered odd nooks and corners. Sleds created a haphazard jumble beside the front steps. Laughing and merrily visiting, they tipped their steaming mugs at her in salute.

Those were the winter people.

She blinked. The scene shifted.

Warm sun gleamed upon noisy families happily lounging upon those same oak porches. The grass was green. The air smelled new; like sunlit flowers and wild mountain pines. Today they were eating fresh baked cookies and sipping iced tea.

The summer people waved and smiled.

She blinked again.

Everyone disappeared.

*Dang. I'm home.*

Abandoned. Yesterday was gone. All that remained of Graystone Heights was a giant empty place haunted by memories.

Feeling disoriented and weepy, she looked at the stables. That big red building was a magical place filled to the rafters with summer families, laughing and smiling hugely. Graystone made dreams come true. Along with tame stable ponies for beginners to ride, her father raised fabulous fairytale Spanish Andalusian Purebreds. Horses so beautiful, Prince Charming himself would have ridden. Winter or summer, rich people flocked to this sturdy sanctuary nestled in wild Montana, seeking a piece of perfection to carry inside their hearts. Graystone Heights was God's untamed haven.

Now, it only held ghosts.

Even God abandoned Graystone.

Shouldering a backpack filled with hastily packed clothes, she locked the Jeep and stuffed the keys inside her jacket pocket.

Okay. That felt like progress.

Next step, going inside.

But sighing, she mindlessly surveyed the thick rock walls bordering the front yard. Ten feet tall, they stretched off into the forest as the last barrier between mountain and man. Fences that should have been tumbling down, ravaged by years of neglect and brutal winter snowdrifts -- weren't.

Weird.

Further up, violet-blue eyes that cried until they remained ugly bloodshot pink were drawn toward the giant attic. A third floor, really. The attic was a grand open space at the top of the house with majestic peaked ceilings, a welcoming granite fireplace, comfortable rose-print furniture, and a cheery pink bathroom with a giant roman bathtub.

The tub had gold legs shaped like eagle talons. She loved that tub.

*My attic. It will be dusty, cold, and empty.*

*A place for ghosts.*

*Perfect. I'll fit right in.*

Encompassing everything beneath it, the attic crowned the three-story mansion. Her bedroom, her space; and hers alone. Guests never ventured there. Big picture windows had become sprinkled with white flecks of winter snow...windows she expected to be hazy with dirt and neglect.

Clean polished glass defiantly glistened.

How odd.

A strange thought sparked. It didn't stick.

They rarely did anymore.

She left the hospital far too soon. Her bruised brain had bounced around inside her skull, becoming useless mush, but hating the hospital, nurses, and doctors, she stubbornly checked herself out. For several days afterward, she rambled aimlessly around a luxurious sprawling Central Park penthouse that felt like a mournful mausoleum, having delirious conversations with no one at all.

It should have disturbed her.

It didn't. Arianna remembered little from the past eight weeks.

Or how she even got here.

Snow layered the estate's black slate roof. *Graystone? Why am I here?* She felt pathetically lost. Her confused breath made frantic white puffs. She tried to recall what brought her to frigid Montana. All her mind could manage was a jumbled slideshow of odd moments.

White roses in a gold vase.

A heart monitor incessantly beeping. Make it stop!

Boxes stacked in silent empty rooms that once had witnessed wonderful moments of great love and warm laughter.

Staring at a stranger in the bathroom mirror, she'd seen a half-dead woman with a long sheet of lifeless coffee-brown hair whose haggard face had become dangerously pale and thin. Familiar blue eyes circled with pallid purple hollows.

It didn't matter. Despite having packed clothes inside a backpack that once belonged to the world's most enthusiastic six-year-old, this was a one-way trip.

Soon she would join her son.

"Go inside," she whispered.

Feet reluctantly moved.

She couldn't quite remember actually choosing to experience this piercing moment in Montana. The desperate days since Ryan's death had finally boiled down to this pivotal instant with her trembling hand pushing open one side of impressively towering wrought-iron gates. An ostentatious entrance for wild Montana: those grandiose gates were designed to inspire respect.

Only the strongest of hearts dared enter here.

Regal and imposing, those scrolling black arches seemed appropriately ominous right now. This was all she had left. A run-down mountain resort with empty stables on 400 acres of treacherous mountain ravines people once loved to ski.

And a limp.

That would probably fade. Eventually.

Here in Montana, there would be no more bright lights or pretty music. At eighteen, she left for New York with big dreams, used her Julliard tuition money to host one fabulous attempt at stardom, terrified of the consequences if it didn't work. That show brought unbelievable fame, as if the world's musical elite had anticipated her arrival. Along with glorious accolades for her original contemporary compositions came her first invitation to play the glistening black grand piano at Carnegie Hall. She boldly bought a fashionable red evening gown, pulled thick brown tresses into a sophisticated cascade befitting a musical diva, flexed her magical fingers, and vowed she'd never see Montana again.

She hadn't...until today.

But wild Montana was her beginning.

Now it would be the end.

These timeless mountains called her name.

The majestic wrought-iron gate squeaked noisily as she pushed against it, loudly proclaiming her arrival.

To whom? The frosty skies? Some grumpy old bear wandering the woods? Moving painfully slow through the courtyard, frozen grass-blades crunched beneath polished turquoise-blue boots that gleamed of money. Watching her own slow gimpy trek toward Graystone's oak doors, praying she didn't fall, the overpriced ladies western boots on her small feet seemed deeply offended she dared expose that precious alligator skin to the snow.

Too flippin' bad.

Life is hard, Gator.

Feeling breathlessly dizzy and ridiculously weepy again, she stopped walking. Panting made her side ache. Well, it always ached, but panting made it worse. Bigger snowflakes were falling. Fat popcorn sized puffs tumbled from the heavy white-gray sky. Looking skyward, the tumbling ice crystals were beautiful but dangerous.

Snow stuck to wet lashes, cooling her hot face.

The storm was coming hard and fast. This was definitely a blizzard. First one of winter. Soon the ground would be a blanket of white.

*Good. Come get me, Old Man Winter.*

Tempted to sit down right here in the front yard and let the bitter cold finish her off, Arianna wiped wet eyes with clenched fists.

She should at least go inside.

Inside, she had a plan: curl up in a dark corner, close her eyes forever and quietly fade away. Besides, dying sprawled out in Graystone's front yard buried in snowdrifts seemed like an unfinished mission. No, the goal was in sight. She should finish this journey and take her last breath with a little dignity.

Not that anyone would care or notice.

She had no one. Not even parents; God embraced their partying souls years ago. No love lost there. Her parents valued celebrations and laughing with strangers, not family. Having a daughter was an inconvenience.

Thus, her attic.

No real friends either. Her best friend was a smiling little boy with twinkling violet-blue eyes and coppery auburn hair.

But now her best friend was gone.

God embraced him too.

She was completely alone in the world.

But...who kept Graystone's front veranda free of autumn leaves? And who mowed the football-field sized front courtyard and lawn? Green blades peeking through white snow looked evenly cut, perfectly groomed. Glancing around at details she completely missed, she saw the boxwood hedges were neatly trimmed.

This was all wrong!

She had stood here contemplating snowy death for ten dreary minutes, but that information just now soaked into her battered brain.

And...ooh! Who nursed and nurtured the red Don Juan roses framing the front steps? Once just tender shrubs, the proud bushes climbed two stories high on a sturdy white trellis. It was stunning.

How did she miss that important fact?

Was her mind hopelessly mangled?

Probably.

Maybe it was an illusion.

Yeah, she decided with a sigh, just another hallucination. Staring in amazement, those gorgeous red roses were exactly how she envisioned they would look when she planted them that final summer. The summer she left Montana. The dozen or so damask smelling autumn blooms would become beautiful ice-rubies by morning.

Well, if hallucinations could freeze, that is.

The old-fashioned social veranda spanning the entire front of Graystone boasted a fresh coat of waterproof stain. Some of the weathered oak planking looked new, gleaming burnish-red against the older wood.

Her mind wasn't working right.

Somehow, all those things meant something.

She couldn't imagine what.

Trudging up the oak front steps, hearing her boots thump on the wood, nostalgia washed over her. *Home.* Rubbing her hand down the worn-slick banister framing those fateful last ten steps, she imagined Ryan walking up these steps too.

Mesmerized with Montana, he would have gasped and gaped at the great towering pines and falling snow. He would have been utterly awestruck by the jagged mountainous glacial peaks soaring up behind the stables.

Ryan would have loved Graystone.

She stifled a heartbroken sob.

"Wuuahh…nnoo…why him?" The funny bungled sound echoed off the empty porch and broke the winter silence.

The sad noise made her feel unbearably alone. Alone on a journey that would end her meager half-life existence and bring relief to the aching heart of Arianna Hartwell.

Oh. But…wait!

At the front door, her hand nervously palmed the cold steel knob.

She wasn't Arianna anymore.

Not here! Not in Montana!

Certainly not at Graystone Heights!

Panic stuck, whipping colder than an arctic blizzard.

*Not Arianna…*

*Oh dang…*

Here on the wide veranda where she ran barefoot as a child, giggling in innocence and joy with long brown hair streamed down her back like a wild heathen; here, at this critical moment with snow falling faster and her breath making frozen white puffs, she became Savannah Graystone again.

*Savannah.*

It felt as cold as the metal doorknob beneath her chilled hand. Plain. Hard. Like simple unprocessed steel.

*Graystone.*

A loveless family legacy she traveled half the world to escape. A name she buried beneath a brilliant facade of worldly glamour and musical prestige. As Arianna Hartwell, she ruled as queen. Her dazzling melodies echoed inside the worlds most exalted performance cathedrals. Her music sending poetic shivers up the most prestigious analytical spines.

Like notes of polished diamonds, they said.

Emotional perfection.

That was the music of Arianna Hartwell.

Her original compositions were zealously purchased and re-produced by talented musicians around the world; an instant guarantee of fame.

But nothing compared to hearing the composer play her own music. Her hands wove sounds on the piano no one else could duplicate. Passionate eternal sounds, transcending ordinary notes; like two hearts flawlessly beating as one upon their turbulent journey through life.

Her right and her left.

The man's deep baritone and the woman's rich soprano.

Asking and answering, talking in the music of love.

"Geezuz, Zeus…you're a worthless old mutt!"

Confronting those stomping feet and deep male voice, Savannah whirled around. She found herself pinned against the solid oak door by a monster!

Oh, my god!

She was black furry face to vulnerable human belly with Death!

And it came in the form of fierce dripping dog jowls!

That enormous Great Dane was a colossal beast from childhood nightmares! The sleek black coat was dappled with fat white snowflakes. The dog's wide bear-like mouth and flesh shredding teeth were an inch away from delivering an extremely painful death.

This wasn't the death she planned!

Savannah couldn't breathe. Or move. The plan was to peacefully fade away; not be ripped to shreds by Satan's servant!

The giant ebony beast calmly sniffed her chest. Hoisting his nose a tad higher, the gentle brown eyes peering up at her were like wise old oaks.

"Oh!" She gratefully exclaimed. "A friend!"

Savannah swore Zeus actually smiled. "Dang. You're a big guy." She rubbed his massive head. The fur was silky smooth. His powerful body felt impressively Herculean beneath her hand. A black tail as thick as her arm satisfactorily wagged.

"Pathetic guard dog! You'd make a better horse." The man sarcastically groaned, stomping up the front steps a bit more forcefully than necessary. "Meet Zeus. A sucker for flowery perfume."

Glancing at his master, then back at her again, Zeus' welcoming black tail happily wagged, in complete defiance to the surly man.

"Traitor!"

Savannah knew that angry voice, although the stern face of its owner remained hidden behind a strategically placed armload of freshly chopped firewood. Even his familiar dusky-bronze head remained covered by the hood of a goldenrod colored ski jacket.

He had been watching her. Obviously.

Snow dusted his thick yellow coat.

Plus, Savannah realized as her mushy-oatmeal brain sparked into action a bit too late; in the quiet mountains her noisy jeep rumbling up that rough road would have been heard from miles away.

But he waited.

And watched.

It felt like an ambush. If Riley Rosemont wanted, he could have sliced her throat without a single gasp.

If he knew her truth, he probably would.

"Well hell, Savage. Born yesterday?" Riley curtly snapped. "Open the damn door before we all freeze."

"Oh. Right. Sorry."

It was unlocked, of course. No one locked up in the wilderness. Not like New York, or London, or anywhere plush and extravagant Arianna Hartwell would call home. Pushing the oak doorway to Graystone open wide, she stepped aside. Riley's hulking figure rudely tromped past. Grumbling not entirely to himself and definitely not kindly, he thumped boot-clad feet all the way to the massive granite fireplace in the living room.

Savannah quietly closed the door behind her.

Riley made enough noise for both of them.

Eyes widened. It was warm inside. And clean!

Oh! Graystone wasn't abandoned! Someone lived here! Nostalgia punched like a fist. Fighting an overwhelming urge to bawl like a baby, Savannah clenched stinging eyes.

*It isn't real! It's just another cruel hallucination!*

Unfortunately, with her eyes closed other senses kicked in, bringing amazingly familiar fragrances. Coffee was brewed recently. She smelled fresh pine burning on the fire. It crackled. A hint of leather mingled with the faint musky animal scent of a dog nearby.

*It isn't real.*

She'd been seeing delirium induced images for days. She was just imagining Riley stomping around and the giant dog…who stood right beside her. Oops! Her aching left hip leaned heavily against Zeus. Reluctantly, she opened her eyes and peeked at him. Yes. Real. Gentle brown eyes looked worried.

Good dog, good heart.

Bless him. Zeus was keeping her from falling down.

*My new friend.*

The simple compassionate act was so touching Savannah wanted to throw her arms around the massive Great Dane and cry.

Graystone wasn't dusty, cold, and deserted at all!

The estate was nicely furnished and comfortably inviting. The grand common room was bigger than she remembered. Yet smaller somehow with that burly discourteous man stomping around shaking snow off his back, growling under his breath about god-only-knows what horrific offenses she had committed.

"Let me help." Dropping her backpack of clothes, Savannah helped unload ax-quartered oak firewood that still concealed a man she hadn't seen in six years, eight months…and two precious minutes.

Angrily tipping his head back, the yellow hood fell.

Bronze-red hair appeared.

If Savannah weren't so emotionally dead inside, her heart would have thumped a rapid ecstatic staccato.

Nothing. Her heart barely sloshed in recognition.

More wood was unloaded. Familiar green-gold eyes widened upon seeing her, but only for an instant. Unceremoniously, Riley dumped the remaining logs into a heap beside the fireplace. Hands fisted at his sides, he glared fiercely at her.

Lovely. Nice to see he hadn't forgiven her.

Or forgotten.

"Why the hell are you here, Savage?!"

Snarling her once superbly pleasing pet-name as though it were abhorrently sinful, he crossly brushed errant wood chips off his snow dampened coat. Quickly shedding it, Riley changed his mind about conversation, tossed the bright yellow jacket across a plush burgundy sofa she'd never seen before and noisily tramped into the kitchen, not waiting for her answer.

All Savannah could do was watch him stomp away.

*Nice buns, Mountain Man…yum.* She suddenly felt ridiculously hollow inside, utterly famished, hungry beyond needing food.

*Wouldn't you make a tasty treat?*

Tall enough he made her willowy five-foot-six body seem fragile, stress-ravaged, and a little too lean; his brawny capable shoulders tapered into nicely trim hips and warrior strong legs.

Riley Phillip Rosemont.

He looked good. Real good. Healthy. Robust. Indestructible. When she was seventeen that gorgeous man promised to marry her. Childish wishes that never came true. Oh how Savannah wished they had!

She was losing it.

*It's just Riley, for heaven's sake!*

*Okay, so he's bigger than I remembered. Tougher. Yummier.*
*Oh good grief! Stop drooling!*

Helplessly submerged in Riley's astoundingly male presence, it took Savannah several seconds to think straight. Maybe it was jet lag, or sheer déjà vu. Oh how life turned in cruel circles! They had run this course before.

The fussing. The stomping.

The inevitable yelling.

She could follow Riley and attempt to make things right…or she could simply slide out that front door and disappear again. *No. Stop!* Halting her instinctive moving feet, Savannah realized she was already halfway there. Her hand hung just over the doorknob.

No. She did that to Riley once before.

Twice wasn't an option.

*Remember who you are. He sees Savannah Graystone. You became Arianna Hartwell, world famous contemporary composer and award winning concert pianist. You traveled the world. You became a star.*

Shoulders squared, Savannah shed her fluffy white parka and marched…well, gimped rather pathetically actually, into the kitchen. She stopped cold. He had remodeled the kitchen. Industrial utilitarian stainless steel pantries and restaurant style worktables were gone. He made it cozy. Personal. Welcoming.

He even built a cozy breakfast nook table in one corner.

Miles of creamy granite countertops now iced gleaming oak cabinets the same hearty color as Riley's bronze-red hair.

Savannah loved that dusky fire-touched color.

"No, Riley." She curtly demanded. "Graystone should be empty. Deserted. Why are YOU here?"

Pouring hot coffee, he snickered. "I live here."

He turned to face her; he looked dangerously handsome in his comfortable denim shirt. White thermals peaked from beneath the half-buttoned neck. Both shirts tucked into faded Levis. Scuffed work boots. Practical boots, with thick grooved soles that gripped the icy ground without sliding, not fancy colored leather like her pampered turquoise gems.

Useful. Traditional.

Riley was exactly how she remembered.

Wholesome. One with the earth. Honorable, like God's hand.

"Here to claim your generous Graystone inheritance, Savage?" He cruelly barked. "Well, you've wasted your time. There isn't one. Your heartbroken Daddy drank himself into the ground after your wayward Momma purposely broke her own neck skiing down slopes no sane person should."

Emotionally broadsided, she wobbled. "What? Suicide?" Fists gripped the creamy granite countertop.

One auburn brow sardonically arched. "You didn't know? Of course not. You disappeared. Until today. You didn't even bother sending flowers to their funerals. Vivian didn't fall. She quit!"

"My mother? On purpose? Why?"

"Her secret affairs were finally common knowledge. The latest fool she cheated with expected her to leave your stubborn old man. But folks like us don't divorce," Riley heartlessly growled, "Marriage is 'til death do us part.'" He hatefully added as if marriage to Savannah would have been his own death sentence.

"She finally got caught?"

"Yep. You and I knew Vivian's secrets for years, but John refused to see it until he caught her bare-assed and dirty-handed. Beat that man to a bloody pulp. Took a pop at Vivian too. Landed himself in jail for a while. It was hard for a small Christian town to swallow that much scandal. Lying, cheating, violence, and then suicide on the slopes. A real messy ordeal. Graystone Heights was Harmony Hills' biggest employer, but within months everyone made excuses and quit. Except me, of course. Without people to run the ski slopes, kitchen, and stables, Big John lost everything in one season," her former lover mercilessly declared. "No paying guests, no Graystone."

This was worse than she envisioned! Her father loved Graystone! Dearer to his heart than anything or anyone, Big John loved his beautiful horses and the legacy of Blackfoot Indian horsemen he represented. Proud, strong as granite, and just as unforgiving; he died a broken man.

Seeing Savannah tremble, the fierce warrior across the kitchen stood a bit taller, almost as if Riley took pleasure in seeing her pain.

"Now you know," he bitterly continued. "Vivian slid headfirst through Devil's Gateway and your iron-willed daddy started talking to ghosts and lost his soul in a bottomless bottle of whiskey. He closed Graystone and never sobered up. John lost everything. Pride. His wife. His reputation. The man was inconsolable. The daughter he groomed as heiress to five generations of heritage land, denied having a family. John didn't have a son, but he had a stable full of horses still needing a master. So he left the whole damn legacy to me."

"You?!" Her stunned squawk made Riley grin. "Legally?"

"Legally. From foundation to the rafters, mountaintop to valley. I own Graystone Heights. I was nearly as shocked as you look."

Savannah unceremoniously closed her gaping mouth.

"Pretty ironic, the judgmental Blackfoot warrior who spent years chasing me out of here, swearing I'd never marry his only daughter and sully his illustrious Native American Graystone birthright with ordinary white man Rosemont blood, was absolutely right. We didn't get married." He flatly stated. "But John gave me all that precious land anyway."

"My. God."

Riley meanly tipped his coffee mug in mock salute. "Hell of a good time you've missed, Savannah." He took a lingering sip. Hazel-green eyes glared at her over the rim. "Now go home."

"Oh...Riley," she sadly whimpered, "I... can't."

All at once, the emotional weight of a thousand snow-capped mountains tumbled down upon her in an icy avalanche of total defeat. Nothing prepared her for hearing the sordid details of her parents final descent into madness from the lips of the one man she spent her whole life loving.

Arianna-Savannah- whoever the hell she was...was falling. Down?! *My legs are gone.* She blinked mindlessly at Riley.

Thoughts became pathetic gray puffs.

The world turned murky and cold as every ounce of steely determination disintegrated; driven downward by love she left behind, love she lost along the way, and reality she just couldn't face anymore.

Riley watched as a valiant woman's broken soul crumbled into a thousand tiny pieces. He saw violet eyes glisten. For an instant, he swore he saw broken shards of light inside her violet-blue eyes.

She blinked. It was only ordinary tears.

But her eyes seemed empty now, her spirit lifeless, destroyed by lies of perfection and illusions of happiness she had created in order to survive.

Illusions utterly destroyed in...two precious minutes.

Nothing.

*Oh, yes. Please, God. Take me too...*

Darkness consumed her.

21

# Chapter Two

"When was the last time you ate? Damn Savage, you're thin as a starved deer!" Raging male fury pierced the soothing balm of gray nothingness Savannah slid into, hoping never to return. However, fate was cruel. Of course, she would still hear Riley's boiling anger along with the sensation that strong arms took her accursedly weakened body...somewhere.

Upstairs. One flight, he briskly trotted. Two.

*He's carrying me?*

Savannah couldn't open her eyes. It only would have produced tears. "I ate," she murmured, "yesterday. I think."

"Now you're a starving model too? I thought you were happy being the modern-day female Mozart?"

How did he know that?

Before her lips could form the question, she felt his hip shove open a door; a door he rushed through a thousand times as a child, bringing his generous smile and gifts of woodland treasures. Today it brought an onslaught of feminine smells: powdery fresh linen, heady pine walls, but also...cinnamon. The pinecones she always soaked in cinnamon essential oil.

Her eyes flew open. "My room!"

Riley flinched and griped her tighter, but took a dozen long strides across the oversized bedroom and unceremoniously deposited Savannah upon the downy soft queen-sized bed that still somehow smelled of...love.

Impossible.

Her imagination was running rampant.

Landing none too lightly, she yelped. "EEOwww!" Squinting tears, she curled up against the pillows. "That hurt."

"Too bad! Why are you here, Savannah?" Riley roared as he leaned down over her, hands braced against the headboard. "What the hell are you doing in Montana?"

"Well, I..." Staring up at his angry but charismatically handsome face, just inches away, she wasn't quite sure why she came to Graystone.

23

Gee, even furious he was lip-smacking gorgeous.

"You look good, Riley."

Hazel eyes narrowed. He hatefully growled.

"Real good."

Another feral threat rumbled inside his broad chest.

"Miss me?"

"No! Miss me?"

"Well...I didn't think you'd..."

"Exactly! You didn't think! How dare you come back here!" Whack! His hand smacked the headboard, making her jump. "In a snowstorm! Have you lost your mind?"

"Uh...maybe?"

Shoving away from her, Riley angrily stalked across the room sounding every bit as threatening as a wild grizzly bear just immerged from winter. "How dare you come back here! My god, there you were standing innocently on my doorstep, looking like a lost black sheep! How dare you!" Long arms waved in exasperation. "Six and a half years you've been gone! And now you expect me to what?!" As he whirled to glare at her, an odd noise of fury and confusion gathered inside his throat. "Do what? Welcome you home?"

Watching Riley rave her fever-seared mind envisioned that not-so-innocent prodigal black sheep. It came home surrounded by cold white snow seeking merciful release from heartache. Instead the lamb found a monstrous angry beast protecting his cave.

The abominable snowman.

With gold-green eyes.

And auburn hair.

For the first time in what felt like eons of lifetimes and millions of impossible wishes, Savannah actually laughed.

Loudly. Hysterically.

Riley just stared.

"I'm not innocent." She giggled.

"No shit." Raking her with a gaze that meant he was convinced she HAD lost her mind, Savannah knew it might be true. Gasped through sword-like pain piercing her wounded left side, she finally gained control over the unexpected hysterics.

"Ha-ha...that was funny."

"Sure. Hilarious. Losing it, Savage?"

"Maybe. A little. It's been a long life."

"Yeah. Ditto."

Realizing he'd been through hell too, she sat up. Slender fingers patted the bed beside her. "Come over here, Riley. We're adults. Let's talk."

But that burly furious man just stood there, as far away as humanly possible, for a full five minutes. She counted.

She had become good at counting precious seconds.

"Talk?" he finally spat, "You left me Savannah! You walked away and never looked back! I didn't exist anymore. Not to you!" Riley's ferocious bellowing was fierce as a wounded lion and just as deadly. "We have nothing to discuss!"

"I'm sorry. For everything. Really I am." Breathing slow and deep to keep from crying, she leaned weakly against the oak headboard Riley once lovingly hand carved with trailing ivy and their initials, underscored by the mantra they lived by since childhood:

*Forever Isn't Long Enough*

Words he'd etched into her heart.

Four years older, Riley worked at Graystone afterschool and weekends since he was fourteen. Savannah was a pesky little heathen running wild; ignored by parents, and too high strung to politely play with guest children. She clattered and pestered, following Riley around, making his workload seem lighter.

That's when it began.

She was ten. He was fourteen. They fed horses and smiled. They raked leaves and laughed. They washed dishes and shared secrets.

In truth, romance blossomed years earlier. Their mothers were friends and when Riley first saw that tiny baby with lush dark chocolate hair, unique violet-blue eyes, and pouty rosebud lips, he boldly proclaimed that someday he would marry Savannah.

He meant it.

Savannah only had one boyfriend. Riley.

Ever. No other boys even tried.

She was claimed at birth. No man dared challenge Riley Rosemont for what was rightfully his. But he gave her plenty of time for innocence. Although they loved each other fiercely, Riley never even kissed her until the summer she turned fifteen. He was nineteen, becoming a man, but he wisely didn't take things any further for another two years.

He was her first, in every way possible.

Savannah liked to think she was his first, too.

Even when he left for college, Riley appeared every weekend complaining about hating the city. Then in May he returned for the whole glorious summer, training Andalusian horses for her father. He was a compassionate savior for an overlooked girl who roamed the mountains like a wild-thing rather than deal with her dysfunctional family.

Riley was her truest friend.

He always solemnly swore that someday, when they were old enough for adult commitments, she'd become Savannah Janine Rosemont.

It had a nice sound. Soothing. Hopeful. Like walking through a sun-drenched wildflower meadow with a gentle verdant breeze tenderly stirring the sublime scent of wild roses

Mountains of roses.

Red roses gleaming in the golden sunlight.

She loved Riley her entire life.

Then one day, Savannah just couldn't anymore.

"You're bleeding," he coldly observed.

Panicked some stray part that was necessary and vital to her barely strewn together body had sprung loose; both hands anxiously felt her wounded left side. Nothing. No broken bones poked through previously grotesque torn skin. Feverishly horrified, Savannah briskly pat down her miraculously pinned-together left leg.

"Not there." Strong arms brusquely folded over his chest. Distrustfully frowning at her frantic misplaced inspections, the tiniest hint of worry flicked in his gold-green eyes. "Can't you feel it?"

Instead of answering, she sighed and gave up. Arms folded over her chest to mimic him, she leaned like a broken rag doll against the sturdy headboard. Savannah refused to explain that no, she couldn't pinpoint just one single place that might be bleeding because her entire body hurt.

Even her brain hurt. Every lucid thought took effort.

A single tear rolled down one cheek.

Still not offering to help, Riley stayed across the room, scowling as though she were contaminated. "Your head, Genius. Just above your right eye. You smacked it on the floor when you fainted."

"Oh." Touching her forehead, sure enough a red smear marked her fingertips. Dabbing at it with her thumb, the blood stopped. It was just a small hairline cut, but bruised. The skin felt hot and tender. Oh well. Her aching head throbbed with a thought-destroying migraine for fifty-seven terrible days. This new bump made it no worse. Besides, there were too many other injured places to fuss over.

"Maybe it knocked some sense into me."

"Doubtful." Riley studied her with discerning forest green eyes brightened in the center by a starburst of gold. She loved those expressive hazel eyes. In the sunlight, they were luminous gold with a mossy oak leaf rim. "You look terrible. Why are you here? You should be in a hospital."

"I was."

"How did you convince them to release you?"

"Convince them? I just left."

"Why?"

"Because. I could. So…I did."

"Who helped you?"

"No one. I walked out."

He didn't seem to buy that. In fact, he looked highly doubtful. "Does anyone know where you are?"

"You do. Unless I'm imagining you...in which case, no."

"Great," he sighed, "and this is real, Savage."

"Wonderful. Reality bites." No one had called her that in a long time. Savage. It felt weird. She wasn't a wild-child anymore. Was she? Avoiding Riley's stern scrutiny, Savannah looked down at her outstretched legs, pathetically searching for some semblance of truth to explain her miserable existence and unexpected appearance into his peaceful life. Instead, she noticed the obnoxious bright magenta socks she put on her feet...sometime. Somewhere.

"Where are my boots?"

"Downstairs. I decided they looked uncomfortable." His hateful snarl had dramatically softened. She couldn't imagine why. "Do you remember the hospital?"

"Not really."

"Tell me what you remember."

"Doctors."

"Anyone else?" There was something oddly hopeful in his voice. "Were you there all alone?" He prodded.

Picking at a funny dirt smear on the knee of her jeans that she truly could not recall falling down and getting, Savannah wondered why he would ask that. "Does it matter what my busted brain remembers?"

"Yeah. To me it does."

She had dreamed of Riley while lying half-dead in the hospital. It was just a misguided fantasy. In her dream, he cared. In the dream, Riley held her hand. Together, they cried.

She really was losing it! Riley wouldn't cry.

Why would he?

He didn't know the truth. Any of it. He had no idea she ran away from Montana and became the world famous composer, Arianna Hartwell. And he certainly wouldn't go to New York City! The man hated cities. Obviously, he hated her. If this unexpected interrogation kept going, he would hear things guaranteed to make him hate her worse.

"You weren't supposed to be here, Riley."

"But I am here. And now, so are you." He sighed in resignation, "Do you know why you were in the hospital?"

"I...there was...an accident."

"Look at me, Savannah."

She didn't want to. Her bruised mind was useless oatmeal sizzling like fried eggs inside her fevered inferno body. She felt so vulnerable. If she looked at him, Riley would see more truth than she wanted to share.

What could she possibly say?

27

*Oh by the way, Riley, I stole something precious from you. I selfishly kept that beautiful gift all to myself. I meant to bring it back, when the time was right. Really, I did. I was keeping it safe, watching it grow. But now it's broken and gone forever.*

"I mean it!" He brusquely ordered. "Look at me!" Obeying, she met his gaze. In the face of the man she once deeply loved, she found only cold loathing. Savannah couldn't stop the hopeless river of tears that streamed down her cheeks.

She'd lost so much.

It only made Riley's frown deepen. "Want some ice?"

"No."

"Tylenol?" He tersely offered, "Morphine?" She shook her aching head. "A hefty shot of horse tranquilizer?"

"That isn't funny. You hate putting down broken animals."

"For you, Savage, I'd happily put you out of your misery."

"You're mean, Riley Phillip."

"And you are definitely broken," he grumbled, but seemed surprisingly apologetic. "Seriously Savannah, what do you need?"

"Nothing. I had pills. I got rid of them."

Green eyes widened. "Just the pain pills, right? You didn't stop taking your antibiotics, did you? You need them."

She started to question how Riley knew she took antibiotics to prevent infection from all the surgeries, but felt overwhelmingly confused.

Had she told him?

Maybe Riley was just another hallucination.

Maybe in reality she was face down on the kitchen floor, knocked out cold. Maybe talking to Riley in her massive attic bedroom wasn't real, at all. Or maybe...she was actually in the front courtyard covered in icy snow, dying a cold lonely death, just dreaming of Riley.

Dang. Couldn't she pick a happier dream?

She thought when people died they dreamed of beautiful angels. No, even in death she screwed it up. She imagined an angry mountain man.

What a mess.

"Savannah," he commanded in a stern parental tone, "Where are your antibiotics? Are they in your backpack downstairs?"

"No. I flushed everything."

"Stubborn Graystone woman," he vehemently swore, pacing the floor. Despite herself, she peeked at him. She watched Riley stomp an angry contemplative circle before the unlit fireplace. He stopped and studied the clean steel grate that hadn't seen soot and ashes for nearly seven cold years. Turning around again, he caught her watching.

Their gazes met.

His eyes narrowed. "Why did you flush your pills?"

"Well...I, uh. Because."

"That was just damn stupid."

Savannah couldn't remember why she dumped them. Everything since the accident was a hazy blur. Thoughts all disconnected and chaotic were sparking randomly through her sweltering brain, getting nowhere. It was frustrating.

Vaguely, she remembered her brilliant plan to curl up a cold dark room in the mountains and fade away.

Looks like plans had changed.

"Why is my room still nice and clean?"

"Is it? I hadn't notice. Maybe you have a concussion."

"I do." She regretfully confessed, wishing bad-dream-Riley would disappear. Rubbing pounding temples, her thoughts were becoming murky gray again. "Or, I did have one. Bumping it again can't be good." Fading fast, Savannah slumped weakly against the pillows and feebly sniffed. "I just need some sleep."

"Some sleep?" His question was as flat-lined as her aching heartbeat. "You came all the way to Montana to get some sleep."

"Uh, yeah. I...think...so."

He finally walked closer, cautiously, as if expecting her to snarl and attack. She wouldn't. Couldn't he see how weak and sick she was? Savannah's heavily blinking eyes told her that gruffly handsome man was getting dangerously close, but she was too overwrought to move. Unconscious curtains were rapidly closing.

"Go away, Riley." Her head bobbed, but she stubbornly righted it.

"It's my house. You go away."

"Okay," she whimpered, "in a minute."

She had traveled so far, emotionally. Utterly spent, Savannah had struggled just to survive. Yet here, with the smell of pine and fresh linens, in the daunting presence of a man whose dusky auburn hair and charismatic face she thought of day and night for too many years...she just couldn't fight anymore.

It felt like falling headfirst into a well of deep water.

Down the dark black hole she went, falling into a place where drowning into nothingness seemed almost a pleasant release from hell.

Violet-blue eyes reluctantly closed.

Savannah sagged into a boneless heap.

In three quick strides, Riley was at her side. "Savage? Hey? Are you alright?" Warily, almost as if reaching through a dream to touch a ghost, a strong man's hand clasped a pale wrist that had become so critically frail and slender his fingers could have easily snapped it.

Her pulse was almost nonexistent.

Riley swore.

She was burning up. Fever!

He should have recognized the signs. Her brightly flushed cheeks blazed against unnaturally pale skin that had a sickly gray pallor. When he carried Savannah up here, she was chilled from being outside.

Now her body was on fire!

"For Ryan…" he softly whispered, gently tucking her lifeless fevered form beneath downy blankets, carefully guarding the left leg he knew had recently been broken in several places. "Only for him. Because he loved you. Not for your sake. You, I will never forgive."

Then the horrible nightmare journey was over.

Savannah Graystone comfortably slept in her own bed.

In her own home.

For the first time in six agonizing years, eight heartbreaking months…and two life-changing minutes.

Guarded by a man who hated her.

# Chapter Three

Morning came too soon, but the instant Savannah's body painfully twitched she realized it wasn't morning at all. It was only a few delirium-tossed hours. Funny how her perception of time was distorted. Since the accident, seconds often felt like hellish forever, but days and weeks sometimes compressed into mere sorrow hazed nothingness.

Lying beneath thick downy blankets, Savannah was sweating profusely. Her body felt like an oven with a broken thermostat, baking at temperatures way too high.

Even her thoughts felt crispy and charred.

Long damp hair stuck to her neck and back, but the air around her uncovered face held a distinct chill. Opening her eyes, she smelled it. Fire. Straight across the giant bedroom, gleaming inside the granite fireplace, bright orange flames crackled over an oak log for the first time in nearly seven years.

Her gaze skimmed the spacious attic bedroom with its lofty oak-lined peak ceilings. Icy white snow blanketed the big picture windows. A brutal storm-driven wind noisily blustered and howled around the house.

A blizzard. Full force.

Grasping the walls, wind ripped around Graystone's solid corners and slithered under the eaves. It sounded like the icy voices of ghosts. Sad and forlorn, they called out to her, wailing over their lost hopes and dreams.

They wanted inside.

But the ghosts couldn't get in. Someone strong and fiercely alive had kicked them out. Listening to the eerie otherworld sounds brutally attack the estate; Savannah heard phantoms moan and shriek, lamenting their broken lives. Souls from ages past wept over love lost. For an instant, Savannah swore she heard her parents, moaning over their wasted lives.

There was a mountain of heartache in that stormy wind.

Screeching over the high peaked roof, wintertime spirits rattled windowpanes and squalled in dismay when they couldn't get in. Let it snow. Let the wind blow. Graystone Heights was impermeable.

Too bad she wasn't.

Moving a little, bones rebelled, especially the broken ones. Healing, yet not fully repaired, her ribs ached. The left femur held together by bone grafts and steel pins still longed for the protective cast she defiantly cut away.

Yesterday? Yes. She hacked it off yesterday in the bathroom of the Park Avenue penthouse she shared with Ryan.

Testing, she wiggled the fragile ankle.

It popped in rebellion, yet remained whole.

She breathed a sigh of relief. And regret. Her body was battered, but her spirit maliciously rejuvenated unwanted memories of the past few hours. Savannah knew exactly where she was and dreaded facing the man who kindly let her stay.

This wasn't her home, not anymore.

Graystone Heights belonged to Riley Rosemont. He earned that heritage. Riley was another strong Montana warrior in a proud legacy of illustrious horsemen. Savannah forfeited her birthright years ago.

Six years. Eight months. And two precious minutes.

*Momma, what happened?*

*That truck hit us. Give me your hand. Are you okay?*

*I can't move. My heart hurts. I'm bleeding, Momma.*

*I'm right here, Ryan. I'll never leave you.*

Savannah relived those two desperate moments a trillion times. Her bruised mind wouldn't let it go. His innocent voice remained so vivid. She smelled hot brake-scorched tires, felt his small trusting hand nestled in hers, and heard worried men frantically yelling. Remembering hell's vengeance, she even tasted metallic fear in her mouth.

Sobbing without willpower or valor, Savannah curled up and lay there mourning, wishing she would die.

"Wonderful. You're awake. Oh joy." A sardonic voice grumpily declared, yanking her away from memories. "Cry-baby."

Wiping her face, Savannah sadly peered through tears.

Riley. Dang it.

He carried a serving tray filled with herbal smelling foods.

Instantly rebellious, Savannah quickly sat up and managed to wiggle her willowy body up against the pillows. "No way are you using that herbal gunk on me!" Scooting further, she was stopped by the unyielding headboard. She couldn't escape. "I can smell peppermint already! And thyme!" She sang out, "I smell THYME!"

"You smell rosemary, you city-slicker goon." He dryly denounced, placing the silver serving tray upon the nightstand. "Thyme goes with beef. This is chicken soup. Rosemary goes with chicken. The peppermint you smell is just hot tea.

"I hate tea."

"Oh? Since when?"

"Since now."

"That's strange. The Savannah I know loves a hot cup of tea. She says it warms her heart." Hazel eyes dared her to deny it. She couldn't. "She likes tea more than coffee." He added three sugar cubes to the steaming cup. "Maybe you aren't Savannah. Maybe you're someone else."

"I'm Savannah! Dang it, Riley! Who else would I be?"

"Hmm…Arianna Hartwell?"

Her stomach knotted. "Who?" She feigned ignorance.

"Seriously? Is your brain so muddled you don't even remember that you ran away from Montana and changed your name?"

"Uh, well…I just didn't think YOU knew."

"Well, I do."

"Did I tell you?"

"Not exactly."

"My head hurts." She rubbed it. "I'm so confused."

"Let's fix that."

Stubbornly objecting to whatever therapeutic remedy Riley intended, she flattened herself against the headboard and pulled uncooperative injured legs tight against her haggardly heaving chest, creeping away from the grumpy Mountain Man and his foul tasting herbal medicine.

Riley sat upon the bed, facing her.

She became caged between his burly body and the headboard. "Feed me that medieval healing crap and I swear I'll…!"

Her objection became a noisy squawk as Riley thrust a digital thermometer into her mouth. Savannah reached for it, intent on throwing the damned thing into the fireplace, but his hands were faster.

"No! Sit still before you pass out again!"

Like a rebellious child, she swatted at him. He snatched both flailing arms. One big hand clasped her thin wrists, holding them together. She felt like a wild animal he'd skillfully subdued. She defiantly clenched her teeth on the thermometer, curling her lips against the unwanted medical instrument.

"Don't bite that!" He snarled, "behave, Savage!"

His harsh command stiffened her spine. Her jaw obediently relaxed. Flipping one wrist around, a strong hand took her pulse.

Methodically, without feeling.

Doctor Riley Rosemont.

Large animal veterinarian who specialized in horses, but for people, he believed in using the natural medicine that God created, whenever possible. Could this angry man have fixed a broken little boy?

The thermometer beeped.

His bronze brow quizzically arched. "Can I check that? Or are you going to thrash around some more?"

"I'm done." It was true. Panting from fighting him, she ached all over and felt alarmingly dizzy. "Nice Savannah," she meekly sighed in defeat. "Good girl."

"Sure."

But he did release her arms.

Freed, but not happy, Savannah contritely folded them in her lap, pouted her lips around the thermometer still stuck inside her mouth and sat there glaring daggers at Riley.

"Cute. You're such a brat."

She relaxed her posture, uncurled her legs, and smoothed the blanket over them, making a decent effort to be a cooperative patient.

"That's better." He shifted, leaned closer, and reached around outstretched legs. She stiffened. His brawny arm was braced against her left hip. Removing the thermometer from her mouth with the other hand, he read the digital gadget.

So close. Too close.

Riley smelled unfairly good; like woodsy Irish Spring soap, pine logs he'd chopped this morning, and soothing food smells from the kitchen. It was hard to be defiant when natural instincts purred to wrap her arms around his neck and smother the man with kisses.

"Congratulations; a sizzling one-o-six point two."

"A hundred and six? Shouldn't I be dead?"

"Probably soon, if we don't lower it." Scowling as if he wasn't convinced her life was worth saving, he placed his palm flat against her forehead. The movement startled her. She yanked away and bonked the backside of her head against the oak headboard.

It made a loud whack, but didn't hurt much.

"Skittish, Savage?" Riley was so close now, the familiarity made her lightheaded. His lips were memorably kissable, stirring up old yearnings. Did he remember too? "How long have you been this hot?"

"I don't know. A day or two."

He removed his hand and softly swore, quite creatively, cursing her intelligence and her stubborn Graystone heritage, all in one sentence. The harsh admonition made her feel like a careless child.

"That wasn't very nice."

"So? You're fighting an infection. A real bad one. Throwing away your medicine was stupid. Real damn stupid. Do you WANT to die, Savannah? Coming here was dangerous."

"Oh. Well, I didn't…"

"Think? Care? Both?" He finished for her. Fingers swiftly felt down the swollen glands along her neck and slid beneath sweaty hair. The examining touch was so unexpected all she could do was blink. His hand felt wonderfully cool.

"Your skin is gray, but your cheeks are flushed hot pink. When I touch you, it leaves white marks." By his disgusted expression, her face must have a truly deathly pallor. This close, he saw it all. There was no hiding frailty from those all-knowing golden green eyes.

"I'm soooo sorry, Riley," tears burned, "I'm sorry that I left and I'm sorry I came back and I'm sorry I never told you…"

"Eat." He commanded, quickly turning to shove a spoon into her hand and a warm bowl of something wonderful smelling before her nose. "Or I'm kicking you out in this wicked snowstorm. Ten minutes of sub-zero temperatures should cool you off."

Pouting at his brusque attitude, her fingers obediently clutched the polished silver spoon. It was her mother's baroque rose pattern. As a child, she loved that scrolling feminine design. To a little girl growing up in Montana wilderness, it seemed elegant, regal, something fit for a queen. Seeing it today brought a fresh sting to her eyes.

Looking at Riley's frown, then at the silver spoon that felt like a cruel reminder of all the good she'd lost, her fingers trembled.

"I'll hold the bowl." Riley gruffly griped. "Your shaky hands will spill soup all over the bed. I don't feel like cleaning it up."

Trying not to cry, Savannah dipped the spoon into the bowl and took a bite. Oh…chicken and fresh vegetables. Homemade. Flavored with rosemary and a faint hint of garlic. The soup immediately soothed her empty insides, making her chest feel cozy warm and loved, instead of achingly tight and all alone.

Grateful tears silently fell.

Riley growled. "Crybaby."

"Sorry." Scrubbing them away with one fist, she greedily slurped down another spoonful. And another. Dipping a piece of buttered toast into the broth, she ate that too.

The angry man held the bowl and watched.

"It's good," she sniffed, "Thanks."

"Not medieval herbal gunk?"

Repentant tears slowly slid down her face.

He sighed and shook his head. "Are you ever going to stop crying?"

"Maybe. Someday."

Riley held the bowl while Savannah doggedly ate every bite, willfully absorbing the healing chicken soup and buttered toast despite the disgusted stare of a strong-willed man she once wholeheartedly adored.

Fine. Let him hate her for leaving.

Riley wasn't supposed to be at Graystone anyway.

But he was here. He owned it now.

Good grief, she wasn't thinking those things, she was remembering. They already argued. Being broken inside was frustrating. *Zeus.* Her unstable thoughts

35

suddenly recalled the colossal black dog. "Where's my giant friend?" The plea sounded wretchedly pathetic, even to Savannah's own ears.

"You have no friends here, Savage."

It hurt soul deep. "That's not true," her chin stubbornly tilted. "Zeus likes me."

"Great. Zeus likes you." He mocked in a singsong voice.

"Grumpy man. You must be jealous."

Riley just grunted at the ridiculous idea.

"So?" She prodded, "Where is he?"

"Zeus?" He looked incredulous, as if he couldn't believe they were still talking about his enormous Great Dane. "In the stables. Where he belongs."

"Oh, well...that's good." Savannah cheekily chomped another bite of buttered toast and sipped peppermint tea. It was laced with something slightly bitter, obviously meant to heal her mushy oatmeal brain and lower her raging fever. Fighting the urge to behave like a willful child and refuse it, she drank the tea anyway, openly defying Riley's icy animosity.

"Can Zeus come see me?" She asked in between sips.

"No. He's a giant dog."

"A very friendly giant dog."

"Not normally. Usually he tears a hunk out'a strangers."

"See? We're friends. Zeus even smiled at me."

"Drooling isn't a smile. That hungry Great Dane was probably trying to find a piece of you that wasn't all boney. Besides, Zeus stinks like outdoors and skunks and lord-knows-what he found while traipsing around in the woods."

"So? Give him a bath. And I'm not boney, Riley Phillip! Don't be mean. Your Momma didn't raise you to be a bully!"

"I'm a grown man, thank you very much," he tartly disputed, noisily plunking the empty soup bowl back onto the silver serving tray. "Momma Emily's rules don't apply anymore. This is my house now. I can be mean to crybaby trespassers if I want." Scanning her figure hidden beneath the blankets, gold-green eyes suspiciously narrowed. "What's wrong with you, anyway? Can you remember?"

Avoiding his eyes, she stared at the spoon still clutched in her hand.

"Savannah? Answer me."

"I've just been...uh, sick."

"Sick? Please. You look like the kiss of death."

Savannah meekly shrugged and handed him the spoon. Okay, so sick was an understatement. Death truly had kissed her. But then the stupid grim reaper decided she didn't taste good enough and took someone innocent and pure instead, leaving her behind as mortally damaged goods.

What did Riley know about the accident, anyway? Nothing. Right? Recalling his questions about the hospital, she wasn't so sure.

It was all so very, very confusing.

36

Her head throbbed. It was all she could do to remember how to breathe. Right now, Savannah just wanted a little warmth and kindness. If a giant black dog who looked at her with loving brown eyes was her only friend at Graystone, then so be it.

"Can I see Zeus? Please?" She begged, as nicely as she could.

"Hell, woman. Next you'll want Diablo up here!"

Savannah perked up, finding energy beyond warm soup and human kindness, no matter how grudgingly stingy. Had her beloved white horse somehow survived? But he was nearly twenty years old when she left, and in his whole life that untamable Andalusian stallion only carried one rider. Her.

And Riley. Just once.

"He's here! You still have my horse? Oh! Can I see him?"

"Damn Savage," he softly swore, eyes narrowed, "the great man died years ago." Plunking the spoon and empty teacup beside the soup bowl on the tray, his frosty gaze held undisguised steely contempt. "Right after you left."

It took a few stinging breaths to comprehend his harsh accusation. "What happened to Diablo?"

"He stopped eating. Just stood there day and night, sadly looking down the road hoping you would return. You never did. One day, he stopped looking. He lost hope. Lay down and never got up. I've never seen a creature feel so utterly lost and all alone."

Breathing stung.

A cold guilty chill shimmied up her spine.

Her valiant Andalusian stallion died of a broken heart, all because she left. Her mother broke her neck skiing slopes no human should have traveled, after the daughter holding their fragile family together changed her name and left. Her father drank himself into oblivion after she left.

Riley's good and gentle heart hardened because she left.

She almost died because she left.

But someone else, far more important had died.

All because she left.

Savannah gulped as brutal clarity suddenly struck, bright and unshakable, illuminating her hazy shocked mind with a cruel spotlight of truth. Riley wasn't just angry because she left Montana, coldly denying their young love.

The pain in his hazel eyes was fresh.

It was every bit as fresh as her own.

Riley looked like his heart had been ripped out of his chest, like his soul tumbled over and over inside a mangle piece of useless mechanical metal that crumpled and squeezed, destroying everything good.

"Oh...noooo," she gasped. Praying she was wrong, Savannah's fist clutched at the dark hole inside that was once a joyful thumping heart. Right now, that empty place was threatening to implode.

"What?"

37

"You know," she could barely whisper, "about Ryan."

"Yes. I knew we had a child."

Her entire existence froze, cold as the blizzard.

That single unavoidable truth should have bound them forever together. But truth held them a galaxy apart, instead. Truth hung there between Riley and Savannah for a million heart-wrenching seconds.

"I also know about the accident."

"No…" she hissed in denial. "You can't!"

"Yes. You were crushed. And Ryan…" saying their beautiful son's name, he glanced toward the crackling fireplace and Savannah saw his fists clench. When Riley silently met her gaze again, she saw the unguarded depths of his soul-wrenching sorrow.

It mirrored hers.

He just handled it differently.

"Oh. My. God," she whimpered, "You do know! How?"

Questions and accusations were trapped for an unspeakable aching eternity between his stolid warrior face and her weakened crybaby violet-blue eyes.

Riley truly knew about his son. The loss was clear in his face.

And he hated her for letting Ryan die.

With every bone in his body.

Riley shifted, intent upon leaving her alone on the bed that had suddenly become their battleground. Lunging at him, she willfully grabbing the front of his shirt, tugging him back with more strength her critically fevered body should have possessed.

"Hey!" He objected. "What the…"

Yanking him close, Savannah knelt on her knees and crushed their bodies tight together, so close he couldn't escape.

"When did you know, Riley?"

"About the accident?" He snarled between gritted teeth, trying to free himself from her grip. "Eight weeks ago, last Sunday. The day after it happened."

"No, dang it." She pitifully cried out, desperate to clarify tangled thoughts. "When did you know that I gave birth to your son? When did you know I was raising our child all alone?"

Face to face, he took a deep staggered breath. It was ragged with unspoken grief. Gripping her forearms, Riley gently pushed away, creating cautious distance between them again. Jaw clenched, shoulders rigid with tension, those expressive forest green eyes answered so truthfully and mournfully that he had always known.

Always. For six years, he knew.

But those eight months alone being pregnant, praying keeping their baby a secret was the right choice, were Savannah's guilty burden to bear. And Riley couldn't possibly imagine the horror of those last two minutes wedged between layers of unyielding steel, fighting crushing pain, and holding a dying boy's small hand.

Overwhelmed, she slumped against the pillows.

"How could you know? I disappeared!"

"I'm not stupid, Savage. You left for Juilliard and changed your name. Except you didn't actually enter Juilliard. You used your tuition money to rent Lexington Music Hall and invited the biggest production names in contemporary piano to a private performance, where you introduced the world to songs you wrote here in our mountains. Arianna Hartwell became an instant star. I suspected, but I wasn't sure about the baby until the newspapers hinted about your mysterious behavior. Secretive, they said," Riley inched close again, taunting her with his own inconsolable sorrow, "almost maternal and protective, how you kept reporters away." Bronze brows furrowed, "Very odd."

Savannah was wheezing. He knew everything!

He crept toward her. Like a cougar seeking vengeance, the man's movements were stealthy. "And then..." his cool hand reached out and gently cupped her dangerously burning cheek. "I finally saw his picture."

"Picture? Impossible. How?"

"Ever hear of the internet?" He gruffly scolded, but manly fingers softly smoothed along her hot skin. That tender compassionate touch was a stark contradiction to his snarling hostility. "I looked forever for proof, but you always kept cameras away. Then I found a video on a fan website. A three-year-old little boy in a white tuxedo proudly held your hand as you left a performance in London."

Her mind whirled. Her heart wanted to explode.

"He had my red hair. And your violet eyes." His thumb stroked across her cheek again. "But his innocent smile was all his own." Savannah felt smothered by Riley's velvet-light hand upon her face. Was it loving? Or was he just fighting the urge to wring her neck?

"Ryan Patrick Rosemont-Graystone." The reverence and devotion in his voice made her shiver. "At least you gave our son my last name."

*Momma, you should call my Daddy. Please? He'll fix us.*

*I will Ryan. When we get out of here.*

*Promise?*

*Yes. Your Daddy is a very good man.*

*Daddy loves me.*

*Yes, my Prince, I believe he does.*

The car tumbled over and over, stealing everything good. Remembering every horrible hellish sound, that awful burnt rubber smell, and every excruciating injury with cruel clarity, Savannah panted in abject agony, mentally reliving those last precious seconds of Ryan's innocent life.

A strong hand gripped her shoulder. Someone was yelling. It was a man, far away. That angry man shook her.

It didn't matter.

Nothing mattered. Ryan was gone.

But that man loudly insisted she return to his reality and shook her ragdoll body so hard her sizzling brain bounced around inside her skull.

"Savage!"

She mindlessly blinked away memories and drew a raspy breath that ironically mirrored their son's last.

"Damn it woman! Stop that!"

His stern voice yanked her tattered mind back to Montana. His hazel-green eyes looked stricken. Riley had seen the horror reflected in her face as she mentally relived those final two minutes.

"What was that?"

Tears fell. "Oh Riley! How could God be so cruel? I couldn't help Ryan. He hurt so bad. Isn't God supposed to protect children from pain?"

Now it was his turn to blink as if stunned. "You remember the accident?"

Confirming the horrid memories, her arms wrapped tight around her thin body trying to stifle the searing grief burning her spirit into ashes. "I live it over and over. I'll never forget it. It's all I have of him now."

Swearing softly for reasons she didn't understand, he wiped slick teardrops off her sizzling cheeks with his thumbs. "Tell me what you remember."

"No. I won't. Those are my memories."

"How did he die?" He ruthlessly questioned, yet his big hands still held her face as light as a china doll. "Please? I need to know. He was my son too!"

She couldn't resist that heartfelt plea. Riley's son. The son he never met, but obviously loved. "His last thought was of you!"

"Me? That's impossible. My son never knew me."

"No, Ryan knew all about you. I never kept you a secret! You were his hero." She confessed, never dreaming that all those lonely worried years spent aching for a man she left behind, Riley actually knew about their beautiful son. "We were trapped inside that car, bleeding all over. But Ryan believed you could fix him. He asked..." Savannah wretchedly sobbed, her chest heaving with the weight of unbearable sorrow, "He asked me to call you!"

"My god, Savage." The shocked words were a gritty feral growl deep in his throat. "I fix animals, not crushed children."

Without warning, Riley tugged her fragile body from beneath the warm blankets and hauled her right up onto his lap. Savannah was wearing a man's blue t-shirt and little else. Even the bright pink socks on her feet were gone. Instead, she saw ugly scars encircling her left ankle and running up her leg in a horribly chaotic spider web pattern.

Riley had changed her clothes.

He'd witnessed Savannah's war haggard body; the surgical scars where steel rods pinned her shattered thigh back together, the jagged torn marks on her left side where ribs broke like matchsticks. The bone-deep bruises that refused to fade.

Sitting sideways across his thighs, she gasped in dismay and embarrassment. "You undressed me."

"So? You were burning up." In one quick motion, his hand kindly smoothed the cotton material of the shirt as far over her deeply scarred leg as it would reach. For one unguarded instant she saw love in his eyes. "Besides, I've seen you naked before." At odds with his tones of gruff indifference, the sympathy in his face made her cry harder. "Stop that. Crying is for babies."

"I...can't." she blubbered.

"Fine. Then tell me how he died." He curtly ordered, returning to his disdainful inquisition. The light of love in his eyes disappeared.

Insulted his kindness was so fleeting, she refused.

His grip on her body automatically tightened. Ribs complained, stealing her breath. "Ryan was my son! You stole him from me! Now tell me what you remember!"

"No!"

Her feeble squirming objection made him angry. As they struggled, she suddenly realized...Riley could end her suffering. He could stop her aching heart. He knew exactly how! It would be fast and quick; one flex from those powerful arms and she could be in heaven with Ryan.

*Please.* Savannah begged with her eyes, praying his vengeful vice-hold would be merciful. Riley could crush her fragile bones around her burning lungs, snap them in half and send shattered pieces flying like arrows through her abysmally empty heart. He could crumple her body just like that moving truck crumpled their car.

*Please, Riley. Please. Just end this.*

She saw him considering it.

Or that's what she hoped.

But in that painful instant when suicidal madness made more sense than survival, instead of releasing her from pain, this great man's hands suddenly wiped away tears from her fevered face. "I lost you once," he hoarsely whispered, brushing a kiss across her burning face, "Don't ask me to let go of you again."

"But I hurt," it was a sad pathetic whimper, "so deep."

"It means you're still alive."

"I shouldn't be."

"But you are. God didn't take you. It wasn't your time. You can't give up and fade away. It's wrong. So, live Savannah."

"Why? I have nothing to live for. You hate me."

Riley swallowed hard and didn't deny it. "Then make things right between us," he softly urged. "Tell me about my son. Help me understand why I couldn't be a part of his life."

"But you were. I made sure of it. He loved you! Don't you see?" Sobbing uncontrollably, she threw her arms around him and clung to Riley. He was strong and she felt weak. She needed him. "Every day, everywhere we went, everything we did...you were right there too! You lived everyday inside Ryan's heart. I made sure of it!"

His big hand slid slowly down her back, caressing the long sheet of dark chocolate hair.

It felt good.

It felt like love.

"And you've both always lived in mine." He confessed.

Freedom as soft as a dove settled upon Savannah's broken soul. Nestled there in Riley's arms, she cried that deep well of misery completely dry. Exhausted, dangerously fevered, and emotionally spent, she eventually slid into an unconscious gray slumber again. But even in that sweltering delirium, Savannah remained stubbornly tangled in the arms of the man she sworn she would never again love.

She couldn't let go.

And that confused man valiantly held her and cared for her, day and night, for eleven sorrow-hazed feverish days.

*Tell me how he died.*

*No, Riley. Death is silence. Life is music.*

*I'll tell you how he lived.*

# *Chapter Four*

*I dreamed of Red Roses blooming in Winter, boldly defying the Ice and Snow. Once, you were my Ray of Light. Now you've become my Storm.*
*~~~ Riley*

I slept in a bed that I hadn't lain upon in years, holding a woman I honestly never thought I would see again.

Or touch.

Or argue with.

Gee. Some things never change.

I truly believed Savannah was gone from my life. Yet for reasons that didn't make sense, last week I scrubbed and dusted, making her spacious third-floor bedroom as clean and fresh as the fateful day she left.

The attic was locked off for years. That oak door opened to a world of memories I just couldn't bear to face. Savannah's room was a sacred space filled with youthful love, haunted by ghosts of lost dreams.

It's true. I've heard them wailing, especially on long winter nights; sad voices in the wind crying out for love lost.

But like a madman seeking salvation I restored everything like new and chased away the ghosts, thoroughly convinced I was losing my mind.

Savannah wouldn't come home.

That talented musical virtuoso didn't need me.

But she did need me.

My beautiful Savage finally came home!

Holding her frail body as we slept, I dreamt of angel songs. Sweet music drifted in iridescent pink-blue waves. It swept in slow undulating surges across glacier-capped mountains.

Where was it coming from?

Graystone. Through the big bay windows encircling the formal parlor, golden sunbeams glittered. I heard talented fingers trill across the piano keys of the white Steinway grand piano. In my dream, I felt so proud of Savannah.

43

She played and played.

The rays of light grew brighter.

Savannah's music made it grow.

My heart soared.

I watched that luminous heavenly gift coming from her hands shimmer like magic. I'd never actually SEEN music before. I'd only heard it. This music had power, a life all its own. It twinkled. In a single amazed breath, her music changed everything dark in my dreary world into pure white snow glistening like fresh cut diamonds. It felt like redeeming radiance, beautifully blinding. It covered everything in sight.

I welcomed it. Musical luminous snowflakes swirled around me, beaconing to my spirit with a melody of love. I threw my arms open wide and embraced her music.

Yes! This was my salvation!

The magical light originating from that white grand piano caught me up and gently carried me into the bright blue sky.

I wasn't afraid.

I felt humbled by Savannah's musical power.

There, perched upon a fluffy white cloud, in my dream I peered down at my mountain world, so very far below. Then, I saw it. In the wildflower meadow behind the stables grew a lush rose garden. Thousands of red buds blossomed, gleaming against the shimmering background of pure white diamond snow.

Red roses blooming in winter.

Defiant and strong, they would survive the bitter cold.

Would I? Would she?

I woke knowing the most glorious God-given miracle of my life had finally returned! Savannah. I've slept beside my broken raven-haired musical princess while she fought a raging fever and traumatized soul for eleven tenuous nights.

And days. Long anxious days.

I thought she might die.

Afraid to leave Savannah alone, I have faithfully nourished and nurtured a delirious semi-conscious woman who tosses in nightmare-tormented sleep, irrationally whispering memories of a child I never met, yet I loved every moment of his short life.

I hate her for letting him die.

She was supposed to keep Ryan safe.

But once, I loved her. Once, forever didn't seem long enough for how much I loved Savannah.

She was my reason. My music. My life.

My beautiful sweet Savage.

But I can't love her anymore! She stole the most perfect thing that love could ever create and she kept that precious gift all to herself. It wasn't fair!

Savannah never told me about Ryan, but I cherished my son.

I knew his innocent joy.

I saw Ryan only once, years ago, and from a distance.

Running toward her in Central Park, they tumbled together in the autumn leaves like two wild things at play. Love lit their faces. To me, they were amazingly beautiful; like witnessing God's angels. Laughing, Savannah covered Ryan with red and yellow autumn leaves. Then she flopped down on the crispy mound beside him.

It was exactly how I used to play with her.

They spent the whole afternoon staring at the hazy autumn sky, talking quietly about nothingness, mother to son. He was truly perfect. That day, after watching Ryan smile and hearing his joyful laugh, I silently walked away.

My son was deeply loved.

It was enough.

He was merely six, yet he already played the violin with the skill of a born-twice master. Ryan Patrick Rosemont, with his mahogany colored hair and unique violet-blue eyes was born to charm the world with supreme musical stardom.

And then he died.

But he wasn't alone.

Savannah was pinned inside that crushed car too.

On a Sunday morning, while waiting for the phone to ring, bringing a brave and curious voice that had become the most important sound in my world; I received another call instead. A freak accident, they said. Driving too fast, the heavily loaded moving van lost control. Careening wildly, it slammed into a silver Mercedes driving down a curvy country road in upstate New York, crushing mother and child.

My child.

And the gifted woman who should have been my wife.

Savannah's broken body told the unspeakable tale. Her crushed left leg is marked by jagged scars that go bone deep. Broken ribs brutally pierced her creamy soft skin. A tiny arrow-shaped scar etches her left cheek from broken glass and another scar runs along her cocoa brown hairline. If I'd been thinking straight that first fateful morning, instead of roaring at her like a troll, I would have stopped an obviously wounded woman from smacking her head on the floor.

No, I yelled.

And meanly watched her fall.

I still see signs of her original concussion; the forgetfulness, the empty stares void of rational thought. She should be healing by now. Problem is; I don't think she wants to heal. Trapped in this life and unable to enter the next, Savannah merely exists.

She talks to ghosts.

"I'm right here," she cries in her sleep, "I'll never leave you, Ryan." She stayed in that car long after Ryan's last breath was gone. She wanted to die too.

Savannah still aches to die.

She tried. But I stopped her.

"Ryan should live. Save him," she declares to no one at all.

In excruciatingly lucid dreams that I don't know how to stop, she relives that single instant of decision over and again. In a split second that should have changed fate and taken Savannah to heaven but given me a life with my son, she turned the car, yanking it sideways to protect Ryan, sacrificing her side to take the brunt of the unavoidable collision.

"Take me," she cries, "Riley will love Ryan!"

Sobbing in her sleep, Savannah murmurs those heroic maternal thoughts with uncanny clarity. She knew I would take care of Ryan. In that terrifying moment while facing her own impending death, Savannah actually thought of me.

A broken mind doesn't lie. It can't.

She knew if she died, Ryan wouldn't be alone. He would have me and he would be deeply loved.

But she didn't die.

And without Ryan, she has no will to live.

She needs something to live for.

Does she need me? I don't know. I hurt too. It's hard to look at Savannah without thinking about what we've lost. Those eyes. Violet-blue, just like Ryan's. Seeing him in her face makes me angry.

I ache.

But my Savage came home. I don't think she consciously chose to come here. Her mind was too bruised for a decision like that. She could have gone anywhere in the world. Montana hasn't been home in years. She didn't know I would be here at Graystone. She thought the estate was deserted.

I think she was guided.

God must have a plan for us.

It was this last realization that late at night kept Riley from tossing a raving shattered Savannah outside into the ever-growing white drifts of snow. Winter was here full force and the snow this high on the mountain wouldn't melt off until spring. Now Riley would be trapped for months inside this giant house with her.

Fate was cruel.

But that forgetful woman painfully cried out at night, curling up like a frightened child in his arms. Kissing his neck, she was grateful for every tiny kindness. He tried to keep some distance, but it was impossible. Mewling softly like a wounded animal, she clung to him. In fevered delirium, Savannah murmured memories of a child long lost to him, yet that secret existence with Ryan had been her waking reality.

There was no one else in her life, only the music and Ryan. Far more possessive than he had a right to feel, Riley questioned her almost relentlessly, pulling bits of tangled truth from a woman so broken inside that she could barely speak. Savannah's heart and valiant life belonged to one soul and one soul only.

Ryan.

A glorious son he never dared touch, yet with Riley's copper hair and Savannah's piercing violet eyes, Ryan was the best of both of them.

But now that goodness was gone.

*Leslie D. Stuart*

# Chapter Five

"Riley?!" An angry voice sharply urged. The lean female body tucked in his arms rebelliously squirmed. "Wake up you big lumberjack! Let go of me! Why are you sleeping in this bed with me?!"

Too exhausted to fight, Riley felt relieved her delirious life-stealing fever finally broke, but he dreaded what was sure to be a rip-roaring confrontation.

She sounded like spirited Savannah again, no longer forlorn and defeated.

"I know you're awake," she wiggled. "Stop ignoring me!"

Although Riley did his best to feed her, a bony hip dug into his side as she defiantly struggled against his grip. Holding her was like wrestling with a ferret; slippery soft and sinewy, but amazingly delightful to touch.

He decided to let Savannah squirm.

He was stronger and she wasn't going anywhere.

But then her movements slid his forearm up and over appealingly mounded breasts that in spite of his determined disinterest, Riley noticed were far more rounded and womanly than they been at eighteen.

"Hold still, Savi." He gruffly commanded.

"We. Are. Sleeping. Together!" She sharply accused, punctuating every word as if it were a prison sentence.

"With. Clothes. On." He countered.

She made a rude disgusted snort. That sleek feline body squirmed again. "Your thermal long-johns are nothing but winter underwear!"

Riley tried not to grin, but seriously liked that she fully assessed their state of undress before verbally attacking him.

"So?"

"And this giant t-shirt you've got me wearing isn't much better!"

Feeling ornery, Riley finally opened his eyes.

Damn she was beautiful.

Trapped in his arms, a long sheet of sinfully rich dark chocolate hair glistened against the velvety smooth skin of a determined face he'd spent his whole life memorizing. He'd done a good job of playing doctor. Her skin wasn't the least bit gray. It was beautiful healthy peach.

But that sweet rosebud mouth pouted like a spoiled child and violet-blue eyes glared at him as though he committed heinous sexual crimes rather than saved her life.

"You're looking real damn ungrateful for a walking corpse."

"What's that supposed to mean?"

"It means, you're welcome," he dryly stated, "I kept you from dying. It wasn't an easy accomplishment. I didn't have much to work with. A little cooperation would have been appreciated, but no…you were determined to die. But I won. You're still alive. Now, I'm exhausted. Cut me some slack and go back to sleep."

Her mouth hung open. "How long have I been here?"

"Eleven days," he coldly proclaimed. "Today makes twelve."

Her brow creased. "I…don't remember. Anything."

"Because your brain was baking. You've been fevered and hallucinating. A real suicidal maniac. You never should have torn off that cast or thrown your antibiotics away and flown two thousand miles in a snowstorm. You should still be in the hospital. But being the obstinate Graystone woman that you are, you defied all good sense and came here anyway. So…I fixed you. Despite your own stupidity, you're still alive. You came to me, Savannah. I didn't hunt you down. Guess all this hostility means you're ready to leave."

Now he did it.

Fight faded from violet eyes. Mournful gray shadows returned. "You fixed me?" She whispered, as he saw horrified memories unspeakably exposed upon her stricken face.

"Yeah. You'll live another eighty years."

"Ryan said you'd fix me."

Tears slid helplessly down her cheeks. Shuddering as if touched by a ghost, Savannah meekly lowered her head, resting her check upon his bare shoulder. His arm remained wrapped around her waist. Eyes clenched tightly closed, she clenched both fists to her broken heart and held very, very still.

Silent tears dampened his skin.

"Now you're staying?" Riley just couldn't be kind.

"Can I?" It was a tiny whimpered appeal.

"You won't try to drown yourself in the bathtub again?"

"What?" Her head popped up in surprise. Holding her how he was, they seamlessly rolled. Just like old times. They always moved with one mind in bed. Or was it one heart? Leaning over his bare chest with her hands braced beside his shoulders, Savannah blankly stared down at him.

"Drown myself? Why would I do that?"

"Hell if I know. You did it the first night you were here." Riley watched Savannah struggling to remember and knew the instant that she did.

50

"Oh," she looked deeply ashamed. "I was counting bubbles."

"Well you ran out."

He would never forget listening outside that bathroom door, allowing her some privacy. But then the soft splashes of a woman bathing stopped. Riley counted too. Silence. Too long. Calling her name, he received no answer. Charging in, fearful of what he might find, under the cool bathwater intended to lower her raging fever, long dark hair swirled around Savannah's pale body like inky ribbons of death. Her violet eyes were open, staring lifelessly up at him from beneath the water.

No bubbles. Only water filled her lungs.

Yanking her up, Riley frantically performed CPR, pumping her heart into motion, desperately breathing life into her unresponsive mouth. Just when he almost gave up, begging God not to take her, Savannah sputtered and violently coughed up the watery death she purposely inhaled.

After that, she never bathed with the door closed.

To hell with modesty.

"If you came here to die, you came to the wrong place." He sharply decreed, wondering if she would shy away if he wrapped his arms around that slender waist again. She'd stretched atop him quite intimately. Pulling her womanly body closer was tempting.

*And stupid.*

Riley stubbornly laced his hands casually behind his head.

Funny mangled emotions played across Savannah's face as she involuntarily studied his calloused hands and those deeply corded arms. Surprisingly spellbound, she looked like she was seeing him for the very first time.

Maybe in her tangled mind, she was.

Unfortunately, Riley had eleven days and nights worth of dangerously fevered memories he wasn't quite sure what to do with.

Plus, eight painful weeks.

And seven lonely years.

Wide violet-blue eyes boldly scanned the hard-work earned muscles of his robustly carved chest and torso, coming to terms with the man Riley had become. No, he wasn't a lanky country kid anymore either. He was twenty-two when she left. The years alone in the mountains made him hard as the granite cliffs, icy as the glaciers shimmering atop Mt. Stimson and just as dangerous.

With a purely feline purr of lusty admiration that Riley found unnervingly provocative, Savannah sighed. Pouty-sweet lips sexily curved.

It was the most sensual thing he'd ever seen.

Heat rushed through places that hadn't been motivated in forever. And he was seriously motivated. She knew. That sexy sweet smile grew. Inching closer, a decadent cocoa sheet of hair swung down, seductively brushing one side of his face like a sinful silk curtain.

"Stop." He ordered, making her blink. "What are you doing?"

"Hmm? Oh. I wanted to kiss you."

"Why?"

"Because...well," surveying him again, she clearly approving of the man lying beneath her. "Because you saved me."

"It isn't my job to keep you alive, Savage. It's yours."

"Mine?" She slowly repeated, her lips hovering a dangerous breath away. "Is that why you're in bed with me? You were afraid to leave me alone?"

"Pretty much."

It was a blatant lie. Truth was, despite the grief-stricken resentment that kept simmering to the surface, Riley felt so eternally grateful to gaze upon Savannah's beautiful face that he could barely breathe.

But being surly and mean was easier than opening his heart.

She left him once.

She'd leave him again. Guaranteed. He refused to give her the power to rip his life apart. Again. "So, if you want to stay, you have to behave. No more Dr. Riley bullshit; I closed up shop years ago."

"Bullshit?" Wide eyed and deeply offended, she sat back, straddling his hips. The movement wedged their bodies tight together in the most delicious way, making him keenly aware she was only wearing panties and his t-shirt. "Am I such a terrible burden?"

Riley answered with a heartless grunt.

Hurt by his cold attitude, Savannah pouted and slid away.

Relief mingled with sharp disappointment. It was a confusing conflicted gut-wrenching feeling, somewhere between starvation and food poisoning.

How could he want a woman he hated?

What the hell was wrong with him?

"Can we sleep now?"

"No. I'm awake." Hands sweetly tucked beside her cheek, she lay on her side in their warm bed and studied him.

They weren't touching anymore.

He missed it.

And hated himself for it.

"You look good, Riley. Have I told you that?"

"Once or twice." He tried to ignore the appreciative light in her eyes but seeing it made his aching heart pound harder and feel eight times too big for his chest. The half-dead woman who arrived at Graystone in a wicked winter snowstorm was gone.

This woman would live.

"You aren't a veterinarian anymore?"

"I was. But I quickly realized that I couldn't fix every broken creature in Harmony Hills. Sam Lawson's son, David became a vet too. He's better than I was. He doesn't get all knotted up inside when he has to put a horse down."

"You've always been kind-hearted like that."

He scowled. Right now, Riley didn't feel kind.

"I like making things live, not watching them die. When John willed Graystone to me, I sold David my veterinarian practice. Equipment, office, customer ledger, all of it. Then I sold the ski lift equipment from Graystone to other resorts and based upon the American Indian heritage in these mountains, I turned this place into a national wildlife preserve giving me government grants that protect Graystone land from hunters. When things get busy, David still calls me, but only for births. Sometimes those brave Momma mares just need someone to sit there and rub their neck. God usually takes care of the rest."

"Horses? You still run the stables?"

"Yep. But no more kid's ponies or amateur riding lessons for rich folks. I raise only Spanish Andalusian Purebreds now. Premium bloodlines, all top notch from Spain. But they aren't a fancy sideshow for guests to gawk over, like John had. I train mine for show and dressage. They perform, with or without a rider."

"Perform? Without a rider? How?"

"They dance to music. When they are just colts, I teach them subtle voice commands using a halter and lead rope. They learn to jump and rear up on cue, performing different steps and small stunts. As they progress, they learn to move their feet to music. They learn to recognize the timing. That's when all their little baby tricks come together into a full-grown dance routine. Movement, to music. With, or without a rider. A few have actually been in movies, running and prancing around, shaking their manes, making the actor look cool. Training them won't make me rich, but doing it feels right and it keeps a roof over my head."

Beside him, Savannah pulled the warm blankets up to her chin and grinned like a cherub. Obviously, she approved of his life choices. "Like Diablo? He could have been a dancing show horse. If he hadn't been so mad at the world."

"Some are his offspring." Their quiet pillow talk felt disturbingly comfortable. "One son is so mean no one can touch him. It's a waste. He'd make a good stud, but he's a spiteful hellion. He bites and kicks: I swear he's insane. I've thought about putting him down, but I just can't do it."

Violet eyes sparked with interest. "No one can touch him?"

"Not since he was a colt. He attacks anyone who comes close."

"Is he really insane?"

"Nah. He just hates the world."

"Oh. Is he white like Diablo?"

"Whiter. Nearly silver, he gleams so bright. Bigger and meaner too. Makes Diablo seem like a bad puppy."

"Really?"

He could see her mental gears turning. If anyone could befriend an untouchable wild beast, it was Savannah. Like Snow White in the forest, all

53

animals loved her. It was her eerie gift; one he never completely understood. It was as if God's Creatures could feel her good and loving heart.

"Can I see him?"

"Maybe. When you're better. And from a distance."

*If you stay.* He sullenly thought.

Bitterness and anger returned.

Sitting up, Riley swung bare feet to the edge of the bed and stood, knowing she would watch him walk away. Let her. Once, she loved the way those gray thermals men in the mountains habitually wore hugged his lower half. Taunting Savannah felt cruel, but he needed to be honest with himself.

They weren't friends.

And they certainly weren't becoming lovers. Again.

But she was still broken inside and Riley felt responsible to keep her alive. "Right now I'm making coffee," yanking on jeans and a flannel shirt tossed over a chair, kept warm beside the fireplace, he turned to find her sitting up, eyeing him with a distinctly lust-glazed expression, "and you're making breakfast. Gotta' earn your keep, Savi. I have hungry horses to tend and stables to winterize."

"Okay." As slender long legs appeared at the edge of the bed Riley saw once again the jagged scars running over her ankle and shin, spider webbing up the left knee and thigh. Some surgical scars. Some not. Standing gingerly, the instant she put weight on it Savannah flinched and bent over. Damaged muscles visibly convoluted into angry tight spasms. Frantically rubbing her leg to massage the cramps away, her breath came in harsh painful gasps.

His heart ached.

But he'd rather shoot himself than show it.

"Now what's your problem?"

"My problem?" she hissed, hunching over a little tighter. Kneading her thigh and knee, she rubbed cramping muscles so hard her fingers turned white and the leg became angry pink. "You haven't been making me walk!"

"So?"

She looked up, accusing him with glistening eyes. "I have to walk! Every day! Or my leg will never get strong."

"Then walk!" Riley considered spitefully tossing her warm jeans, bra, and sweater across the room, seeing if she could catch them. Somehow, he found himself standing right before her, offering the clothes like someone who actually cared. "Walk this damn house 'til you drop! But a strong leg won't matter if your every second thought is a wish to die."

"I don't want to die."

"Yes, you do."

Her chin stubbornly tilted. "I know what you're doing." Her angry snarl was low and threatening. "You're making me mad so I'll fight and heal faster."

"Nope. I don't play reverse psychology games. Truth is: I just don't give a damn." Her jaw dropped. Eyes watered. Her hurt feelings lay naked on her pretty face. He hated seeing it. Brusquely handing Savannah the bundle of warm clothes, Riley quickly sidestepped away.

"If you don't care," she questioned, "why did you bother yanking my head out of the bathtub?"

"Because I have my own conscience to live with. I won't be held responsible for you." He slid on his own socks and work boots. "So walk, if you can without falling. Walk this house on that pieced-together leg they probably should have cut off." He ruthlessly ordered, knowing the hateful words would strike a wound deep inside her soul. "But don't you dare go tumbling down those stairs, or make me carry your sorry ass back up them again. If you take a swan dive on purpose just to break your neck, you're a bigger fool than I thought. You know as well as I do, suicide is neither heaven nor hell. It's being cursed to walk this earth eternally damned, unseen and unheard, yet trapped forever living inside the misery of your own mistakes."

She shuddered. From head to toe.

"You can't fix mortal mistakes without a body, Savannah. God doesn't allow it. And he doesn't give souls who throw away their life, second chances." Threatening her with religious ideology they both feared since tender childhood, his hand was upon the bedroom door.

Watching him seething, Savannah couldn't breathe.

The truth Riley tossed at her was too harsh. Ghosts were lost souls. Ghosts were cursed. Good spirits didn't become ghosts! Only bad ones! Lost souls. Only a miracle got suicide spirits through the gates of heaven.

"I don't want..." but the denial caught on a sob.

"Yes, you do want to die!" He sternly countered, "You've begged me to help you a dozen times. I won't! So stop asking! Giving up won't bring you closer to Ryan. You'll be trapped even further away from his sweet spirit as you are right now. It wasn't your time, Savannah. If God wanted you, He would have taken you. But He didn't. So live, damn it! God still has plans for you. Appreciate the life He gave you! When you're strong enough to walk downstairs by yourself, then you can leave Graystone!"

Slamming the door, he angrily stomped downstairs.

For ten horribly guilty minutes after Riley left, Savannah stood there shivering in shock and fear. Who knows what the Great All-Mighty actually did with people who messed up their own lives. Maybe in His infinite Love, He took pity on them, after a few years of ghostly existence and offered a way to fix mistakes. The living saw ghosts sometimes, right? Was that their second chance? Or maybe life went round and round, from birth to death and over again, until you finally got it right.

She didn't know.

But Riley knew what she believed.

55

One of the damned.

Suicides were voices in the wind, crying eternally.

Somewhere in these wild mountains, her own mother's wayward spirit whispered. Savannah felt sure of it. And her father? His bellowing voice and boisterous partying laugh was drowned in a bottle.

Suicide. Both of them. Giving up. Lost.

Damn Riley for knowing her heart! Damn him for being here sexy-as-sin in a house she thought had long sat empty! Damn him for saving her pathetic life! Damn him for looking like someone she deeply loved, but behaved like her enemy!

Damn him.

No. Damn her.

Suicide was no longer an option.

# Chapter Six

Riley returned late that evening carrying food he begrudgingly offered. During the day Savannah had showered, then dressed in jeans and a white sweater she found inside Ryan's travel backpack that she didn't actually recall packing.

She walked. All day.

Shoving chairs and furniture around to form a walking track, she gimped painful loops around the giant bedroom until her leg violently trembled. Kneading the muscles into action again, she piled another oak log onto the fire from the huge stack of wood she found on the stairway landing, she mulishly walked a few miles more.

She cried.

No one saw and no one cared.

Lonely and depressed, she peered forlornly out the oversized attic windows. Her father installed them when she just a noisy curious child. A pest, always in the way of their nightly celebrations. He called them her 'Princess in the Graystone Castle' windows. A romantic fanciful notion, but even then, Savannah knew the giant attic bedroom and glamourized view of the world was her prison keeping her secretly tucked away while self-serving parents entertained guests with alcohol and loud music.

Once again, she was imprisoned.

Graystone's first floor rooms were buried, surrounded by a frozen barricade of glistening white snow. The storm wasn't over. Fat white popcorn sized flakes still fell from the frozen sky. Sometime in her fevered eleven days, her blue jeep parked outside the front gates had disappeared beneath snowdrifts.

"Are we snowbound?" She asked Riley, tenderly settling in one of the two plush rose-print armchairs situated by the fireplace.

"For now."

Riley handed her a warm plate filled with roast beef and mashed potatoes. Grateful, smiled and she balanced it on her lap. The food smelled heavenly. He poured her hot tea from the thermos and set it on the accent table, within reach. "For how long, do you think?"

"Until spring thaw, I suspect."

"Good grief! We're stuck here until March?"

"Or April. Depending on the weather." Standing before the warm fireplace now, Riley dispassionately stared at the crackling flames. He kept his back turned to avoid making eye contact.

Dang he looked good. Healthy. Strong. Formidable.

And angry.

"Eat." He ordered, "Your food is getting cold."

"Oh. Right." It did smell good and her belly felt hollow. "Thanks for this, Riley. I really was hungry."

He just indifferently grunted and nudged the burning oak log with the toe of his boot, shifting it so the core of the wood would burn better. By morning, that hardwood stump would be a bright orange bed of coals.

Taking a bite, the roast was tender and wonderfully seasoned with generous amounts of thyme and fresh ground pepper. Oh! It was good. She knew thyme was a natural antibiotic, but what was black pepper? Knowing Riley, it had a purpose beyond flavor. Maybe the spicy heat would boost her immune system. Medical supplement or not, the savory meat practically fell apart in her mouth. He must have cooked it in a crock-pot, which explained why Riley left her without food all day long.

When was the last time she ate?

She honestly didn't know.

Before waking this morning in Riley's arms, her last memory was arriving here and even that was a numb blur. Taking another bite, slowly chewing to savor every delicious morsel, she decided the roast was worth the wait.

"This is delicious."

"It's just roast and potatoes." He condescendingly sighed, "You're just half-starved from not eating all day."

"Maybe. But the food is good."

Tempted to greedily wolf up the pieces on her plate then selfishly demand more from the angry gorgeous man pretending to ignore her, she ate slowly instead.

Good...so good.

And Riley cooked it for her.

Savannah's eyes stung. What was wrong with her? Now eating Riley's roast made her cry? Gee. She really was a crybaby.

"So...how were the horses?" She sniffed.

"Warm. Hungry. Spoiled."

Curt and to the point. Conversation obviously irritated him. Well, too bad. She felt like talking. "How'd you get out there? Snowshoes?"

"Through a steel tunnel."

"A tunnel? Really? Underground?"

"No. Above ground."

She couldn't envision it. "Like a temporary hallway?"

"Yeah. A solid steel arctic-rated dome shaped hallway surrounded by snow," he sarcastically described, "with walls so thick and heavy they are nearly bulletproof, just like they use in Alaska."

He meant to belittle her with nasty sarcasm, but Savannah found the idea of safe passage between the house and barn fascinating. "Where'd you get it?"

"I bought it surplus from an oil company."

"Surplus? Like used?"

"Wholesale. New. It was overstock. I bought it cheap."

"Smart."

Reluctantly, he turned around. Although watching the firm masculine curve of Riley's well-shaped backside was pleasantly entertaining, Savannah definitely liked seeing those familiar hazel-green eyes.

"The tunnel goes from the back door of the house and connects with the stables. It's airtight and storm proof. I put it up last week while you were sleeping. Its rounded top makes the snow slide off so it isn't crushed by the weight. But if this damn blizzard keeps up, eventually the whole thing will be buried in snow, just like a long igloo."

"Sounds cool."

"Icy cold, mostly." The smallest hint of a smile teased, making him look wonderfully kissable. "After I put it up, I shoveled out the snow, but the ground inside was already frozen solid. Where I walk is nothing but slick ice."

"Can I see it? Sometime?"

"Maybe." In his back pocket, a cell phone rang. "What?" He rudely barked into it. Surprised he had cellular service this high on the mountain, Savannah ate more roast and listened to Riley grouch at his older brother Paul. He kept reassuring his worried family that everything was just lovely up here at heavenly Graystone.

Yes, he had enough food. The big walk-in commercial freezers downstairs were fully stocked, as was the giant pantry.

Yes, he still had electricity. The generator was ready, if necessary. He had plenty of fuel in the storage tanks. No, dang it…he didn't need Paul driving the city snowplow up the damn mountain!

Riley didn't want rescuing.

"No. I'm just fine." He curtly repeated several more times, just as irritated sounding with Paul as he was with her. Grumpy man. Growl, growl, growl. But…as near as she could tell, Riley hadn't told anyone that he was snowbound with company.

"You get cellular signal up here?" She asked after he hung up.

"Yeah. I let Sprint put a relay tower up on Broken Arrow Bluff. For a big fat fee, of course." His mouth twitched into a tiny smile. "That communications tower gave them a monopoly on service for all of Harmony Hills and insured that I always have a phone."

"Smart." She ate another bite, but somehow the roast didn't taste magical anymore. "Uh, does Paul know that I'm here?"

"Not yet." The corner of his mouth quirked, but this time it was mean. "Here," he spitefully offered the small black cellular, "call Paul back. I dare you to tell my family where you are and why you are stuck at Graystone with me."

"No thanks."

"Thought so." He shoved the phone into his pocket.

Having devoured the roast, she dived into mashed potatoes richly flavored with butter, extra calories designed to put a little weight on her sickly body. Savannah appreciated the gesture but really didn't like Riley's surly silence.

"Don't the horses need exercise?"

"I lunge them in the indoor arena. It's bigger now."

Sipping warm peppermint tea, she thought about what he did with the once-thriving vacation lodge. It was too big for one man. Yet Riley made Graystone his home.

All alone.

"But isn't it cold inside the arena?"

"No. The stables are as storm-proof as this house. I reinforced the walls and modernized the heating system. It stays a constant seventy-two degrees in there, year-round. Those pampered horses have no idea they live in icy Montana."

"Wow. That sounds impressive." Especially considering the fact that Graystone was already an impermeable fortress. "Where's Zeus?"

"In the barn," he nastily grimaced, "where he belongs."

The beef and potatoes comfortably soothed her hollow insides, making her feel stronger and a little bit defiant. "So? Can I see him?"

"No. You cannot."

"Well good," she chattered, mostly just to hear herself talk. "At least Zeus is inside and warm; right? You are taking care of him, aren't you? He might be a big dog, but even great Danes need a nice safe place to stay warm and dry, somewhere away from the icy snowdrifts. Is he pure Great Dane? He looks like he's half Big Foot. Or horse. That is one giant dog. He's a good boy; I know he is. Zeus deserves to be protected. Is Zeus safe, Riley? Is he sheltered from the storms? Is he warm enough inside the barn?"

"Good hell, Savannah," he scowled at her nonsensical clatter. "Why do you like him so much?"

"Because Zeus likes me. So, I like him."

"If a pig liked you, would you befriend it too?"

"I don't know. I've never met a pig. Do you have one?"

"No, Charlotte," he quipped, "I do not. Thank God too. If I did, you'd name it Wilbur, tie a string to its tail so everyone thought it was 'Some Pig' and then you'd want its stinky ass living up here too."

The Charlotte's Web image made her grin.

And snicker. Just a little. It felt good to smile.

"Eat," he ordered, "and drink your tea."

Slurping up the delicious gravy with pieces of buttered toast, she peered cautiously at the towering auburn man standing by the crackling fire. He sternly pretended to ignore her again but he looked lost. Hazel eyes watched fat white snowflakes fall outside the bedroom windows. Judging by his solemn expression, Riley was contemplating something very painful and unbearably sad. The misery and unhappiness in his face made Savannah yearn to wrap him in her arms and take away all the hurt, forever.

"Ryan looked just like you."

His head whipped around. For several awful anguished moments, she watched her child's father bite back vengeful words.

Criticism was coming.

She was ready. She could take it.

Hands shoved deep into his front jean pockets, his gaze riveted on the floor; Riley finally sighed in defeat and said nothing.

"Pouted just like you too."

"I'm not pouting. I'm listening."

Considering the quiet resignation in his voice, she carefully rose. Testing her weight on the leg that felt achingly feverish again, she slowly gimped across the big room and calmly set her dishes on the oak vanity table beside the door. She made it the whole way without having to stop and hiss-breathe through the pain. Savannah felt hazel-green eyes analyze every wounded move.

She shouldn't be snowbound in Montana.

She should be in a hospital.

Determined to show Riley she really did appreciate still having that achy leg to walk on instead of an amputated stump, she lamely hobbled back across the room without a single whimper. Savannah triumphantly stood beside him at the crackling fireplace. Walking without letting pain win was a small victory, but inside it felt enormous.

"Would you like to hear about your son?"

Again, she watched him struggle not to use words as weapons. His jaw clenched. The internal battle sparked angry heat in his eyes. Finally, shoulders slumped, Riley let out another sigh. Sparks faded into sad shadows. Like two warriors reaching a semi-hostile truce, he reluctantly eased his stance.

"It wasn't fair, Savannah. You stole everything good."

"God punished me for that, didn't He?"

Finding no sympathy in his face, and not wanting any, she shuffled over until she eased her bottom back into the fluffy cushions of her favorite plush armchair and propped her feet upon the fat leather ottoman. Her ankle popped noisily. Savannah stared at it for a second, half expecting the damn thing to fall off.

"I'm being punished too." Riley argued.

"By me. I hurt you, not God. Be mad at me, not the One who made us."

"I definitely am," he sternly affirmed, bringing a sharp sting to her eyes. "You took Ryan away from me long before God did."

"I'm sorry," she sniffed, "really I am." For years, she dreamed of Riley, hoping they might get a second chance.

This wasn't what she envisioned.

"So, we're trapped here. Together. Bet you hate that too."

"It doesn't make me happy."

"Then let Paul drive the city snowplow up here. You could kick me out, Riley. I wouldn't blame you. Then…I would be gone and you could get on with your life." Savannah suddenly realized that she really didn't want to leave Graystone. Or Riley.

"I've considered it."

"Why don't you? And don't give me some hellfire and brimstone religious doctrine about feeling guilty if I died and being responsible for my eternal salvation."

That stern face finally softened into a sly amused smile. "Huh," he half-laughed. "That little barb has been under your skin all day, hasn't it?"

"Like I rolled naked in poison ivy."

Riley's grin broadened.

He was so amazingly handsome when he smiled. It was an earthy wholesome, genuinely amused grin. Watching that simple curve light his face made her heart feel deliciously warm.

No, she didn't want to leave. Not at all.

In fact, Savannah wanted to stay right here and find ways to make Riley smile.

"Interesting image," he chuckled, finally relaxed enough to sit down. "Itchy and painful." Sinking that long powerful body into the other plush fireside chair, his gaze scrupulously raked over her. "But you're too damn skinny and scarred up now for my taste."

"Gee, you're so nice."

Wishing he still found her beautiful, determined not to cry again, Savannah focused on the agonizing task of rotating her sore ankle, seeing if it would pop. It didn't, but she felt the bones unhappily grind. "So, how many times have you changed my clothes or given me a bath while I was a raving suicidal lunatic?"

"A few times."

"And? You don't have any more heartless observations about the revolting physical state of affairs in 'Savannah-ville' that are guaranteed to make me cry?"

"No." Something in his apologetic tone made her look up from studying her foot. "You cry enough without my help."

Riley looked ashamed.

"You have more battle-lines etched into your body than a gladiator," he quietly empathized. "But those scars aren't just skin-deep. You're still battling yourself." Surprisingly compassionate, Riley leaned forward, resting his elbows comfortably on solid knees. "Giving up is for losers, Savage. Don't try it again."

"I won't!" She tartly replied, not liking how his sympathy weakened her. "I've decided that I'd rather be a thorn in your side." Auburn brows arched, questioning her sudden defiance. "Irritating you gives my life profound meaning and great spiritual purpose."

"See? You found something to live for."

Forest green eyes smoldered mischievously. So handsome. The gruff resentment in his stern face faded away. The old gentleness she loved miraculously returned. Savannah didn't understand what made that rare magic happen, but she love seeing it.

"I like this."

"What? Irritating me?"

"No, I like talking to you. It's nice."

"Good." His smile was actually appreciative and kind. "Now tell me about my son. Please. But tell me only happy things," he softly begged. "Like birthdays, and trips to the zoo, and how he learned to play the violin. Tell me how he lived, Savannah. Please?"

Her broken mind click-clicked on something here. It was important knowledge; she sensed it, but yesterday's memories were misplaced and jangled.

"How did you know Ryan played the violin? Did I tell you?"

"No. I know lots of things you think are secrets."

"Like what?"

"Ryan was my son." He benevolently rationalized, "He may have lived in New York City with you, but I was still very proud to be his Dad."

She studied him. He looked peaceful. Almost sociable. *Very proud to be his Dad.* She liked that. Too much. It softened all her raw edges. Oh well, let Riley be mysterious. A few rare moments of friendliness were worth savoring. "You'll listen? You won't say mean things that make me cry?"

"I just want to hear about Ryan."

"Alright." Trying to decide where to begin describing their wonderful son, she snuggled deeper into the comfortable chair, remembering so many good times.

She began at the beginning.

"I swear he was born smiling," she revealed. "Ryan was so curious; always watching the world around him with those big blue eyes, listening to everything and taking it all in as if each moment was a miracle. Constantly happy, he always had this expectant look on his face, like he was on some grand vacation and couldn't wait for the next wonderful surprise."

"Was he a good baby?"

"He was perfect. He rarely cried."

She shared with Riley all those important firsts: his first bath, Ryan's first steps, his first almost-word. It was hard. Her mind wandered easily. The memories were so vivid, so much a part of her soul.

In her moments of quiet contemplation, Riley sat there patiently waiting, trying to envision his son's life.

Then began his endless questions. Hesitant at first, his soft requests broke their reflective silence when she was lost in memories, gazing forlornly at the crackling flames.

"What was his favorite food?"

"Anything with peanut butter. Sandwiches and cookies mostly. Sometimes Ryan ate it straight out of the jar with a spoon."

"I do that sometimes."

"I know. He was very much your son."

That earned her a tiny approving smile.

A while later Riley asked, "What was his favorite color?"

"Mahogany. I don't know why. Most kids like plain old blue or red, but Ryan found it in his crayons and mahogany became his favorite color. He saw it everywhere; on autumn leaves in Vermont and old brick buildings in Boston and in gemstones at the Smithsonian."

"Ahh, Savi..." Riley deviously grinned, making her feel wonderfully dazed, "you miss a really big clue."

"I did?"

"Ryan loved the color of his hair."

"Oh." She smiled too. It felt good, as if that simple curve of her mouth magically pulled together a few of her shattered pieces. "He did," she softly realized. "Ryan loved the color of his fiery-brown hair."

They both considered that for a while. Riley felt proud that his son thought their bronze-red hair was special and Savannah sat there wondering what other subtle clues she might have missed.

"Did he like animals?"

"He loved them. He was gentle and loving, never rough. We had two cats, but Ryan wanted a dog. He would have loved Zeus. He would have ridden him around like a pony." They shared another smile. A few more pieces of her broken heart tentatively slid together. "But he wanted a rabbit. And fish. Oh, and a talking bird."

"Sounds like you needed a bigger apartment."

"We compromised. I bought two horses instead. We kept them out in the country. He loved learning to ride."

That's where they were that terrible day. Riding in a meadow on a beautiful September morning. Riding Brandi in big circles, they had been talking. Ryan laughed like a sweet cherub over something silly she said. Savannah could still hear that innocent sound; it was embedded inside her soul. His bronze hair glint in the sun like smoldering fire.

It was a perfect morning.

"What are you thinking, Savi? Share your memory. Please?"

"That last day…" blinking back hot tears, she forced herself to remember only the good. "Ryan was riding his horse. We were talking about you. He decided he wanted to meet you. I had promised whenever he felt ready, I'd bring him here. I told him that he should call you." There his sweet gleaming face was in her mind. Ryan's playful grin beamed. "He laughed and said that was a great idea. A phone call would help you become friends. He said that very soon, he would call you."

Instead of making Riley unhappy, for some odd reason, it made him smile. "I wish Ryan would have called me."

"Me too. I really do. It might have changed…everything."

"Maybe." For a few moments, he studied the flickering fire. "Would you have wanted a second chance?"

The innocent sounding question hit her so hard at the core of everything important; her heartbeat stumbled. "Second chances? Us? You and me?" He simply nodded and patiently waited for her to breathe right again. "Well, isn't this our second chance?"

"I guess."

"It's a weird one." She honestly acknowledged in the ensuing awkward silence. "Not exactly what I envisioned."

"I agree."

They talked until late evening. Riley left only long enough to bring up more mashed potatoes, buttered toast, and hot tea. The kindness felt so good she obediently ate the fattening food and told him more about Ryan. As storm-driven nighttime winds began to howl outside Graystone, he grew restless, watching her with an odd uncertainty in his eyes.

"Ask me, Riley." Savannah yawned and stretched like a sleepy cat, "I've answered every question. I'll answer this one too."

"I don't want to fight."

"We won't." He had obviously dosed her tea with white willow and valerian extract beneath a soothing-sweet chamomile and honey disguise. The pain in her body was subsiding. Savannah felt calm and superbly dreamy inside.

"I can't fight. You doped me."

"Herbs aren't drugs."

"Just because God created it doesn't make it any less effective."

"So? It looked like you needed a little pain relief."

"I did. Thanks." She flashed a mischievous grin for needling him and yawned hugely again. "So? What's your big dilemma?"

"Uh, well…it's real cold outside."

"Yes. It is. Probably twenty below."

"Heat rises."

"Earth-shattering news, Riley Phillip."

He always did that. Confusing man. Whenever something important bothered him, Riley avoided it by making odd evasive comments that jabbed at an errant dust cloud halfway to Jupiter. Gradually, if you were patient enough and asked the right questions, he might work his way back to the real problem. Or he would drop the subject entirely and leave you wondering what had been on his mind.

It was frustrating.

"Get to the point, Mountain Man. I'm too sleepy to talk in circles. Just tell me what's bothering you."

Still, he hesitated.

"Is it so terribly awful?" She prodded.

"No. Well…maybe."

"I'm a big girl. I can take it."

"Alright." His expression grew stern and defensive. Obviously whatever he needed to say, he expected an argument. "I'm not heating the rest of the house. Only this room. Graystone is too big and empty to run the central furnace. Usually in wintertime, I seal off all the upper rooms with thick oak doors installed at the base of the stairway. I only live downstairs, in the first floor. But since you've been here, we've been…uh, staying up here."

"You mean, we've been sleeping together in the same bed for eleven nights and this morning was the first time I've complained."

"You were too fevered to care."

"Sorry. I'm better now. Thanks for fixing me."

Those honest hazel eyes sought refuge in the flickering flames. "In your dreams you still talk to Ryan; as if you're walking though memories together. You cry as if your heart has shattered into a million pieces. Today you were better, but we've stirred up some painful memories tonight. Who knows what will happen when you sleep. So I'm staying with you," he staunchly met her gaze, daring her to object. "To keep you sane and to keep me warm."

"Alright."

He scowled as if she'd lost her mind. "I didn't dope you that much. Why no fight?"

"Maybe I like sleeping in your arms," she cheekily flirted wishing he'd stop being surly and pretend he liked her.

"That's not what you said this morning."

"As I recall, I tried to kiss you this morning."

"We aren't like that anymore."

"How are we?"

"I don't know. But kissing is a bad idea."

"Okay." She thought for a second and the image from their past that her wounded mind produced felt wonderfully right. "Remember when you were nineteen and I was still only fifteen? We loved each other fiercely. You spent the whole summer sneaking into my bedroom at night, just so we could curl up together and sleep?"

The firelight's amber glow revealed that Riley did remember. They were good memories. She watched him fight back a slow sexy smile. "Your Dad never suspected. John just liked that I was always, miraculously, the first one to work. He even gave me a raise and put me in charge of the horses."

"Good times."

"Yeah. Life was simple."

She wholeheartedly agreed. "Not once, that whole summer, did we get naked," she softly decreed. "Not once did we do anything wrong. We slept together innocently; like friends. We'll be like that again. Except I'm not a little girl anymore and you won't have to sneak out of my room just before dawn."

# Chapter Seven

"He wanted to fly jets."

The crackling fireplace kept her giant third story bedroom toasty-warm but the gentle acceptance in Riley's charismatic face made Savannah even warmer. They weren't touching. They rarely did. The days rolled together into a reliable routine of diplomatic ceasefire.

Six vividly lucid days they had been housebound together; plus eleven fevered ones she couldn't quite remember.

The icy snowdrifts were still growing higher.

Winds still howled. The storm still raged.

Yesterday they lost electricity, but Riley turned on heavy-duty generators that gave power to the house and stables. They had six-month supply of fuel in the military grade reserve tanks her father installed. Graystone took pride in being completely self-sufficient, but even Riley voiced that he doubted Big John envisioned weathering out a blizzard as vicious as this.

Good thing he installed the steel tunnel going to the stables.

The only way outside now was through the second story balcony.

At night almost predictably, they crawled into bed together, huddled up for warmth. A few hours later, she always woke screaming and gasping for air, fighting the blankets, yelling for someone to save Ryan.

Riley was always there, patiently soothing away bad memories. At night, there were no harsh words or gruff reprimands, only gentleness. Ridiculously innocent, they slept together in her bed with their heads lying just beneath the words "Forever Isn't Long Enough." He didn't ask permission and she didn't object.

Sleeping together was pure survival.

By morning Savannah always found herself clinging to Riley, curled up like a frightened child in his arms. Neither mentioned it. They didn't talk about bad things or her leaving Graystone; they only talked about Ryan.

"He loved flying. Whenever we traveled, we always got off the plane last. He liked to talk to the pilot and thank him for the safe ride. But Ryan wanted to be a doctor when he grew up, so he could be like you."

"Did Ryan know I'm a veterinarian, not a people doctor?"

"Yep, but a doctor's a doctor to a child." She snuggled deeper under the blanket covering her legs and lovingly stroked Zeus on his clean-smelling head. She won, of course. But Zeus took a seriously sudsy bath before becoming her pampered Shetland pony sized shadow and Riley gave him strict "doggie-bathroom is outside" rules to observe.

His bathroom treks atop the snow were record-breaking fast.

"Was he a city kid?"

"Not really. He liked the country better. Ryan had his game systems and laptop computer, but he enjoyed being outside. We went camping in the Ozarks a few times. He loved hiking. When we traveled, we loved to explore new places. He made up stories about the places we saw. When we were in Scotland last year for that promotional tour, we stayed in an old castle. Ryan loved it, but he swore it was haunted by a great knight who lost his ladylove in a terrible battle, but now in death, they lived happily together in that castle. He had a fantastic imagination. In Ireland he tried to catch a leprechaun." Remembering that day, Savannah giggled. "Ryan thought if he caught one and was real nice to the cute little man, the leprechaun might show him how the rainbow shines out of the pot of gold."

Her normally stern companion smiled, "Isn't that backwards? Don't you follow the rainbow to find the pot of gold?"

"Well the pot isn't just gold, silly. Its priceless jewels too," she informed him, "Jewels make the rainbow shine; not sunlight hitting the raindrops. That's just what scientists believe because they lack imagination."

There it was again. That cozy approving grin.

It made her chest feel warm and tight.

"Interesting ideas you planted in his head."

"Well, we're only little once, when the world seems fabulously magical and miraculous. Then we grow up and learn explanations that steal the innocence. The magical feeling disappears. I wanted Ryan to feel amazed with life, for as long as possible."

"The kids at school would have teased him."

"Ryan had a private tutor. Our world was very private and protected. He knew kids from all over, but they were involved in music and had private tutors too."

"So his life was just like theirs."

"Yes. To him our life was perfectly normal."

Relaxing for the evening, after working with the horses all day, Riley kicked off his boots and propped his feet on the big leather ottoman too. As he noisily plunked down his brown Tony Lama work boots, they landed beside her chair. Savannah spied a big Bowie knife in a black leather sheath tucked inside his right boot. She yanked it out.

"What's this?" Brandishing the nearly foot long steel blade like a pirate, she swished it back and forth in the firelight making the impressive silver and black-handled weapon dangerously gleam.

"Stop waving that around! You'll cut your head off."

"Ha! I'm amazed you haven't cut your foot off."

Riley tried to snag it from her, but she chucked her tongue and deftly flipped the blade end over end, catching it again by the black hilt.

He completely missed, and Savannah still proudly held his Cold Steel Natchez Bowie knife in her fist.

"Nice try, Mountain Man." She was no amateur. "But my hand is quicker than your eye. Planning on scalping me in my sleep?"

"No. I'm pure white man. You're the Blackfoot Indian."

"Only half." She corrected, "Mom was white, even paler than you. So I ended up with dark brown hair instead of black like Dad's, and I got her pale skin and blue eyes."

"So you aren't a Savage after all," he teased, "You're just a skinny little half-breed pale-face."

"Ha, ha. Very funny. Poke fun at the wounded warrior." Sticking her tongue out at him, he scoffed at the childish gesture. She was fascinated with the knife. "Where'd you get this?"

"Your dad gave it to me." Politely wiggling man-fingers asked for the knife back. She naughtily twisted the blade out of his reach. "I always wear it. You just haven't looked inside my boot."

"Doesn't it irritate your ankle when you ride?"

"Nah, it reminds me to keep my feet straight in the stirrups instead of tucking them under next to their bellies like you do when riding bareback." Inspecting the deadly weapon, testing the grip and balance with little flicks, Savannah twirled it between nimble fingers, making Riley frown.

"I like this knife. It has good weight to it." She swished it, slicing the air several times. "That big blade is like something a mighty war chief would use. No wonder Dad gave it to you. Good handle too," she noted, finally returning the razor sharp Bowie knife to its leather sheath home inside Riley's right boot, "it fits into your fist like an extension of your arm. Not like those pretty pocketknives that most men carry. Those break too easy and feel like a tool, not a real weapon. Nice toy, Riley."

Green-gold eyes had purposely focused upon the gleaming fire, avoiding her gaze. She watched Riley lick his lips and stubbornly fight back a satisfied grin. "Remember when Sam taught us how to use those throwing knives?"

Sam and Millie Lawson. She hadn't thought of them in years. The Lawson's owned the neighboring ranch and had hearts as big as Montana. Sam spent years quietly teaching Riley and Savannah how to survive life on the mountain. Savannah's parents were too self-involved to bother and Riley's folks mostly stayed in town, tending the store.

The Lawson's had two boys of their own, David and Luke, but Sam taught all four kids to shoot and defend themselves in the wilderness, to understand animals; both wild and domestic, and tossed in enough parental cowboy wisdom to make Sam their honorary godfather.

"We sliced the hell out of our poor oak tree target." She happily remembered. "We spent all summer practicing, learning how to throw those knives."

"You were always dead on; better than us boys. I was jealous."

Smiling, Savannah appreciated Riley's honesty. "But you could throw it farther and harder. You were meaner than David and Luke. It didn't matter if your aim was a little off, if that target had been a living thing, it would be dead." She shrugged, "It made me feel like a wimpy girl."

"You are a wimpy girl."

This time, Riley truly grinned. Finally. A real smile. It made him look so sexy. So kissable. *Yum.* Not wanting to ruin it, she just sighed and watched his handsome face glow, letting the moment happen without disturbing its perfection with childish banter.

"What?" He asked.

"Nothing. Just remembering, that's all."

"Good things?"

"Very good."

It was getting late and Savannah felt comfortably sleepy. Outside, a bitter wind blew ice and snow against the house, but inside they were safe and warm.

"Would Ryan have liked Montana?"

"He would have loved it. Ryan thought Montana was this great wonderful wilderness with giant grizzlies and cougars and wild buffalo. He liked hearing about the times when Indians still lived at Graystone in teepees and how his ancestors were famous Blackfoot Indians. Ryan had a chief's headdress with real eagle feathers he liked to wear. I pained his face with eagle symbols and he ran around the house threatening me with a toy tomahawk, screeching wild war-whoops. Sometimes, I dressed up like Pocahontas. I let Ryan paint my face too. He loved it. We threw a blanket over the dining room table to make a teepee and camped out."

"You were more than his mom," Riley softly complimented, a respectful light gleaming in his eyes. "You were his teacher and playmate. You were Ryan's best friend."

It was the nicest thing he could have said. Tears threatened. "I tried. I promised him that whenever he was ready to stop being a secret, we would visit Montana. Ryan always said, 'when I'm older. That way Dad can see what a big strong man I am.' I built you up into quite a hero. I think he was afraid you'd be disappointed."

"Never. I love my son."

"He knew that, Riley."

Savannah's wandering memories became lost in the crackling flames, so she missed the fleeting shadow that crossed her bronze-haired companion's stern face.

"Somehow," she wistfully added, "Ryan knew he wasn't a secret."

Leslie D. Stuart

# Chapter Eight

I should tell Savannah the truth. I know I should, but I just can't bring myself to do it. Those were my memories, my moments.

The only contact I had with Ryan.

Riley's cell phone rang one quiet Sunday afternoon last spring, changing his heart and life forever. It was an old phone number, forwarded to his cellular from the cabin he kept in town. He used that number as a veterinarian. Wondering why someone would still call it, Riley formally answered, "Dr. Riley Rosemont."

"Oh! My!" A small curious voice declared. "You sound so big! I found your number in Momma's cell phone. I tried calling a few weeks ago but no one answered. I was too nervous to leave a message." He rapidly jabbered, not giving Riley time to speak. "It's really you! Oh! I'm so excited! Do you really live in Montana?"

"Yes. I do. Can I help you, son?"

A tiny gasp. "Son?" That bated silence created an odd lump in Riley's throat. "I am! I am your son!" The excited boy sputtered. "How did you know it was me?"

It took only a stumbling heartbeat. "Ryan?!"

"You know my name?" He breathlessly exclaimed.

"I do."

"Oh wow! This is so cool," he gulped on the news, "I can't believe it." Suddenly shy now, the excited jabbering abruptly ended as Ryan nervously hedged for something to talk about. "Uh, New York City is a real long way from Montana."

"It sure is."

"Different too."

"Yep." Riley could hear Ryan breathing, fast and excited, and wasn't quite sure what to say either. His son had called him!

"Momma is half Blackfoot Indian. Did you know that?"

"Yes."

"But her skin isn't dark and her eyes are a funny violet-blue so most people never guess that she's part Native American. One woman, in an interview, asked if she was Hawaiian. Momma just laughed. She never told her the truth."

"Your Grandpa John Graystone was a Blackfoot Tribal Leader." Riley calmly explained, following the easy chatter. "His grandfathers were proud chiefs that raised horses. But your Grandma Vivian was born in Portland, Oregon. Her family came to America from England. She had light skin and blue eyes. I'm mostly Irish, originally. I guess that makes you…"

"Something special!" Ryan burst out giggled so happily it made Riley's heart melt. "I play the violin," he staunchly declared with a distinct touch of pride in his voice; just naturally expecting his father to keep up with his erratic thoughts. He did. Whenever tackling conflict, Ryan thought exactly how Riley did, in little hops and careful skips with carefully placed statements of irrelevant facts that jumped all around the real problem.

"I didn't know that you played the violin. Is it hard?"

"Nah. The violin just does what I hear in my head. It obeys me. I hear the music in my head and draw the bow across the strings, and there it is. Ta-dah! Music! Just like in my head. Momma says I play like a twice-born master. I don't know what that means, 'cept I make her proud."

"It means you are really talented."

"I guess so. I just like playing it. Last Christmas, I played Ava Maria for our church, all by myself. It's a really big church. The chapel has tall pillars with a giant white statue of Jesus holding his hands out to the people. There are big stained-glass windows behind Him, like the doorway to heaven. I like our church. I like that statue of Jesus. He looks friendly; like he really loves me. I don't like ones where He's nailed to the cross. I saw those in another church where Momma performed. Seeing Jesus hurt made me sad. Do you know that song, the one that I played?"

"I do. It was written by Franz Schubert. A long time ago."

"You know music?"

"Some. I used to listen to your Mom play." That memory put an odd lump in his throat. "Does she know that you called me, Ryan?"

"No, but we're okay. This is her cell phone and she has bunches of minutes. She's practicing her piano. Sunday is our quiet time. When she's writing music, she lets me call my friends. I have friends all over. We meet lots' a nice people. Most play music just like me." He hesitated, sounding far more mature than any six-year-old should. Riley felt proud Savannah did such a good job raising their son.

"Um…will you be my friend?"

"I'd love to."

"Oh good! Can you hear her playing?"

He could. In the background. Riley could hear the piano laughing and asking questions. It almost sounded like a woman's voice instead of a musical instrument of wire and wood. "She's amazing. Is that new?"

"Yep. We're writing it together. I already know my part. It's easy. I just play 'Twinkle Twinkle Little Star' on the violin in these different funny ways making the violin ask questions. She plays bits of other songs that people recognize, answering me. Together, we're gonna make people smile."

"Are you going to perform it?"

"Yep. Next week at Carn'gee Hall."

"Wow. Carnegie Hall? That's a really nice place."

"Mmm, it's big." Ryan obviously didn't revere the historical musical status symbol. To him, it was just another place to play music. "My friend plays the flute there sometimes. Andre; that's his name. He's twelve. He plays in a kid's orchestra. Momma plays there bunches, but she always plays alone. Or with a symph'ny, like she did last Christmas. I'm a surprise." He thought for a second, then stated, "In pictures, you look tall."

Riley almost choked. "You have pictures?"

"Yep. Bunches and bunches. I like looking at them. Momma framed one. The first one. Ever. It sits beside my bed. You were a little boy like me. You were holding Momma. She was a tiny baby with all this crazy thick brown hair sticking out all over her head. She says your families were always good friends and in the mountains, life is hard sometimes, so good friends become like family."

"It's true."

"She tells me stories 'bout Montana. Like, your dad's store. I like how everyone calls him Papa Rosemont and your mom is Ms. Emily 'cuz it makes her feel young. She sounds like a funny lady. In my room, I have a picture of you riding this big white horse named Diablo. But you were older then, almost grown up. You look so tall on Diablo. Momma loved Diablo. He was wild but she tamed him. All by herself. Diablo loved Momma. In the pictures of you and Momma together," he wistfully added, "you look like you really loved her."

Savannah had told Ryan all about him! His sweet son, who was supposed to be a secret, knew all about his father's life.

Riley wasn't sure which part of that was safe to touch.

"Well, I am tall. Six foot two. Papa still runs the Mercantile and Ms. Emily is your grandma, but she doesn't let anyone call her that. You have five cousins: two girls and three boys. They all call her Ms. Emily."

"Cousins!? Really? Wow. A real family. Uh..." he suddenly sounded terribly anxious, "are you married? Do I have any brothers or sisters?"

"No. I live all alone on the mountain."

"Sooo, you really are a Mountain Man. I thought Momma was just teasing." He softly chuckled. "Do you have a beard?"

"No. I look more like a cowboy. I run a stable full of horses."

"Really?! Any white ones like Diablo?"

"Some are his offspring. Others are gray with dappled spots and some are pure black. Mine are Spanish Andalusian horses. They have long wavy manes and tails that reach clear to the ground. I teach them to dance to music."

"Ooh! Like the Lip'zzaner Stallions? I saw them last year. They jumped way up in the air, just like Peg'sus."

"Yeah, like those. I train mine as show horses. Mostly they just dance around and look pretty. I teach them a trick that makes it look like they're running, but they don't actually move forward at all. It's like dancing in the air. Some leap real high and kick their legs like flying, but that's hard to teach. Several of my horses have even been used in movies."

"Cool! I love horses. I can ride without falling off. Falling off hurts."

"It sure does."

"I wanted to learn, so Momma bought us two horses. We keep them at riding stables in the country. They're really spoiled." Ryan happily burbled, laughing a little. "We ride every Saturday morning. We leave New York City before the sun comes up and I sleep in the car. Momma always times it so we get to the stables just in time to watch the sunrise. I like that part. It feels special. Then we ride horses all day long."

"Sounds like fun."

"Yep. Bunches and bunches. My horse is brown," he explained, "her name is Brandi. She's good with kids. Not like Wizard. That's Momma's horse. He's gold with a white mane and tail. I can't ride him. He bounces too much. But Momma sure looks pretty when she rides him." He suddenly became quite wistful sounding. "She films me. We film everything, even dumb stuff. For memories. Memories are 'mportant, you know."

"She has a video recorder?"

"Yep. We use it every day. Momma saves the movies on these little disks; permanent, so they can't be erased. Because someday," he wisely proclaimed, "someone we love might need to see what we thought was just an ordinary moment. To them, our ordinary day will feel very special."

Wondering why Savannah told Ryan that, Riley didn't know what all this excited jabbering was leading up to, but it was definitely going somewhere important.

He heard Ryan take a deep pensive breath. And hold it.

"Go ahead, son. It's alright. Just ask me."

"Okay," relief lightened his voice. "How did you know my name? Momma thought I was a secret."

"No Ryan, you aren't a secret. I have known about you almost your whole life. I'm very proud of you, son."

"Ohhh...so I'm NOT a secret." He slowly repeated. "Son. I like that." Riley could even hear Ryan's beautiful sweet smile. "I'm six. My birthday is Feb'uary second. That's when I'll be seven. Momma took me to the Smi'sonian.

It was waaay cool. I saw dinosaur bones. Real ones; older'n dirt. My hair is red like yours but my eyes are blue, like Momma's. Um," getting to the point of his fact-filled chattering, he took a deep courageous breath, "didn't you ever want to see me?"

"Yes Ryan, I did. I think about you all the time and wonder how you're doing. But I live in Montana and you live in New York City so you can play music for people. There aren't any places like Carnegie Hall in Montana. Where you live is very special. Your Mom takes good care of you. I trust her to teach you right and keep you safe."

"Her real name is Savannah, you know." Ryan sagely announced, "I like it better than Arianna. That's just her fancy stage name. Savannah Graystone, that's her real name. But Momma named me after you. I'm Ryan Patrick Rosemont-Graystone. You're Riley Phillip. We have the same initials, 'cept my extra G, of course." He giggled, "And see…Momma let me keep her family name too. She says the Rosemont's are good people and the Graystone men were strong warriors, so it's an honor to have both names."

The whole matter-of-factness of it all blew his mind. Savannah was utterly honest with their son. "So, what do you call her?"

Ryan hooted as if that were hilarious. "Momma."

"Of course you do." Riley sheepishly grinned and laughed a little too. Ryan was so knowledgeable and mature it was easy to forget this was just a six-year-old child. "Would you like to see me, Ryan?"

"Someday. When I'm bigger. I'm kind'a small, Dad."

Dad.

Overwhelmed by that simple poignant word, Riley slid weakly against the wall and thump…he was sitting on the floor. His heart raced. His eyes felt wet. He had to clear his throat. "Have you played at Carnegie Hall before?"

Now it was his turn to dodge emotional bullets.

"Nope. I have two songs. The Twinkle one, then we'll play a duet Momma wrote…uh, she wrote it for you, Dad."

There it was again. The honorary name that made his knees feel weak and his heart seem eight sizes too big for his chest.

"Savannah wrote a song for me?"

Good thing he was already sitting on the floor.

"Yep. It's called 'Second Chances.' It has words, but at Carn'gie we'll only play the music. No words. Everyone knows the words anyway. A famous lady sings them on the radio. A man in Hollywood used "Second Chances" in his movie and that lady and Momma won big 'mportant awards for it. Last year she went to Hollywood and thanked everyone for liking it. I stayed in New York with Marcus; that's Momma's agent. He's nice, kind'a like an extra Grandpa. We watched her on TV. Momma wore a sparkly white dress and kept her hair down. She looked so beautiful. She flew home the very next day and we celebrated her award by going to Disneyworld in Florida. That was cool. She made me feel like I had won an award too!"

*Second Chances.* He had heard that song on the radio. If Ryan hadn't summoned the courage to call, he never would have known Savannah wrote it or that 'Second Chances' was about him.

Riley wondered what movie Ryan meant.

A love story, undoubtedly.

No wonder Savannah had won awards. That heartfelt melody stuck in your head from the very first notes. It was an unforgettable message about love gone wrong and life coming full circle so love could live again.

"Savannah wants second chances? With me?"

"Yep." To his credit, Ryan just softly laughed at Riley's shocked question. "Wanna know a secret?"

"Only if telling me won't get you into trouble. Calling me took courage, son. It was a huge grown-up step. I'm really glad that you did it, but I don't want Savannah to get mad at you."

"She won't. Momma said it's up to me to decide when I want to come visit you and if we should be friends. I've been thinking…maybe we should try."

"I'd love that, Ryan."

"Good." His childish triumphant giggle was distinctly pleased. "The secret, Dad." His voice took on mysterious conspirator tones. "Wanna hear it?"

"Sure."

"Forever isn't Long Enough," his son reverently declared, stealing all the breath right out of Riley's lungs.

His mind couldn't function.

Savannah taught Ryan their private maxim, the one that meant absolutely everything when said to the right person.

"When you love someone with all your heart," Ryan solemnly explained, "forever doesn't feel long enough to share with the people that you love. Momma still loves you, Dad. Says she always will. But our life is here in New York and that life makes us happy, but you are happiest living in Montana."

This was hard. So much harder than he ever imagined. Savannah still loved him. Or at least, that's what Ryan thought.

"We talk about you, Dad." Ryan seemed to like saying that word, and Riley definitely liked hearing it. "Momma knows keeping me a secret was wrong. But now, she says, the damage is done. We can't go waltzing back into your life expecting miracles. These things take time. Rushing too fast would ruin our second chances."

"Oh. Wow. This is a lot to absorb. Uh, do you want second chances?"

"I never had a first chance, Dad."

It was so painfully true his eyes stung. "Now you have one."

"Thanks! Ooh! I'm glad you know about me! This is exciting! My heart is jumpin' in my chest! Are you really glad I called?"

"Ryan, I'm so happy that you called, my heart feels eight sizes too big for my chest, and I'm sitting on the floor."

"The floor? Really?" He squealed, "Me too!"

"I love you, son. With all my heart. And forever really isn't long enough, not for how much I love you."

That thrilled gasp meant everything. But Savannah's voice called in the background, asking Ryan to please come and help her practice, because she was stuck between 'Devil and Sunshine'; whatever that meant.

"Go ahead, she needs you. Call me anytime, Ryan. Maybe someday soon you can come see me in Montana."

"I'd like that! I'll call next Sunday! I promise! Bye, Dad! I love you!"

"I love you too!"

For almost an hour afterwards, Riley sat on the floor reliving every precious word, praying he would hear Ryan's voice again.

***

"Dad! Dad! Guess what?!"

Oh how Riley had anxiously awaited that joyful voice! "What?"

"I played my violin at Carn'gie Hall!"

"You did? When?"

"Last night! The people laughed." And Ryan happily giggled.

"Were they supposed to laugh?"

"Oh yes! I made them laugh so hard it made my eyes burn, 'cuz I wanted to laugh too. But I kept playing. I got excited and messed up one part. I shouted the Twinkle words instead of playing them with my violin. The violin was s'posed to be the voice, not me! But people laughed and Momma made the piano laugh at me too! It was great. I laughed a little then. The people heard it in the microphone. I couldn't help it. But the people cheered. I didn't want to stop playing that funny Twinkle music that made everyone smile, but when we were done they clapped real hard."

"Wow. That sounds incredible."

"It was. When the room got quiet again, we played them your song. I swear I heard a million hearts break. Well, maybe not a million," he honestly admit, "but there sure were bunches of people listening to us play. Their eyes were all shiny and bright. I could see them. I wore a white tuxedo and stood in a spotlight, so I know they saw me real good too."

"Cool. I wish I could have seen you."

"Me too. We recorded it, so you really can see it sometime."

"I'd love that."

"After we played 'Second Chances,' I gave Momma a bunch of red roses. They clapped so hard it sounded like thunder. My chest felt all tight and warm inside. They clapped so long; Momma asked if they wanted another song. They did! They clapped and stomped and some people even whistled. It was crazy! So I sat beside Momma on her piano bench. I picked out the high notes while she

81

played 'Baby Steps.' That was my song, Dad! My song! And she played it for all those people! We didn't plan it at all, but it sure was fun!"

"Amazing. You play the piano too?"

"A little. My fingers are still too small. The violin is easier."

"You are truly astounding, Ryan. I love you so much!"

"I love you too!" His voice squeaked with excitement. "I like talking to you, Dad. Feels like we're already friends."

"It's because you're a part of me, so we understand each other."

"Dad?" He mischievously snickered, "are you sitting on the floor?"

Sure enough, Riley was. He hadn't even noticed.

"Yep, I sure am. I think I slid down here when I was picturing you in my head, standing on that stage playing music for all those people, making them smile."

"It was the coolest," he happily gushed.

"My chest feels all tight and warm inside too, Ryan."

"Are you smiling?"

"You bet!"

And that's how it started. Every Sunday for three exciting months, Riley anxiously waited for that wonderful call where he ended up sitting on the floor and spent several days afterward reveling in the glory of his son, daring to hope that maybe he had been given a second chance. For the first time, Riley felt like he did the right thing by letting Savannah keep Ryan. He was so happy and loved. Their musical life was filled with joyful adventures that were magic to a kid.

Ryan toured castles and saw amazing places. He met famous people, but found them all to be very nice, especially to little boys.

The extraordinary life he lived seemed quite ordinary to him.

Riley was in awe.

Ryan was completely convinced that magical fairies lived in the forests and if you sat real still and closed your eyes; because fairies were terribly shy and frightened of big people, you could sometimes hear them laughing.

Ryan was a musical prodigy and special beyond words. He deserved the wonderful life Savannah was giving him.

Then one day, the call never came. It felt all wrong. Hearing the truth from Marcus Seabourne was the darkest moment of Riley's life.

His beautiful son was gone. Forever.

Riley felt mortally wounded, as if someone ruthlessly sliced out his heart with his Bowie knife. Even now, with Savannah here, he was walking around with a big empty useless hole inside his chest.

Riley let himself really love Ryan. With all his heart.

His son wasn't just an image in his head, but a real boy whose laughter felt like music; a talented boy destined to play the violin in grand cathedrals and live life to its fullest. For three very short months, Ryan Patrick Rosemont-Graystone was the miraculous epicenter of Riley's life.

Then he was gone.

He should have had six years with Ryan, not three months.

Riley should have held his son in his arms, just once.

He shouldn't have stood alone beside his small ivory casket lovingly covered with masses of white roses, and stoically watch the most precious gift God ever created be slowly lowered into the cold dark ground.

For that, Riley would never forgive Savannah.

# Chapter Nine

Savannah suddenly appeared in the kitchen on the first sunny morning they'd had in weeks. Twenty-one days, trapped inside Graystone. Quiet days. Winter held Montana in a frigid post-blizzard grip.

She was still shaky and moving slow but finally gained a few pounds, filling out her comfortable baggy gray sweats and a heavy white sweater a little better. Her gaunt pale face was pretty again, all healthy peach and flourishing. Today her hip-length tresses were twisted up into a thick Chinese knot.

Like forbidden silk.

"What the hell are you doing down here?!" Riley loudly groused, then he noticed Zeus watching his beloved mistress with worried brown eyes and knew who helped Savannah down three flights of stairs.

"We're housebound. I should cook."

With that defiant declaration, she celebrated her triumphant trek downstairs by preparing fresh biscuits and creamy cheddar potato soup. It tasted just like a hot baked potato smothered in butter, sour cream, and cheese. Cooking took her a while. Riley sat at the kitchen table and watched, gruffly telling her where to find the right pans and utensils, staunchly pretending to be annoyed.

Truth was; he liked watching her.

Lately, he even watched her sleep.

As firelight flickered across her smooth face, Riley often wondered how he survived the years without Savannah by his side.

"Not bad," he grinned, poking a buttered biscuit into his second bowl of her luscious tasting soup. He wouldn't admit it, but her cooking abilities far surpassed his. "Maybe you'll come in handy this winter."

"Pfft," she roughly scoffed, "Handy? Like a good broom? Or a nice copper pot? Wow. Quite a compliment, Mountain Man. Soon as this snow clears away so I can find my stupid Jeep again, I'm out of here. Then you can get back to hollering at Zeus and training horses; or whatever you normally do whenever you aren't stuck babysitting me."

Silence. His smile disappeared.

85

"What? I thought you hated our little situation."

"Uh, well," he frowned and glanced away, "In spring I'll plow up the whole backyard and plant a vegetable garden." Playing with another biscuit, Savannah noticed he wasn't eating anymore. He wouldn't look at her either. Obviously, whatever was bugging Riley had nothing to do with planting vegetables.

Moody unpredictable man.

Why couldn't he just say what he meant?

Instead of being irritated, Savannah decided to play along. "Gee, that's a ton of food for just one person."

Riley mildly shrugged. "My Mom called."

She shook her head. What did his mom calling have in common with her soup? Or a vegetable garden? Nothing. It was total randomness, avoiding the real problem. "Really? And what did Ms. Emily have to say today?"

"She wants to visit. Dad bought her a new snowmobile. She might come next week, if the weather clears so she can ride here safely."

"Good. Then I'll have someone friendly to talk to."

"I'm friendly!"

Having just gulped a mouthful of rosehip raspberry tea chock full of natural vitamin C that her body needed, Savannah started laughing so hard at his defensive tone she almost sprayed tea all over the kitchen. "Good grief, Riley. What's eating you? Are you pouting?"

"No." He was. A full-blown childish pout creased his brow. Unhappiness puckered his mouth. "I'm just thinking."

"Well please, Riley Phillip," she urged, trying not to giggle and make him angrier, "share those profound thoughts."

It took him a minute. He looked away at nothing, then back at her, and then looked away again. Savannah knew he would rather toss out odd comments that made no sense whatsoever than get straight to their real problem.

But she called him on it. Now Riley had to be honest. Obviously, it wouldn't be easy. Turmoil darkened his expression.

Savannah patiently waited.

Riley silently contemplated life and stirred his soup. Crumbled a biscuit into inedible crumbs. Silence stretched on forever.

Whatever this was, it must be good.

Or really bad, depending on the viewpoint.

At last, he reluctantly sighed. "We need to talk Savannah."

"We are talking, Riley."

"I mean talk about us."

"Us? Hell, everything about us makes you angry."

Riley finally looked up from intently studying his half-eaten soup. She was stunned by the tangled emotions stirring in his eyes.

"We were really good once."

"Yeah, when we were children," she rationalized, "back when life was simple and revolved around horses and hiking the mountain and eating boysenberries until our faces were stained purple. Life was easy. Our biggest worry was staying away from my Dad when he drank and our biggest gripe was my unfaithful Mom. But you kept me away from all of that. You were older and did cool things like ride motorcycles and shoot guns. So I followed you around, learning. I was a noisy pest, but you were nice to me. No one else noticed I existed. I was grateful. It was easy to get along."

"Damn it." He restlessly growled, "You weren't a pest! I never saw us like that. Never!" His fist struck the oak table, making his bowl bounce. "We were good because being together was right!"

What was he saying? Suddenly he liked her?

Impossible.

Riley was barely tolerant of her company. He'd make it quite clear he had no interest whatsoever in getting cozy. He was an emotional iceberg: except for when she shared stories about Ryan. Then, he calmly listened.

But that one perfect thing keeping him occasionally civilized was also the one thing that hurt deep, making him snarl and growl.

"We've both changed," she quietly tried to make sense of his outburst and not antagonize him further. "You've been polite about it, but I know you hate having me here. Everything I do makes you angry."

Scowling, he grumbled a strange conflicted denial.

"See? We can't even have lunch together without fighting."

"We're not fighting. We're..." he couldn't finish, because denying it would have been a lie. Back to studying his soup bowl. It made her want to cry. Why did he insist on being so temperamental? Was being nice so hard? Apparently, yes.

"I'm better now." Savannah was determined to be realistic and calm, even if he couldn't. "It's sunny today. The top layer of the snow will melt in the sun and tonight it will freeze into a hard layer of ice. In the morning, it will be solid enough that I can safely ski into town. I'm stronger now. I should go."

"You're better?" He roughly snarled, "You managed to walk downstairs holding on to Zeus! Or," he glanced at the giant dog lying near her feet, "did you ride him?"

Ashamed, she quickly looked away from Riley's critical glare. Of course, she rode Zeus down the stairs. Her limp wasn't just from clumsy wounded muscles that were still trying to heal, but from a bone-deep pain she was beginning to think would never fade.

"See? You cheated."

"So? Stairs are hard."

"And skiing isn't? You wouldn't make it twenty yards before you fell and shattered your leg into a million pieces! You made lunch," he raged, "that's great. A week ago, you couldn't. Your head doesn't hurt anymore. You can

87

think straight again. That's good too! But you and I are a little too volatile for your taste so suddenly it's 'Bye, Riley?'" He mocked in a hateful sing-song voice that made her want to bawl. "Thanks for yanking my head out of the bathtub when all I wanted to do was die.' I don't think so!"

Without warning, the uncivilized mountainous brute yanked her up from the table. She resisted but he proceeded to drag her by both hands across the warm kitchen.

"Stop, Riley!"

"You're better? Then prove it."

"How? Where are you taking me?"

She managed to free her hands from his grasp. He just growled low in his throat and snagged one powerful arm around her lean waist. Riley carried her through the house. Despite loud protesting, they continued past the oak entryway. Kicking and fighting through the vast living room, Riley took her down the back hallway. Finally, he stopped deadly still at the doorway to the pristine entertainment parlor.

"Stop this! Let me go!"

He obediently set her down. She wobbled. He scowled. But despite the odd fierceness that suddenly possessed Riley, his hands protectively clasped her waist, keeping her from falling to the floor.

"What the hell has gotten into you?" Savannah smacked him in the chest. Hard. Twice. It only hurt her hand. Riley didn't even grunt. "You big brute! Why did you haul me in here?"

Glaring, he flipped on the light.

Savannah gasped. Her piano!

It was still here!

The hardwood floors of the parlor were meticulously polished. Her beautiful white Steinway grand concert piano held center court in front of the ceiling to floor bay windows.

Normally, those majestic windows would have displayed a breathtaking view of the mountain. Through the glass that formed a graceful semi-circle around her piano, no sun gleamed.

All she saw was a white wall of snow.

Her knees felt weak.

"There." Riley raspily breathed, tugging Savannah tight to his chest in a calming embrace after the ardent struggle she ensued, "Play Spring, by Vivaldi; or Fur Elise by Beethoven, or Mozart's Op#9. Play your songs. Play anything, but play it with real feeling and heart, just like you used to."

"Play? The piano?"

"Yeah. If you can," he gruffly challenged. "I'm betting that you can't. I'm betting the music inside you is nothing but a jumbled up mess. Do this one thing to prove you're really better inside, Savannah."

"Oookay. Why?"

"You want to leave?"

"I, uh…"

"Well this is your chance. With the snowplow attached to the front my four-wheel drive truck that is parked inside the garage, we can drive over the snowdrifts. Play music like God intended you to do. Play, then I'll put chains on the off-road tires and we'll drive into town. I'll stick your ass on the first plane out of here. You can escape Montana and forget all about me."

"But, I…leave you?"

"Yeah. Leave me," he viciously snarled, "leave me forever! And never look back! That's what you want, isn't it?"

She just shivered.

The tremor started at her toes. Holding her how he was, Riley felt that wicked quiver shoot straight up her spine. He didn't know what it meant and frankly, he was too damn angry to care. "Play music, Savannah. God gave you a gift. Use it. Play from the heart. Prove that you aren't still broken inside. Prove you appreciate the life you've been given. Prove you won't drown yourself in a bathtub the minute I'm not around to stop you."

Tears fell. "Dang, Riley. I'm past that. Really, I am."

"Prove it. Play. That. Piano," he sternly emphasized, pointing at the gleaming white musical instrument holding center stage in that pristine sacred room. "Then you can leave Graystone. Forever. I promise."

"But I…"

"Play!" He released her. Savannah gripped the doorway. Stomping loudly through the house, noisily slamming closet doors, he yanked on his goldenrod ski jacket and sharply whistled for Zeus.

Then Riley left her.

Savannah stood in that doorway all alone, staring forlornly at the gleaming white grand. It was her first Steinway concert piano. Her truest friend. That piano never judged or ignored her. That piano just obeyed. She wrote countless songs in this elegant room.

She couldn't remember a single one.

The notes wouldn't come.

Determined to prove Riley wrong, she tried running through songs in her head. Touching an invisible keyboard in the air, she tried to play the notes but her silent fingertip melodies were garbled, amateurishly lost, and unspeakably sad.

She couldn't touch those black and white keys. They were sacred now. She couldn't even step foot inside that room.

The music inside her died with Ryan.

Without his joyful love, Savannah felt nothing.

Riley found her late that evening sitting in the parlor doorway looking lost and far lonelier than any woman should ever feel.

She never wore her waist-length hair loose anymore. She always twisted it into some foreign knot; just like her shadowy twisted soul. She rarely spoke. Quick statements. Muted apologies.

Unless she talked about Ryan.

Or they were arguing, of course.

But even then, she was a little too agreeable. He was tired of hearing rational calm submission. He was tired of Savannah trying to appease his turbulent moods. If she were truly better inside, he knew she'd stand her ground and smartly tell him off.

She never did.

He was sick of seeing hurt in her face. She'd tip that stubborn chin and pretend everything was just fine. It wasn't fine. Not even close. She wasn't dead, but she wasn't alive either. This was his Savage, a beautiful wild-thing that once ruled these untamed mountains.

Shadowy half-life didn't suit her.

Savannah was wrong.

All those years growing up together, she wasn't walking in his shadow. He walked in hers. At nine, Savannah climbed on top of the scariest white-lightning horse Riley ever saw and she grinned at her big bad thirteen-year-old hero for being afraid. She could shoot better, climb faster, and run for longer than he could. Animals loved her, like she was some God-sent angel, something sacred to be cherished and protected.

She was his miracle, blessed with a gift of music so pure it transcended ordinary realms and touched the heart with sounds so burningly bright, hearing Savannah play brought tears of joy.

He knew.

He stood in her parlor doorway forever, hovering at the edge of musical perfection, utterly in awe of her glorious talent.

Once, he loved Savannah with all of his heart.

Forever wasn't long enough. Not for them.

Forever was just the beginning.

Maybe he was broken inside now too. Okay. He knew he was. Riley couldn't seem to let go of the anger. He wanted to, but rage tore at the good like a beast with an evil mind of it's own. He struggled to tame it.

They had it right once.

They could do it again.

"Hard, wasn't it?" Not giving her time to think or resist, Riley scooped her willowy body off the floor and carried Savannah into the warmth of the living room.

"I," she shivered, "I'm cold."

"I know. I'm sorry." He was too angry this morning to remember to close the heavy doors to the stairway, keeping all the warmth trapped downstairs. "I closed off the stairwell now and built a big fire. It should warm up soon."

Standing her up on those wobbly achy legs, he quickly wrapped a heavy blanket around them both and held her close to his chest, encasing their combined body heat inside a snug cocoon. Stroking rich chocolate hair until the twisted knot tumbled down, he angled her chilled form toward the blazing fire he'd built.

"Better?"

"Yeah." She was plastered against him. "Thanks." Arms around his waist, she lovingly rested her head upon his chest and sighed. Tonight they would stay in his bedroom down here. Riley knew it would be a long and mostly sleepless night. She would toss and murmur memories, driving them both insane.

"Did you play?"

A shudder ran through her whole body. "Nnnoooo."

"Okay. So tomorrow will be easier."

"Tomorrow?" This once fearless woman actually trembled. Riley felt his own heart nearly crack in two.

"Tomorrow we'll try it again. God sent you here to heal. So, do it."

"God didn't send me."

"Like hell, He didn't. You definitely weren't in your right mind. No way did your fevered mind rationally choose to jump on a plane and come to Montana. God brought you here. He deposited your broken soul right on my front porch. And if you can't play music, then you're still broken inside. If you're still broken, I can't let you leave Graystone."

"I'm fine, Riley!" Shoulders squared, glistening violet eyes angrily glared up at him. The defiant stance tipped her face closer. She looked so beautiful. All Riley could think about was kissing her.

Maybe he should. That would get a real reaction.

Something besides politeness and tears.

He'd probably get slapped for it. Hard.

Hell, it might be worth it.

"If I play the piano, you'll let me leave?"

"Yeah." His voice seemed a little too husky. Pouty-sweet lips unintentionally begged to for his taste. The lean female body pressed against him had some highly desirable curves. He liked how her waist naturally scooped inward at just the right place. Hips sloped outward. That curved spot fit the palm of his hand perfectly. Riley fought the urge to run his hands further down her backside and let himself truly appreciate the ripe womanly swell of her butt.

Riley liked those forbidden female curves.

Too much.

He'd spent every night for weeks innocently cuddling up with those sweet curves, secretly enjoying how Savannah's deathly thin physique was becoming wonderfully healthy and amazingly appealing. Again.

Innocent. Hell. Who was he kidding?

Only himself.

"Play music like you used to." Clearing his throat, Riley decided he'd better get those very adult urges under control. "Then you can leave."

Blue eyes narrowed. Lips pursed.

But she didn't march into the parlor and prove him wrong. Laying her head upon his chest again, she sighed in defeat. Her arms around him actually tightened.

"Then you'll let me leave?" She wearily echoed.

"That's the deal."

"Play, then I can leave Graystone."

Savannah didn't seem to notice or even care that Riley really wasn't holding her captive. They were alone in a giant house encased twelve feet deep with drifted snow, huddled up together for comfort and warmth, but his custom 4X4 Chevy Avalanche LTZ was built to conquer the mountain. Flashy red and slick as hell to drive, the oversized 22" steel-studded winter tires and heavy-duty engine were no match for the ice and snow.

Besides, it wasn't storming anymore.

They could leave now, if she really wanted to.

Away from the house, the thick snowdrifts weren't as deep. Around the backside of the barn where it was open to the forest, the wind leveled it smooth. Just yesterday, he'd walked through it with Zeus. It only came up to his thighs. With the arrow shaped snowplow blade attached to the front of his truck, it would have been drivable.

Up here, the towering stone fence around Graystone's front gate held the snow in, keeping the wind from blowing away.

Sorrow held Savannah captive.

And they were surrounded by ghosts.

# Chapter Ten

Going crazy locked inside the house, Savannah desperately wanted to see the horses. They argued. Riley refused. She pouted. He tried to make her play the piano. Shoulders slumped in defeat she sadly gimped away.

One day of torture was enough.

She wasn't standing in that doorway again.

So she puttered around Graystone's first floor rooms that she stupidly managed to trap herself in, completely bored out of her mind.

Although, she had to admit, Riley's big bedroom downstairs was much nicer than her sprawling childhood attic. She liked his choice of solid oak furniture and heavy manly bedding. She loved falling asleep watching the flames flicker inside the rock-lined fireplace. It used to be an entertainment hall, but he'd turned it into a wonderfully spacious bedroom.

It felt cozier than her attic. Friendlier.

It was warmer down here too. The airtight winter doors closed at the base of the stairs locked in the heat. The ground floor encased in insulating snow stayed comfortable from constantly blazing fireplaces in the bedroom, the living room, and from the potbelly stove in the kitchen.

Riley had strategically modernized the old guest sitting room into a charming den with a billiard table, walls laden with hundreds of books, and a large HD flat screen TV with three-hundred satellite channels.

Watching TV made her mind wander. Riley found her one evening staring mindlessly at it, utterly lost in memories, crying pointlessly. He curtly turned it off and hid the remote. He declared that until she stopped being a hopeless crybaby, she'd lost her television privileges.

So everyday Savannah walked the halls trying to get stronger; avoiding the parlor, of course. Their one sunny day was simply the light in between storms. Another blizzard blasted the mountains keeping cheerful Ms. Emily trapped in Harmony Hills and Savannah locked inside Graystone Heights.

Trying to give Riley some well-deserved space, their first night downstairs she stubbornly curled up on the couch to sleep, but later found herself in his warm bed, tucked tight against him.

He carried her in there, claiming he was cold.

After that, she quit resisting.

Savannah cooked and cleaned, trying to be useful. During the day while Riley worked in the stables with the horses, she played the billiard table all alone; mastering the world's most spectacular bank shot. She learned to make a bull's-eye on his dartboard. Perfect, every damn time. She challenged Riley to beat her. He couldn't. He tried, but after losing several games, he got mad and stomped away. In between all that fun and excitement, Savannah read books until she was cross-eyed.

For two ridiculously long weeks, their silly battle to see the horses waged. Neither gave in.

November flew by.

December crept along.

She never touched that piano.

In the morning over breakfast, she begged to see the horses. Riley always coldly refused. Then he would stay away all day long, not even returning for lunch. At night, after obviously punishing her for being an annoying blight in perfectly peaceful life, Riley would finally return, smelling wonderfully of horses, hard work, and contentment.

She would rationalize why she should see the horses and make excuses that he quickly rejected, pestering all evening until exhausted and worn-down they innocently crawled into bed.

There, Riley always held her close and Savannah let herself pretend it wasn't just to keep warm.

She won, of course.

Finally venturing outside through the arctic rated steel tunnel linking the house to the stables, she was bundled in her white parka, leather gloves, and a fluffy white beret she'd found in her backpack, but of course, didn't remember packing.

"Interesting hat." He teased; toying with the fat white poof perched atop her head. "Did ya' steal that from a polar bear?"

"It keeps my head warm."

"That's good. Wouldn't want your thoughts to freeze."

"Nope."

With that first slippery step out the back door and into the steel tunnel, Riley automatically reached for her gloved hand to keep her from falling on the frozen ground. "You're a stubborn woman."

"Ya' think?"

"Hell, honey. I know."

Savannah happily giggled. The tunnel was freezing cold. Their frozen breath made funny white puffs that seemed to shimmer like magic. It was taller than she'd envisioned; nearly twelve feet tall at the center of the metal roofline arch. Lights gleamed from the ceiling. Industrial strength and cold rated, the bulbs stayed turned on all the time, just so they wouldn't shatter from the fridge air. The minuscule heat the lights created was completely lost to the uncompromising icy cold.

"I feel like an Eskimo in here."

"You look like one too." He playfully tugged at the end of the thick white scarf wrapped around her neck. "Where'd you find this?"

"In our lost and found box."

"We have a lost and found box?"

"Yep. In the basement. Along with bunches of party supplies, cases of booze we'll never drink, and a five-thousand piece puzzle that I put together."

"Gee, you passed on getting rip-roaring drunk and opted for the puzzle?" He grinned because neither of them drank. Her partying parents guaranteed that. After witnessing their self-centered lifestyle, alcohol held no appeal.

"I was bored."

"Obviously. What was the puzzle of?"

"Hawaii. A beach in Kauai, I think."

"Sounds warm." Unlike Montana.

Their voices eerily echoed as they walked. Trotting ahead to end of the airtight tunnel that was locked flush against the stable wall, Zeus looked back at the slow moving pair and barked, urging them to hurry.

It made a tremendous rumbling noise.

"Thanks, Riley."

"For what?"

She gave his gloved hand a squeeze. "For letting me come with you."

"Let you? Please," he snorted. "You were driving me crazy."

Laughing because it was true, her left boot skid precariously on the icy pathway. That turquoise alligator skin slithered away so fast it seemed alive.

She felt surprised by Riley's quick reflexes as he caught her. Suddenly she was incased by strong arms. His worried face was just an inch away.

"Easy there, Savage." His deep voice was wonderfully husky. "It's just cold enough, if you fall, you'll shatter."

"Like Humpty Dumpty?"

"Worse," he slowly released her, "walk slowly. Plant your feet evenly, not heel first. Don't slide around."

"Okay. No ice skating." But his hand stayed hovering near her elbow as he protectively walked beside her the remaining eighty-seven steps to the stable doorway.

She counted.

It felt good to count the steps toward freedom.

Riley spent every day out here, grooming and tending his pampered friends, but this seemingly ordinary event was thrilling for Savannah. Escape from Graystone, at last! As they slid open the heavy steel doors to the stable and stepped inside the warmth, twenty horses nickered in greeting and stomped their hooves in excitement.

"Oh! Holy Cats!" A huge tiger-striped tabby as big as a bobcat, mewed and rubbed against Riley's legs. Yanking off her gloves, she hung her fuzzy white hat and thick jacket on the coat rack.

"Who's this?" Eager to touch, Savannah knelt and rubbed healthy thick fur. The big cat gazed at her with appreciative yellow-green eyes and noisily purred.

"Goliath. He runs the joint."

"Hi'ya, buddy." She knelt down. The cat eyed her.

"Careful. He scratches."

"He doesn't look mean." Proving it, the tabby walked right up to her hand. "Gee. You're humungous." She greeted, stroking down his powerful body. "Mmm, soft. Wow. Your fur is so thick. I like petting you." Pleased, the enormous cat flopped over on his side and became a happily motoring rug. She laughed and vigorously rubbed his whole body with both hands. Goliath seemed to grin.

"Don't you have any small animals, Riley?"

"Nope."

"Goliath likes me."

"All animals like you."

Charging past Goliath's welcoming committee of one, Zeus ignored the big purring tabby and went straight for the bowl of dog food waiting for him. "Ah, there's your breakfast." She observed, "No wonder you wanted me to hurry." Crunching noisily, her big friend wagged his thick black tail.

The stables were warm and thriving with life.

Savannah grinned.

Original old creaky wooden floors were now a solid cement slab with modern drains to keep everything clean. Lighting as warm as the summer sun gleamed from the lofty rafters two stories above them. Each extra-large paddock stall had sleek half-door gates of modern galvanized metal, replacing the old chewed up wood slats her father's bored stable ponies notoriously gnawed on. New decking on the upper hayloft smelled like fresh cut wood and a circular access staircase that twisted skyward gleamed burnish red with new planks of oak.

"It's incredible, Riley. Just beautiful. Dad would be jealous." She gushed, genuinely impressed by the improvements. "The stables are so modern now. You've done so much work."

"Wait 'til you see the stallion corridor I added to the north side and how I enlarged the arena out back. It's three times the size it was before."

Picking up a bucket that he filled from the storage bins, Riley offered extremely sociable horses sticking their heads over the wide paddock gates generous handfuls of grain, a loving pat, and sliced apples.

"This is Duchess," he introduced, "I just weaned her last colt, so she's feeling a little bit lonely." He lovingly rubbed a dappled gray broodmare on the forehead. Eager to touch the sweet mare, Savannah rubbed her too. Duchess welcomed all the attention.

"She's a good Momma. Aren't you, Duchess?"

Riley looked at her funny. "How do you know?"

"I can see it in her eyes. She knows how to love."

All down the wide hallway, on both sides of the wide clean corridor, other horses eagerly nickered, shuffling around in their comfortable straw-layered stalls, anxiously waiting for Riley to say hello.

"And this is Eclipse." He moved to a sleek black mare with a gorgeous wavy mane. She affectionately rubbed her face against his chest. As Riley stroked her muscular neck, she arched it proudly. "Eclipse is straight from Spain with a truly impressive pedigree. Old blood, dating back a hundred years. She's pure black; not a hint of gray or white on her anywhere. She arrived this summer. I plan on breeding her this spring."

"What color is your stallion?"

"Black as night."

"Oh. Then their foals will be beautiful."

"I hope so."

Introducing her one by one to regal horses straight out of romantic fairytales, Savannah couldn't stop smiling.

And touching.

Andalusian horses were naturally gentle, curious, and incredibly intelligent. The mean ones like Diablo were a rarity. Each eager dignified face she rubbed literally beamed with acceptance. She had forgotten how thick their wavy manes were and how sleek their aristocratic faces looked. Powerfully built with stunningly shapely bodies and gorgeous long ballerina legs, they were horses fit for kings.

Just touching them made her breathless.

They were so beautiful.

Riley kept the lights and heating environment carefully controlled inside the stables. In here, his pampered babies never grew shaggy winter coats. Even in wintertime, their muscular bodies remained sleek and smooth. The protected horses had no idea the outside world was dangerously freezing.

She met and happily loved on all twenty of them.

"Want to see what I've been training them to do?" Riley finally asked. She'd spent nearly an hour meeting every horse and was back to rubbing Goliath's belly, who wouldn't leave her alone.

"Sure. Wanna watch, Goliath?" She questioned her newest furry friend, "Me, you, and Zeus? We'll be Riley's audience. Can you clap?"

The big cat noisily purred.

"He hates people, you know." Riley gruffly clarified.

"Well, he likes me."

"Obviously. Crazy cat."

Riley clipped a lead rope onto the halter of a beautiful dappled gray named Mirabelle. He opened the paddock gate and led her out of her stall. Strutting out into the wide central corridor, the leggy mare sidestepped and impatiently pranced.

"Wow," she gushed, "She's moves like a dream."

"Mirabelle is a real dignified lady; a born dancer. Mirabelle's a smart ballerina, aren't you honey." He affectionately ruffled her impressively long silvery-gray mane. Strands gleamed as if woven with sterling silver threads. As Riley fussed and affectionately talked to Mirabelle, running his hands over her chest, belly, back and legs to medically inspect her body in a way that the mare only found loving, not intrusive, Savannah realized how much he loved these horses.

It was there in his gentle voice.

In his compassionate touch.

And in his luminous gold-green eyes.

"Come watch," he urged at the pair turned and Mirabelle strut down the long corridor, "she's learning her Spanish Airs."

"What's that?"

"Choreographed dance moves," he called back over his shoulder, "for horses. She's mastered the Piaffe, the Passage, and now she's learning to Capriole. You jump way up there, don't you, Mirabelle? Just like flying."

The mare tossed her silvery head, nickered, and bounced sideways in anticipation. "Okay, okay. We're going." Riley proudly grinned, leading the way into the arena. "Coming?" He glanced back to make sure Savannah was still following.

She was, just slowly.

With Zeus and Goliath at her sides.

"Mirabelle does everything from voice and ground controls. Oh, and music; she really likes dancing to music." He declared, his long legs keeping pace with the enthusiastic prancing mare. At the end of the wide corridor, he flipped on several automated switches along the wall and stuffed a remote control in his pocket. Then Riley opened the chest-high steel gateway to the arena and took Mirabelle through it. Turning back around he flashed Savannah a wolfish sexy grin that stole her breath, then latched the gate again and disappeared.

By the time Savannah caught up to the pair, Riley stood in the center of a modernized dirt floor arena. It was huge now.

Her father would have been extremely jealous.

The previously simple sloping roofline now soared skyward with reinforced steel ceilings that arched like a giant circus tent. Hundreds of lights hung from the rafters. The dirt floor was packed perfectly smooth, not a single pebble anywhere.

Using the remote, *March of the Sugar Plum Fairies* blared through the integrated sound system. Without saddle or rider, only a soft cotton halter and a slender forty-foot lead rope, Mirabelle began prancing giant circles around him.

Just by talking, Riley made her gait change.

Fascinated, Savannah leaned against the metal gate and watched. Zeus lay down by her feet. Goliath jumped on top of the fence and perched himself on a wide crossbeam. Pretending to ignore everyone, yellowy eyes became narrow half-slits. Even over the music, she could still hear the curious big cat purr.

Mirabelle's ultra-slow-motion embellished Passage cantering movements were rocking horse dreamlike and breathtakingly elegant. So graceful. Hooves lifted, legs arched, then reached and planted again. Slowly. Like a waltz. On and on her body rocked, taking Mirabelle in beautiful slow circles around Riley. In perfectly calculated leisure rhythm to the music, her gleaming black hooves gently thumped upon the hard-packed earth. Muscles drawn tight, every calculated step revealed the incredible strength it took to obtain such utter physical control.

So glorious.

That silver-gray dappled mare was every little girl's dream.

Or one girl's.

But that wild-hearted little girl owned a fearsome wild stallion instead.

As the renowned ballet masterpiece ended and the easily recognized introduction to Tchaikovsky's thunderous 1812 Overture took its place, Riley clucked his tongue, motioned with his hand ever so slightly for Mirabelle to stop.

But she didn't stop.

Mirabelle kept moving those long shapely legs and amazingly…she wasn't going forward anymore!

Ballerina-sleek joints kept delicately arching and dramatically lifting into a perfectly placed Piaffe. Mirabelle looked like she was slowly trotting in place. But it wasn't the jerky up-down running movements like people would do. Her beautiful long legs were still gracefully reaching forward in exaggerated flourishes, but at the last instant before she hit the ground, each hoof zipped right back to the same spot where it started.

The effect was stunning.

As the music became more dramatic, Mirabelle snorted with excitement. Clearly, she recognized the pounding musical shift. With an exuberant flip of her long silvery tail the dancer broke out of the Piaffe stride. While Riley held the lead rope slack so she could have a few moments of have freedom, Mirabelle enthusiastically sidestepped an immense eighty-foot circle around her master, tossing her gorgeous thick silver mane with each step. Tail proudly held aloft, the thick tresses trailed like a decorative banner behind her.

Something big was coming.

Mirabelle's silvery body tensed with anticipation.

Savannah could see Riley talking to her. But his voice was so low and soft, only the dancing mare could understand his words.

Mirabelle loved this. The music, the movement, and the attention. That beautiful horse loved the man who patiently taught her how to dance. It was there in everything she did. From her pert flicking ears constantly listening to Riley's quiet voice, to the way she arched her powerful neck and puffed her muscular chest with pride when she did something right.

Mirabelle wanted to please Riley.

The synchronicity between man and horse was astounding.

There. It was coming. Mirabelle knew it and her body responded.

The music triumphantly thundered.

Savannah saw those sleek dapple-gray muscles begin to bunch in preparation. Mirabelle broke into a brisk canter, yet every graceful movement remained carefully controlled. Just like before, black hooves landed where they started.

Such power.

Such control.

The beautiful mare only moved forward by inches.

Talented legs became a whipping tornado of extraordinarily restrained motion. She'd never seen anything so exhilarating.

Such amazing strength! It was magnificent!

At the perfect moment with the evocative music, Mirabelle was suddenly airborne. Straight up, she went. All four legs left the ground. Her hooves were higher than Riley's head! How could a horse jump so high!

At the height of the dramatic leap, the mare quickly tucked her front legs tight into her muscular chest. Proud head thrown high, her neck arched like a mighty warrior. She thrust her hind legs out in a dramatic kick that truly looked like flying. Her body hung there, suspended in air for one perfectly magical moment in time.

Then Mirabelle came down from the sky, earthbound once again, but just as nimble and graceful as Pegasus.

Watching, Savannah felt a little weak-kneed.

She'd been holding her breath.

The next one stung.

Riley had forgotten all about her. He turned, utterly focused, the pivot point for Mirabelle's acrobatic performance. He only had eyes for the prancing silver-gray star.

This was his amazingly exquisite, perfectly synchronized world. He looked so handsome and happy out there working with Mirabelle.

No wonder Riley was angry she'd disrupted his life.

No wonder he stayed out here all day.

He hated being around her.

Riley hadn't hardened his heart to the world. Only to her. Riley still loved. He just didn't love her! But here with these magnificent horses, this was a world overflowing with love!

His world. His beautiful perfect equestrian world.

Riley wasn't gruff and grouchy just to needle her. He simply hated every moment they were together. He was trapped here with a woman he truly couldn't stand. Whatever occasional kindness he grudgingly displayed was simply because deep inside, Riley Rosemont was a genuinely compassionate man.

He just couldn't bring himself to kick aside the broken sparrow that fluttered to his door one cold October day.

A good man. A man who truly cared about life.

A man who loved deeply. Who used that kindness to teach beautiful magical horses how to dance. Horses that loved him so much, they flew, just because he asked.

A man who hated her.

The truth made Savannah overwhelmingly ashamed.

"Hey!"

She blinked at the stern male voice. The music had stopped.

"Are you alright?"

Savannah realized she'd slumped forlornly against the metal gate. How long had she stood like that? Probably a while. Everything had blurred into a miserable dark abyss of self-pity and regret.

"Uh, yeah. I'm good."

Lifting her forehead off the top of the gate, Savannah saw Mirabelle standing obediently across the arena, right where Riley left her. But the auburn haired man leaning down with his charismatic face just inches away from hers was frowning.

"I'm okay. Really."

"Good hell. Are you crying?"

She was. Big fat wet tears. How pathetic. All because she finally realized how deeply the goodhearted man that she loved honestly hated her.

"Sorry."

Riley grimaced as if her apology offended him even more than her crybaby tears. "Why are you crying? Last time I looked over here, you were grinning like a kid in Disneyland."

Savannah didn't know how to answer. She was furious with herself for spending weeks daydreaming about second chances. All these weeks she'd been secretly praying that beneath Riley's gruff defensive attitude, somehow he still loved her.

He didn't. He hated her.

He was just too good of a man to kick her out.

It broke her heart, all over again.

Sobbing now, she wiped cheeks soaked in regret with the back of her hands. That didn't help at all. Sniveling, she turned her head and dried them with her shirtsleeve. All that accomplished was to smear tears on her shirt. Her face was still getting soaked.

Riley sighed in disgust. "Get in here, crybaby." Opening the gate to the arena, he tugged her inside with him, latching it behind her. Using the tails of his own blue flannel shirt, he dried her puckered face, making her feel like a child.

"Talk to me. What's wrong?"

"I, uh…" she pointed, indicating Mirabelle, "she's soooo beautiful." The spluttered words came out in a forlorn broken sob.

"Yes. She is. The finest dancer I've ever trained."

"She fff…flew. Just like Pegasus."

"Yeah. Pretty cool, huh? Now, why are you crying?" Shamed into silence, she just shrugged one shoulder and looked away. "But you were so happy." He objected, "Amazingly happy. Now you've decided to throw a major boohoo party. Are you losing it, Savannah?"

"Maybe."

"Okay. Fine." He sighed, patiently playing along. "Then tell me what's brewing inside your crazy head."

*You hate me.*

*Bunches and bunches.*

*You'll always hate me.*

*And I'll always love you.*

"I should go," she sadly blubbered.

"Go?" Riley abruptly stood. Hazel eyes glared in utter disbelief. "Back into the house? Right now? But you were dying to come out here!" Riley looked more than a little miffed and quite a bit unfriendly.

"Not back inside the house, dang it." Shaking her head, trying to clear garbled thoughts, she sniffled. "I should leave here. I don't belong at Graystone. I just drive you crazy."

"So? I drive you crazy too. I'd say we're equal. Doesn't mean anything at all, except that we're both a little broken right now."

It was so unexpectedly straightforward and unlike 'evasive Riley' that she blinked in stupefied amazement and gaped at him.

"What?" He finally asked.

"You feel broken?"

"Every damn day."

Again, it took Savannah a few stunned seconds to digest his unvarnished honesty. "Just since…Ryan, uh…the accident?"

"No. I think it started the day you left."

"Oh. God. Sorry. No wonder you hate me."

Scowling as if she'd said something incredibly dumb, he click-clicked his tongue against the roof of his mouth. Mirabelle nickered, eagerly trotting to her master's side.

He'd trained her well.

"Good girl. You are a beautiful dancer, aren't you honey?" Riley affectionately rubbed that aristocratic silvery face. Big brown-sugar eyes gleam with pride. "You fly just like an angel sent down from heaven." Relishing the attention, the mare practically glowed. Snapping the lead rope back onto Mirabelle's halter, he thrust the soft cotton coil into Savannah's hands.

"Quit overanalyzing everything, Savage. Come help me."

Savage. She loved when he called her that.

Everyone affectionately called her Savi.

Only Riley thought she was strong enough to be a savage. A wild woman. Untamable. Like these mountains. Like Montana.

Her home.

"Will you teach me what to do?"

"Will you stop boohooing over flying horses?"

"Yeah. I'm really sorry, Riley. For everything."

"And stop apologizing about every damn thing! It's annoying!"

"Okay. Sorry."

Riley uttered an exasperated growl. "Shut-up, Savage." But the husky way he said it spurred warm butterflies in her middle. "You're helping me. Not crying. Got it?"

"Okay. I'm good." Savannah vigorously scrubbed puffy red eyes with her fists. "No more tears. See? All gone." Making sure her face was dry, she forced a broad childish smile.

"Cute. Brat." The corners of his mouth quirked upward, just a little. "Now move your crazy butt so Mirabelle can work. We have dancing to do."

She obeyed, gimping to the center of the arena, leaving Zeus and Goliath waiting at the gate. While Mirabelle danced giant circles around them, Riley stood right beside Savannah and patiently taught the gentle commands and subtle hand movements he used to cue the regal horse into action.

"Talking is your connection. Instead of a bridle and saddle and the weight of your body on her back to control her, use the power of your voice. It doesn't really matter what you say. Just make sure Mirabelle hears either praise or authority in your tone. At this point, all she really needs to hear is approval."

Going through the whole routine again, by the time the exquisite mare flew magically through the air and kicked out like she was soaring high above the clouds, Savannah was laughing aloud.

She even earned a huge approving smile from Riley.

It felt wonderful.

Afterwards, she hugged Mirabelle's neck and rubbed her sleek aristocratic face, gushing quite sincerely about how beautiful and magical she was. Savannah didn't give her rope back to Riley. She insisted upon leading her back into the stables. She brushed Mirabelle until she gleamed and rewarded the enchanting horse with slices of apples.

Next Riley let her work one by one with Alcatraz, Domino, and Bijoux; three yearling colts still learning basic dressage steps and beginning voice commands. Keeping a watchful eye on her, he rode a long-legged black mare named Jinx that flaunted a graceful Flamenco all around the outer edges of the massive arena.

Her shapely legs proudly strut like a sexy lady.

Satisfied Savannah didn't need him to supervise; Riley finished riding Jinx and saddled a sultry reddish-black dancer named Voodoo. The mare had starred in three different movies. Later he rode Encore; a mischievously jazzy silvery-spotted mare, and then Absolute, who was so black she gleamed; letting the fancy ladies stretch their long muscular legs.

The work was fun and exhilarating.

Savannah forgot all about leaving.

They were busy all morning and well into the afternoon, but her thigh and ankle ached so Riley let her groom horses in the paddocks while he rode his prize black stallion, Merlin, inside the arena. She had yet to meet Merlin, but she heard him in there thundering around like a mighty gladiator. She wanted to watch, but decided it was better to keep busy.

Finally, Riley joined her.

They didn't talk much. Once, he walked right over and casually offered her an apple. A nice one. All juicy red that he washed for her. Granted, he gave the horses apples too, but she grinned and happily ate it. Occasionally, she felt Riley watching her with that "Doc Rosemont" look in his eyes, but Savannah just kept working.

Busy hands drove away depressing thoughts.

Even if he did hate her, Riley was kindly sharing his wonderful equestrian world. The rare experience was worth savoring. No sense losing the good of this special moment by focusing on bad things she couldn't change.

Be grateful for now, she told herself.

Make today count.

This moment matters.

Then amid contented horses crunching and munching, with her hand rubbing the velvety muscled neck of a sweet creamy-white mare named Moonlight, came the one question she had been dreading.

"Why did you leave me, Savannah?"

She didn't want to answer.

Honesty tumbled out anyway.

"Because I was mean and selfish. I needed a grand adventurous life. I craved those audiences. I loved making music so beautiful it made people open their hearts and glimpse heaven. I couldn't do that here, with you. But you belong here, living under this big Montana sky, riding magic horses and traipsing up those unconquerable mountains. I didn't want grand adventures all alone. So… I took a little piece of you with me."

Silence. For another whole hour, they brushed horses, shoveled stalls, then put down clean wood shavings and straw for bedding.

Finally, he stopped working and walked up behind her. Out of the corner of her eye, she could see Riley leaning his arms over the stall gate. She was inside grooming Eclipse, making the mare's black coat gleam.

He looked stern and suspicious.

"Are you saying you got pregnant on purpose?"

Savannah turned and looked him square in the eye. "Yes, Riley. I did." There, she finally said it. The last big secret.

It took him several stunned seconds to breathe. When he did, air noisily whooshed through his lungs. "You planned it?"

"Yes. I wanted your baby very, very much."

His face blanched. "But you didn't know you were pregnant when you left? Right? You found out later, in New York."

"No. I knew I was pregnant for two whole weeks before I left. That's why I picked stupid fights with you so we would argue and break up. I knew you needed to stay here in Montana. But I needed to take our child and go make music."

She waited to hear the verdict of his eternal condemnation. She could take it. She was prepared for all kinds of hateful things. But those words never reached his lips. Riley looked at her and opened his mouth, then shut it again.

Frowning, he angrily looked away.

"I hated you for leaving." He finally murmured while staring at the straw scattered on the paddock floor.

"I know. You still hate me. You're just being a gentleman about it."

"I'm no gentleman."

"Yes Riley, you are. You are the finest man I have ever known." Tears threatened to fall big-time but she had promised not to cry, so she resumed brushing Jinx. "I loved you very much. I was proud to have your child."

It felt good to tell him. It was true. She still loved him. Regardless of how he felt, Savannah knew she always would.

But telling him wasn't necessary.

"I'm sorry my selfishness ruined your life. I'm sorry that I hurt you. I'll go soon, so you can be happy again. I promise."

That seemed to make him even angrier. The dark emotions stirring in his hazel eyes rocked between cold fury and a pain so deep it made her feel ashamed. She didn't understand. Savannah couldn't look at him anymore. Riley leaned against the paddock gate for a while, watching her. She could feel him simmering, but she focused on brushing Jinx.

Finally, he silently stalked away.

Too soon, it was time to go inside. They had been out here all day. It was well past dinnertime and her empty belly growled. Donning her heavy white jacket, fuzzy hat, scarf, and leather gloves again, she stood beside the coat rack for a moment with her eyes closed, smelling well-loved horses and listening to their shuffling animal sounds. Savannah tingled with good memories. She felt grateful for the rare day.

Unfortunately, Riley was waiting and scowling.

Apparently, he passed judgment after all.

Her sentence? A life without his love.

Locking the wind-tight outer doors behind them to protect the horses, they reluctantly trailed through the icy snow-encased steel tunnel. Zeus had fallen asleep inside the stables and was obviously staying there tonight.

"Why did you come to Graystone?" His frosty question finally broke their silence. "You didn't think that I knew about Ryan. You thought our son was a secret."

Blue eyes narrowed. Something blisteringly dangerous stirred inside. The fact that Riley actually knew about his son and did absolutely nothing to acknowledge Ryan's presence made her angry.

The fact that he loved Ryan, but hated her made it worse.

Something inside Savannah snapped.

"Because for two very precious minutes I held your son's hand and talked to him while he died." Angry breath made eerie white puffs. "His last thought was of you. I couldn't figure out why. Obviously, that question stuck inside my battered brain. Maybe I needed answers."

They stood mere inches apart in that cold corridor, like enemies making a final stand. His expression was grim and hard, but his gaze met hers without wavering.

She had told Riley how Ryan lived.

Now inside this frigid steel tunnel, with an icy knot of regret frozen inside her gut, she finally told Riley how his son died.

"Those two minutes felt like forever. I couldn't save him." Her voice cracked, but she refused to cry. Instead of sorrow, intense rage simmered, boiling over her broken heart, filling the empty spaces with something dark and bitter. It felt strong. Right. She clung to it. Rage felt so much better that regret. Savannah stood a little taller, letting the powerful furious heat inside grow.

Anger. Real anger.

For the very first time.

"We were covered in glass and blood, trapped inside a car that had become nothing but twisted metal. A tomb. But he didn't panic. Ryan said his heart hurt and admit he was scared. There were men shouting, desperately trying to rescue us, but all I heard was Ryan asking me to call you because he felt sure that you could fix us."

Green-gold eyes glistened.

Riley loved his son. It was right there in his face.

She'd lost a son too!

And in those two minutes, she also lost Riley, forever.

Forever wasn't long enough to heal this much hurt!

Hell had stolen everything good.

Savannah wanted to hit something!

"It should have been me that day!" She shouted, furious at the brutal injustice life had dealt. "Ryan should have lived! Ryan should be living in Montana with you. He should be here! Not me!" Flinging her arms, rage replaced sorrow completely. "Ryan should have seen Mirabelle dance like Pegasus today. He should have watched her fly. If I had brought Ryan to Montana before the accident, maybe we could have been a family. But you hate me now! All the good is gone!"

That fateful moment of hell in upstate New York stole too much. Her son. Her music. And her second chances with Riley. Furious with the whole unfair world, Savannah turned and marched away.

"Why did his heart hurt?" Riley quietly asked.

"I don't know. They never told me."

She stomped on a slick spot of ice and skittered a bit. The man walking behind her hissed but his warning didn't faze her. *Let me fall.* Physical pain was nothing compared to the desolate ache inside her heart.

"I only know his whole chest was soaked in blood. He wheezed. It was awful." Seeing his small mangled body again in her mind, eyes glazed. "He suffered, in those last two minutes." She coldly declared, no longer holding back the grim details of Ryan's death. "Making an innocent child feel such terrible pain was the cruelest thing God could ever do!"

Her boot slipped on the icy ground. Her foot flew right out from under her. Savannah squealed. Flailing her arms, she wildly spun. But she only fell halfway before her body stopped.

Riley protectively caught her.

"Damn, Savage." He breathed against her face. It was warm and her heart was cold. Being pinned against his solid body felt right, but the rightness of it made her furious.

He hated her. Why would he bother being kind?

"Are you alright?"

"Wonderful! Fantastic! Let go of me!"

Regaining her footing, Savannah meanly yanked herself away from his grasp, brushing herself off as if trying to get remove the feel of his touch. "I don't know why you caught me. You should just let me fall and shatter into a million unfixable pieces," she snarled up at him. "Then you could dump my useless frozen shards in the trash and thank heaven for relieving you of the whole Savannah Graystone mess!"

"Sure," he dryly decreed, far too tolerant and calm sounding for the rip-roaring quarrel she was burning to have. "That would fix everything. We lost our son. It messed us up inside. Can we just stay focused on figuring that out?"

"Fine! Let's figure out why God would steal an innocent child and make his last moments so painful, when I was perfectly willing to go in his place?"

"I don't know why. But He did."

"It was cruel."

"I agree."

Well, gee. How could she declare war if Riley just agreed? Seething, she changed tactics. "Want to hear the part that baffles me the most?"

"Go ahead, tell me." He stuffed his hands in the pockets of his yellow jacket. "Get this monster off your chest."

He was too patient, too purposefully composed, and too emotionally controlled while she was on the verge of hysterical screaming.

Did he really not give a damn?

No. She already knew that answer. Riley cared about his horses. Riley loved Ryan. But he didn't care about her. He hated her.

He'd been telling her that by word and deed for weeks.

"Ryan knew that you loved him! You were his dying thought. YOU, Riley!" She poked him in the chest. "Not fear. Not how much his body hurt. Ryan didn't even cry. He just thought about his Dad and had faith that you could fix him. A Dad who, as far as we knew, didn't know his son existed. But Ryan loved you, Riley!"

The abysmal guilt she felt for Ryan's death iced her entire soul, leaving nothing inside but bitter chilling fury.

"His last thought was of being saved by his hero. You! He said, 'Daddy loves me.' Then, he took another ragged breath and our beautiful son was gone. The silence was deafening! The whole rest of the time that I was trapped inside that mangled car with broken bones sticking out of me and bleeding all over the place, screaming for God to bring Ryan back, I couldn't stop wondering how that sweet little boy knew you already loved him."

Riley awkwardly looked away. What was he hiding? Something big enough he wanted to protect it. The truth was there in the defensive tightness around his jaw.

"For the record, I didn't come here to find you, Riley." Freezing despite her heavy parka, she turned and started walking again. Slowly. Determined not to fall.

"Then why are you here?"

"I came here hoping to curl up in a dark corner and die. I wanted to see Ryan again. I thought death was the answer. But here you were!" Outraged her plan went so terribly wrong; she flung her arms in the air as she stomped. "What a shock! And until you slapped me in the face with what suicide really meant, I still would have given up. But I don't want to become a voice in the wind. I don't want to be a lost soul. I want to see our son again. Someday." She firmly declared, hearing Riley's boots crunching on the ice behind her.

"So I'll wait until God decides to take me. I'm not asking your forgiveness or looking for closure. I never meant to stay here. I'm sorry that I've been such a terrible burden. You've been more than hospitable, especially considering how much you hate me."

Behind her, Riley made a funny noise.

She didn't care.

"I should leave Graystone," she rationalized, "The storm is clearing again. On ski's I can make town in four or five hours. I won't fall. I'll be fine. You don't deserve the pain that I've brought you. You deserve to be happy. You haven't done anything wrong. I have. I ruined everything. And I'm really truly sorry."

The man behind her was silent for several steps.

"Where will you go?"

"Somewhere. Anywhere. Does it matter?"

"That's a real dumb question, Savannah Janine."

His deep formidable snarl made her spin round.

Riley never used her middle name.

Hearing it from his lips was shocking.

Hands stuck deep inside his jacket pockets, Riley stopped walking. He'd been trailing just a step behind her. Now they were several yards apart. Shoulders had squared into a rigid stance that made him seem imposingly tall.

"Why is that dumb?"

Forest green eyes gleamed with something she didn't understand as he met her startled gaze. He swallowed back truth. Glancing down at the icy pathway between them in avoidance, he thought of something. His eyes swiftly sought her face again.

"I never married."

His odd statement hung there like frozen breath. "So? I'm sure you have had plenty of beautiful girlfriends keeping you pleasantly entertained."

"No." He denied, "There's been no one."

"And that's somehow my fault?"

"Maybe. Partly. Yes, it is your fault. So now, you're back. And I think you should stay here with me. Permanently."

"And what?" Her harsh scoff created an icy puff. "Marry you?"

"If you want. Yeah…" he quickly decided, "marry me."

She was so shocked her spine quivered. "Are you serious?"

"Yes. Marry me, Savannah."

"Have you lost your mind?"

"No. We should get married."

109

"Hell of a proposal." Frustrated hands flapped skyward, "Married to a man who hates my guts! Why? So you can spend every damn day of forever reminding me how you wish I died instead of Ryan? Well I wish it too! I know losing him was my fault! Marriage sounds like a sadistic punishment. No thanks!"

"I never said it was your fault."

"Very true. You never *actually* say what you really think! But your actions say it every damn day!"

Hurt and confused, Savannah stomped away with more agility than she'd felt in months. Angry adrenalin charged through her veins, numbing the pain.

"I mean it. Marry me."

"Marry you!? You HATE me!" She yelled, enjoying the way her sharp fury echoed inside the icy tunnel. "What a twisted mean-hearted thing to say!"

"Marry me, Savage." He repeated with more conviction. Riley didn't know why, exactly, but now that marriage was on the table, the idea seemed incredibly right. It would fix them. He felt sure of it. "I should have married you years ago."

"Bullshit! Lair! Meanie!"

Arriving at the house, Savannah threw open the oak door with such force it shook big icicles off the eaves. They dropped onto the outside of the steel tunnel like frozen missiles. Riley instinctively ducked. When none penetrated the thick walls, he looked at that furious woman standing in Graystone's back doorway and softly laughed.

She looked amazingly beautiful. And wonderfully alive.

"Finished fuming?"

"Not even close. Angry feels good! I'm sick of crying!"

"Good, no more cry-baby. Now marry me, Savannah Janine."

"Go to hell, Riley Phillip!" She shouted and angrily stomped inside.

Wow. Go to hell.

Riley grinned. This was definitely progress.

Watching Savannah flap her arms and fume, Riley followed her inside their warm house and quietly closed the back door behind him. She was seriously offended. Why? Was the idea of marriage to him that terrible? Or was it just the way he asked?

Man, she had been spewing a ton of emotional gunk on their slow walk. Poison, that's what guilt had become; a dark toxin simmering inside. Those last moments of Ryan's life poisoned her soul.

In the living room, she was still spewing guilty junk. That low feral snarling hiss sounded dangerously like outlandish lunacy. That's okay. They walked the road to craziness for weeks. It was becoming comfortably familiar territory.

Removing his yellow ski jacket and gloves, Riley hung them inside the coat closet, slid off his boots and left them beside the door.

At last, he had finally gotten beneath her sad emptiness. Boy, was she raging. There were no apologies and meek compliance coming out of her mouth now.

About damn time.

"Marriage!" She hollered, stomping around the big living room.

Okay, so maybe it wasn't the world's most romantic proposal, standing in a frozen tunnel where their breath made funny white puffs and it was so cold he couldn't even kiss her. But obviously, judging by the stormy female tirade raging and criticizing the ridiculousness of white roses and love songs, such stupid romantic notions still mattered.

Good.

Watching Savannah rave and splutter to herself, Riley considered his options and decided he had better tiptoe very carefully around the very dangerous thing that he actually wanted to say.

"We didn't celebrate Thanksgiving."

"I cooked ham!" She spat like a hostile wolverine. "We didn't have a turkey! Celebrating seemed silly. What do we have to be thankful for, anyway?"

"Well, let's see..." he calmly tossed fresh kindling and a thick oak log into the fireplace, making orange coals sizzle as the smaller branches burst into flames. "We're together. That's a good thing." She made rude sarcastic sounds of disagreement. "We're alive. That's worth being thankful for."

"Oh joy. Alive! Wonderful consolation prize for surviving a near-death experience that took everything good," she furiously clamped her hands together several times, making angry motions of smashing a tin can, "and crumpled life into a tiny useless wad of..." staring at her frustrated empty gloves, Savannah seemed at a loss for words, as if her frazzled mind just couldn't find the right adjective.

"Shit?" He offered in a helpful tone.

"Yeah! Shit!"

Trying not to smile at her vehemence, he watched Savannah flop down on the couch and attempt to yank off her sleek turquoise boots even though she was still wearing her heavy white parka and gloves.

Crazy woman was undressing backwards!

"Piles and piles of horse manure," leather-clad fingers awkwardly tugged on her boot. "That's what life gave me," she grunted, finally yanking it free. "Shit to wade through."

"Maybe you should keep your boots on."

Holding one stylish turquoise boot in her gloved hand, Riley knew she was considering throwing that overpriced hunk of leather at him. He almost smiled. This was the Savage of old.

This woman had fire inside!

This woman wanted to live!

Not just live; this woman wanted to fight and laugh and play, letting the music of life flow through her wild-hearted soul.

Standing before the crackling fireplace casually warming his chilled backside, Riley silently dared her to throw it.

Violet eyes glared.

A feline snarl rumbled in her throat.

God, she was beautiful.

"Go ahead, throw it at me. But if you miss and that boot goes into the fire, I won't fish it out."

Muttering to herself about bad luck and timing, she yanked off the other one and slung both turquoise boots across the room. They noisily chunked into a heap beside his scuffed Tony Lamas.

"Good decision."

"Shut up, Riley! Just shut the hell up! Your opinion is NOT wanted!" Then the anger-obsessed woman sat there grumbling incoherently, staring at her wiggly toes. On her small feet were those same bright magenta socks she wore that fateful first blizzard ravaged day, but now the left one had a tiny hole. She inspected it, twisting her foot around, making sounds of disgust. The woman might have great taste in boots, but she definitely needed more clothes. She had to do laundry every three days just to have something to wear.

"Christmas is coming."

"Christmas is coming?" She echoed with wide-eyed incredulity, "What does that have to do with anything?"

"Just saying," he nonchalantly half-shrugged. "That's all."

Jumping up again, Savannah cast him an irate scowl that included a warning growl and flung off her leather gloves. One skimmed across the floor, nearly into the kitchen. Next came the white parka. She only tossed that across the couch. Must have been too heavy to fling across the room.

"Christmas IS coming." He casually emphasized.

"So? Who are you to be so concerned? Santa Claus?"

"Nah. I have flying horses, not reindeer. Although my truck is red," he noted, rubbing his hands across his backside that was nicely warm from the fire, "it would make a lousy sleigh."

"Jackass!"

"Raving lunatic."

"Heartless...grumpy...troll!"

"Crybaby."

"Big mean BULLY!"

"Scrooge."

"Dang it! I do NOT hate Christmas!"

"Hmm, that's good to know." Riley fought back a winning smile, "Then I think we should have prime rib. I have one in the freezer. And scalloped potatoes. Maybe we'll make some hot apple cider and sit by..."

"Good grief, now your planning Christmas dinner!?"

"Well, sure." He pretended to be puzzled by her temper tantrum. "It's the happiest day of the year."

"GRRrrrr!" Glaring at him, livid his unexpected marriage proposal had upset the fragile balance of the ethereal numb existence she'd been wallowing in, Savannah stomped around the entire living room spluttering furiously.

Apparently, she forgot the white scarf trailing from her neck and the plush white hat was still cozily perched upon her head in a way that was almost comical.

"Irritating Mountain Man! You never say what you really mean!" Arms flung wildly in exasperation. "You just toss pebbles into mud puddles, creating emotional ripples that have no significance to the real problem at all. Why don't you take whatever confusing thing you ACTUALLY have rolling around inside your head and go jump in a lake?"

Riley finally grinned. Wide and proud.

She understood how he thought. He seriously liked that she did. It made his heart feel warm and tight; eight sizes too big for his chest.

She was right. He *was* tossing pebbles into puddles, carefully gauging their effect. But the emotional lake Riley spent two months cautiously edging his way up to was dark and deep. Once he created ripples in that placid surface, there would be no stopping the waves.

"You forgot your polar bear hat."

"Shut! Up!" Finally yanking off her fuzzy white hat, Savannah tossed it onto the couch. She must have snatched the hair-tie too, because the long brown hair she kept braided all day tumbled loose into a wavy chocolate sheet. Remembering the scarf, she angrily yanked if off her neck and threw it across the room. It sailed and billowed like a long white ribbon.

"We should decorate a Christmas tree."

Violet eyes gleaming, she vicious whirled on him, "I never married! Christmas is coming! Decorate a tree?" Small feminine hands flailed skyward with baffled vehemence. "Have you lost your mind? Who the hell cares?"

"You care."

Without preamble or warning, Riley marched forward and gathered a startled Savannah close, pinning her slender body tight against his. "I saw you looking at the calendar yesterday. That's why you want to leave. You don't want silence and sad memories. You know you'll miss that little boy's joyful laugh and spend the holidays crying."

"I cry every day," she rebelliously squirmed, "Christmas is no different!"

Cupping her face in his hand, he declared. "I don't hate you, Savannah." He said it so sincerely, violet eyes bugged.

"Huh? You what?"

"I don't hate you," he truthfully reaffirmed, "not at all. Quite the opposite, in fact." Fingers gently stroked across her soft cheek. He liked how smooth her skin was. "Maybe I'm all twisted up inside about losing Ryan, but I'm twisted up inside over you too."

"You are? But Riley, you grump around like I'm the worst thing..." her beautiful face puckered. She couldn't continue.

"Sorry I've been so harsh. I haven't handled things very well." Tilting her stubborn chin closer, he lovingly traced her pouty bottom lip with his thumb, finally touching Savannah exactly how he'd envisioned doing. With his other hand holding her waist, he felt her taut spine quiver. "We should be friends, not enemies. We used to be friends. You were my best friend, Savage. We should have been friends forever."

The tender honesty made her eyes water.

Riley gently folded her into his arms, hugging Savannah in a compassionate cocoon of love. She stiffened, but then she sighed and accepted it. Arms laced around his back, she gave in. Holding him close, her pretty face lay right against his heart.

It felt so right.

This morning when he saw her slumped against that gate, crying her broken heart out, his soul ached too. But he gruffly pushed her past it; and she had a great day. Smiling and loving on those horses, she spent hours beaming like she was trying to savor every second.

Beautiful. He loved watching her.

Savannah deserved the truth.

"I never married because in my heart, I still belonged to you." He gently confessed, "I understand why you left. You were right; Montana wasn't big enough for your music. Maybe it felt selfish to steal Ryan from me, but I understand that too. You still loved me. Your acceptance to Julliard was your golden opportunity to shine. Problem was; you couldn't envision me living out there in the spotlight too. So, you took what you could from here and did what you were destined to do. And you loved our son with all your heart."

She was crying. Softly. Trembling in his arms.

"I haven't been honest. I let you go. I could have stopped you from going to New York City, but I didn't even try. All that glorious talent, trapped here in the mountains with me felt wrong. You rose so fast to stardom. Tours and concerts and recordings; it was everything you deserved."

Caressing her hair, he still felt that warm pride of knowing she'd made it. "After you changed your name, you were careful. Your picture was never on your CD's. I understand that too. You needed a clean break from Montana, from your parents...and maybe even from me. You had to become the woman God intended. Untarnished by the past. When Ryan was three, I went to New York determined to claim my son. It's a real big city. But I found you."

Looking up at him, her mouth dropped open.

"Right when I had worked up the courage to bug your doorman, you and Ryan came out those glittery glass doors, laughing like best friends. You were

114

completely engrossed in one another. The two of you walked right past me. It felt weird to be that close, yet so far. I followed you. For one near-perfect afternoon, I watched my beautiful family playing in Central Park. You ran with Ryan and played silly chasing games. You always let him win. You fed popcorn to the ducks and waddled around imitating them. It made him laugh so hard he said his side hurt."

"You were close enough to hear us?"

"Close enough I memorized his smile."

"I never saw you."

"You only had eyes for Ryan."

"Why didn't you talk to me?"

"I considered it, but when Ryan got tired, you buried my sweet son in a big pile of red and gold leaves that you scraped together. It was exactly how we used to play. Then you flopped down in the leaves beside him. That's when I knew you were just trying to give Ryan a piece of what we had together. You wanted him to experience that innocent joy and unconditional friendship we shared. I watched you two lay there until almost sunset just talking and inspecting leaves, finding funny shapes in the clouds, and laughing about goofy things."

"I was tempted to walk over and say 'Hey, Ryan. I'm your Dad. Can I join you?' But I just couldn't bring turmoil into Ryan's life. I knew we would fight. Ryan belonged in that wonderful life with you. You made him happy. I didn't think you loved me anymore. So, I came home. Alone. Without the people that I have *always* considered to be my family."

She looked utterly ashamed and terribly distraught.

"I'm so sorry," she needlessly apologized, "I wish I'd seen you. We could have…oh, Riley. I feel just awful," her chin puckered. "Talking to you would have changed so many things. Ryan would still be alive if…"

"No," he abruptly countered, "You can't second-guess God. We can't live like that. It's wrong."

Her brow furrowed in confusion. "Then why are you telling me this? I know I screwed everything up. I should have called or written a letter; something to give you a choice. But I didn't. That's your point, isn't it? You were right there. I had a chance to fix everything, but I was too blind to see you?"

"No, honey. I could have fixed it. But I walked away. *That* was my point." He tenderly acknowledged. "I'm sorry. Leaving you alone was wrong."

Warily, expecting her to smack him and dart away, Riley tipped her face up. Violet eyes were wide. He almost smiled. Instead, he lowered his head and gently kissed her.

Soft. Just a tender plea for forgiveness.

At first, she resisted. Then she whispered his name.

*Riley…*

Warm lips softened under his. She whimpered. Eyes closed, feminine fingers eagerly skimmed up the broad plains of his chest and laced around his neck. Clutching the back of his hair in joyful sliding-fists, she actually drew him closer.

It had been a long time.

Too long.

Yet her pouty-sweet mouth tasted so familiar.

He liked how Savannah stood on her toes and instinctively pressed against him. He loved when her fingers clasped and stroked his hair. Possessively running his hands down her backside to cradle jean-clad hips in his palms, she groaned with need.

*Yeah, baby. Me too.*

Still trickling his hair through her fingers, she let the fistful slide through her hand. He loved when she did that.

It felt good. Real good.

Taking that as a positive sign, Riley tasted and teased. Hands memorized the shape of Savannah. Up her back and around her ribcage. Wanting more, he appreciatively cupped feminine curves that he hadn't touched in years. She let him. In fact, those curves arched into his hands, as if she needed this stolen recklessness too.

Her body felt slender in places, amazingly rounded in others, but definitely not fragile anymore.

Savannah Graystone used to be the strongest woman he had ever known. Inside, where it really mattered. She could be strong again.

He could help her.

Or he could keep tearing her down and let guilt poison everything good. In that kiss, with mouths and bodies eagerly became reacquainted with one another, Riley decided he had best get his priorities straight and quit acting like a heartless troll. He didn't want to be surly anymore. He didn't want to see Savannah cry.

What he really wanted was to feel exactly like this.

All the time.

Marriage would fix them!

Being married was a promise.

It would make all the wrongs right. He felt sure of it.

He needed this beautiful woman to be his wife. Forever.

"Oh...my..." she huskily exclaimed as they reluctantly drew apart. In her eyes, a miraculous violet light overpowered the sad lavender-gray. He had seen this light before. It could only mean one thing.

Savannah still loved him!

"On Christmas Eve, I'll put snow chains on the tires of my truck and we can drive into town," he softly proposed. "We'll look at the holiday lights in Harmony Hills. That should get us into a proper holiday spirit. We'll visit my parents and have dinner at Paul's steakhouse. I'll buy you more clothes. And I'd really like it," he sincerely begged, "if you would please marry me. We can live here, or I'll sell Graystone and we'll buy a ranch in New York. I can raise horses anywhere. But I won't lose you again, Savannah."

She sucked in a great noisy gulp of air and grinned. She was laughing. Real honest sultry-husky laughter. This wasn't the hysterical kind he heard before, this was velvet pleasure and tickled-pink amusement wonderfully intertwined.

It made him want to kiss her again.

And strip her naked.

"I have clothes. Tons of clothes." Then, just as unexpectedly, she sternly pulled away and frowned. His arms felt barren and cold.

"Married? You don't even like me, Riley."

"A pair of sweats, three sweaters, two blue jeans, a few socks and underwear does not constitute a full wardrobe, Savage. Besides, I just asked you to marry me. Nicely. I believe that means I like you. I even agreed to live anywhere you want. Didn't you catch that part?"

"I heard your crazy idea."

"So? What's the real problem?"

She nervously licked her lips. "I left New York. Our penthouse apartment sold fully furnished in two days. I even sold my piano. They gave me a month to move out, but I hated being there alone. I went crazy and packed everything. Our clothes. All of Ryan's things; toys, books, even his laptop. I shipped everything to your Dad at the mercantile. It's all there, Riley. Our whole life is waiting for you in carefully packed boxes."

"My dad knew that you were coming?"

"Not exactly. I addressed them to you, no return address. The instructions said to give you those boxes on Christmas Day." She reluctantly confessed, "I didn't expect to be alive when you opened them. I hurt so deep. I just wanted to curl up in an empty corner and die. Inside, I was already dead. I couldn't sleep and I didn't eat. I thought leaving the hospital would help. I was so alone. I felt frantic. Everything reminded me of Ryan. I just walked around from room to room, crying and remembering. It made me feel like I'd already become a ghost."

A teardrop slowly rolled down her cheek. She had stepped only a few feet away, but that small distance felt like a deep canyon isolating her from everything good. Offering his hand, Riley felt relieved when she reluctantly laced her fingers into his and came closer again.

"So I dumped all the pills, tore that cast off my leg and got on a plane. I knew of a dark empty house in the mountains. A place for ghosts. Except Graystone wasn't empty and someone strong had chased away all the ghosts. I don't remember flying here. I don't remember driving up the mountain. My brain completely flat-lined until the instant I stood on your front porch, wondering why I'd come home. But it was too late. You were growling at me and Zeus had me cornered against the door."

"Are you really sorry that I kept you alive?"

"No. I'm very grateful. Thank you."

Considering everything she said, everything they lost, and everything he still wanted from life, his mind whirled.

"I meant it, Savannah."

"What? That I need more clothes? I agree." She grinned, wiggling pink clad toes with the hole shining through. "I used to be much more fashionably attired."

"I meant, crazy woman; will you marry me? Please?"

"I..." her chin quivered, "I just can't."

"Why not?"

"We're a mess."

"Maybe we're not doing great right now, but we can heal. We'll heal together. We used to be very best friends. We used to be great lovers. We could be really good again, I know we could."

Staring at the floor, nervous fingers toyed with his. When she met his gaze again, he saw uncertainty. "Would you like to see pictures of your son?"

"Pictures? Really?"

"And digital videos. Tons of them. I filmed everything. Every day of his life, I filmed something. Just for you. Because I knew that someday those ordinary moments would feel very special to you. On Christmas Day, you can have them. As a present, Riley. Not as a memorial."

\*\*\*

"Good heavens this house is cold."

Savannah heard a melodic voice proclaim from somewhere downstairs. A female voice! Flinging open the bedroom door of her upstairs attic, frigid air hit her. Curious, but half convinced she'd imagined it, she limped to the edge of the stairs and peered over sturdy oak railing that trailed along the edge of the freezing rectangular stairwell.

She walked too much yesterday. All night painful muscle cramps kept convoluting her left leg into tight spasms. Riley gave her prescription strength Tylenol, but the pain shooting through new bone and healing nerves was excruciating.

Rest today, Doc Rosemont ordered.

So today, she was trapped inside the house, all alone. Today there would be no warm stable, no beautiful dancing horses, and no Riley.

Feeling awful to the core and grumpily baffled by yesterday's bewildering events, Savannah convinced Riley that the walls of snow encasing the first floor of Graystone were making her claustrophobic and she missed gazing through her big attic windows.

Actually, she felt he deserved some space.

But seeing the sun shining upon the frozen white world did make her feel better. After weeks of blizzards, it felt like God had finally smiled.

They stayed in his bedroom downstairs last night, but this morning after she noisily complained about having cabin fever, Riley helped her upstairs. Well, half carried actually. He'd been nice about it. Too nice, proving once again he was a genuinely good man. It made her apologize profusely, which of course just made him frown.

Last night they ate a late dinner and didn't talk anymore about Ryan or getting married or how great that impulsive lusty hot-blooded kiss had been. And he didn't try it again. When it was time for bed Riley just built the fireplace in his bedroom up to a nice warm glow, climbed into bed, draped his arm around her waist, and dropped into a deep sleep.

Yesterday was wonderful and confusing.

Riley didn't want to marry her! He couldn't! Why? It was all some misguided notion to right childhood dreams gone wrong.

More mumbling.

Something heavy scooted around on the second floor.

"Drifts half as high as the house!" The woman complained, "This is crazy!" The humming Savannah heard wasn't Riley's chainsaw! It was a snowmobile coming in through the second story balcony!

They finally had company!

"Ms. Emily?" She called down, "Is that you?"

"Oh!" Feet scampered. A perky female face and slender body swathed from head to toe in a red snowmobile suit peered up the stairwell. She took off her snow goggles. Pink cheeks and hazel gold eyes smiled. Riley's eyes. "Savannah?" His spunky mom asked. "Why are you up there? Riley always closes off the upstairs in winter."

"Well...um, it's warmer up here and the sun is so pretty today. I can't walk down..." she honestly didn't know how to finish that.

Did Riley's parents know about Ryan? The accident?

Oh gee, this reunion was going to be terrible.

"You mean you can't walk down the stairs until your leg heals?" Ms. Emily knowledgeably grinned.

"Uh, yeah. Riley has to help me. Or Zeus. I ride him, sometimes."

Ms. Emily laughed. "You ride that big dog? I'd like to see that."

"Riley says it's cheating."

Ms. Emily waved a gloved hand as if the idea were utter nonsense. "Where is Riley? Good grief my youngest son has no manners. Leaving you alone up there like some princess locked away in an ivory tower. Bet he's even been a big grumpy bully too; pretending he doesn't care."

"Well, sort-of." How did his Mom know? "Wanna come up?"

"In a bit. Let me unpack the supplies I brought and get out of this goofy Santa Claus suit Papa makes me wear. He couldn't have ordered me a pretty pink one. Or white," she grumbled, yanking thick gloves off small fingers in a fidgety-fluttery little bird way that Savannah always found endearing. Next came the red hat and a thick braid of auburn hair appeared.

That's why Papa bought her red.

He loved Ms. Emily's flame colored hair.

Redder than Riley's dusky auburn, the bright hue was now streaked with touches of gray. Watching the perky woman fume, Savannah smiled to herself.

Ryan would have loved his Grandma.

"No," Ms. Emily still ranted, entirely to herself, "I have to ride around the countryside looking like a silly red elf. People can see me coming from miles away! It's embarrassing. Good thing Christmas is coming. I'll fit right in."

Savannah sighed. Was everyone going to say that?

Yes, Christmas was coming and on the day Riley would receive a gift like no other. His son. Except that wonderful joyful little boy was gone.

Riley wasn't nearly bitter yet.

He would be.

Watching Ryan's life would sear hatred into his heart forever.

She had stolen his son.

"Oh, sorry dear." Ms. Emily contritely looked up, hearing Savannah sniffle. "I'm rambling." But seeing her teary eyes, she sighed. "I'll bring you some hot tea." The sweet face offered a comforting motherly smile, finally looking her fifty-something years. "Now go back into your bedroom and stay warm."

"Ahhh? Ms. Emily?" But red fluttery bird had already disappeared.

"Yes?" She bounced back into view.

"You knew about…my accident?"

"Well of course. You were right to come here. New York is a sea of strangers. Just a terrible lonely cement jungle with no heart and soul at all. Montana will heal you." She beamed as Savannah gaped at the surprisingly accurate description.

"How did you know I was here?"

"I call Riley almost every day. His tone changed. He became secretive. Of course, it took him a while to admit you were here, but I always knew." She wisely tapped her temple, "He may be a grown man determined to have a private life, but he still can't keep secrets from his Momma." With a girly giggle, she noisily scampered away again leaving Savannah leaning over the railing in wordless bewilderment, wondering what terrible things Riley might have said.

Bad things, for sure.

She shivered. Then gamely limped back inside her room.

Until yesterday's kissing-apology-marry me madness, Riley definitely hated her. Afterwards, he acted as if nothing happened.

Baffled, she decided the whole incident off was a simple demonstration of male prowess. The fact that she liked his touch only meant she was…*Oh please. Who are you kidding?*

120

The moment Riley kissed her she melted.

He could have stripped her naked right there in the living room and she wouldn't have objected. In fact, she would have rejoiced. Even now, her body still craved the way his hands cupped and caressed, claiming the reckless moment like a man who wanted more.

What a mess.

If Ms. Emily knew she was home, the whole town knew. The woman was sweet as honey, but loved to gossip.

Sharing, she called it.

But Ms. Emily seemed genuinely happy to see her.

How much did Riley share? Did she know about Ryan?

Savannah couldn't decide what was worse, Ms. Emily knowing about her lost grandson, or having to tell her. Waiting for what felt like a torturous eternity, when footsteps finally came trudging up the stairs, she threw the bedroom door open wide.

It was only Riley.

"Oh. It's you." She closed the door behind him.

"You were expecting someone else?"

Disappointed to the core, she just shrugged. Obviously, Ms. Emily had been fully informed about Savannah's heinous crimes against the Rosemont family and changed her mind about being friendly. Leaning against the closed door, she wanted to bawl like a baby.

"So... she left already?"

"Who? That bossy little woman down there messing up my clean kitchen? No. Mom is busy ordering me to be nice to you and making her famous Fudgy-Cocoa Peanut Butter cookies. What a gooey mess."

"Be nice to me?"

"Mom has this insane notion that I've been a big bully."

"Well, I uh..."

Riley playfully laughed. Suddenly, Savannah found herself nestled against his warm strong body, trapped by burly arms. Oh! It felt so good. He just showered. Dark auburn hair was still slightly damp. He smelled crisply clean. Like woodsy soap, green apple shampoo, and a unique dusky-male warm-skin scent that was pure Riley.

"So, you were happy to see my funny Mom?"

"Yeah. I was."

"I'm glad." His big hand slid possessively up her back. He rebelliously smiled, daring her to resist. This genuine change in attitude was so refreshing she felt a little lightheaded.

"Were you really disappointed to see me?"

"No. It's just that I heard her voice downstairs and I talked to her and...well, I realized how much I've missed her. We were good friends. Once."

"You still are."

Being this close to him, seeing that wicked golden glint in his green eyes, all she could think about was how fabulous it would feel to slide her arms around Riley's neck and kiss that handsome smiling man until they just couldn't breathe.

A real hot-blooded passionate kiss, not a friendly apology.

Although the apology was nice too.

"You told her what I did?" She nervously toyed with the buttons on his denim shirt. At the neck, cream-colored thermals peeked through. Vaguely, she wondered how fast she could rip off both shirts. "Does your Mom know that I stole her grandson?"

"Sure. She knew all about Ryan. I didn't keep my son a secret."

Okay, it was official.

Savannah was going to bawl.

"Damn. I always say things wrong!" He rushed to explain, "You didn't steal him. Mom understands why we had to lead separate lives." Riley gently caressed her quivering chin. "Don't cry, honey. Please. I asked her to come here today."

Confused, she forlornly blinked. "Why?"

"I thought maybe if you two talked for a few days, you might feel better. You've been so sad. I know you tried to save Ryan. I know you turned the car to sacrifice yourself. He was just too small. His little body couldn't take the collision. The car flipped five times. Did you know it was that many?" She shook her head and wondered how he possibly knew that fact. "Mom's your friend. Please don't be upset. She loves you. She always will."

It was the kindest sweetest gesture he could have made and before Savannah could stop herself, fingers twined pleasurably into Riley's bronze hair, standing on her toes, her mouth pressed firmly against his. He froze. Then a low sound of manly approval rumbled in his chest and they were kissing.

Without reservation. Passionate and needy.

Just like old times.

She loved the familiar slant of Riley's hungry mouth eagerly taking hers. The demanding nibbles and playful caresses of his lips and tongue and teeth, with strong hands earnestly roving over her back and sides made Savannah's aching heart swell eight sizes too big.

Where had she heard that before?

Ryan. He asked if she ever felt that way. She told him quite honestly that only Riley made her heart want to burst.

Only Riley.

With his hands stroking her body into a revved-up accelerated celebration of remembrance, pressing her curves tight against his hard body, making her spine tingle and the rest of her yearn for more.

Only Riley could make her feel like this.

And it was shocking as hell.

"Well now," he grinned as they finally drew apart, both breathing like they'd just climbed a high mountain, "that was interesting."

"I'm sorry...I didn't mean to..."

His mouth quickly claimed hers again, silencing any pretense of apology, proving the only honesty they shared for weeks was this moment wrapped in each other's arms opening their hearts to something better.

A second chance.

And she wanted it with all her bursting heart!

*More! More!*

Answering, he gripped her butt with both hands and bent his knees a little. Pushing her back against the door, Riley lifted her up, hoisted her into the cradle of his hips in a way that was both superbly intimate and provocatively promising.

He wanted her! Lovers!

Savannah had no objections.

Wrapping her legs around his waist, he growled approval and tucked her closer. Yes! They were good at this. Real good.

Every movement felt like sugar-coated sin.

But just when hands had impatiently crept under clothes and the kisses and friction between their bodies made her blissfully breathless and lightheaded, Riley swore, set her down, and suddenly stepped away.

Way away.

Nearly across the room.

"We can't go backwards, Savannah. We aren't kids anymore." Wiping his mouth, he made a rough sound of shock and quickly tucked both of his shirts into his jeans again. She hadn't even realized she'd undressed him.

"Your shirt is unbuttoned." He declared in a tone that made her feel dirty. Looking down, the comfortable blue flannel she habitually wore every few days was open all the way, revealing her white bra and smooth stomach.

"Oh. Gee. How did that happen?"

Hazel eyes rolled. "Hmm, go figure." Riley sternly glared as if she somehow seduced him and he was innocent of any wrongdoing.

Ashamed, Savannah quickly buttoned it.

So much for second chances.

Once again, she somehow did something to make him turn cold. The two extremes were hard to keep up with. "I said I was sorry for kissing you."

"I'm tired of apologies! Be Savage again, damn it!"

She didn't understand. "I wasn't trying to..."

He took three quick strides. She was back in Riley's arms with that hungry mouth devouring her once again.

Confusing man. Fine. Let this be about pure instinct or lusty sexual weakness. But once upon a time, as their over-heated bodies both clearly remembered, they made beautiful music together.

"I'm leaving," Riley groaned, reluctantly dragging his mouth away from hers, "before I do something stupid." From hips to chest, she was pinned against him. He wasn't letting go. Even his hand cupped her backside, pressing their lower halves tight together.

"Stupid? Kissing me is stupid?"

"No. Maybe. Hell, I don't know." He released her. Her hopeful heart plunged. "We'll talk when I get back. You'll be fine here with Mom for a few days. Behave yourself."

"Okay," she blinked; a little dazed and a whole lot confused.

Suspicious gold-green eyes narrowed. "What? No fight? You're not mad that I kissed you?"

"I kissed you first. You are just reacting," she logically rationalized. "Besides, whenever you get back from wherever it is that you are going, I'm sure you'll decide to regret this crazy little episode and find reasons to hate me again. So," she sadly shrugged, still tasting Riley's warmth on her lips, "don't worry about it. I already know that you don't like me."

"It isn't that simple."

"Yes, it is. We were incredible once, but I royally screwed it up."

"I kissed you first yesterday."

"Only because we were fighting and that was a great way to win." He started to object but she wouldn't let him. "Forget it, Riley. This never happened. No harm done. I'm not mad. We are what we are. A mess. Now go."

Savannah opened the door to let him out, determined not to cry for being such a softhearted wimpy fool. She wondered if Ms. Emily would track her down if she "borrowed" the snowmobile and disappeared from this frustrating man's life for good. Could her leg handle that heavy machine? Probably not. Damn thing would probably shatter and she would freeze to death on the mountain. Alone.

It might be worth a try.

Staying here hurt just as much.

Only in different places.

He didn't leave. He was watching her. She couldn't look at Riley. If she did, he would see that deep yearning inside for something beautiful she already destroyed.

The good between them was gone.

So what if he kissed her? Big deal. It just proved the man was human. She started it today by kissing him first. Yesterday's marriage proposal wasn't real. He only did it because she dropped that bomb about intentionally getting pregnant, so he dropped one about hunting them down.

Truth was, Riley would always hate her for leaving and for losing Ryan. He'd always say contradictory things that made her crazy.

Staying here hoping for love was just plain foolishness.

"No." He decided after tense moments of silence. Reaching over her shoulder, Riley quietly shut the door. "I'd get back and you'd be gone."

"How can I go anywhere? I'm broken."

"You'd find a way." Cornered against the closed door, she couldn't escape. Strong fingertips gently tipped her stubborn face up to his. She tried for as long as possible not to look at Riley, but when she finally did, Savannah saw wisdom in those gold-green eyes.

"This did happen." He solemnly decreed, "I won't forget kissing you. I liked it too much. And I don't regret it. Any of it. Not at all."

She couldn't do this! The tenderness in his touch and the honesty in his handsome face just created a deep need for Riley to love her.

He wouldn't.

Love and hate couldn't sleep in the same bed.

And sex, no matter how passionate, didn't spark love.

It was just heat. That's all.

"So," determined to salvage her sanity, she rudely shoved his hand away from her face, "where are you going?"

"Over to Sam Lawson's. He called this morning. I have a mare going into labor. I've already warmed up my four-wheel drive Avalanche and put the snowplow on it."

"You're going to Sam and Millie's?" She perked up, eager to see her honorary godfather. "Please, can I go with you?"

"The road between our ranches is too rough. I don't want you being bounced around, hurting from the ride. That's another reason I asked Mom to come stay with you. Besides, she was busting for an excuse to use her new snowmobile."

He'd considered her feelings and needs. What did that mean? Probably nothing. "You keep horses at Sam's too?"

"Brood mares, mostly. I don't have enough room here. I trust Sam. Hell, he and Millie practically raised you. Sam taught me more about horses and life than anyone."

Still hovering over her, Riley was too close, too handsome, and far too friendly. That soft glow in his eyes had once meant he really cared.

Now, she didn't know what it meant.

"I have to go, Savannah. I don't want to, especially right now, but Ivory is carrying twins and she's having contractions six weeks early. Sam is sitting with her, but I can't risk losing those babies. It takes years to build a profitable bloodline and raise enough colts you can afford to sell some. People don't just buy pretty Andalusians. They want magic horses that dance. Training takes four years; sometimes five. This summer I'll finally have a few horses I can sell. But these twins, I plan to keep for their bloodlines."

"Twins are rare."

"It's true. This is Ivory's first delivery. She is Diablo's last daughter." He softly revealed, smiling when she gasped. "Venus was her mother. Do you remember how pure white she was?"

She did. "Venus glittered like a goddess. Do you still have her?"

"Yes. She's happily living out her royal days as the spoiled queen of Sam's stables." Seeming drawn to touch, his hand caressed her hair. "This spring, after the roads clear, I'll show them to you."

This spring.

Savannah looked away again.

Her heart clenched.

"Please," he whispered, leaning down until his warm breath brushed along her cheek, "be here when I get back. I know I'm hard to live with. I've yelled and grouched around, making life miserable for you. But that isn't how I really feel. I'm just confused inside. I'm bitter, but we need to heal, not fight. Please don't leave me again. Please, give us a second chance."

She gulped on that raw request. A second chance. Oh! How she wanted that! Savannah fought the burning urge to fling her arms around his neck and start the whole "kissing Riley" madness all over again.

"Are you taking Zeus?"

"No. Why?"

"Take him. That way, if you two get stuck in the snow, Zeus can pull you out or you can just ride my big friend home." She unflinchingly met his gaze, hoping you couldn't see how much she prayed his little speech was sincere. "Give Sam and Millie my love. And be safe. I'll be right here. Okay?"

Riley wolfishly grinned, popped a quick kiss across her mouth, and decisively marched through the door. Listening to him trot down the stairs, those footsteps sounded much happier than how he trudged up.

Maybe she would stay. At least a little while longer.

Besides, chatting with Ms. Emily might be fun. And educational.

# Chapter Eleven

Educational was an understatement. Within the first hour of "sharing" Ms. Emily casually divulged that Riley was an uncle several times over and the entire Rosemont family still lived in Harmony Hills. His roughneck older brother Paul refined his wild ways, married the mayor's only daughter, Melanie, and became a successful businessman. They owned a prosperous steakhouse called Savory Grille that served a mouthwatering breakfast menu too, so it naturally became the community convergence point for daily gossip.

His sister Julia married Jacob McIntyre; a gregarious mountain adventurer she met in college. They ran a thriving bed and breakfast, owned a dozen rental cabins, and hosted overnight hiking expeditions that Julia wisely advertised over the internet, keeping them constantly busy.

Everyone else from Savannah's childhood either moved away or dug deep roots with families and businesses that helped Harmony Hills thrive.

"But you were our shining star, Savi. You shot for the moon and got the sun instead." Ms. Emily happily complimented. She'd propped cute purple-socked feet on the ottoman, warming her wiggly toes by the fire.

"We knew Arianna Hartwell was really our very own Savannah Graystone. When your first CD came out Papa cleared a special wall in the store, just for you. We ordered a hundred copies. They sold out in three days. We ordered more and Papa made this fancy copper display rack for your sheet music. Those sold fast too! I'm glad you wrote easy versions of each song that beginners can play. Those young girls taking piano lessons dreamed of being just like you." She gushed as excited hands fluttered.

"Before long, the whole town knew your songs. People walked around humming 'Serenity' and whistling 'Heaven Help Me.' In church Pastor Davenport let the choir sing 'Angels Among Us,' even though it wasn't intended as religious music. He told the whole congregation that you'd wrote that beautiful song while living in our mountains. It was wonderful. You made me so proud."

127

All this happy approval was overwhelming. Savannah felt unworthy. "Weren't you mad that I left Riley?"

"Heavens no. God blessed you with a gift and He needed you to share it with the world. You didn't leave Riley because you wanted to. You were answering His call." Her lips pursed as she frowned a little. "But I was plenty mad at Riley."

"Why? He didn't do anything wrong?"

"Oh yes he did! My son let you go away and have that baby all by yourself! I told Riley you'd left here six or seven weeks pregnant, but he claimed that wasn't possible since you two never slept together." Hazel eyes dramatically rolled. "Please. Love like yours just naturally grows up. The day you were born Riley loved you; and he had been a grown man sharing intimacies with the woman he loved for nearly a year. Pretending innocence after the fact was just plain insulting."

Savannah's jaw dropped. "But...I wasn't showing. I never took a pregnancy test. Everyone in Harmony Hills would have known if I bought one."

"True. Small town. People like to talk." Ms. Emily naughtily grinned. "I saw it in your eyes; that special womanly glow. YOU knew you were going to be a Momma. That was the only test necessary."

"Gee. I thought I was so sly."

"I knew for sure when you two started hollerin' and fussin' at each other, tearing everything good apart. It wasn't pretty to watch, but God needed you to walk a different road; one far away from Montana."

It was a relief that Ms. Emily understood.

"I thought if we broke up," Savannah conceded, "Riley would move on with his life. I even figured he'd marry and have a family," she gulped, "with someone else."

"Never. You two are destiny. After you left Riley worked himself near-crazy trying to forget, still denying you took a part of him with you. Months went by. He wouldn't let anyone talk about you, but Julia kept watching birth records on the internet; you know-- the ones local papers publish, whether you want them to or not? Well, you left Montana in June," she counted Savannah's eight months alone on her fingers, "and on February 2, the New York Times announced Ryan Patrick Rosemont-Graystone was born." Ms. Emily looked quite proud of herself for figuring it out. "I told stubborn Mr. Riley Phillip that he best haul his butt to New York City and find his family. But he's a mule-headed man," she muttered, shaking her head. "He was convinced you didn't love him anymore."

"But I did love Riley!" Savannah blurted. "I still love him."

"Of course you do." A knowledgeable smile creased her sweet face, making small crinkles at the corners of compassionate gold-green eyes. "A Montana mountain woman doesn't purposely have a man's baby without a whole lot of forever-type love inside her heart."

"Wow. You really get it. I just told Riley yesterday. He was shocked. He didn't talk to me for a while, and then we...uh, argued."

And kissed.

And Riley asked her to marry him. Nicely.

Why? A ridiculous sense of duty? After the fact? Probably.

"Guess Riley never did the math," his mom cheerfully giggled. "Bet that made Doc Rosemont feel just a teensy bit silly." Ms. Emily munched on another chocolaty-peanut-butter cookie. Savannah had reached her sugar and cocoa limit.

"Did you know Riley came to New York?" She was curious. How much did Ms. Emily know about her son's choices?

"Sure." She readily nodded, "Tore him apart. He came home as broken as you were; just in different ways. Riley locked himself at Graystone and buried himself in grief. I told him when we were at the hospital that without Ryan to love you'd be coming home to Montana now, and he best open up his heart and give you someone else to love. But he's been calloused and cold, hasn't he? I've heard it on the phone: grumbling instead of loving. Big dumb man."

It took Savannah a whole minute of bug-eyed astonishment to comprehend what Ms. Emily just revealed.

"The hospital?" She stammered, "Riley was there? With me? In September? This September? You and Papa actually went all the way to New York City?"

Her chatty companion blanched. "We did." Fluttery fingers clamped into fists in her lap, as if clenching them could somehow take back the truth she inadvertently revealed. "Terrible noisy place. Don't you remember, honey? We were with you for two weeks."

"Oh. Gosh. Dang. Riley too?"

"Actually, he stayed by your side for thirty-two days."

Stunned breath stung. So did her eyes.

"Thirty-two days." She whispered, feeling that truth slowly sink in. "I kind-of remember him. I thought it was a dream. I had a terrible concussion. Even when I got to Graystone, I wasn't thinking right. I wanted to die, Ms. Emily. I had a raging fever and I...well, I tried to drown myself in the bathtub."

Somehow, telling her humiliating secret felt right. Was that how Sharing worked? Ms. Emily shared a secret, so Savannah shared one too?

"You tried to drown yourself?"

"Riley saved me. Later, after my fever broke so I could think straight again, he told me what my Mom really did to die, how she fell down the ski slopes on purpose and how Dad buried himself in whiskey and gave up. It scared me. I didn't want to be just a voice in the wind. I just wanted to be with Ryan. Now he's just stuck with me."

"Oh. My. What a drama you two have shared!"

"He hates me for stealing Ryan. I really don't blame him."

Ms. Emily tsk-tsked. "Riley doesn't hate you. He can't. Hate goes against everything right inside."

129

"He sure has a funny way of showing it."

"Well, men are…men." Ms. Emily shrugged as if there really was no legitimate excuse for their behavior. "Riley won't like that I've shared so much. He's a private man. He keeps his own counsel. Always has. 'Cept for Sam," she sagely decided. "Riley respects his opinion. Might be good that he's spending a few days with Sam. I hope he shares, just a little. Sam will know the right things to say. He always does. Not like me," she regretfully conceded. "I jabber too much."

Staring at the flickering firelight for awestruck moments, Savannah thought about everything she had just learned about the surly man she was living with.

Yesterday she was convinced Riley hated her.

Today, he kissed her. Because he wanted to. Several times.

He even begged her to stay. Nicely.

Remembering the deliciously amorous gleam in Riley's forest green eyes and the way his powerful body ignited the need to take more, Savannah's chin defiantly tilted. "I'm glad you told me the truth, Ms. Emily."

"He should have told you, not me," his Mom softly apologized. "It wasn't my place to chatter about Riley."

"Too damn bad." It felt good to be defiant. "He's had weeks to tell me that he came to New York City."

"Maybe he was waiting for the right time."

"No. He had tons of chances. Trust me. We talk about Ryan almost every night. And dang it, I deserve the truth! Even though I can't remember it, I deserve to know that I wasn't alone in that hospital. Being alone felt awful! It helps to know you and Papa were there. I'm very grateful. So, thank you…for telling me the truth. Thank you for coming to New York. And thank you for coming here today. I really needed an honest friend."

Ms. Emily sighed in deep relief. "We're more than friends, honey. We're family. Always have been. Always will be."

"I wish Riley was as understanding and forgiving. He just grouches around like I'm some horrid biblical plague."

His mom giggled. It was girly and cute. It seemed impossible the feisty redhead was fifty-something. "Well, he's a tough Montana mountain man with a strict code of how men are supposed to behave. But he has an awful big hurt inside that he isn't quite sure what to do with." Ms. Emily wisely explained, proving she understood Riley's enigmatic indecipherable heart too. "He truly loved Ryan. When Riley told us about the accident and asked us to go with him, I watched him fall apart. He couldn't talk. On the flight out there, he turned to steel, buried sadness and clung to anger. At the hospital, he spat fire and brimstone at your doctors. Even shot off a few hot-blooded remarks to that very nice grandfatherly man, Marcus Seabourne. Maybe harsh words are the only truth Riley can bear to feel right now."

"He yelled at Marcus? My agent? But he's the sweetest man on the planet." Savannah couldn't imagine Riley yelling at the blue-eyed New England native who had become her adopted family. "What did Riley say?"

"Something about you shouldn't wear scratchy hospital clothes. Riley sent Marcus and his wife Cynthia to your apartment and made them bring soft cotton t-shirts, clean undies, and nice blankets so you didn't have to use the hospital ones."

"Oh. I wondered who did that."

"See? He isn't quite as tough as he pretends. He cared enough to come to New York City when you were hurt. He stayed with you, Savannah." Leaning forward, she adamantly explained, "My son sat with you in that hospital room, day and night. He rarely left. Papa and I got a hotel room, but Riley didn't bother. He slept on a rollaway bed the doctors gave him. He even showered there and the nurses brought him food. He refused to leave your side. That counts for something, doesn't it?"

"I guess so. Wow. This is such a revelation. Riley stayed with me. More than four weeks? Dang. I wish I could remember."

Imagining Riley there in that sterile hospital, stubbornly keeping her company while she teetered in death's doorway, hope warmed her.

"He saved my life when I came to Montana burning up with fever. I had a bone infection and hurt so bad. I was a sick raving lunatic. Instead of tossing me out in the snow like I probably deserved, Riley healed me." In spite of her cautious pessimism, Savannah felt herself grin. "So, he cared. Right?"

"Oh he cares." Ms. Emily kindly confirmed, nibbling on another cookie. "My son cares about you more than he knows what to do with. Someday, you and Riley will get things straight; I just know it. Someday, you'll be Savannah Rosemont."

"We'll see."

Savannah didn't share that optimistic enthusiasm.

But for two days of sharing, fragile hope grew inside, keeping her heart delightfully warm. Visiting with Ms. Emily was like having a sleepover with a wonderful giggly friend. They laughed and told secrets and had a wonderful time.

But Papa kept calling Ms. Emily's cell phone. He missed his vibrant sweet wife and complained about sleeping all alone. So too soon, their chatty girl-time was over. Leaving Savannah with an ice chest full of food and plenty of firewood, Emily Rosemont reluctantly bundled up in her funny red snowsuit and drove her noisy snowmobile back to Harmony Hills.

Somehow, being alone wasn't so bad now.

Riley would come home tomorrow. Maybe the next day.

Savannah looked forward to it!

# Chapter Twelve

"Savannah...honey? Wake up, babe. I need your help." Riley whispered, surprised to find her upstairs, all alone. The sleeping woman stirred, grumbled incoherent complaints. The bundle in his arms nervously squirmed. "Easy, Sugar. We'll get you fed."

"Not...hungry." Savannah sleepily murmured.

He flicked on the bedside lamp.

Squinting, she sat up and rubbed her eyes. "Oh! You're back!" Reaching to hug him, Savannah breathed a whiff of dirty sweaty horses and something else far worse. She immediately drew back in repulsion.

"Uugh!" Fingers covered her nose. "Eeew! You smell awful!"

"I'll shower in a minute. Where's Mom?"

"Papa missed her." She stated in a nasal voice, keeping her nose plugged. "She went home. She tried calling you, but your phone was off. She called Millie, who said you and Sam were busy helping Ivory."

"Extremely busy. Look..."

He slid back the blue stable blanket concealing the precious cargo bundled in his arms. Lamplight revealed a tiny white newborn foal so weak and small she looked like a frightened fawn. Her eyes were a sad sightless blue-gray. Pert pointed ears swiveled, listening intently.

"Oh Riley! A baaabyyy!" Forgetting all about the offensive barnyard stench that clung to his skin and clothes, her hand flew from covering her nose to pull the blanket back a little bit more. "Girl or boy?"

"Girl."

As Savannah's fingers gently touched her, the premature filly curiously sniffed. "Dang, she's small. Too small."

"She's six weeks early."

Holding her fingers before her tiny muzzle, Savannah let the filly smell it. Baby nostrils flared, but taking another whiff of the gentle woman, she sighed heavily and weakly dropped her heavy head upon Riley's forearm.

"Oh, poor baby. Its okay, Sugar," she lovingly cooed, stroking her velvet soft face. "She's so fragile." In the pale lamplight, Riley saw violet eyes sympathetically glisten as she sadly whispered, "Is she going to die?"

"I don't know. Maybe. Her brother was healthy and strong, but I think she's partially blind. Her Momma completely rejected her. Ivory wouldn't even let her nurse. And her heart has an awful slushy sound. I probably should put her to sleep, to save her from suffering, but I just can't do it. She's alive. To me, that means God has a purpose for her. Please Savannah," he softly begged, "will you help me with her?"

"Me? What can I do?"

"You're so good with animals. They trust you."

Her fingers still lovingly stroked the white coat. The filly relaxed. Eyes were open wide, but her breathing was slow and calm.

"Until right now, she's been terrified, but look, she likes your touch. She isn't fighting at all. She likes it. If we're lucky, she might actually live a few days. But they don't have to be bad days. We can make her comfortable. I just can't let this tiny baby suffer and die, rejected and all alone. Although her time here might be short, she deserves to be loved."

"Yes. She does!"

Scrambling out of bed to yank on jeans, Riley noticed Savannah was sleeping in one of his flannel shirts. Several sizes too big, that red-checkered material looked damn sexy hanging to mid-thigh over her slim form.

Had she missed him? Maybe.

She had definitely been excited to see him.

"Thanks, Savage."

"You're welcome." With her back turned she pulled jeans up over her hips, but he caught a glimpse of temptingly curvy skin. "Am I?"

"What?"

"You're Savage?"

"Since birth." The question caught him off-guard. Truth tumbled out unchecked. "Do I still have that right? To call you mine?"

"Maybe. If you're nice to me." She teased. Glancing his way through the shadows, she naughtily grinned. Riley smiled too. It felt good.

"Let me warm up the room." Grabbing the steel poker, she stirred orange coals in the smoldering fireplace and added fresh wood, building it up to a nice crackling glow. He liked watching that sweet feminine silhouette move around in the near-dark. Hip-length dark chocolate hair hung loose in a heavy sheet that swung free behind her. It gleamed seductively against the orange flames.

So beautiful.

They had some serious unfinished business.

Later.

Right now, they needed to save their premature foal.

134

Savannah grabbed an old pink velveteen blanket from the closet. "We'll use this." Shoving back the chairs and leather ottoman, clearing a spot on the floor, she spread the blanket out before the warm fireplace and planting herself at one end. "Bring her to me. The blanket you have her wrapped in is rough and stinky. This one is soft and smells good."

Riley carried his cargo across the room, knelt down, and gently unwrapped the precious package. The tiny filly whimpered. Panic-stricken at being released from the safe blanket cocoon, gangly white legs frantically sprawling out, kicking in all directions. Holding around her small belly, Riley set her down in the middle of the fresh pink blanket.

"There. Now cover her up."

Savannah quickly gathered the corners together, capturing the frightened foal into a neat comfortable bundle. She scooped her up, right onto her lap. Murmuring soothing reassurance, she wrapped her arms around the filly and held her close to her own warm body. The small white head sticking out of the blanket was nestled against her chest.

Pressing tight against Savannah as if feeling her body meant safety; the filly curled up, uttered a trembling relieved sigh, and stopped struggling.

"That'll work."

"There sweetie, you're alright now." Savannah softly cooed, lovingly caressing that tiny trusting white face. For the first time since her traumatic birth, the premature foal completely relaxed. Riley was in awe.

"Has she tried to walk?"

"Not really. She's too weak. Just keep her warm and calm. Her little heart can't take too much. I'm running out to the stables to get a bottle of colt formula. And vitamins," he decided. "I'll bring her a shot. Or two. Maybe some antibiotics. That might help."

"And something that smells yummy to get her interested in eating. If she hasn't nursed yet, she might not know how."

"Good idea. I can crush some apples. They smell strong and sweet."

"Not too many. Just enough to stimulate her appetite so I can get the milk into her. That's what she needs." He nodded, agreeing completely. "Oh, and Riley," she giggled, far happier than he expected her to be, "bring some newspapers to cover the floor. She might get messy. I doubt baby horses make very good house pets."

"Okay. If I can find some."

"And please," she impishly beamed up at him from her position the floor, "take a shower. No way will this baby have an appetite with you smelling like an icky stable."

"Am I that bad?"

"Worse. You're covered in dried blood, Doc Rosemont."

"Oh. Right."

He finally looked down at his disgustingly stained jeans and blood smeared shirt. While helping Ivory give birth he wore long delivery gloves, but forgot to protect the rest of his body from the mess.

"I was in a hurry. For two whole days, we thought Ivory was having false labor. We hoped she'd carry full term. Then the contractions hit hard. Everything happened fast. Her brother was born first. He was just fine. But when I saw how fragile and pretty this little girl was, all I cared about was bringing her home to you." Praying he did the right thing, Riley turned to leave, but then glanced back at the woman sitting on the floor. "Don't be sad if she dies, Savage. We can't play God. He'll still take her, if He wants to."

"I know. Life is hard sometimes. At least Bitsy will be loved."

"Bitsy." He smiled, feeling worry ease for the first time since he helped deliver that tiny premature bundle happily snuggled up in that beautiful woman's arms. "I like that. Baby Bitsy. It fits."

Cooing at the filly about being dainty, Savannah grinned.

When Riley finally returned from the stables, he had taken the time to shave off three-day's worth of bristles and thoroughly scrubbed his body with Irish Spring soap. His skin felt tingly clean. Hopefully, his smell-appeal had improved.

Not for Bitsy's sake.

For Savannah.

Opening the bedroom door, the woman and foal were still on the floor, right where he left them. Firelight cast shadows that danced in the dark. The bedside lamp created a faint circle of light around the bed.

Savannah was humming. Softly. Soothing sounds. Bitsy's face lay against Savannah's chest. Eyes half-closed, basking in the attention, the tiny filly was in heaven.

The music had returned.

At least a little.

The door creaked, as it swung open. She looked up and smiled. Welcoming. Pleased. It did funny things to his heart.

"Did you bring a calving bottle?

"I did. I couldn't find any newspapers. I think we've burned them all. If she makes a mess, we'll just clean it up."

Walking toward her, Riley set his overflowing medical bag on the oak floor. Savannah sat slightly hunched over Bitsy, holding the filly tight in her arms. Bitsy may be comfortable, but he knew that position was killing Savannah. Without asking permission, he automatically sat down behind her, stretching long legs out on either side of her hips.

"You smell much better." She quietly complimented, careful not to raise her voice and startle Bitsy. "Almost likable."

"Almost? Then I used too much soap. I was aiming for barely tolerable." Gently clasping her shoulder, Riley leaned Savannah back into his solid chest where she could just relax and hold the filly without growing achy and tired.

His stronger body became the backside of her chair.

"Gee, barely tolerable and considerate too."

"You looked uncomfortable."

"I was. Thanks."

Bitsy's eyes were open, listening to them talk. It was cute. He'd never seen a foul so tiny. Her face was pretty. "How is she?"

"Happy. She knows we'll take care of her. Bitsy isn't completely blind. She keeps watching the firelight. If I move my hand over her face, her eyes follow it."

"Good. Shadows and light are better than nothing. Maybe her eyes are just hazy." He speculated, hoping. "See if she's hungry." He offered a warm calving bottle. "I brought a cup of mashed apples too, if we need to coax her into eating. But she really needs the milk. I put vitamins in the bottle, instead of a giving her a shot. I couldn't bring myself to hurt her, even a little."

"You've got a soft heart, Doc Rosemont."

"Don't tell anyone."

Savannah smeared a glob of the thick gooey formula on one finger, then brushed it over Bitsy's lips. "Here, honey. Try this. It's good for you."

Smelling it cautiously, a pink tongue shot out and licked it up. Nudging her mouth open, Savannah squeezed the bottle. Nickering with delight as those first drops of warm milk hit her throat, Bitsy sucked greedily.

"Well, gee. She didn't need coaxing at all."

"It's because she trusts you."

Bitsy made a funny nickering sound. It didn't take much to fill her tiny stomach. After several minutes of chugging the milk, gray-blue eyes sleepily drooped. Riley set the half-empty bottle aside. No longer scared and hungry, Bitsy comfortably curled up, snuggled closer to Savannah, and happily closed her eyes again.

"You did good, Savage. Now Bitsy has a chance."

"Hope so. She sure is sweet."

Slowly, expecting the woman leaning against him to tense, Riley slid his hand purposefully along her hip and ran his fingers down the outside of Savannah's right thigh. Glancing over her shoulder, she suspiciously arched one eyebrow, questioning the possessive move. "Careful," she warned in a dusky feline purr, "I'm not sweet. I bite."

"Hard?"

"Well, no. Nibbles mostly."

It made him grin. "I think I can handle it."

"Can you?" A mischievous sexy glint warmed violet-blue eyes. "I haven't nibbled in a long, long time. I might get greedy. So you'd better not get too friendly, Riley. You smell just yummy enough; I might turn you into a midnight snack."

"Really? I might like that."

"That's the idea."

The image of her hands and mouth roaming over his bare skin was deliciously sinful. He knew she wouldn't bite. Not at all. Savannah would lick and taste him all over, truly savoring every shared intimacy. That's just how she made love. Slow and sensual, as if being naked together was a thing of beauty, something she cherished.

Wouldn't it be wonderful to forget caution and good sense, forget the past, and simply wallow in pleasure? Envisioning how amazing they would be together, a heady buzz kicked inside.

Wanting her felt so much better than bitterness.

"You're wearing my shirt." The top two buttons were open. From where he sat behind her, peering down, he had a healthy view of ripe female curves.

"Should I take it off."

Riley didn't touch that temptation, but he did grin. The last time they'd seen each other, he'd been almost rabid with need. He still felt guilty for unbuttoning her shirt so fast. His reckless need to run his hands over her silky smooth skin was an intoxicating urgency. He'd startled himself. He ached to claim her. To feel her sleek body slide against his, to taste and touch and smile and feel whole.

"How was your girl time with Mom?"

"Informative."

"Usually is."

"I heard about your nieces and nephews; how cute they are and how well they do in school." Suddenly uneasy, she looked away, studying the firelight. Feminine fingers lovingly stroked Bitsy's white coat. "I heard all about everyone living in town; who is married to whom, who works where, and how many kids they have."

"Typical Harmon Summit gossip." He accurately judged.

She nodded to agree. "She...talked about you too."

He should have expected this. Waiting for her to continue, Savannah remained silent. "And?" He prodded, "What did Momma Emily share?"

Her face tipped away from him. She merely shrugged. Hiding her face, a satin dark chocolate sheet of hair swung down against her cheek and midnight shadows concealed whatever she was feeling.

Uh-oh. This wasn't good.

"So what? You learned that I'm a terribly crabby?"

"No. I already knew that."

"You discovered I hate cauliflower. And liver grilled with onions, like your Dad used to make." He pretended to shudder. "That stuff stunk to high heaven."

138

She sighed heavily and seemed to slump a little. "We didn't talk about that either. But I agree; Dad's grilled liver was gross."

"Did he make you try it?"

"Once. I gagged and spit it out. Dad swatted my butt and sent me to my room for the night without any dinner. I was only four or five, but I still remember how mad he got."

"John had quite a temper."

"Especially when he drank."

It was true. Savannah's childhood wasn't pretty. She'd spent most of it locked in her bedroom by people who didn't give a damn about raising a little girl.

At least, until Diablo arrived to Graystone.

Then she roamed the hills on the white stallion to escape. Unless she was at school busting her ass to get good grades that might earn a smidgen of approval or playing the piano, she rode away on Diablo at sunrise and did not reappear until after dark. It was safer that way. Bears and wolves were kind and loving compared to her parents.

"Then what juicy dirt did Mom share?"

Finally, she took a deep breath and pent-up words he'd dreaded hearing tumbled out of her mouth in a rush.

"You were with me at the hospital! It wasn't a dream."

"No, it was a nightmare." He grumbled, instantly angry his secret was exposed. "I can't believe she told you that."

"Ms. Emily thought I already knew."

"I told Mom you had a severe concussion, that you forgot things. Guess I should have been more explicit."

The heady rush of friendliness evaporated. Riley felt a bitter chill grip his heart. Unexpectedly cornered with the truth, his emotional steel walls returned. Cold. Hard. Just like the frozen winter snow.

"Why didn't you tell me?"

"You didn't remember. So, I decided it matter."

"It did matter! I thought I was all alone in that awful place, hurting, but you were there. Ms. Emily said you stayed for thirty-two days. That means something, to me. Were you ever going to tell me?"

"No, but you've asked, I won't lie."

Petting Bitsy, she became silent again. Her tucked face remained hidden behind that sheet of hair. For a long time the only noise in their darkened bedroom was the crackling fire.

"Say it." He gruffly ordered, almost daring her to challenge him. "Whatever you are thinking, just say it."

"Why did you come to the hospital?"

"Your agent, Marcus called, telling me about the accident. Then your surgeon called, saying you were critical, but stabilized. Then your attorney called. All within an hour of one another." A soft-spoken grandfatherly man, Marcus Seabourne was the only person in Savannah's life that Riley actually trusted. "Marcus was genuinely upset. The other's just wanted someone to make decisions about your medical treatment."

Slumping a little more, her voice trembled with sorrow. "You came to New York only because they called?"

"I had to go. Your legal papers listed me as Ryan's next of kin and your emergency contact. You have no other family, Savannah. Just me."

"Oh," she sniffed, "I forgot about my living will."

She seemed deeply disappointed that he hadn't come to the hospital simply because he cared. This was a tough one. No matter how he felt about Savannah, Riley just couldn't lay down his heart.

She left him once.

As soon as the snow cleared, she'd leave him again.

He'd be alone. Again.

Just thinking about how easy she walked away the first time, disappearing into her perfect musical world without caring how he felt, made him angry.

"Did you see Ryan's headstone?"

"I did. It's beautiful. I couldn't figure out how someone knew to put 'Forever Isn't Long Enough' on it. I didn't remember ordering it. But then, everything was so jumbled up inside my busted head, who knows what I did or said."

"You asked for it, actually."

"Well, thanks for listening." Sitting in front of him, hunched over as if she wanted to disappear, her body was somehow getting smaller, pushed down by the burden of heartache and shame. "So…you handled Ryan's services?"

"Yes. Since you couldn't leave the hospital, we kept it small and private. It was just me, Marcus Seabourne and his wife, Cynthia. Mom and Dad were there too."

She sniffed and wiped her face with one hand. Head bent, her humiliated tears stayed hidden behind that sheet of glossy brown hair. Dark strands drifted over Bitsy, in sharp contrast to that pure white coat. Riley felt her spine tremble as she tried not to cry. He should have felt sorry for her, but for reasons that made no sense, he felt vindictive.

She didn't bury their son. He did.

It would haunt him forever.

He wanted to make her pay.

Why were his emotions so extreme? A few minutes ago, he'd wanted sex, love, and laughter. Now he coldly wanted to make her cry.

"I had to make decisions for you too."

Her head jerked up. "You did? Like what?"

"They wanted to amputate your leg."

The body leaning against him stiffened. Rigid. Horrorstruck. Appalled. Savannah sucked in a great gasping lungful of air, stifling a heartbroken sob. Wow. That was by far the coldest thing he ever said. To anyone.

It was too late to soften that blow.

She wanted the truth. Well, this was it. The cold hard truth.

"I wouldn't let them."

Cautiously, she peered over her shoulder. Violet eyes glistened. "Those surgeries: pulling bone out of my hip to repair the places that were shattered, putting the pins inside my ankle, and the steel rod in my thigh...you made them piece me back together?"

"What choice did I have? I can't even give Bitsy a shot without feeling awful. I couldn't be responsible for your leg. You're strong. I knew you'd heal. When you started becoming lucid, I came home. You were healing. I thought you'd continue your wonderful life in New York City. But like a stubborn Graystone woman that you are, you checked yourself out of the hospital and flew all the way to Montana in a blizzard."

"So...you just did what you had to do," her voice was tiny and distressed, "and then left?"

"Pretty much. I knew you only put me on those legal papers because of Ryan." He coldly divulged.

"You didn't expect to see me again?"

"No. I honestly believed you and I were through."

She looked away and shivered from head to toe. Hiding her face again, she sat there for another long tense silent hour, rubbing that silky white sleeping filly and occasionally sniffling.

Riley felt guilty.

Where had the good gone?

He'd ruined it.

He'd hardened his heart, used words as weapons, and made Savannah cry. His hand still lay upon her thigh, but now he felt like a trespasser. Why was he so cruel? Did hurting her relieve his own pain? Hell no. It only made it worse.

"Sorry, Savannah. I should have told you nicer."

She just shrugged as if feeling she deserved it. Riley couldn't see her face, but her shoulders and head hung in a defeated cower.

"Can I ask you something?" He gently questioned.

"I guess." But her voice was strained and tight.

"Earlier, you said you thought it was a dream. Do you really remember us being together at the hospital?"

"A little."

"What do you remember?"

"In my dream, you held my hand," she swallowed hard, "and we cried over losing Ryan. But that can't be true. You don't cry. So...I guess I don't remember anything at all. My broken mind just wished it."

141

But it was true.

Most days Riley slept slumped over the side of her bed, just holding her hand. The only part of her he could touch. She'd been so broken, in so much pain. They really had cried together. Many times.

Her one dream was actually several heartbroken weeks.

"It was real." He confessed. "All of it."

"You cried with me?"

"Yes. I did. I never left your side."

"Why?"

"Because I couldn't. I was afraid if I left that room, with that heart monitor beeping, I'd come back and that beep would be gone."

"You thought I'd die?"

"Everyone did. Your survival was a miracle. That's why I was furious at you for coming here. I left, thinking you were safe. You would survive. Instead, you tempted death, even begged for it to take you. It made me furious. You didn't appreciate living or having two working legs. I know I've been a bully. I know I should have told you the truth. I've handled everything wrong. Sorry, Savannah."

Wiping wet cheeks with the backs of her hands, Savannah straightened a bit. "Can I ask you something? And will you answer honestly?"

"Sure."

"Why did you kiss me? Not the first time, when we were fighting, and you asked," she gulped and omitted the part about marrying him. "The other day? Before you left. What was that?"

Another loaded question. Wonderful. Riley sighed. She deserved at least a piece of his carefully guarded heart. "Maybe sometimes, Savage," he benevolently confessed, "I really miss how good we were."

"What are we now? Seems to me you've been thrown into my messy life without a choice. I'm living here at Graystone because I traipsed all this way to die. Now you're stuck with me. That can't make you happy. You came to New York City because I put you on some stupid legal papers. You even had to bury our son. Alone. I know you're mad. I feel it in everything you say and do. Hate just keeps boiling up inside you. Yet, sometimes…like tonight," she sniffed again, "bringing me Bitsy…you do the nicest things. It's confusing, Riley."

"Bringing you a tiny premature filly that will almost certainly die and make you bawl for days is nice?"

"She's alive right now." Savannah stubbornly defended, "And Bitsy's happy to feel wanted and loved. Her time here might be short, but being loved matters."

Yes, it did.

Love did matter.

Without hesitation, Riley dropped his left shoulder. Leaning against him how she was, Savannah automatically tipped sideways into the cradle of his arm. She gasped and stared up at him. "Riley?"

"We were good together, weren't we?"

"Yeah," she whispered, "we were great."

"I miss it. Every day, I miss how good we were."

Violet eyes glistened. "Me too. So much."

Riley kissed her. Soft. Honest. Not half-crazed like before. Lingering and tasting, nibbling just a little.

The kiss deepened.

Murmuring approval, Savannah slid one hand up to lovingly stroke his face. Slowly, soft fingers trickled through the back of his hair and gripped it in gentle fists. The sweetness of that affectionate touch made him ache for all the good they had lost.

Could they get it back?

He didn't know.

Did he want to try? Yes.

As he reluctantly drew away, the pretty face staring up at him was utterly mystified. Then she grinned. Bitsy grunted, squirming closer, trying to regain contact with the comforting woman who had moved.

"Now look what you did," she giggled. "You woke up the baby."

"Sorry."

Grateful she wasn't overanalyzing the impulsive kiss; Riley sat her up and slid away. Escaping the reckless moment, he stood and gathered his stethoscope from his medical bag. He walked around the blanket and knelt down again in front of the pair.

Firelight lit Savannah in glorious shades of amber and gold. She looked like a divine rescuing angel with that tiny white horse bundled in her lap. Glossy chocolate hair flowed over the pink blanket and around Bitsy.

Offering the vitamin-enriched milk, the filly sniffed it. Recognizing the smell, Bitsy nickered and guzzled greedily.

"Good girl," he softly soothed. "That's a good girl."

Gently, he pulled back the blanket so he could check her. Riley stroked a white coat so innocently pure that it glistened in the firelight. Over and over his hands rubbed. Comforting. Massaging warmth and life into her weak body and legs.

Savannah just held her while he helped the baby eat.

"Mmm, so tiny." He talked to Bitsy, smiling as her ears flicked in his direction. "Bet that makes you feel better. You were hungry again, weren't you? That's good. You'll get stronger now." When she was full, Riley continued a soothing flow of conversation and slid the stethoscope under her chest.

Bitsy didn't struggle, but lay there trusting with slender legs tucked beneath her. Those pointed white ears swiveled toward every quiet sound. With

143

his stethoscope he listened to Bitsy's tiny heart sluggishly churn instead of thump-a-thump. Wishing he'd heard something hopeful, he sat back on his heels and sighed.

"The look on your face says she needs a miracle."

"She is a miracle." Riley tucked the pink blanket into a velvet cocoon around Bitsy's fragile body. "She shouldn't even be breathing."

He watched violet eyes glitter. For some dumb reason Savannah's tears seemed unfair. Why was she allowed free expression of heartache?

If she felt sad, she cried. Boo-hooed like a baby.

He couldn't.

Men were supposed to swallow pain whole and move on.

Life sucked sometimes.

"You should get up and walk around." He gruffly commanded. "Sitting there will make you crippled."

"I am NOT a cripple!"

"Damn." He sighed, ashamed. "I didn't mean it like that."

"Sure. Whatever."

Kneeling between Savannah and the fireplace, Riley saw every wistful expression on her face disturbingly exposed in the firelight. She stubbornly tipped her chin. She closed her eyes.

She swallowed that pain whole.

Eyes opened, gleaming, but not overflowing.

But that raw wound remained. Just tucked inside now. Where pain would fester. Where she could recall it and later cry, all alone.

Riley realized how much he had hurt her.

Not just right now with his thoughtless words, but he had inflicted pain with every calloused cutting cruel word since she arrived.

And she'd taken it. Why?

"I am sooo sorry, Savannah." He truly meant it.

"For ordering me to walk around?"

"For pretending that I don't care and then kissing you," he tenderly clarified in a voice that made her bottom lip pucker, "which just proves that every harsh thing I've said and done since you got here was mean and wrong. And a lie."

A single tear slowly slid down one cheek.

She whisked it away with a shirtsleeve.

"Why do you take crap from me? In the old days, if I hurt your feelings you would have slapped me across the face and told me to go to hell."

She just glumly shrugged as if she deserved the verbal punishment he'd been dishing out. Not meeting his gaze anymore, she concentrated on petting Bitsy.

"Do you know why I brought Bitsy home? Because she does need a miracle. You're her miracle. Look how sweetly she's curled up with you. That tiny filly might be dying, but Bitsy can feel your love. She trusts you. Love gives her reason to fight. You loved Bitsy from the first minute. I saw that light shine in your eyes. That light changes things, Savage. You've always had a connection with animals. Somehow, they just feel your good loving heart. Like Zeus…my big tough guard dog took one look at you and fell in love."

"You said Zeus wanted to eat me."

"Hell, he'd never bite you. You're his queen. Haven't you noticed that he sleeps on the floor, right beside you? You can't even get out of bed in the morning until he moves."

"My side is closer to the fire. Zeus is just staying warm."

"No. He's there because he loves you. He's protecting you. Maybe you're too sleepy to notice, but if you go to the bathroom during the night, he walks right beside you with this worried look in his eyes."

"I lean on him to walk." She glumly confessed.

"See? He helps you. You didn't train him to do that. He didn't ask. Zeus does it because he cares. Right now he's out there in the stables," he pointed toward the barns, "howling his fool-head off because he's too damn dirty to come inside the house where he can be with you, and I won't take the time to bathe him. Did you know that?"

"I wondered where he was." She scowled as though Riley was a heartless hardened criminal for locking out her giant friend.

"Goliath loves you. I've never seen a cat so in love."

"He just likes to be petted."

"No. Goliath hates to be touched. He hisses and scratches at me."

"Maybe you rub him the wrong way."

"I probably do. I rub everyone the wrong way."

That earned him the tiniest Savannah smile.

"You did it with Diablo too. You were only nine years old when your Daddy spent a fortune shipping that wild Andalusian here from Spain, dreaming about raising good bloodlines. That stallion thundered off that horse trailer and into the corral like white lightning, biting and kicking anyone in his path. John believed Diablo was tame. They lied. Your Daddy was so mad; he marched into the house and brought out his gun, fully intending to use it. To hell with the money. He was a proud man. He wouldn't take being swindled. But you cried and begged him not to shoot Diablo."

"I remember that day."

"I, for one, will never forget it."

"Why?"

"Because that day changed everything. John didn't mean it when he told you that frenzied stallion was your problem now. He was just mad. But you believed him. We spent all day standing outside his corral while you just talked to Diablo. That wild stallion charged that fence, hollering, threatening to run you down. But you weren't scared. You just kept talking. In one week, you made that angry horse your friend. Diablo loved you. He ate apples right out of your hand. A month later, you climbed upon that scary white stallion's back. Your Dad was so happy someone could control him, he officially said Diablo was yours."

She nodded, remembering.

"Diablo still raged and snapped at everyone else, but for you, he acted like a docile kid's pony. He was abused. The men in Spain whipped him. He carried deep black scars all over his beautiful white body. Diablo hated people, hated everything and everyone, but this sweet little girl loved him. So...he protected you. That simple love made the big man whole. He gave you his heart."

Riley was going somewhere with this, but putting his highest truth into words wasn't easy. It meant admitting that every mean thing he said to Savannah and the heartless way he had been behaving was all just to hide his fear of losing her again.

Swallowing his pride was hard.

He wouldn't lose her again.

Now was his chance.

"And me, Savannah," he softly confessed. "I'm not immune."

"Please, just stop," she sadly begged, "I get it. I'm good with animals. Occasionally, I'm good with people. You loved me once and that love made you happy. You had big dreams for a lifetime of love. Our love made you whole. Then I left. Worse, I stole your son. Losing him hurt deep. Now, you're bitter and vengeful. This is just another way for you to rub it in my face that I broke your heart and ruined everything good."

"I still love you."

Her mouth hung open.

"I never stopped loving you. Ever."

Her lips were working but no sound came out.

"I think I'll love you forever, Savannah."

"Oh...Riley."

"That's the real reason I went to New York. Because I love you. That's why I pretended to be your husband, raising hell all over that hospital so those damn judgmental doctors wouldn't take the easy road and leave you broken."

"You told them we were married?"

"Yeah, honey. I did."

Violet eyes suspiciously narrowed. She wasn't buying his sudden emotional surrender. He'd already been too cold and mean. Riley knew by her doubtful expression he had a ton of wrong to make right, between them.

"Why bother pretending? You had legal authority."

"Because I cared. Too much. Part of me wanted it to be true."

"But Riley," she skeptically argued, "you came back to Graystone and left me all alone! People who care don't leave! That isn't love!"

"I know." He felt ashamed to the core. She deserved love, real love. "I'm sorry. I left because bitterness was easier than clinging to anything good. Whenever you were awake, you'd just cry. The doctors claimed you didn't remember the accident. You were in so much pain. I was right there, right beside you, but you cried out for Ryan instead. We'd been apart for so long, I didn't think you needed me. I misunderstood. I didn't realize you were crying because you DID remember the accident. I thought you were rejecting me. Again. So, I got angry. And I've done my best to stay that way. Finding fault was easier than opening my heart."

Her doubtful frown became a sad pout.

"But now sometimes when you look at me," he earnestly explained, "I see that light in your eyes that means you do care. Deep inside, I want it to be true. I want to believe in love. Our love. And that's why I kissed you."

Breathing slow and deep, she sat there watching the firelight flicker. Riley knew she didn't want to believe him. Savannah didn't want to be hurt anymore. She'd been through so much. He saw every mangled emotion play across her face.

"You fought with them for me?"

"Yes. I'd do it again too. Except I wouldn't leave you in that hospital all alone and make you find your way to Montana hurt, wanting to die. I'd stay. I'd tell you how much I love you, how much I need you. Then I would bring you home with me to Graystone Heights, your home; our home," he softly added, "and give you reasons to live."

"But Riley, you don't even like…"

"I love you, Savannah." He honestly affirmed in a voice that left no doubt, "You should have been my wife. I've loved you since the day you were born. I loved you every day you were gone. I can't imagine not loving you."

It was so true, his heart clenched.

He couldn't lose her again.

He had to make things right. "Forever isn't long enough, not for us. Do you think, maybe, you might still love me? Just a little?"

Eyes gleaming, she reluctantly whispered. "Maybe. A little."

"Please, will you marry me?"

Taking a deep staggered breath that caught on heartache and flinched, revealing too much buried pain, she studied the orange flames as if that crackling warmth making shadows dance across their darkened bedroom was the only lucid reality she could trust.

"You're tired," she decided. "It's late. You should sleep."

"Answer my question first."

"I don't want to."

"Don't want to marry me, or answer?"

"Answer."

"Okay. Fine. Then think about it. Please." Instead of letting himself get mad, Riley walked over to their bed, stripped it of heavy blankets and pillows, and dropped them on the floor beside her.

"Tonight we'll right sleep here."

"Why?"

"Because Bitsy needs to be near you. And whether you believe it or not, I do too." Without asking permission, he spread two thick comforters out on the floor for them to lie upon and another one to cover them up. It was warm by the fireplace and the cushion he made wasn't that bad.

"You're a stubborn confusing complicated man."

"Crawl in there, Savage." He brusquely ordered, "And slide Bitsy so she can touch you. We'll talk about being stubborn tomorrow."

She groaned and carefully moved her aching left leg. Bitsy complained too, but Savannah took off her jeans, leaving only his shirt. She rubbed her thigh for a minute, then scooted into the makeshift bed. She settled on her right side and reassuringly placed her hand upon Bitsy's neck.

The tiny white filly nickered happily and curled up in a ball. It was cute. Like a kitten with hooves, gray-blue eyes, and pointed ears. Savannah lovingly smoothed the blanket over her fragile body. Bitsy sighed and closed her eyes.

Satisfied this would work, Riley climbed in beside her, leaving his clothes on too. "See, we're camping out."

"Real funny, Mountain Man," she snickered, "Last time we camped out, I was seventeen and we spent the weekend at Lake Pleasant with Sam and his boys. You went to sleep in your tent, like a nice young man should, but woke up blissfully naked in mine. Sam nearly caught you creeping back into your own tent."

"He knew. I know he did. But he never said a word."

"Of course not. Sam's a very smart man."

Considering some of the soft-spoken wisdom Riley recently received from Sam Lawson while playing mid-wife to Bitsy's Momma, he knew that aging cowboy was dead-on with many of his keen observations.

Love wasn't complicated. Love was pure.

People made it complicated.

"He is smart," Riley conceded, "And I was being reckless."

"Maybe. But you gotta admit; we sure had fun."

"Yeah. We did."

Savannah yawned hugely and closed her eyes. And she didn't squirm away when Riley possessively wrapped her in his arms.

# *Chapter Thirteen*

Tick. Tick. Tick-a-tick. Something noisily tottered just a few feet away from Riley's head. Tick-tick. Lying on his side, he groggily squinted. It was already morning. Already? Gee, hadn't he just closed his eyes. Daylight came way too soon.

Despite the two thick comforters beneath him, his body ached in odd places from sleeping on the floor. With her back to him, Savannah's warm backside was cozily tucked tight against his front. Her curves fit his in the most amazingly pleasant way. Arm around her waist, the flannel shirt had lifted.

His left hand lay upon her smooth stomach.

Skin. Oops!

Across the bedroom, the tiny white miracle he brought home last night was unsteadily walking around. As she stepped and daintily sniffed the world she couldn't see, Bitsy's tiny black hooves ticked upon the oak floor. Slowly inspecting and finding it safe, the curious filly carefully stepped forward again. Currently she was familiarizing herself with the odd obstacle being created by the coffee table.

"Savi," he whispered against the nape of her neck. "Are you awake, honey? Look at Bitsy."

"I know. Isn't she beautiful?"

Rising up a little, he leaned on his elbow so he could see her face. Violet eyes were open and alert, glistening with that wonderful miraculous heavenly light that changed lives and opened hearts.

Love. Pure unconditional love.

Riley ached to see that light when she looked at him.

"You're beautiful, Savage."

"You must still be dreaming." But she grinned with girlish pleasure and glanced back at him. The light in her eyes actually brightened.

Love. For him? Maybe.

"No, you're definitely beautiful. Especially this morning."

"Some mornings I'm hideous?" She teased.

"Honey, you're so beautiful and sweet, some nights I stay awake just so I can watch you sleep. I love you, Savannah."

Violet-blue eyes gleamed. She swallowed hard and he knew she still didn't believe. Taking a chance, Riley buried his face into the warm curve between her shoulder and neck, playfully nibbled tender skin.

She didn't object.

Instead, Savannah closed her eyes and blissfully sighed.

Her body grew warmer. Softer.

Molding against him like velvet pleasure.

It was encouraging. She even arched her chin a bit so his mouth could thoroughly capture that erotic spot behind her ear that was certain to make her shiver.

When she did shiver, mewing with delight, Riley gripped her tighter and kept right on proving he meant everything he said last night.

He loved her.

He wanted to marry her.

Marriage would fix them.

Sometimes words weren't enough. Or sometimes too much. Sometimes a man needed to say what he meant in other ways.

He'd show her the depths of his heart.

When they were young, he spent years memorizing Savannah, gauging her reactions. Slowly they learned how to physically love, teaching each other about pleasure. It all began with nothing but tender kisses. Then those loving caresses gradually became something more. There was no need to rush. Preserving every ounce of innocence, two years after that very first breathless kiss, he finally made love to her, claiming her forever as his own.

He would do it again.

He would earn her trust.

Slowly. Making all the wrongs, right.

"Ahhh, Riley…" she huskily purred, reaching back to grip the side of his hip, "you remember what I like."

"I do remember. You're mine, Savannah." He kissed the nape of her neck, "My beautiful sweet woman." She wasn't wearing jeans. Only panties and his flannel shirt. Her warm backside snuggled tighter, fitting right in the cradle of his hips. "You always have been. You always will be."

"Does that mean I can have you, too?"

"Yes. I belong to you, too."

"Ohhh…hmm…yeeesss." Taking those sultry satisfied sounds as an invitation, his fingers on her stomach slowly slid. Up. She wasn't wearing a bra. As his hand inched upwards, her hips rocked in reply.

His hand molded around her round full breast.

God her skin felt good. So firm and velvety smooth.

A woman now; no longer a girl.

She'd matured magnificently.

Blood boiling dangerously, body barely under control, he wanted so much more than tender caresses and slow physical awakenings.

He wanted passion. Hot and needy. He wanted Savannah.

Damn. He needed to slow down.

Breathing faster, she groaned and female fingers at his hip tugged at his jeans. "Hold still." He quietly urged.

"I can't hold still," she arched into his hand as his fingers lovingly stroked her skin, "I love when you touch me. I love your hands on my skin. I remember too! Oh…Riley… I've missed you!"

"I know baby, I've missed you too."

"I need you. Now!"

Suddenly Savannah rolled to face him. She devoured his mouth. The kiss so hot and demanding Riley couldn't think.

It was incredible.

Hands were everywhere.

She wanted him. All of him. Now!

Her red flannel shirt miraculously disappeared.

Skin. Beautiful sweet tawny-peach Savannah skin.

That yearned for his touch.

Tugging urgently at the clothes between them, she laughed with delight as he rolled her on top of him, so she straddled his stomach as he slid off his jeans and threw away his shirt.

"Better?"

"Perfect."

Much, much, later…he couldn't quite remember how that one zealous kiss changed everything between them, but as they lay naked and physically spent in the tangled blankets, his mind finally kicked back into gear.

Riley realized what they had done.

"My…God…Savage," he struggled to think.

She made love like a wild thing, tasting and touching, nibbling and licking; taking great pleasure in reacquainting herself with his adult body. Smiling. Laughing. Murmuring profound satisfaction. Taking exactly what she wanted.

But she gave great pleasure too.

So much, it still made thought impossible.

She was amazing.

Even now, the sultry sweaty woman collapsed across his chest seemed a bit like a starving tigress and he just became her breakfast.

"You…we…oh, God."

She lifted her head and happily giggled. It was the happiest sound in his world. "That good, huh?" As she moved, a sheet of luscious chocolate hair draped seductively across his bare skin. It was cool and sleek, wickedly scintillating. "We have an audience." She nodded across the floor.

Curled up on her pink blanket again, Bitsy lay several feet away, quietly listening. Somehow, she had returned. He never noticed. He was too busy with Savannah.

His Savage.

And holy saints, how she grew up!

"What just happened?"

She huskily laughed and rolled off him. Riley immediately missed her silky warmth. "I took advantage of you on the floor. Several times. Let's call it breakfast, since obviously, we were both famished. Maybe later we can do lunch." She giggled at the bad joke that promised more silky skin and tangled sheets. "Are you already having regrets?"

"No. I just, I didn't think...do you love me, Savannah?"

"Riley," she beamed, divine light glistening in beautiful violet eyes, "forever isn't long enough for how much I love you."

"Honestly?"

"Honestly. Truly. Cross my heart." Smiling, she crossed her naked breast. "I love you, Riley. I always have. I always will. You belong to me."

Getting up, she shamelessly walked across the oak floor and into the bathroom, giving him a full view of long slender legs, sweet female curves, and firm full breasts that still bore pink marks from his greedy hands and mouth.

Riley didn't see any scars at all.

He only saw a beautiful woman with peach-satin skin and a sensuous cocoa mane swinging down her slender back. Glancing back at him, Savannah grinned triumphantly.

She seemed quite proud of herself for conquering the mystified naked man she left lying on the floor.

Well hell. He should be deliriously happy.

Why wasn't he?

By the time she returned, dreamily smiling and dressed in pink panties with one of his blue flannel shirts draping around her willowy frame, he had angrily yanked on his clothes. All of them. Even boots.

Why was he so upset? The way he felt was madness. Angry? Why? This morning a stunningly beautiful woman pleasured him into sweet delirious exhaustion. A woman he loved.

He should be content. Cheerful.

Like any normal man.

What the hell? Angry? Really? Was he hopelessly broken?

Riley had wrapped Bitsy up in her blanket. He now held the tiny trusting filly in his arms. "Her heart sounds stronger." He couldn't keep the sharp edge out of his voice. "Even her eyes look clearer. Since she seems stronger, I'm going to see if any of the brood mares in the stable will accept her. Duchess still has milk. She hasn't stopped producing yet, from her last colt. If she'll accept Bitsy and let her nurse, Momma's milk is healthier than formula."

Savannah looked completely baffled by his rough tone and brusque manner. Clearly, she expected they'd enjoy a few warm kisses and after-glow cuddling; maybe even share quiet pillow talk that could mend the broken past and pave the way to a brighter future.

That wasn't happening.

The shattered expectations in her face made him even more furious. He watched her swallow hard and knew she was swallowing a big chunk of pride. "Well...yes," she decided, the blissful light of love fading from violet eyes, "I guess we should take care of Bitsy."

"Yeah. She comes first."

"Okay. Can I come?"

"Who should I carry down three flights of stairs?" He angrily bit, "You or Bitsy? I can't do both."

That pert bottom lip started to pout. Violet eyes watered. Then her chin stubbornly tilted. "See? I knew you didn't mean it."

"What?"

"All that 'I love you' crap."

"It wasn't crap."

"Sure. That's why you're so charming. Again."

"I just..."

"Shut up, Riley!" She held up both palms to block out his voice, "I don't want to hear it! No more lies!" Pulling on her jeans, she glared at him. "Now take Bitsy downstairs. Then get your mean-hearted bully-butt back up here to help me downstairs too. I'm going with you!"

He started to object.

"I'm not playing games with you, Riley Phillip! I mean it!" She plopped down in a chair. Slamming bare feet into pink socks, she angrily yanked on her turquoise boots. "Whatever your problem is, get over it! I'm sick of you running hot and cold. It's bullshit! And mean! Just stay cold. Ice cold! It's easier to deal with than hot-blooded lies." He opened his mouth, "Shut the hell up! Let's take care of Bitsy. Can you manage that without griping?"

Not sure what else to do, he left.

Downstairs, he wandered around holding Bitsy. He halfheartedly gathered Savannah's parka, gloves, white scarf, and fluffy hat. Not wanting to face the woman upstairs, he put them on the couch. Stalling, he even found a sturdy gold-handle cane leftover from when Graystone had guests.

Then, for one truly mean moment, he considered leaving her up there.

What was wrong with him?

They just enjoyed the best mind-blowing sex EVER and here he was stomping around fuming. About what?

He honestly did not know.

Leaving Bitsy bundled on the floor near the base of the stairs, she fussed, but Riley knelt and calmly stroked her soft body to reassure. Satisfied she was safe and loved; the trusting baby curled up to wait.

He only made it halfway up the stairs before he saw Savannah, determined as hell, gingerly taking each stair tread one by one. He noticed her white-knuckled death grip on the handrail. Good god, she could fall and break her neck! Her left leg shook.

Walking level surfaces was one thing, but putting weight on those bones while stepping downward was extremely painful.

Their eyes met. Riley swooped her up. With a cry of alarm, she wrapped her arms around his neck.

"I do love you." He declared, "But you could get pregnant and then what? Will you leave me again? What we did was stupid."

"Is that what's eating you?" Grinning in relief, she laughed a little at his ridiculous tantrum. "I took care of it. Your worried Momma brought me enough foamy contraceptives things for a brothel."

"She did?"

"Yeah. It was embarrassing."

"Oh."

"She was convinced we might need such things."

"So…you can't get pregnant?"

"Nope. Ms. Emily even brought six months' worth of a birth control prescription that she wrangled out of Mr. Anderson at the pharmacy in Harmony Hills. So," she playfully rubbed her nose along his bristly cheek, "I can start taking those little magic pills if you'd like to occasionally get friendly. Or," she rolled her eyes, "you can keep stomping around, being a troll, acting like we just did something awful."

They reached the bottom of the stairs. Still frowning, Riley carefully set her down, holding her waist until both legs were steady.

"You've changed, Savage."

She looked at him funny.

Damn. That wasn't what he meant! Why couldn't he ever say what he felt? Why did everything important always become jumbled up inside?

"You were different."

"I was? How?"

"You knew things." Wonderful. Another crappy explanation.

*Come on brain. Work right.*

Suddenly Riley knew exactly why he felt so angry. Rolling the reasons over in his mind, weighing evidence against allegations, he felt totally justified.

"You weren't…uh, shy."

"Oh. That." Kneeling down, she rubbed Bitsy, who nickered happily under Savannah's soothing touch. She didn't answer right away. Her head remained sadly bowed. When she did reply, her voice was as truly brokenhearted as he'd ever heard.

"You didn't like making love with me?"

"I did! Too much! Who taught you to be like that?" He roared the poisonous judgment eating him alive inside, "Who else have you been with?"

Savannah stood and Riley knew she wanted to slap him.

"You!"

"And? Who else?"

Her mouth gaped. "You honestly think I've slept around?"

"Sure. You were too confident," he defended his suspicions. "The old Savannah never would have taken charge. You didn't just make love; hell woman, you devoured me!" Too vividly, he recalled those luscious stunned senseless sensations when she held him captive by no more than her busy mouth and loving hands. The sheer perfection of those pleasurable moments made him angrier.

"You even threw off all the blankets and let me watch our bodies moved together. Why? Because you knew I liked it! Who taught you to be so uninhibited?"

"How dare you!" Standing tall and defiant, violet eyes flashed with righteous fury. "Just because I knew what I wanted and knew how to please you too, you automatically assume I've been with someone else? Why? Because you liked it too much?"

"Well, I…"

"That's the most screwed up thing I've ever heard! If you liked it, you should take it as a compliment, Riley! I had a damn good teacher. You!"

"Just me?"

"Only you," one finger angrily poked him in the chest, "you bullheaded jackass fool! One man. Ever! All my life! Only you!"

Riley knew she wasn't lying. His gut clenched.

He'd just made a huge mistake.

"But forget it!" She screeched, "It won't happen again! EVER!"

Shrugging into her white parka, she plopped that fuzzy white hat on her head. Eyes glared, she dared him to say she couldn't go to the barn.

Riley didn't say a word.

The only thing on the tip on his tongue was *I'm sorry.*

But he didn't say that either.

He picked up Bitsy instead.

Seething, Savannah spied the walking cane and angrily snatched it up. "You were right! Getting naked together was stupid! Real damn stupid! Dumbest thing I've ever done! But don't worry, Riley," she sourly decreed, "I won't ever punish you with wild uninhibited sex with me ever again!"

The whole rest of the day, she didn't talk to him.

155

She talked to Bitsy and loved on all the horses. Savannah gave each one their morning greetings and moments of her undivided attention. She congratulated Duchess for accepting that fragile white filly as her own newborn foal. She watched Bitsy nurse on her adopted Momma and gave Duchess handfuls of extra grain as a reward for taking her parental responsibilities seriously.

A giant tabby cat followed around, rubbing on her legs. He nearly knocked her over. Savannah scooped up Goliath and loved on him too. He purred so obnoxiously loud, Riley could hear that blissful feline motor clear across the stables.

She loved on Zeus, of course. "Guh! You stink!" She firmly declared and gave Zeus a sudsy bath in the oversized cement shower stall where Riley normally rinsed sweaty horses. Water gurgled down the metal drains.

It was noisy raucous bubbly fun.

Her squeals and laughter echoed through the stables with joy, making the pit in his stomach feel abysmal. Curious horses hung their heads over paddock gates to watch. Even Goliath perched himself high upon a wooden ceiling crossbeam, too bewitched with watching that crazy woman to seek refuge from the water.

While Riley worked several restless horses in the arena, Savannah wandered around the two massive nicely heated buildings using that gold handle cane, happy as a lark to be free of her Graystone prison.

He felt awful.

And real damn stupid.

Savannah wouldn't even look at him. But she happily visited everyone else. She spent the entire day patting and loving, cooing on those animals as if they were her very best friends.

Zeus followed her step for step.

The big dog definitely sensed something was wrong.

He'd look at his mistress with worried brown eyes, then glare at Riley with disapproval. It just served to compound his guilty conscience. Savannah didn't seem to notice the peculiar undercurrent between man and dog.

Keeping a watchful eye on Bitsy, she was satisfied to see Duchess licking her adopted baby clean. Bitsy nursed until her small belly bulged. She tottered around the straw-covered paddock, happy to be alive, healthier than he dared hope.

She was a miracle.

When Riley quietly joined Savannah, pretending to check Bitsy's heart, she frowned and gimped away with her Great Dane guardian. She must be hurting. He noticed she was leaning on both that cane and Zeus.

"Just ride him, if you're hurting." He called out.

"Shut up, Riley!"

After that, he didn't see her again. She completely disappeared. He looked for her, but only found her white parka lying on the floor in the tack room. No woman anywhere, and no sign of her faithful dog and cat fan club. But he definitely didn't like seeing the heavy western saddle that was tugged down off the rack, flopped on the floor.

That only meant one thing.

She wanted to get as far away from him as possible. He couldn't imagine Savannah could carry that heavy saddle, let alone lift it above her head, swing it onto a horse, and riding away. Could she even ride anymore?

Probably not.

Would she leave him? Somehow?

Maybe.

Well, maybe being left all alone in the unforgiving icy Montana mountains was exactly what he deserved.

A beautiful woman made love to him with all the selfless joy in her unbridled heart and he'd accused her of being sleazy.

What an idiot.

What did she call him? A bullheaded jackass fool.

He had to agree.

Riley found her late that evening in the north corridor where he kept his prize black stallion, Merlin. The metal gate was slightly ajar. Her gold cane hung on one of the crossbars.

This time, he'd catch her. She couldn't avoid him forever.

Riley silently crept through.

Merlin's paddock door stood wide open.

His heart lurched.

There was a reason Merlin lived separate from the rest of the horses. It wasn't just because he was male. The big man was too high-spirited to have neighbors. He liked to frisk around, wild as a colt, to prove he was king.

It was best if he ruled alone.

Draped on a brass wall hook was the black stallion's cotton halter.

Free? Oh hell. Where was Savannah?

He didn't see Merlin anywhere.

It was quiet. Too quiet. Did that big stallion trample her? Cautiously, he stepped closer and peered around the wall.

The mighty Andalusian as sinfully black as Satan's soul stood calmly inside the roomy paddock, nibbling sugar cubes from her small hand. Merlin didn't seem concerned that the gate to his prison was wide open or that he was free from all physical restraints.

Escape wasn't as fun as hanging out with that crazy woman.

She had braided his thick wavy mane in a dozen places and tied the long strands with bright red ribbons. Ribbons? Gah. Poor Merlin. She must have found those in the tack room. Merlin seemed ridiculously happy to be her giant playmate. Those big brown eyes looked a little dopy. As she lovingly rubbed his black aristocratic forehead, he sighed.

Great. Another love-stuck fool.

Standing in the paddock gateway, Riley finally had her cornered. She couldn't gimp away from him this time. "Hey, there you are." He cheerfully greeted. "Looks like you've made another friend."

She completely ignored him.

The giant tiger-striped lump covertly crouched upon the wooden crossbeam above Riley's head opened yellowy eyes.

Goliath. Still shadowing Savannah.

Creepy cat. He looked evil perched up there.

"We didn't eat anything today. Are you hungry?" He asked as nicely as he could. Shifting her body, keeping her back toward him, she shook her head. Then added another red ribbon to Merlin's rather unmanly collection.

"Bitsy's doing great. She looks stronger. Healthy." Riley casually commented, "Did you see her walking around?"

Nothing. Not even a shrug.

Goliath grumbled low in his throat.

And Merlin was starting to give him the evil eye.

"Duchess is a wonderful Momma." He amiably chatted and hoped discussing their tiny miracle foal might help Savannah warm up to him. "Although her colt was weaned recently, she's still producing plenty of milk for Bitsy."

Merlin earned another braid and red ribbon.

Riley earned nothing.

Not even a sigh.

"I checked Bitsy's heart again. It still has a slight murmur, but it's better. I think she just might make it. Her eyes have even improved. The cloudiness is turning the prettiest color of baby blue. Maybe in another week or two, she might be able to see. Do you believe that? A white horse with blue eyes. She really is a miracle."

The lumpy pile of straw in the back corner of the oversized paddock stirred. A freshly bathed black Great Dane looked up and scowled.

Good grief, Zeus was guarding her too.

"It's dinner time. I'm going inside the house to clean up and eat. Will you please come with me?"

"No!" she finally snapped.

Holding onto Merlin's strong body with both hands, Riley knew Savannah's leg was killing her. Gripping the stallion's body so she didn't fall, she slowly inched around that towering black horse.

She disappeared behind his muscular backside.

Riley held his breath.

She reappeared again beside Zeus, where she lifelessly dropped into the pile of straw, utterly fearless that she'd pinned herself behind Merlin's very dangerous hooves.

"Go away, Riley." Violet eyes glared at him. No light of love glimmered. Only hurt. "I'm staying right here with my friends. I ate some apples. I'm not going back to my Graystone prison and I certainly won't go anywhere with you!"

Angry, he took a step inside the oversized paddock, intent on forcefully carrying Savannah out of there.

He was suddenly face-to-face with an extremely hostile Merlin.

"Hey." Riley shoved a hand against his forehead, "Move it, big guy."

Challenging his authority, Merlin snorted and boldly stepped forward, forcing Riley backwards out of the paddock. He wished Savannah had left the halter on the stallion's head so he had some control. Muscular chest puffed with pride, Merlin arched his neck like a threatening warrior. That black horse proudly filled the entire opening.

His powerful body suddenly seemed colossal.

"Fine. You want to play games?" Riley reached for another blue cotton halter hanging on the gate. Before his hand reached it, Merlin flicked it with his nose. It dropped just inches away from the stallion's front hooves.

Wow. That nifty little trick was actually impressive.

"Wonderful."

He considered reaching for it anyway.

Merlin defiantly put a big black hoof on it, ending that option.

"Come out of there, Savannah. Please, honey." Riley sincerely begged, "Merlin's unpredictable. He might hurt you."

"The only unpredictable man who hurts me is YOU!"

Her newest guardian arched his powerful neck in agreement. He grunted deep in his chest as a show of force and towered over Riley.

God, had Merlin always been that tall? "I'm sorry, Savannah. I didn't mean to hurt you..." Merlin tossed his regal-ribboned head in warning. "Really, Big Guy? Seriously? You want a piece of me?"

The formidable black stallion issued a menacing "Pffft," through his nose. He snapped his teeth. Riley flinched.

The sound was sharp and defiant as those teeth only met air.

Savannah laughed.

And Riley stomped away.

Mad as hell.

With no one to blame but himself.

## Chapter Fourteen

She had a long time to think today. Too long. Too much to think about, too. Savannah sagged wearily into the prickly straw, not caring too much about comfort, and closed her eyes.

A hefty furry body thumped down, grunting as it dropped into the straw beside her. Smiling, she hooked her arm around Goliath and scooted the giant tabby closer.

The cat purred.

It felt good to relax. Her body ached terribly.

But her heart ached even more.

What a horrible confusing turbulent day!

It started out amazing. Glorious!

Making love with Riley was the magical remedy that pulled all the shattered pieces of her heart back together again. It healed every wound. Confident of his love and lost in his arms, she hadn't felt broken anymore.

She was wonderfully whole.

But afterward, something went horrendously wrong.

Her heart shattered again.

Savannah admitted she shocked herself this morning, attacking Riley like some wanton jezebel in heat.

Poor man didn't stand a chance.

All because he said, so convincingly, that he loved her.

*"You are mine, Savannah. You always have been. You always will be."*

*"Does that mean I can have you, too?"*

*"Yes. I belong to you, too."*

She wanted that. She was pathetic. She needed Riley's love like some emotional junkie. This morning she threw caution to the wind simply because he nuzzled her neck just right, sending shivers up her spine. Reckless. She seized that reckless moment of pleasure like there was no tomorrow. Ahh yes, she seized the moment alright…taking and taking.

Giving too. Giving all her love to him, all at once.

Now, she would deal with the consequences.

Why would he naturally assume she had been intimate with someone else? It was dumbfounding. Because he liked it? In truth, Riley made love with just as much gusto and mind-numbing 'can't-get-enough-of-you' exuberance as she did.

Maybe more.

Remembering made her sassily smile.

She wasn't the only one whose body shook and quivered with profound fulfillment but had greedily come back for more. Several times. He'd always had great stamina. She never dreamed Riley could be so passionate.

It wasn't just sex.

Every touch felt like a promise of forever love.

Savannah spent years remembering every nuance of their loving, yearning for his familiar touch, aching for a second chance. Maybe that's why she was so enthusiastic today. Her body instinctively remembered everything Riley ever taught her about pleasure and in one rambunctious morning romp, she gave him a full hands-on demonstration of her accomplished sexual repertoire.

A repertoire designed to please one man only.

And he was extremely pleased.

Riley roared like a lion, making her mew like a kitten.

But then later…he decided to be angry.

Confusing complicated stubborn mountain man!

Always before, he treated her like a fragile little girl who needed to be tenderly seduced. Today? They were real adult lovers.

The man definitely knew what to do in bed.

Or on the floor.

Huh. That wasn't quite as funny as it sounded rolling around inside her head. But my god! It was exciting! Riley's hands and mouth were everywhere, devouring her body like he hadn't touched…

Suddenly, Savannah sat straight up in the straw.

Goliath went flying.

"Oh!"

Riley was so upset this morning because in all the years they were apart, he HADN'T been with anyone else.

He hadn't touched a woman in years.

Oh, gee. This was bad.

They had both been faithful, staying physically committed to people they believed they would never see again.

For six and a half long lonely years.

How completely screwed up was that?!

Rubbing sleep from her eyes, Savannah realized that sometime in the past few hours while she was curled up sleep-thinking and contemplating the evils of life, Merlin The Magnificent had flopped down beside her in the straw. Lying on his side, his aristocratic face almost touched her hip. He looked like a gigantic black dog. With hooves. And red ribbons braided into his kingly mane.

Big dangerous warrior. She grinned.

Well, not too dangerous. The mighty wizard was snoring.

And there was Riley.

Sitting with his back braced against the opposite corridor wall, he hadn't left her, after all. Knees bent, elbows resting upon those long-legged knees, he watched her with gorgeous green-gold eyes. It melted her heart. Bronze hair was slightly ruffled, as if he'd been sitting there with his head in his hands.

Sleeping?

Probably not. He looked sad. And all alone.

"Hi, Riley. You look tired."

"Now you're talking to me?"

At his deep voice, Merlin flicked his tail and grumpily stirred.

Carefully, Savannah crept out of the straw, leaving her ebony guardians behind. Her thigh ached too much to walk. Bone-deep pain throbbed with every heartbeat. She quietly crawled all the way to Riley and leaned against the corridor wall beside him.

He looked surprised. And deeply relieved.

"I finally understand why you got mad today," she whispered.

"That's good. At least it made sense to one of us," he softly apologized. "I'm sorry, Savannah. I have no idea what came over me."

"I do."

"So, enlighten me. Why did I act like a jackass?"

She thought about that and couldn't decide how to approach their delicate little dilemma. Riley wasn't a jackass. He was jealous. And being jealous, even if were completely unfounded, meant he truly cared.

Problem was…Savannah might be wrong about her 'dual celibacy theory' where neither of them enjoyed physical loving in all those lonely years. If she were wrong, and he'd been involved with someone else, then she would be forced to agree he'd been a major jackass and she would be furious with Riley, all over again. It would mean he ruthlessly accused her of playing around, when in truth he wasn't faithful to their love at all.

A double standard wasn't like Riley, but right now, she didn't want to fight. "What time is it?" She asked instead.

"I don't know." He dejectedly sighed, casually plucking pieces of straw out of her hair. Seven pieces. She counted. Then with one thumb, Riley gently rubbed a smudge of dirt off her cheek. It struck her as one of the sweetest gestures, ever.

"It's sometime after midnight, I suppose."

"Good. Its tomorrow," she proclaimed with renewed enthusiasm. "A brand new day. Now we can start all over again."

Riley scowled as if she were crazy. "You stink."

"Well, aren't you romantic?" But she grinned. She was a brat today. She ignored Riley. She let Merlin bully him. Then slept half the night in a stable like some homeless scarecrow. She deserved a little needling.

"You really do love me."

"Apparently."

Savannah giggled at his dry tone. "Did admitting it hurt?"

"I've been happier."

They were being watched; both Zeus and Merlin were awake. Curious heads lifted. Suspicious, they were listening to their quiet conversation. Goliath was perched atop the crossbeam on the ceiling again. Yellow eyes glared out of the shadows.

"Tell your bodyguards I'm harmless." Riley gloomily declared. "I won't drag you out of here. If you prefer sleeping with those three giants over sleeping beside me, so be it."

"They're fine. We're only talking."

She took Riley's hand and saw everyone relax.

Especially the man.

Well, Zeus couldn't be more relaxed if he tried. Sprawled out on his back in that pile of straw, his giant legs were stuck straight up, like crooked black trees waving in the air. The dog slept weird. But closing his eyes again, he definitely looked happy.

"Riley," she tentatively asked, praying her celibacy theory was right, "am I the only woman you've ever slept with?"

For a tense heartbeat, he looked guarded. She knew his answer would be defensive and mean. She cringed. Then light dawned in hazel eyes as he realized where she was going with this.

"Yes. You're the only woman I've been naked with."

Her heart felt lighter, brighter, and blissfully full.

"All those years, you stayed faithful to me?"

"I did."

"Is that why you got so mad this morning? You thought that I hadn't been equally faithful? You really believed I had been intimate with someone else?"

"Yeah," he glumly sighed, "I did. Sorry." He contritely grumbled, but his gaze never wavered. "It was dumb. We were apart nearly seven years. But deep down, staying faithful mattered, Savannah. Dang it, you're supposed to be mine."

"You've said that our whole lives."

"Well, it's true." Hearing it again felt wonderful. Grateful, she smiled and gave his hand a reassuring squeeze. "Which also means," his voice dropped to a smoky near-whisper, "I belong to you too. I meant it this morning. I love you, Savannah. I need what we are together."

The emotion in his face was raw and utterly honest.

"I need it too."

"Enough to give me a second chance?"

"Maybe. Why did you stay faithful?"

He sighed and looked discouraged, but honestly answered. "You know, all my life the only thing I've ever felt completely sure about was that we were supposed to be together. Even when we were young, I knew no matter what life brought, you'd be by my side. And then...you just weren't here anymore. I guess I didn't deal with that very well."

"Sorry."

Riley offhandedly shrugged. She knew that lonely pain felt mild compared to the current ache inside his heart. "After you left I buried myself in work and kept hoping that someday life would come full circle so we could be together again. Other women just weren't an option, for me."

"You didn't even look?"

"Nope. Wasn't interested. But look at you, Savage. You're beautiful." She scoffed, making harsh noises of skepticism. "When you don't stink like horses and a giant dog, that is. And Goliath, whatever mutant species he is."

"Brat. He's a cat. He likes me."

"Everyone loves you, babe. Even me. You're irresistible." He finally half-smiled. That tiny approving curve of his mouth made her insides warm. "Why didn't you let a man into your life?"

"No one offered."

"Impossible."

"Alright, a few asked. But I never even went to dinner with anyone."

"Because?"

"Because I didn't want another man." He didn't seem convinced. "What we had was great, Riley. We were two hearts beating as one. Not just in bed, but all the time. I didn't want second-rate music with no dynamics and a choppy emotional rhythm that lacked synchronicity. I wanted a grand dolce appassionato." She dreamily described, letting the romantic words flow from her lips like a private song.

It earned her a wide smile. So handsome.

"We were a harmonic unison, two lives wonderfully synchronized. We flowed through turbulent forte crescendo days and into peaceful adagio nights like a magnificent symphony. I wanted that flawless precision from love, or nothing at all."

"So to you...we're music." Riley's hazel-green eyes glowed with keen admiration. "Great music."

"A masterpiece," she gushed. "What are we, to you?"

"A miracle." The reverent word came without hesitation, making her feel unworthy. "You are all I've ever wanted."

"Then we both clung to what should have been, but wasn't."

"Looks like it."

It was another long confusing day. Savannah tried to decide what to say. Thinking, she brushed straw off her jeans and picked wood chips off the flannel shirt she borrowed from him this morning.

She glanced at Riley. Patient and kind, he was watching her.

They were like one now. It wouldn't last. Eventually something would irritate Riley and he would hide behind those emotional steel walls again.

But she had right now. This moment.

A moment worth cherishing.

"You were amazing this morning," she boldly complimented, "The way you touched me…I couldn't even think."

"Me neither," lips curved, slow and sexy, kindling that sweet passion she craved. It made Savannah want to kiss Riley senseless. "I didn't want to think. I just wanted to savor you, us together. It had been sooo long." Raw honesty gleamed in the starburst illuminating his forest green eyes. God, how she loved those eyes. "You really learned all that fun adult stuff from me? No books? No raunchy porn flicks?"

"No. Dang it," used to being defensive; it took a heartbeat to realize he was only teasing. Hazel eyes glint with playful fire. It was actually a compliment. "I wasn't raunchy," she clucked her tongue and perkily replied, "I was enthusiastic."

"Extremely." His dusky appreciative tone made her blush.

"Guess that means you liked getting naked with me."

"Loved it. You were phenomenal."

"We were phenomenal," she softly corrected. "Together."

"Maybe we should try an encore, sometime." He huskily suggested. "After you take a shower, of course. And we check on Bitsy." He stood, and was far more nimble about it than she could be. "And eat. I was hungry hours ago. Now I'm starving."

"Uh, Riley?" She nervously asked after he scooped her up by the waist and gently steadied her sore feet upon the floor. "Just because we're super-amazing at one thing isn't going to fix everything else."

"I know. But at least we have something right."

Bitsy was nursing again. Legs were sturdy. Her fragile body stronger now, her fuzzy white tail flipped happily as she sucked. Duchess seemed motherly and proud. Bitsy turned her head to look at her rescuers.

Savannah gasped, "Her eyes ARE turning blue! Baby blue!"

"Cool, huh?"

"God sent us a snow white horse with angel blue eyes."

"She might not ever see perfectly," Riley explained, "but maybe the cloudiness is from being a preemie. But Duchess has good milk; it's already making her strong. Bitsy will spend her whole life being pampered and safe. Her heart still sloshes a bit, but maybe that will heal too."

"I'm so glad we gave her a chance."

"A chance..." hands shoved in his front jean pockets; Riley leaned one shoulder against the paddock wall and looked away. The golden light illuminating his eyes faded. He was obviously mulling something over. Something bad. She just waited. When those hazel eyes finally found her face again, she saw disappointment.

"What?"

"I don't want to fight."

"We won't." His expression remained doubtful. "Just say it, Riley. I promise whatever it is, we won't fight."

"Do you love me?"

She did, but for some odd reason the words stayed stuck in her throat. She'd said it once, and meant it with all her shattered soul. Then things went to hell. She couldn't say it now. Savannah nodded instead. "And you?"

"Yes. I do love you."

"Then tell me what's eating you."

"Okay. Fine. I found your jacket," he dryly conceded.

"Really? Where? I can't remember where I put it down."

"It's in the tack room. Right beside the saddle you thought about tossing on Merlin so you could ride away from here."

"Oh." As they walked down the long corridor to retrieve it, Savannah felt deeply ashamed. "I wasn't taking Merlin." She tried to clarify her earlier actions, "I was taking Mirage or Jinx. Besides, I know how important Merlin is to your bloodlines."

"Gee, thanks for considering my bank account."

He was bitter again.

So much for happiness and great music.

They arrived at the carefully organized tack room with twenty saddles and bridles hung up along the walls. Her white parka lay on the floor, beside the heavy western saddle she managed to hoist off the wall. But the bulky heavy thing had toppled onto her. She got no further. Instead of saddling a horse to ride and disappearing from his life, she sat on the floor crying over broken legs, broken hearts, and Riley.

"Are you going to leave me again, Savannah?"

"No."

"What was this?" He hooked his thumb toward the saddle.

"I was just mad. And confused. That's all."

"And now?"

"I'm just really sorry."

Picking the heavy western saddle up with one hand, Riley slung it back upon its steel wall-rack. He made it look so easy. No way could she saddle her own horse. What was she thinking?

Well, she wasn't.

She'd been too busy grieving.

Strolling back to the doorway where she contritely stood, he frowned down at her and sighed. "We should get married."

"Huh? Married? Your thoughts are so hard to follow. Why would you want to get married?"

"It would simplify things."

"But we're a mess together."

"I thought we covered that part." Taking her hand, Riley walked beside her toward the outer doors, kindly slowing his long-legged pace to match her achy limp. "I was faithful. You were faithful." He rationalized their bizarre shared vow of celibacy, "I love you. You love me. That means we belong together."

"But we drive each other crazy."

"Only because I've been mean and dumb. But I'd rather be like this…" in one swift decisive move, Riley turned and grasped her hips. She was tightly pinned against that powerful male body. Arms locked around her, his head lowered. That adamant kiss left her head spinning, her heart thundering, and her soul aching for more.

"Oh. Wow. That was…yum."

"Give us a second chance, Savage."

She wanted to. "But you still haven't seen Ryan's video diary."

"How will that change anything?"

"We talked to you. Every day, like you were simply away on a business trip and would come home soon. That's how we kept you in our lives. I guarantee seeing it will hurt. Ryan was easy to love, so happy and sweet. Now, he's gone. Seeing those movies will make you hate me."

"I won't. I love you. Marry me."

"Stop saying that." But she grinned at his persistence. "We should go inside. I'll shower; then we'll eat something and sleep. Or we could roll around naked and make music together. That's more fun than arguing."

"I'm serious."

"No, you're delirious; low blood sugar or something."

"Fine. We'll eat." He stubbornly agreed, "But tomorrow morning we're driving into town. I still have the snowplow attached to the front of my truck. We're not waiting for Christmas. We'll watch those movies, together. And while we are in Harmony Hills with my family, I'm making an appointment with the preacher. You will marry me, Savannah."

"I can't marry you tomorrow!"

"Why not?"

"Because I haven't even said yes."

"Yet. Will you? Soon?"

"We'll see."

***

The drive into Harmony Hills was tense and slow. Riley's heavy-duty four-wheel drive Chevy Avalanche progressively plowed through mounds of frozen white snow. It towered so high above the ground he had to pick her up, lifting her into the passenger seat.

The snowplow didn't blow snow away like the big automated one that Paul voluntarily drove for the city of Harmony Hills. Their industrial strength, arrow-shaped snowplow was a solid steel grading blade. Wider than the truck and as tall as the hood, the top edge was angled further away, making the blade tip forward. Instead of pushing snow aside, it compressed it down, pushing it beneath them as they moved. Like creating a huge snow ramp. The big truck snarled like a giant red mountain goat, but easily climbed over frozen compacted mounds.

Savannah found it fascinating. Straining against her seatbelt to peer out the windshield, she watched the walls of snow squish beneath them.

"Sure we can make it?"

"Positive."

"But we're climbing up and over, not through."

"The snow is too deep to push aside. This way works fine."

"We won't sink?"

"Nope. The heavy blade gets rid of air pockets, crushing everything ahead. The angle of the blade smashes the snow. It's like paving your own road." He explained, shifting gears from rumbly first gear into growly second, "We won't get stuck. Trust me."

"Okay."

The oversized tires on his Avalanche didn't have ordinary tread, but thick snow-paddle grooves. The rigid rubber caught the snow, compressed it tight, then gripped it hard making a sloggy swoosh-crunch-squish noise as they chugged along.

Riley was right, away from Graystone's gated enclosure wall, the icy drifts weren't as deep. During the blizzards they endured, the resilient stone entrance fence had been a fortification defense, blocking wind from buffeting the house. But those walls also became a confining menace that trapped swirling snowdrifts tight around Graystone Heights, locking them inside an impassable prison.

Freedom from walls felt sublime.

Inside the truck, they were toasty warm. But the frigid white world around them was unforgiving and dangerously cold.

Riley was a patient driver, vigilant and experienced with Montana winters. The Avalanche sometimes skittered and shimmied on the thick patches of condensed ice, but he never lost control as they trudging down the rough twenty-five mile road that twisted and curved toward civilization at Harmony Hills.

Well, at least she assumed they were on the road.

They hadn't hit any pine trees. Yet.

They only slept a few hours. Innocently. While she showered, scrubbing away the turbulent day, Riley heated bowls of leftover stew. Food soothed the edges of her frayed soul, warming her cautious heart. After the hearty meal, they were both too exhausted and emotionally drained for anything more entertaining than a few tender kisses.

But last night in his big warm bed downstairs, in the room he declared they would share permanently after they were married, Riley tucked her body tight against his, holding her all night like he really meant it.

"You still haven't answered my very important question."

"Which one?" She teased, "You ask so many."

"Come on, Savage, don't be cruel."

"I'm not cruel. I'm practical. And I'm practically convinced you've lost your..." they spun on slick ice. Before Riley could stop it, the truck made a complete circle. Savannah didn't squeal or cling to the door in fear. She simply laughed.

"Oh boy, Disneyland."

Riley flashed a bright boyish grin. "Like that?"

"Yep. It was fun. Especially since we didn't wreck."

Still smiling, he righted the big four-wheel drive. The engine growled with impatience. He shifted gears, plodding forward again.

A bit slower this time. Like a snail, instead of a turtle.

"I wasn't kidding when I asked you."

"You mean your insane notion about being my husband?"

"It's not crazy. It's the right thing to do. Marriage will fix us."

"Uh-huh. Sure."

"Marry me, Savannah."

"If won't fix us. We're beyond fixing."

"Maybe so, but I still want you to be my wife."

"You know Riley," she giggled at his foolhardy persistence, "if you just need a naughty naked roll in the hay now and then, I won't complain."

"Sleeping with me is a punishment?" While he turned to glare at her, the truck slid down an embankment.

Okay, so they were on the road, after all.

Now, they definitely weren't.

Riley swore at winter and snow in general, roughly yanked the steering wheel and gunned the engine. They quickly bounced back onto the semi-level surface again.

"Was sex a punishment?"

"For you it was," she defined; glad she was buckled up tight. "You said I'm too skinny now. Not your type."

"I lied. Besides, there's meat on your bones again."

"Uh, well..." she glanced out the passenger window. It fogged with her breath, "but I have too many scars. They're ugly."

"That's not true. I don't even see them."

"But you said I have more scars than a gladiator."

"I said tons of stupid things. Doesn't mean any of it was true."

Zip, they caught black ice and skid sideways. Fast! The truck didn't have any intention of stopping. Riley fought it, using the big blade and the deep tread tires to control the slide, but they came to rest facing east instead of south.

"Damn snow!" He glared at the towering pine trees they'd narrowly avoided hitting. "That was close."

"So…you lied."

"Huh? Oh yeah. I lied." He agreed, wondering why Savannah insisted on playing this game. Especially right now, while he was driving. "How many times have I asked you to marry me?"

"In my lifetime? Or just since you lost your mind?"

"Savannah!"

"But…you deserve a beautiful woman."

Riley clucked his tongue to disagree. Her excuses felt ridiculous. He just wanted to get married. How hard was that? "I do? A beautiful woman? Well, hell…" he shifted into reverse and gunned the engine, making the truck snarl, "I thought I deserved a swift kick in the ass."

That made her smile.

Riley liked seeing it. All morning her face had been tense, her pouty lips tight. She never said a word about it, but he knew she was nervous about going into Harmony Hills. Whatever waited for him in the boxes she mysteriously shipped to his Dad's store, Savannah wasn't looking forward to dealing with.

"I love you, Savage."

Doubt flickered in her eyes. "Just drive, Riley."

Easing the Avalanche backward, carefully navigating the slick surface as they turned around, they inched forward again. For another slow mile, both were silent as Riley concentrated on the road. The snow wasn't as thick now. Navigating their way down the mountain was becoming easier.

"So, what's the real problem?" He finally asked, feeling they needed to resolve this. Soon they would be in town and face his parents. He needed Savannah to commit. He felt sure marriage would fix all the wrongs between them. "Why won't you say yes?"

"I'd be a terrible wife."

"Why?" He prodded.

"Riley, dang it!" She spluttered, "Just because we got crazy once and made beautiful music together doesn't mean you'll stop being angry with me over dumb things. We were great together, but perfect music doesn't just happen in bed. It needs to be all the time. But we just don't harmonize anymore. You're playing a war march and I'm playing a sad nocturne."

"Maybe we're just out of practice."

It was all Riley could do to keep from stopping the Avalanche right there and showing her a few perfect notes.

171

"We could be great again." He coaxed, "I know you love me. You said it once. Now you're scared to say it again. But I still see that light in your eyes."

He got her with that. She did love him. That sweet honesty was right there fully exposed, illuminating her pretty face.

"Yes Riley, I do love you. But officially becoming Savannah Rosemont isn't necessary." She calmly rationalized, "Sharing your name won't change anything. Our relationship is what it is. Marriage won't make me love you any more…or any less. It's just a legal piece of paper."

"Fine. Don't marry me." He sulked, feeling marriage was quite necessary and vital to fixing everything broken in their bewildering relationship. "But you're living with me, Savannah. Permanent. We are together now. Got it?"

"Alright. I now officially live at Graystone Heights."

"With me." He sternly added.

"Yes, with you." She melodically agreed, "Riley and Savannah, forever and ever, 'til death do us part, Amen." Solemnly making the sign of the cross over her heart, even though they weren't Catholic, she quirked a naughty garish grin and laughed, "You can just tell your good church-going, God-fearing Christian parents that we've decided to live together in sinful bliss. That should make them verr-rry happy."

Did she really think he cared what people thought? He didn't. "I will tell them. Today. We'll tell them together."

Her rebellious smile dissipated. "Today? But I…"

"No, I like this idea. Sinful Bliss. Marriage is boring. Instead of an ordinary wife, I get a sexy Mistress! I can't wait to tell my family!" He gave her an enthusiastic naughty smirk that made violet eyes widen. "From now on, we won't innocently sleep together just to stay warm. If I want to strip you naked, have my wicked way with you, and enjoy some Sinful Bliss…I will. Over and over. All. Night. Long."

"Ooh," her cheeks flushed pink, "is that a threat?"

"No. A promise. If you won't marry me respectably, standing before a preacher to show God, the community, and my family that you love me, then you can show me your devotion every wild night in our bed."

"You're funny." Giving a nervous jittery laugh, Savannah rubbed Zeus who insisted on squeezing his massive body into the small space by her feet, just to be near her. "We've been living together for weeks. Ninety percent of it, you've been mad. Now I have to choose between hot scandalous sex or the holy bonds of matrimony? I think you have a bad case of cabin fever."

"If we weren't sliding sideways down this icy road I'd prove you wrong." Riley challenged.

"Sure." She grinned, enjoying the hell out of their adventurous little ride. This tempting banter was much more fun than sulking around a giant house trapped inside sad memories. Beneath them, tires snarled with delight as they finally gripped solid pavement.

"Yea!" Hands clapped, "We made it."

"Did you ever have any doubts?"

"Well, once. When we spun circles."

On the icy two-lane highway, Riley turned the truck south toward Harmony Hills. It had obviously been snowplowed by a more efficient blade than the wide steel arrow attached to his Chevy Avalanche, but the road was empty, deserted. The asphalt surface gleamed with a dangerous layer of black ice.

Pulling into a roadside clearing, Riley jumped out and removed the big steel Graystone grading blade, leaving it beside the road for later. When he climbed back inside the warm truck, his jeans were covered in snow up to his thighs and his breath made white puffs.

"Where are we staying tonight?"

"I have a cabin in town. We'll stay there through Christmas."

"Christmas?!" She squawked, "I thought we were only staying tonight! What about the horses? And Bitsy? We can't leave her! I thought we were getting my clothes and Ryan's movies, going home tomorrow."

"No. Christmas is the most loving holiday of the year. We should be around family, not locked away alone on the mountain."

"Riley! The horses will die all alone!"

"Honey, relax. Those Andalusians are the most pampered horses on the planet." Shifting gears to tackle the highway again, the big four-wheel drive chugging forward. The tough off-road tires noisily crunched on thick layers of ice. "Bitsy and Duchess are just fine. That Momma is thrilled to have another baby to love."

"But...she's so fragile!"

"Not anymore. I checked her. Bitsy tottered around this morning, happy as any healthy newborn. Her eyes are almost completely blue. Barely gray at all. She watched me, not just listened. Even her heartbeat is better. I wouldn't have left Bitsy, if she needed us. She's in God's hands now."

"What about food and water and..."

"I programmed the automatic feeders and turned everyone loose so they won't be cramped inside dirty stalls. Bitsy and Duchess have the main corridor all to themselves. The big practice arena divides into sections. Alcatraz and the other rowdy yearlings are in one end; Mirabelle, Jinx, Eclipse, and Voodoo are in the middle. My dancers. All the broodmares have the rest, including Merlin's hallway. I opened that too."

"All of the brood mares and Merlin? Together?"

"Sure. It'll do him good to socialize. You saw how bored he is."

"But he'll fight with them."

"Nah. He won't bite and kick a lady. Gladiators only play rough with men. There are no boys to bully. Only pretty girls to love."

She made a funny sound, "Did you forget what will happen with that big black stallion happily wandering around loose in your cozy warm ultramodern horsey-Hilton with a dozen lonely mares? Horses don't use birth control, Riley."

"I hope they do get friendly. I bought all those mares from different places to diversify the bloodline. Merlin has dominant traits, so his colts will be black, or near-black with red hints, like Voodoo. The black Andalusians don't sell for as much money as pure white horses, but Merlin is the only stud I have."

"Your little herd will probably double next year."

"Good. You can help me deliver the foals, and train them. By then, you'll be strong enough to ride. You're light enough they can carry you a year before me. Plus, animals love you. Training will be easy. If you wanted," he optimistically planned as they drove; "we could enter dressage shows. You can wear a slick modern riding suit for ladies; a pearly white one with rhinestone sparkles. The saddle and bridle should be white too. White frosting on a black horse. You'd wear your hair down and curl the ends into thick chocolaty ringlets, like you used to do."

"I'm surprised you remember that."

"I loved it. Your hair is so healthy and glossy. The curls gleam. You'll need a white lady's hat with a white feather in the side. That would be impressive. Icing on you, too. The horses will dance. You'll be perched on their back like a beautiful crown jewel. Then…those black horses will sell for a small fortune."

Savannah couldn't hide her grin. She missed riding. Shows! Oh! The thrill. The magic. A dozen foals next year! She loved their gangly legs and innocent eyes. Like Bitsy. So trusting and pure. Then they grew and needed lessons in manners. It took years to teach horses how to perform under saddle and bridle, to dance like glorious earthbound angels, like Mirabelle.

But training was Riley's gift. He knew how to open their hearts.

So gentle and kind, he tamed wild things with patience and love.

Just like he once tamed her.

"Okay, you win." She conceded, "I'll marry you, Riley."

He almost skid completely off the road.

They stopped, tilted at a dangerous slant. His side of the truck leaned precariously into a deep snow bank. From that awkward angle, Savannah hung by her seatbelt, hands braced against Riley's shoulder.

"Well," he impishly taunted, "You look comfortable."

She groaned as Zeus decided he had enough of the cramped foot-space and scrambled unceremoniously over her body to find a safer spot in the back seat. "Uh! Zeus! How rude! Come on, Riley. Straighten us out!"

"No. Say it again. And mean it." Using the steering wheel for leverage, he grabbed it and defiantly pulled himself up the slanted truck interior until their faces were a breath apart. "Not because I win. Marry me because you love me."

"Riley Phillip," she purposely purred his name, straining against the taut belts that kept her from falling right into his lap. "I love you. I've always loved you. I've spent years praying we'd get a second chance. I stayed faithful to our love. I've stayed faithful to you, in every way possible. You're the only man I ever want to make music with. Please, Riley Rosemont," she softly begged, "will you marry me?"

For thirty-nine drawn out seconds he just stared at her.

She counted.

"Soon. A six and a half year unofficial engagement is long enough."

"You mean our 'I'm faithful-- your faithful; we're both ridiculously screwed up' years? Was that our engagement?"

"Yes. And our punishment for being stupid."

With that firm declaration, he threw the big red Avalanche into reverse. Tough snow tires tore up the ice, flinging white shards everywhere. Zip...he popped them right back onto the paved road. Savannah bounced around, but ended with her butt securely nailed into her own seat.

Riley shifted into park and unsnapped his seatbelt. In a heartbeat, that determined auburn man was right in her face.

"Do you love me?"

"With all my heart." Softly, she kissed him. Twice.

"Tonight you'll sleep with me for real?"

"Is your cabin warmer than this truck?"

"It can be."

"Then yes. Tonight I will gladly rip off your clothes and show you how much I love you. And I will marry you, Riley." Her sincerity made him smile. "I'd be honored to be your wife. But only," she decisively added, "after you watch Ryan's video diary."

His brow furrowed. "Why is that a condition?"

"Because we should reconcile grief," she feathered another loving kiss across his mouth, "so we can fully dive into joy."

"Joy," he huskily whispered. "I want that."

***

Is there anything better than being locked in the arms of the woman you love? Naked. Exhausted. But deeply satisfied? Could anything compare to having a beautiful musical princess sleep across your chest where she happily collapsed after you thoroughly ravished her body into sublime euphoria? A feeling that was years overdue? Was there any sweeter sound than her soft sighs of profound contentment?

Riley didn't think so.

In fact, he couldn't remember another time he'd been this happy. Ever. Was this joy? He sincerely prayed it was.

After their weird sideways confrontation on that frozen highway, he drove straight to Rosemont Mercantile to see his parents. Savannah was wide-eyed and jittery, but Riley stayed close, his hand situated possessively at her waist, giving silent reassurance.

Overjoyed the illusive couple had ventured into civilization, his parents closed the store, called Julia and Jacob, and demanded they all traipse through the snow to Paul's restaurant.

Savannah blanched in traumatized horror. A Rosemont family reunion definitely wasn't expected. She hedged, made silly excuses. Riley held her hand, making her follow him to the back of the store, where they could talk in private.

"What's the real problem?" He quietly asked, kissing her gently to verify he wasn't mad, only concerned.

"Are you telling them we're getting married?"

"Why?" He bristled, "Have you changed your mind?"

"No. I promised to marry you, and I will."

"Then we'll tell them at Paul's restaurant. Together."

"I'd like that. But my problem is: I want to look nicer." She glanced down at faded jeans she wore every third day for nearly two months and her slightly threadbare gray sweatshirt and seemed embarrassed. "I have pretty clothes. Really I do."

"They don't care, honey. They're just glad to see you."

"It isn't for your family." She met his confused gaze with an adoring smile. Love. Sweet unconditional love gleamed bright and pure in her beautiful violet eyes.

It made his heart feel eight sizes too big for his chest.

"I want to look pretty for you, Riley. If you're determined to marry me, then I want you to feel proud of your wife. You deserve a beautiful woman, not a homeless rag-a-muffin."

That pleased him through and through.

He proved it, kissing her until they were both a little breathless and he wished they were truly alone.

"Hey, Dad?" He called out, "Where are Savannah's boxes?" He didn't bother pretending ignorance of the hidden shipment. "She wants to change her clothes."

Silence. Then funny twittering as his parents whispered to each other. "In the back storeroom." His Dad finally answered. "Want help, son?"

"No. We're good."

They found the storeroom stacked ceiling high. Breaking open several labeled boxes, Savannah gathered up an armload of clothes and beauty supplies. Riley patiently waited in the hallway while she locked herself inside the bathroom by his Dad's office. She reappeared wearing a plush lilac sweater and stylish plum colored jeans. On her small feet were sleek black sharkskin dress boots. They must have cost a fortune. She even curled her hair into elegant cocoa waves, exactly how he liked, and applied just enough makeup to make her eyes appear sultry violet.

She looked amazingly beautiful.

He told her so.

Showed her too.

Riley was tired of her feeling sad and guilty.

Tired of him feeling cold and angry at the world.

Kindness was the cure.

Worried and clingy, Savannah followed him down the snowy street into Savory Grille. The minute they walked in together, Paul's wife Melanie enveloped them in enthusiastic hugs and greetings.

Big tough burly Paul took one look at Savannah, affectionately welcomed her with a warm brotherly hug, and decisively closed down the steakhouse for the day.

That never happened either.

"I'm sorry about Ryan, Savannah." Paul sincerely offered, making her gape at the normally pokerfaced man's forthright condolences. "Losing him must have been awful for you and Riley. I'm glad you came home to us. You belong here. We've missed you, little sister."

Another giant brother-bear hug left his fiancé sniffling.

It was eye opening. For him.

Everyone understood.

Except for his Mom's prophetic insights, that Riley adamantly denied until he just couldn't deny them anymore, the Rosemont family had never openly discussed Ryan. But big steely mountain man Paul compassionately broke down barriers. He brought their unspoken truths out into the open with one sincere hug.

It made Riley proud of his family.

Ryan wasn't a secret.

They'd all lost him; he saw it in their faces.

Julia rushed in the back door, her bright red hair caught up in a hasty ponytail. She grabbed Savannah from Paul. "You're here! You're home!" Julia was so excited that she twirled Savannah in a circle. "Oh, Savi!" His younger sister gushed, "I've missed you!"

He brought Savannah home.

To her family. To the people who loved her.

"We're getting married." She proudly told them, not waiting for him to make the formal announcement. That brought fresh hugs, congratulations, and excited female jabbering about marriage plans. It was wonderful. Soon, they were all laughing.

Savannah held his hand and beamed.

Overwhelmed by his family's unified admiration; Riley liked how his beautiful sweet Savage kept constant contact. Hands. Her hip. The side of her body gratefully pressed against his. Her funny relieved smile shining up at him that said more to his heart than words ever could.

She needed what they were together.

Love illuminated her gleaming violet eyes.

Love. Forever love. For him.

He felt unworthy.

This was so different from being bitter, Riley felt euphoric.

This amazingly gifted woman promised to marry him!

Once, when he drifted away to talk to Jacob, she went too, keeping her hand tucked into his back pocket. When Melanie asked him for help in the kitchen, Savannah automatically followed, deftly contributing to the big family meal. She grinned up at him, making it impossible to pretend he didn't love their alliance.

Savannah was his best friend.

Had been, since the day she was born.

Soon, she'd be his wife.

Forever wasn't long enough. Not for them.

He liked their phenomenal togetherness far more than he openly revealed. Until they were alone. Then, with the fireplace blazing, they made love with a frenzied appetite that surpassed his most vivid erotic dreams.

God how he loved her.

"Riley?" She whispered, "What are you thinking about?"

"You." Caressing that thick sheet of glossy rich-cocoa colored hair, she happily sighed. His hand trailed down her bare back. "Did you mean it? Are you really going to marry me?"

"Nah." She huskily giggled and slithered bonelessly off his chest until they lay face to face. "I just wanted sex. Lots of it. Fun and Hot, and Ooh-so-delicious. Sinful Bliss. Yeah. That was wicked. Thanks for obliging."

"But… you promised."

She burst out laughing. "Gee Rosemont, you are one seriously obsessed man." Clucking her tongue at him, she saw his stern expression and lovingly ran her hand along his face. "Enjoy the moment, Riley. Cherish here and now. This moment matters."

"I know, but…"

"We're together. Naked. Like adults. We aren't sneaking around like reckless kids or hidden away in the mountains. By now, your sweet Momma has probably told all of Harmony Hills that we're engaged to be married. Everyone knows exactly what we're doing right now; that we are celebrating our love, celebrating our second chance. They approve. Doesn't that make you happy?"

It did. But he spent too many years alone to settle for just here and now. "Marriage is a promise, Savage. An important one."

"I promise to love you." She teased in a melodious throaty bedroom voice. Soft hands fluttered across his chest, working their way down his stomach. "I promise to drive you crazy. All. Night. Long." She taunted him with his own words.

Riley sucked in his breath, gritting his teeth as those hands explored a bit lower on his anatomy.

"Ooh…my. Nice."

Marriage wasn't the only important thing on his mind.

"I promise to be the best…"

Riley rolled, pinning the sultry giggling woman beneath him, searing her rosebud mouth with the honesty of his fierce need to claim her.

Again. And again.

For the rest of his life.

"Just promise me this." Ready and willing, he slid deep inside sleek velvet heat, making Savannah's nails grip his back as she arched into the private union.

"Music, Savannah," his gentle tempo made those beautiful violet eyes jubilantly glazed, "promise me, we'll always make beautiful music together."

"I promise," she vowed in agitated little pants.

The slick body beneath him was tightening, needing not a waltz, but a grand dolce appassionato symphony.

"I love you, Riley Phillip. With all my heart." She pledged, "Forever isn't long enough. Not for us."

"That's exactly what I needed to hear."

*Leslie D. Stuart*

# Chapter Fifteen

"None of these are 'Montana' worthy." Savannah declared, dropping a heavy box of designer clothes and expensive hats by the doorway to Papa Rosemont's office.

"Oh? Why not?"

For the past few days, she had noisily sorted through boxes he'd discreetly hidden inside his storage room. Meanwhile, Papa sat at his desk pretending to work on accounts receivable. Although Ms. Emily fussed about it being unfair and complained about wanting to help Savannah, he made his wife work the front of the store, running the cash register.

He loved Emily dearly, but protecting his future daughter-in-law from sad story telling was the right thing to do.

Enough hearts had been broken.

Enough tears were shed. No more sad stories.

Now it was time to heal.

"These clothes are too flashy for mountain life." To demonstrate, Savannah held up a white sequined evening gown. "I wore this at Carnegie Hall." It shimmered with iridescent flashes of light as she wiggled it. He could imagine under the spotlight, she looked like a million bucks.

"Wow." He appreciatively whistled.

"See? Flashy."

In his years of running the Mercantile, Papa had grown to appreciate well-tailored clothes. He fingered the hand-sewn sequins. "This dress must have cost a small fortune. Looks like something fit for a queen."

"Well, I'm no queen. I'm just plain ol' Savannah Graystone."

He liked her modesty, "Was Arianna Hartwell a queen?"

"On stage she was glorious, worthy of roses tossed at her feet. The rest of the time she was just an ordinary Momma named Savannah." Papa respected that she didn't feign away from the truth. "For New York City, this dress was great. But for Montana, it's ridiculous." She hooked her thumb toward the storeroom. "There's more, too. Shoes and dresses; overpriced gunk I'll never wear again. I need to find good homes for my clothes."

Papa truly appreciated that Savannah was wholeheartedly dedicating herself to her new life. And to Riley.

Getting rid of these clothes closed a door.

It meant she promised she'd never leave again.

New York was the past. Montana was her future.

"Well, look at this number," he picked up a fancy russet leather Fedora from the box, "this sure is nice."

"I wore that in England. It rained almost every day. Ryan picked it out from a fancy hat shop in London. It's actually a man's hat. I just didn't have the heart to tell Ryan. Try it on, Papa."

Grinning that she'd offer, Papa Rosemont plunked the leather hat upon his graying head. He tipped his head to the side and curved his hand to his cheek the way Ms. Emily did when she was showing off. "Is it me?"

"Dar'lin, it's stunning." She drawled like a southern belle, playing along. Violet-blue eyes happily twinkled. "Makes you look like a rich man, Papa. Or a wild adventurer. You just need a leather hunting jacket, Riley's big Bowie knife gripped in your fist, and a gun holstered to your side."

"He still carries that thing in his boot?"

"Yep. Every damn day." She rolled her eyes and actually laughed.

It was nice to hear Savannah laugh.

Most of the past three days she spent shifting through boxes, reminiscing. Papa heard her sitting in there crying. Usually Riley was right beside her. He heard them in there together, quietly talking. Right now Riley was somewhere with Paul.

Papa never bothered her. Well, once he did, when he discreetly handed Savannah a box of Kleenex. He hadn't made a fuss. Later, she'd thanked him and offered a framed picture of Ryan to sit on his desk.

His grandson.

Then, they'd both been a little weepy.

Studying him wearing that beautiful bronze leather Fedora, she grinned with approval and decided, "It needs something."

Fumbling through the expensive clothes, she produced a gleaming black silk dress. Holding it up to her body, it was sleek and extravagant, fitting like a second skin. The floor-skimming hemline flared into a regal princess train embellished with black raven feathers. Carefully, she plucked two feathers from the hem, snatched the fedora off his head, and stuck them into the hatband.

"There. Much better. Now it's officially yours." As Papa leaned forward, she placed it back on the head of its new owner. He liked Savannah. Always had. Always would. Riley was a fool to let that sweet woman get away. "Perfect."

"Don't ya' think it's too fancy for an old country man like me?"

"Nope. It's very dashing. Come look." Dragging him away from his desk, Savannah tugged on his hand, taking him to the nearest display mirror.

Admiring the russet leather hat and the not-half-bad reflection of the man he saw in that mirror, Papa Rosemont grinned. It *was* dashing. If he could have chosen any hat in the world, it still would have been this exact one. The color of the leather matched the parts of his hair that wasn't streaked with gray. The little black feathers stuck on the side made it look sophisticated.

"I'll wear it with pride." He announced, which seemed to please Savannah. "So, whatch'a gonna do with the rest?"

"Well, I thought since Christmas is coming, other people might like my fancy duds. Everything is tailored to fit me, but all you do is pluck out the side seams like this," she gently tugged on the end of a hidden thread. Temporary stitches inside an Armani cocktail dress melted away, making the garment instantly larger, "and it goes back to being normal."

Fascinated by the ingenuous tailoring, he inspected the dress. The hidden stitches making it fit slim Savannah's body pulled free without leaving a mark. Now it could easily be re-tailored to fit nearly any woman.

"That's the coolest thing I've ever seen."

"I had all my performance clothes tailored that way. Just pull the strings and they unravel. Sometimes, I only wore a gown once. Letting fancy duds hang in my closet felt wasteful, so Marcus Seabourne's wife resold them on EBay, cheap. Then my dresses went to women who normally couldn't afford something special."

"Is that what you want to do with these?"

"Yep. Even country women need to dress up and feel like a queen, now and then. Wanna help me distribute them to worthy new owners?"

"Sure, honey. I'll help you pull strings."

"And sell them. Cheap. Real cheap. I want you to help me advertise. We'll make it fun. I think Ms. Emily's tired of running the front of the store, anyway."

"She is." They both looked across the mercantile and saw the fluttery woman bustling around with customers, chatting amiably about nothing at all. But clearly, Ms. Emily was bored. "Ya' ready to turn her loose on Harmony Hills so she can go tell stories?"

"I guess so. Besides, she has a wedding to plan."

"That she does."

Releasing Ms. Emily from cashier duty, Savannah and Papa went to work. By afternoon, the new storefront displays Papa boldly designed made cars screech to a halt in front of the Rosemont Mercantile. People sat in their cars and gawked. Then, without fail, they would curiously park and come inside, pretending to be casual shoppers simply needing basic supplies.

But they were all wide-eyed and snoopy.

Mannequins seductively posed wearing glitzy Prada evening gowns were not the usual sight in Harmony Hills.

"BIG SALE!" The bold red sign hung across the front store windows proudly announced. "Savannah Graystone's New York City Closet. Arianna Hartwell retires! Welcome home, Savannah! EVERYTHING MUST GO!"

"Ten dollars!" Ladies gasped, clinging tight to Valentino sequined evening gowns worth a hundred times that much. "Are you kidding, Papa Rosemont?"

"Well, if that price doesn't seem fair," he lazily drawled, a twinkle in his green eyes at Savannah's clever idea, "she's willing to trade. She needs mountain clothes and gear. Why? Well, 'cuz Savannah's living in Montana now. Yep. It's true. She says these fancy New York clothes will just sit in her closet collecting dust. It's a waste really. Such pretty things. Did you know she's living up at Graystone again? With Riley?"

Ladies would ooh and ah over the revealed secret.

"Yep, they're finally getting married. When? Oh sometime soon, I expect. Ms. Emily's busy fussing around, making all kinds of silly woman arrangements. Flowers and cake and such nonsense." Papa would wink and grin because everyone knew how much he adored his fluttery wife. "It's just destiny, I s'ppose." He proudly philosophized to curious shoppers, "Those two have loved each other their whole lives. Music? Well, that's in the past. Being in love is more important."

The idea worked. Within days Savannah became the proud owner of two heavy leather jackets, three dozen pairs of jeans, and five pairs of slightly used cowboy boots some of the local teenage girls had outgrown. Of course, Papa was careful with the trades, making sure all the clothes and shoes fit her willowy body and small feet. Trading her fancy dresses away for more functional outfits was genius. She now owned enough jeans, sweaters, and flannel work shirts for a year.

And the town?

Harmony Hills became a ridiculous parade of happy peacocks strutting around in designer clothes.

And at Christmas, Papa knew the whole town would be receiving extravagant gifts from one another that they couldn't normally afford.

It was brilliant.

People kept their pride.

And Savannah looked like a mountain woman again.

She had truly come home.

# Chapter Sixteen

Every precious moment of his life was right there. Riley watched it all. First steps. Ryan playing. Savannah tucking Ryan into at night. Bedtime stories. Prayers.

He watched them tour castles in England, and Ireland, play on the beach, and walk through forests. Quiet days. Fun days.

Learning music. Listening, Ryan's beautiful violet-blue eyes closed as his mind absorbed sounds. Creating music. Laughing. His face lit with joy.

The whole time, Savannah and Ryan talked to Riley as though he were simply away on a business trip and would soon come home.

"Riley," her very first video began, "I know you aren't going to like this, but I'm pregnant with our child."

The camera aimed, balanced on a tripod. Savannah sat stiffly in a straight-back wooden chair. She looked nervous, unsure. One hand rubbed her small bulging belly. Protective, already.

"I made decisions we probably should have made together. But this child isn't just mine," she quietly affirmed. "It's yours too. But we just can't live life together, Riley," she was crying, soft sad sniffling whimpers. "I wish we could. This is where I belong. Your home is in Montana. But I've only been here a few months and already I have concerts and an agent and…people love my music. Can you believe that? It's a dream come true."

Wiping her wet face, she bravely continued, "Someday you'll see this video diary. I'm going to film something every day. For you, so you can share our lives. I love you, Riley. I always will. Forever isn't long enough for the love I have for you inside my heart. I pray someday God will give us a second chance."

Savannah showed him things; like her first modest apartment, or a glittery red performance dress carefully cut to disguise her growing tummy, or the first sonogram pictures of Ryan.

That day, she said nothing.

She simply smiled. That radiant grin meant she had a secret. Placing them in front of the camera, Riley saw those first fuzzy pictures of his son. Sometimes she played the piano, letting the camera run in the background. Her tummy was growing. She showed it to him, lifting her shirt to reveal slick round curves that had been smooth and flat.

Then there was the day Ryan was born.

He missed the actually labor and delivery. Riley knew no one held Savannah's hand. No one reassured the frightened young mother everything would be fine. There were only doctors and nurses, doing their jobs.

She gave birth to Ryan all alone.

But the next day, judging by the date in the corner of the screen that read February 3$^{rd}$, she proudly showed Riley his newborn son.

She looked pale and weak. And a little scared.

His heart ached.

"He's beautiful," she reverently whispered to the camera. Holding the sleeping baby in her arms, she kissing baby-fine auburn hair. "Thank you, Riley. I love you. Our child is perfect."

After that, her daily messages seemed almost therapeutic; a way of reassuring herself that she wasn't raising this child all alone. She filmed Ryan sleeping and eating, sitting in his baby swing, lying on a blanket in the grass.

So sweet.

Having made a small fortune already, she moved into an upscale penthouse apartment overlooking Central Park. Riley toured it in virtual reality, room by spacious room as she narrated. He agreed, the view of Manhattan from their posh living room windows was worth a million bucks.

She talked about being worried to leave Ryan with babysitters while she practiced piano and performed.

A few days later, she solved that problem by hiring an older woman Mrs. Ambrose as a nanny; but only when Savannah needed piano time, not every day. Riley met her too. The round-faced woman with smile crinkles around her brown eyes looked reliable and kind, but slightly confused to be saying hello to a digital camera.

Savannah talked about being apart. She wondered aloud if he would ever forgive her. She doubted it. She didn't blame him.

Savannah talked about everything.

But she showed him even more.

It was almost like being there. Almost.

Some things, Riley replayed over and again, watching that precious moment in Ryan's life until heartache either spilled over into silent tears or eased enough he could move forward again.

He didn't know how long he sat in their darkened cabin, remote control in hand, but felt grateful whenever a fresh glass of water or cup of hot tea appeared.

He numbly ate the sandwich placed upon the coffee table, without ever realizing Savannah was in the room.

Finally, somewhere in the fifth year of life, Riley shut it off. He couldn't absorb a single minute more. His insides were thrashed, shredded by memories he should have witnessed first-hand, not years later.

That piercing truth hit hard.

His neck and back ached. His head throbbed. But his heart felt mortally wounded. He vaguely wondered how the ravaged organ continued to beat inside his chest at all. He didn't know what time it was; or even what day.

It didn't matter. Ryan was gone.

Stumbling toward the shower, he didn't see Savannah anywhere around the cabin. Glancing into the darkened kitchen, the microwave clock read 3:19 am. He expected to find her curled up in bed. Checking, she wasn't.

Where was she?

Had she left him all alone?

He watched Ryan's life for almost three days straight.

Eyes closed; too mentally drained to care the bathroom was chilly in sharp contrast to the soothing heat of the shower, he rinsed his hair. Hot water pounded on his head, bringing Riley slowly back from the past. He was tired. Bone tired; the kind of soul-deep exhaustion that left an inner scar. Leaning against the chilly ceramic tile wall, his thoughts were muddled and hazy.

Riley needed to sleep.

Just sleep until morning, he told himself, then he would watch again. He had to see every precious minute. He had to complete that heart-wrenching task.

Right now, he couldn't even imagine talking to Savannah.

Behind him, the glass shower door quietly slid open. Cool air skittered across his skin. A soft hand touched his back.

He didn't have the energy to even flinch. Groggily opening his eyes, the room was blanketed in thick clouds of steam. The bathroom felt warmer now. Arms wrapped around him from behind. Bare breasts press against his back.

He couldn't do this.

Sex was the last thing he needed.

But Savannah didn't hug him for long. This obviously wasn't seduction. Reaching around him for the bar of soap on the shelf, she wet it beneath the spray and silently rubbed slick bubbles over the stressed-out muscles in his back. His whole body was tight with tension and grief.

Her hands rubbed. Slowly. Massaging.

Then she rinsed him.

It felt good. Like she really loved him.

"Go away, Savannah."

"Sshh, you don't mean that." Female curves hugged his back again. Hands laced over his heart. Still half-leaning his shoulder against the wall, he felt the hot water spill over his back. Her cheek lay against his skin. It soaked her too.

Releasing him, she wiped her wet face. Soaping his back again so the skin was slick beneath her hands, she kneaded his arms and shoulders for so long he knew her fingers must ache. She finally grabbed the showerhead and rinsed away soap and stress, heating his body back to life again.

"Such a good man." She quietly murmured over the sounds of falling water. "Such a good heart." Rinsing him for a few moments more, she rubbed his body with her hands. She never once made a move he considered seductive.

Just loving. Concerned.

He gradually relaxed. Riley felt sleepy and warm. Loved. Her undemanding kindness soothed the frayed edges of his soul.

"Let's go to bed." He gruffly ordered and turned off the water.

"Uh…okay." Obediently opening the enclosure door, Savannah handed him a fluffy white towel. She was wet too and just as naked as he envisioned. But she wasn't trying to seduce him. In her soft violet-blue eyes, he saw apologetic worry and more unconditional love than he could comfortably accept.

"You should be sleeping." He grumbled.

"So should you."

Drying off, he wrapped the towel around his waist. Riley watched Savannah dry off too. Then almost repentantly, she hustled to the bathroom hook and discreetly hid her naked body inside the fuzzy pink bathrobe she'd unpacked from the storage room boxes. The one with big red hearts that Ryan picked out last year for Valentine's Day.

Riley knew because they told him on the video diary.

"Ryan gave that to you."

"He did."

"It's nice. It looks comfy."

"It is."

Mind half-numb, he watched her brush damp brown hair. "Want help?"

"No. I'll get it." Savannah looked nervous. "You should go to bed."

"Alright. In a minute." But Riley didn't leave. Instead he took the brush from her hand. Her eyes widened. "Turn around, babe. Let me help you." In long gentle strokes from the top of her head to thick ends reaching her hips, he slowly removed every tangle.

"Thank you." Keeping her back turned and her head contritely bowed, she hung up the bathrobe. On the hook was a plain cotton nightgown that she quickly slid over her head. Then seeing herself in the mirror, on second thought she rewrapped herself inside the fuzzy pink hearts too, as if trying to prove she wasn't demanding anything from him.

He felt bad. She deserved better.

She deserved to be loved.

"Do you want to be alone?" She anxiously asked.

"No. I want to sleep in your arms."

Taking her hand, they silently walked through the darkened cabin. Except...the lamp still glowed in the living room. Reaching to turn it off, Riley discovered where Savannah had been.

She never left him alone.

A nest of blankets and pillows swathed the furthest corner of the room. Wadded up Kleenex filled a small wastebasket and littered the floor.

He must have walked right past her.

She stayed with him the whole time, watching and silently crying, but trying hard to give him some space.

"You wanted to see Ryan too?"

"I did." Violet eyes watered. "Sorry."

"Don't apologize. Just come to bed with me."

Later, Riley didn't remember actually climbing into bed.

He vaguely recalled coaxing Savannah out of her clothes.

But he would never forget how good it felt to make music together.

Their bodies moved together in a slow mournful ballad. The gentle soothing melodies healed the broken past and left Riley sleeping with his head over Savannah's heart, wrapped tight in her loving arms, breathing quiet sighs of hope.

\*\*\*

"Wake up, Savage. You have a blood test to take."

Savannah groaned and buried her head under warm blankets. She'd heard Riley up for a while, but hadn't moved.

His phone rang and she cringed at the noise. "Today," he declared, murmuring instructions about boxes and something about Zeus. Not knowing what it meant and not caring, she'd kept sleeping.

"Savannah." His stern voice yanked her awake. "Get up."

"No." She murmured from beneath the covers, "Come back to bed."

"I mean it. Get up."

Sounds like Riley was back to being grumpy and demanding. She seriously preferred the gentle loving man who opened his heart and made love to her last night with such compassion. She had cried tears of joy. Riley fell asleep with his head resting over her heart.

"You need to take a blood test."

"Blood test?" She griped, not moving, "For what?"

"Rubella. You know, German Measles. Real nasty stuff."

"Don't be dumb. I don't have rubella."

"Well, in the great state of Montana you have to prove it."

"I don't want to."

"Then I guess you can't become my wife."

Sliding the blanket down, frowning, she blinked at him. Far more revived from the past few emotionally grueling days than she felt, Riley had pulled on Levis that he hadn't buttoned all the way.

The top two buttons remained open.

That resilient body was etched in the most delicious ways, making her mouth water. Male hips were strong and solid. His belly was smooth and carved with a tempting downward slide of taut stomach muscles that always felt wonderfully sleek beneath a woman's hand.

So damn sexy.

But that confusing unfairly gorgeous man was noisily sliding hangers around in the closet, inspecting the few dresses she kept.

"What are you doing?"

"Finding you a wedding dress. Got anything warm and pretty that's white?"

"I can't wear white, you dope. I'm not a virgin."

Riley chuckled. "Few brides actually are." Again, his chest rumbled with content amusement. It was an unexpected relaxed sound. She couldn't fathom the source of his good mood. He selected a strapless white formal gown she'd worn on stage in London. "How about this?"

"It's sleeveless."

"Does it have a little jacket? What about this lacy thing?" He held a decorative white lace bolero jacket up to it.

"That skimpy thing is about as warm as a snowflake."

Putting it back, he resumed noisily sliding dresses and inspecting. "How about this?" He chose a white silk dinner dress.

"Turn it around, Romeo. Look at the neckline."

He did. It plunged halfway to her navel. "Cool."

"Sure. I'm sure your parents will be thrilled to see half my breasts."

"I wouldn't mind."

"Riley!" Undeterred by her resistance, he just huskily laughed. "Come back to bed," she yawned. "Besides, I've changed my mind about marrying you. You're too grumpy at night and too damn happy in the morning. We'll just live together in sinful bliss."

Casting a sly look over his broad shoulder, Riley grinned. "We're getting married at my parents' house. Today. No more sinful bliss."

"But I like bliss," she pouted, "Come back to bed. You're friendlier in here."

"It's nine-thirty. Now get your naked ass up and help me."

"Oh Riley stop," she yawned hugely. "Besides, we need a license."

"Got it last week while you were busy trading off your fancy clothes to all of Harmony Hills. I'm sure some of those fancy dresses will reappear today."

Surprised he noticed what she did with her New York clothes, Savannah sat up. "And a preacher," she rationalized, "We need someone to marry us."

"Pastor Davenport is expecting us at five o'clock."

"It's Christmas Eve. No one will come."

"The whole town is already invited. Momma Emily made sure of it."

"Oh. Well. Dang." Knotting the sheet in nervous hands, she fished for excuses. "We need flowers," he arched a brow and she knew Ms. Emily handled too, "and a cake."

"Done. Melanie ordered it. Julia took care of music and my tux. Dad, Jacob, and Paul are cooking our wedding dinner. We're having prime rib; the specialty of Savory Grille."

His family had been busy.

"We need two gold rings!" Ahh-hah! Savannah felt smug. No way could he sidestep that very important stipulation to marriage.

"You really want a ring?"

"Yep. I do. With a diamond."

Reaching into his side of the closet, Riley fished through the pocket of the black leather jacket he'd worn last Sunday to dinner with his parents. She'd known all evening he had something on his mind, something important, but somehow they ended up naked the minute they were alone.

Whatever he wanted to discuss was forgotten.

Turning around, he opened his palm.

In Riley's hand were three rings. Two were unadorned gold bands, one wider and larger, but the third was a beautiful diamond solitaire.

He had her attention now. "Rings? For us?"

"Yes. These are our wedding rings. I bought them seven years ago," he quietly confessed. "Right after you were accepted to Julliard. I was coming with you."

"You were?" she spluttered, "You wanted to marry me?" So many years wasted. "Dang, Riley. Why didn't you say so?"

"I never got the chance. We started fighting about stupid stuff, yelling like enemies and slamming doors. We broke up. Then you were gone." He sat down beside her on the bed. "I just spent two days watching years filled with memories that should have been mine too. God gave us a second chance. I won't lose you again."

Caught off guard, she nervously toyed with the sheet covering her bare chest, "maybe you should watch the rest of Ryan's films first. Then you can decide if you want to marry me. You were pretty mad at me last night."

"I wasn't mad at you. Not at all." His head shook, "I was mad at me."

"You were? Why?"

"Because I let life slip away. The whole time I watched, I knew I should have been there too. I could have been. I didn't even try. I convinced myself letting go was right. It wasn't right. I never married because in my heart I already had a wife. She just happened to live in New York City so she could write fabulous music and she raised my son, all alone. But you never should have been alone, Savannah. I should have married you years ago. Today is Christmas Eve. Today we should make things right."

"Oh. My. Wow!" That was the finest speech he'd ever given. "When you finally get to the point about how you feel, it's impressive."

Taking her left hand, he slid the beautiful marquis cut diamond on her finger. "Now it's official. You're my fiancée." It made her smile. Riley tipped her fingers so the diamond caught the light. "Like it?"

"It's perfect."

"Do you love me?"

"Forever isn't long enough for how much I love you."

Smiling, Riley held her face in his hands and drew her close. His kiss was a promise. "Will you please pick out a dress and become my wife?"

Savannah wanted to, but she had one more very important thing to negotiate. "If we're getting married, I want more kids."

"We can't replace Ryan. It's wrong."

"I know that. Each child will be special and unique." She selected the wider wedding band from the remaining pair and slid it on his left hand. Then laced their hands together. "If I marry you, I want the whole package; a big noisy Rosemont family, each one with different personalities and different needs, and us working hard to raise them right, and then us spending seventy or eighty years growing old together in these mountains."

She caught him unprepared. His face blanched. "But…your music is important." Sidestepping the issue, Riley wouldn't meet her gaze as his mind churned over the idea of a family.

"Maybe someday I'll play music again. I can't play until God sends me something. If He does, then you and I will decide how to share it with the world."

He seemed satisfied by that. "How many?"

"Songs? Well, that's up to God, don't you think?"

"Kids. How many baby Rosemont's do you want?"

"Four or five would be nice."

"No, they'd be demanding little babies. Then they'd grow up to be…"

"See!" She brindled, gathering the sheets tighter around her naked form, "I knew you weren't serious! All this marriage business was just hot-blooded talk! It changes the whole romantic thrill when you see the big picture doesn't it?"

"No, Savage," he sternly declared, holding their joined hands. Her diamond caught the light, "I definitely see the big picture. I've seen God's plan for us my whole life."

"Have you? Marriage is forever. You said it yourself; people like us don't divorce. We always say forever isn't long enough, but forever isn't a romantic whim. It's God's way of binding two souls together for all time. And marriage, in God's eyes, also means raising a family."

"We've never talked about kids." He anxiously hedged, but he wasn't fighting. He was thinking. "Ryan just…happened." This was serious. She watched Riley study the beige carpet, then the white bedroom wall. Finally, his eyes met hers. Emotions gleamed. The handsome rugged face she would eternally love; that hadn't shaved in three heartbreaking Ryan-filled days, was etched with worry.

"It's your body, Savannah."

"My body is yours. So is my heart."

Five haggard life-changing breaths. She counted. Their entire future hung on those decisive seconds.

"Childbirth isn't easy." He reluctantly acknowledged.

"Is that what you're agonizing over? Good heavens, Riley, I wouldn't offer more children if I didn't mean it. I loved raising your beautiful son. Maybe next we'll have a daughter. Or," she perkily hoped, "maybe a whole house full of boys. I'd be the only girl. Wow, wouldn't that be a noisy crazy riot?"

"It would."

"Besides, I did just fine giving birth to Ryan. Delivery wasn't that bad. I was just scared because I was all alone. But next time, you'd be right there with me. You'd be the first one to hold our baby." Manly forest green eyes were definitely getting misty. "Don't you want to be a real Daddy?"

Slowly, he licked his lips. "I'd love to." Shielding his own tender feelings from scrutiny, Riley leaned over and kissed her full on the mouth. "But only with you," he huskily ordered. "Our children. Our life. Our family."

"Yes." She agreed, "Our love. Our forever. Our home."

Knowing he'd won both the battle and the marriage war, Riley triumphantly grinned, "So, how soon will you want a baby?"

"No rush. Whenever God sends one. I already started taking the pill. I'll stay on it until we're both ready for another heart to beat in our lives."

"Another heart." The corners of his mouth curved wider and she was rewarded with another heartfelt kiss. "I like that."

"Then help me find a white dress."

That afternoon in a private ceremony, with the Rosemont family and Sam and Millie Lawson present, Savannah and Riley were finally married. Paul was his best man. Julia was her bridesmaid. It was perfect.

Riley looked incredibly handsome in the white tuxedo. Maybe he was right, maybe marriage would fix everything between them that was broken. The hopeful way he looked at her made Savannah feel like a queen.

As Riley recited his vows, he was so solemn.

She felt the momentous weight of his promise.

He promised his life. He promised his love. Forever.

Officially sliding that shiny gold ring on her hand, a jubilant gleam lit those gold-green eyes. He looked like he had wanted to make this promise his entire life. It made her want to kiss that perplexingly complicated man until he cried.

Which would probably take an act of God.

Their first official kiss as man and wife was unforgettable. Riley gathered her against his warm welcoming chest as she nervously gulped great gallons of air.

She married Riley Rosemont.

Just before their lips met he huskily whispered, "Forever isn't long enough, Savage. Not for how much I love you."

Then, he kissed her.

Savannah wanted to live inside that fervent loving kiss for all of eternity. Longer! She never wanted to lose the feeling that Riley truly loved her.

She received all his heart. All his love. All at once.

For quite a while afterwards, she drifted in a delirious daze, holding his hand and smiling. She finally became Savannah Rosemont.

Savannah. Like miles of verdant green grass gently swaying in a springtime breeze. Rosemont. Mountains of beautiful red roses.

The reception was comfortably casual with lots of smiling faces. The whole town seemed to have suddenly "decided" to visit Ms. Emily's big warm house on Christmas Eve. The feminine floor-length Prada performance gown she wore for their wedding ceremony felt inappropriate and gaudy at first, but everyone sincerely approved of its graceful elegance.

For one night, Savannah was a queen.

Riley never left her side and stole a million happy kisses. Every time the doorbell rang, he welcomed someone important into their celebration.

A private wedding, but a wonderfully social reception.

"Let's dance," Riley murmured in her ear, guiding her toward the expansive family room. Furniture removed, the room became a dance floor. They'd already cut their cake. They laughed at apple-cider toasts made by Papa and Paul. Now romantic music warbled through the house.

"Do we have to?"

"One dance wedding," he ardently promised, guiding her around the room. They were already swaying. As one. People were watching. "Then we'll leave for our honeymoon."

"Where will we go?" She hadn't considered a honeymoon yet.

"Our home. Back to Graystone. Where we belong."

In that anxious heartbeat, Savannah knew Riley already managed to get her boxes of clothes and Ryan's movies secured inside their house in the mountains. It made her nervous and uneasy.

The worst was yet to come.

That last day of Ryan's life.

She had been shimmering in happy excitement of marrying Riley. Now reality hit. Her heart faltered.

"What's wrong?" He whispered. "Talk to me."

He slid her into a gentle waltz. She was in awe of his finesse. "I'm just...overwhelmed by the crowd."

"Liar. You've played piano around the world, for thousands of people." He softly kissed her as they moved. It was so romantic, but she just couldn't enjoy it. "Your spine is stiff and you aren't smiling anymore."

"I'm just..." but his hand slid up her back, forcing her to look into his loving eyes, "I'm scared. You haven't finished watching the video diary. What if you still decide to hate me?"

"Impossible. I love you too much."

Just like that, Riley decided it was time for them to leave. Waving goodbye, they trudged out into the snow. His shiny red Chevy Avalanche was decorated with silly pink streamers and a trail of noisy tin cans. Since the truck was up so high, Riley romantically lifted her into the passenger seat.

Everyone cheered.

Leaving happy people behind, she felt exultant, but was grateful he decisively regained their valuable privacy. Slow and careful, Riley drove along the icy roads. The inside of the truck was bitter cold.

"Mom put our wedding quilt in the back seat, along with our other presents." Turning, she found a plush ivory quilt neatly folded atop a pile of gifts. It was handmade. Thick and velvety soft, each stich was a stich of love. Savannah gratefully wrapped it around her legs and tucked the other side over Riley's lap and around his chest.

"You must be cold, too."

He nodded. "A little. Thanks."

It was nearly midnight and so dark outside that from the muted dash lights, she could only see the silhouette of his handsome face as he focused on navigating the icy road. Finally, the heater warmed up and they quit shivering.

"Better?" He asked.

"Yeah." It felt good to be going home. "Where's Zeus?"

"Already in the barn at Graystone. He rode up with Paul this afternoon. He cleared our road with the big city snowplow, so the way up the mountain should be easy now. He even hauled the one we used back to Graystone; in case we need it again."

"He took my boxes?"

"Yep. Everything. You officially live at Graystone. Paul checked on the horses. He said Bitsy looks fantastic. She trotted right up to him, healthy as any young colt. Her eyes are completely blue now. Paul said she can see just fine."

"She really is a Christmas miracle."

"Yep." Silent for a while, listening to the big truck engine growl in the night and the icy road crunched beneath heavy-duty tires, they each mentally relived their life-changing Christmas Eve wedding.

"Savannah Rosemont," he softly mused. "I really like that."

"Me too. It's prettier than Graystone. Such a cold steely name. Rosemont is hopeful. I always envision mountains of red roses."

"Hopeful? Roses?" He chuckled, "You're a funny woman."

Savannah snuggled beneath the warm quilt and grinned. "Merry Christmas, Riley." The digital stereo clock read 12:08. "It's officially tomorrow."

He frowned, "I didn't get you anything."

"You gave me a wonderful present. Your name."

"I did." His smile was warm. "I love you, Savannah."

Hearing the sweet sentiment felt wonderful. "Thanks Riley. For everything," she happily gushed, "I know if I had been more cooperative, I could have helped you with our wedding, but somehow, you made everything just perfect."

"Honey, all you and I did was show up to our own party. Mom, Julia, and Melanie planned it all, right down to the music. I simply told them I wanted it to happen on Christmas Eve."

"Really? Wow. They worked so hard for us. The cake was so pretty. Your parent's house was filled with flowers. Our wedding was beautiful."

"You were beautiful. Still are."

"Thanks. You made me feel like a queen."

Reaching the road going up the mountain to Graystone, there were no snowdrifts, thanks to Paul. The way ahead was icy but smooth.

"Do you love me, Savannah?"

"Of course!" His shadowy profile looked stern. It was insulting. "I just married you, didn't I?"

"Then watch the rest of Ryan's movies with me. Soon. But don't sit in the corner, quiet and forgotten. I want you sitting right beside me. You are my best friend. Now you are my beautiful wife. This is our second chance. We'll grieve together. That's the only way we'll ever find true joy."

"Oh Riley!" She breathlessly whispered. Maybe marriage really would heal everything broken inside. "I love you!" She wished Graystone wasn't so far away. Oh how she wanted to touch him! She'd show him how perfect second chances could be. "When we get home, I'm going to make you soooo happy that you married me!"

In the pale yellow dash-lights, she saw his sexy smile curve. "Promise?"

"With all my heart."

Savannah made good on her promise. She attacked her apprehensive husband the instant the fireplace was properly lit. Riley pretended to grumble about being cold but she wrapped herself around him, kissing him senseless, warming him body and soul as she enthusiastically proved her devotion.

Smiling like a king, Riley stripped away her pretty dress and his formal clothes. They made love wrapped in their velvety soft wedding quilt that he hastily tossed down in front of the warm fire.

But the fun didn't end there.

Christmas Day was just the beginning of their honeymoon celebration.

Riley loved her. Their love was destiny.

He knew it the day she was born.

Their second chance was perfect. For six blissful honeymoon days, they basked in the glow of the warm fireplace, wore little more than blankets, and whispered softly of their beautiful joyful forever.

*Leslie D. Stuart*

# Chapter Seventeen

"Don't forget this thing," Riley reminded, tossing her the fuzzy white beret she always wore to keep her head warm. "Unless you want to donate it to our snowman."

"Not a chance. I love this hat."

New Year's Day, sunlight beamed on their frozen world. Everything looked blindingly white. It was a positive sign for a brilliant new year. Savannah was determined to build a snowman. Although Riley swore she was crazy for wanting to leave warm Graystone and play in icy snow, he agreed to indulge her childish whim.

"Got a carrot for his nose?"

"It's in my pocket," Riley reassured, "along with charcoal briquettes for his mouth and eyes. Got everything else?"

"Yep. Right here in this bag."

Gingerly, she stepped out the second story balcony and onto the densely packed snow surrounding Graystone. It felt weird to see only the top half of the house. Cold. So cold, even with the sun.

"Aren't you coming, Zeus?" She asked the black Great Dane who stopped just short of putting his feet in the frozen snow.

"Wrrrhhhooof!"

Riley laughed. "He says you're nuts."

"Rrrr." Zeus turned tail, thundered back inside.

"See? He's staying where it's warm."

Savannah shivered. "It is cold. Maybe this is a bad idea."

Already shaping a big lump of snow into a ball, rolling it around the powdery surface to make it bigger, Riley snickered, "No way. You made me get dressed. I was perfectly happy wandering around our house without clothes. I had a warm bed. A warm fire. And a warm woman. What more could a man want?"

"A New Year's Day snowman?"

"Not exactly first on my list of wishes." Rolling a volleyball-sized snowball around on the yard, he laughed. His enthusiastic grin was boyish and teasing. "Now, crazy woman, come help me push this thing. Rolling snow will warm us up. We're building the best snowman Montana has ever seen."

"Then we're getting naked again."

"Absolutely."

It took a while to roll the first snowball big enough for Frosty's rotund lower half, but it was fun exhilarating work.

"Pack it tight," he instructed. "He'll last longer."

"I am." Working together, Savannah patted the snow with gloved hands. Snow stuck to the ball as Riley rolled it. It was tightly frozen.

"I want him to live clear 'til spring."

"Better make him big."

The ball was nearly a yard across and so heavy they both grunted as they struggled to move it. Riley declared it was big enough.

"Where do you want Frosty?"

"At the edge of the yard, under the shade of those pine trees." She pointed to a towering stand of ponderosa. "That way he'll last, but I can see him through the attic windows."

Next, she got the job of creating Frosty's head while Riley rolled a medium sized ball for his belly. All over the front yard were funny round trails where they rolled the three giant snowballs. Once, Riley popped her with a small fistful of snow, but only in the back.

"Hey, Rosemont!" Savannah laughed.

"Hey, woman. You're a Rosemont, too."

Despite the frigid cold, she felt hot pride sear tender places inside a freshly healing heart. Riley was right, marriage cured them. They weren't broken anymore.

"It's true. I am. I am Savannah Janine Rosemont. So be nice to me, Husband!" She tossed a snowball back at him. Expecting it, he caught the ball, sending a white shower of splintered snow all over his bronze head.

"Ha ha! Got you!"

"Nah, baby. I got you. Forever." The approving possessive gleam in Riley's gold-green eyes was sexy and smoldering. Ever since she'd said 'I do', he'd worn that amorous thrilled-senseless expression. Seeing his unspoken love felt wonderful.

"Yep. Savannah and Riley," she happily chimed, reveling in their wonderful new relationship, "forever and ever."

"Amen." His grin was wolfishly proud.

Thrilled by his bountiful affection, Savannah shivered.

"Wanna go back inside?"

"Nope. I'm good. Just happy, that's all."

"Oh sure." He dryly teased, "I always shiver when I'm happy."

"Actually…sometimes you do."

He grinned and didn't deny it. Just this morning, in their bed, she'd made him shudder with sincere passionate bliss. A warm bed sounded good. Determined to finish their project, she bent over and shoved her growing snowball again. Frosty's head nearly reached her knees and probably weighed fifty pounds.

"Gotta build Frosty. Then we'll go get naked and warm."

"Warm first. Then naked."

"Okay. Can't make good music if our bones are chattering."

"Nope."

They laughed, panting from the effort as they shoved heavy snowman parts round and around the front yard. It was fun to play like kids. She felt young, her spirit light. Finally, the giant head and fat middle were just too heavy to move.

"He's huge!" Savannah exclaimed after Riley placed Frosty's round white head atop the other two. "Nearly as tall as you!"

"But fatter."

"Definitely. Not sexy at all."

"I'm sexy?"

"Of course!"

Happily chattering like the best friends they were born to be; together they decorated Frosty with a red scarf and a gaudy plastic gold crown Savannah scavenged from old party decorations in the basement. Then they shoved a pair of bright yellow rubber rain boots into the front of him for feet. Making arms out of two pine branches, Riley turned one upward.

It looked like Frosty was waving.

"I like that. Nice touch, Riley."

His carrot nose was long and slightly snobbish. Frosty's charcoal eyes and the wide curve of his black briquette grin stood out against the white snow.

Savannah thought he looked marvelous.

"Frosty the Snow King."

Admiring their creation, Riley noticed she was shivering uncontrollably now. But would she admit it? No. Stubborn woman.

"I'm freezing," he declared, offering his gloved hand. Cheeks rosy pink, but lips slightly blue, Savannah's breath made white puffs. "I need a warm fire." Her leather-clad fingers laced between his. "And a warm friendly woman."

"Me too. Happy New Year, Riley. This was fun!"

He wholeheartedly agreed.

Together they raced across the frozen yard and back inside Graystone where they celebrated the New Year and became very warm indeed.

***

"I want to ride again." Savannah declared one morning in January as she watched Mirabelle prance giant circles around Riley. He looked like the proud ringmaster in the center of the practice arena.

Marriage was wonderful. They worked together, played together, and curled up every night to blissfully dream together. They never argued, not even once.

"Do you think my leg could handle riding?"

"Maybe. You hardly limp anymore."

"I don't?"

"Not unless you're really tired."

Savannah grinned. She hadn't noticed the chronic limp was fading. Riley noticed. His awareness felt good. "Can I try riding Mirabelle?"

"She's pretty bouncy. You might fall off."

"I won't."

Compliant with her desire to ride, Riley saddled the sleek dappled gray dancer. He lifted Savannah onto the mare's back. Hands released her. She settled into place and already wanted to cry. Curving her thigh around Mirabelle's body was excruciating. The angle required for her knee and ankle to rest properly in the stirrups sent pain screaming through the leg.

But she bravely tipped her chin and sucked back a sob.

Riley immediately saw. "Nope. Not happening." In one swift move, he hauled her off Mirabelle. "I saw those tears."

"I'm fine! Put me back!" But as her feet met the ground, the left leg mutinously collapsed. "Uughh," she groaned, toppling.

Riley caught her arm. "Stubborn woman."

"Maybe I just need practice." She argued, standing firm again.

"Maybe you need more time to heal."

After that, no matter how hard she begged, Riley refused to let her try again. Once, when she was alone with Merlin, she urged the giant black stallion over to a fence and climbed upon his towering back. Once again, the pain was unbearable. Defeated, she'd slid off, crumbled into a sad heap in the straw.

She hated being broken.

January waltzed by in a sublime rhythm of Married Bliss. This was so much better than sinful bliss! They worked with the horses, flirted and teased all day, as fun foreplay to joyful nights spent making love.

Riley wanted to finish watching Ryan's movies. Together. Savannah made excuses. She was too happy. Why ruin bliss with tears of regret?

February second came.

Ryan's would-have-been birthday.

That morning Riley woke before her, at sunrise. She didn't hear him unpacking the precious moments from the past. Savannah couldn't stop him from turning on the TV. She didn't know Riley sat alone watching Ryan's final days until it was too late.

"What the?" She spluttered, waking to hear a child's laugh. Familiar, so familiar. It ripped opened old wounds! She raced down the hall into the entertainment room. "Riley!" Hazel eyes stared at the screen, glazed and lost. "What are you doing?"

He didn't answer.

Ryan was dressed in his little white tuxedo. They were backstage at Carnegie Hall. Nervous yet brave, he was talking to the camera, telling Riley about his role in the night's performance.

"I'll start by playing 'Twinkle Little Star' on my violin, over and over in funny ways, like the violin is asking questions. The first time, Dad, when I play the 'wonder what you are' part Momma will answer on her piano with 'You are My Sunshine,' all loud and happy. We'll keep playing bits of songs that people already know. One time, Momma's piano will tell me to 'Follow the Yellow Brick Road,' and my violin shouts 'Zippidy-do-da!' It's funny. I'll play bits of 'Old MacDonald,' and 'Yankee Doodle,' and 'This Old Man' too. Momma plays harder stuff like Beethoven. To finish, I'll play the whole violin chorus of 'Devil Went Down to Georgia.' Do ya' know that song, Dad? It's crazy fast and really cool." He proudly grinned. "People will be shocked I can play so good."

Riveted to Ryan's voice and face, Savannah felt herself sink down onto the couch beside Riley. She had completely forgotten the outrageous childish medley she'd written.

Glancing over, suddenly aware he wasn't alone, Riley wrapped his arm around her, tucking their sides tight together.

"Why are you watching this?"

"Because today is his birthday. I need to see him."

Now Ryan stood on stage, as viewed from the professional filmed concert version that Savannah edited right into their video diary. His mahogany red-brown hair gleamed in the bright spotlight. He looked so small, yet stood tall and unafraid.

Then, he played it.

The audience roared with approval.

Neither of them said a word.

They watched in silence. People cheered. Ryan bowed like a gentleman to the enthusiastic crowd. Then he sat beside her on the piano bench. They played a duet, "Baby Steps," a lyrical happy song Savannah wrote for Ryan.

They continued watching right through the last days of his life.

Neither spoke. Neither moved.

They became a pair of sad statues.

Then...the final day of Ryan's life. This was the last recording. His horse trotted around the grassy meadow. His bronze hair gleamed glossy-red in the sunlight. Ryan's chestnut brown mare snatched a bite of grass. The little boy grinned.

"Brandi wants to eat." He said.

"She's spoiled, Ryan. Brandi isn't hungry; she's just testing your authority. It's your job to keep her going." Savannah's voice came across the microphone as she held the camera. "Just talk to her, like I taught you."

Round and round the pair circled the wide meadow. The mare reached for grass, but Ryan nudged her sides with his heels, scolding her. After Brandi obediently moved forward again, he patted her neck, saying her how good she was.

"I'm getting better." He happily declared and urged the lazy mare into a gentle gallop, circling the meadow. He rocked in the saddle like a pro.

"Next summer Mom, can I go see my Dad?"

"If you want."

"We'll fly to Montana?"

"Yep. It's too far to drive."

"How long can we stay?"

"As long as you'd like." She promised. "So you're getting serious about meeting your Dad?"

"I am. Do you think Dad will like me?"

"He'll love you, Ryan, with all his heart. Maybe you should call your Dad sometime. That might be a good place to start building bridges."

"Call him?" Ryan laughed as though she just told a funny joke. He stopped Brandi and walked the horse toward Savannah. "Why didn't I think of that?" Still grinning with his happy secret, he waved at the camera and winked. "Maybe I'll call him next Sunday."

But that call never came.

\*\*\*

For two solemn weeks, Ryan's last days of life haunted Riley, gnawed at his gut, devouring everything good. He tried to shake it, tried to pretend everything was fine, but the past held him. Bitterness dug icy claws in deep. Again.

Savannah knew.

He saw guilt on her face.

Withdrawn, he barely spoke anymore.

So much for honeymoon bliss.

February rolled by. Silent. Solitary. Except occasionally at night, when he found a few fleeting moments of joy in her arms.

Riley felt awful.

Savannah said nothing.

March came. The sun decided to shine on Montana. Snow melted into muddy slush, except around Graystone's walls. Towering drifts merely shrank, unwilling to relinquish their hold on the house. In the front yard, Fat Frosty still bravely waved. Every day he saw Savannah visit Frosty. She patted down his round body, compressing the frozen snow tight together to make it last.

She even talked to the snowman.

Jabbered away about nothing.

Riley watched her, from a distance, telling Frosty burdens no snowman should have to carry. Crazy woman.

"He won't last much longer." he gruffly declared, striding across the snow. She looked uneasy as he approached; unsettled and shocked he had decided to follow her. "I don't know why you fuss over him. It's just a snowman."

"But he's our snowman."

"So?" Trying to swallow bitterness and be kind, he reached up, adjusting Frosty's goofy gold plastic party crown.

"I like him." She defended. "He's special."

"Because?"

Hands on her hips, she turned to face him. "Because the day we made Frosty we were amazingly happy."

That truth hit hard. Guilty, Riley couldn't look at her.

They'd been insanely happy that day. Delirious, giddy in love.

Then he watched Ryan's final video diary. His heart closed. Her fears of rejection were justified. They should have comforted, healed together, but steel walls locked his grief inside, locking Savannah out. Grief killed happiness.

"Can I ask you something, Riley?"

"I guess."

"Are you going to divorce me?"

So blunt. Damn. His mind hadn't even wandered that far. Yet. But her crestfallen expression proved Savannah did.

And was convinced she knew his answer.

"No. I'm just a mess inside over Ryan. Seeing his last days was hard. I can't shake it. I'm stuck in the past. I just need time to heal. That's all."

"It was hard for me too."

"I know." He struggled for the right words, knowing he owed her an explanation. "Bitsy's strong now; stronger than I ever dreamed she'd be."

Violet-blue eyes narrowed at him speculatively. "What does Bitsy have to do with us and Ryan?"

"Nothing." He was avoiding. He knew it. She knew it. Glancing down at the white snow then at Frosty, he confessed.

"Ryan called me."

"Huh?"

"Last summer. He called me every Sunday for three months."

Her lips formed a small "O" as his truth sank it. "That's how Ryan knew you loved him. You told him."

"I did. Every week."

"That's why you grieve." She wisely summarized, "You miss him. The real boy; not just an idea."

"Yes. I do miss him. We were great...I loved..."

He couldn't talk about this anymore. Couldn't say Ryan's name. Couldn't tell Savannah how cheated he felt. He only had a dozen precious phone calls with his son. She had years! It wasn't fair! Torn in a dozen different emotional directions the awful aching icy knot inside fisted unbearably tight.

It stung. His eyes burned.

Men don't cry!

Anger sparked instead, fierce and defensive.

"You know what…I'm sick of thinking about Ryan. Sick of hurting. Ryan is all we talk about! All we think about! No more, Savannah." He shouted, letting the beast inside rage. "I don't want to talk about him anymore. No more! Ever! Not again! Don't tell me stories. Don't talk about the past. Got it?"

Shocked, hurt gleamed in her eyes. "Fine!"

"We're married." He firmly added, "We're staying married."

Brindled for a fight, her cheeks had flushed pink from the cold, but her eyes sparked fire. "Fine! We'll stay married. But I won't sleep beside a man who hates me! The attic is mine! All mine. You can't come up there. Sex isn't a cure. It's just a Band-Aid. I deserve better!"

Nights spent reveling in her arms was the only thing holding him together. She wanted to take that away too? Hadn't he lost enough?

"Sleep wherever you want. I really don't give a damn."

Leaving her gaping, he stomped away.

They didn't talk the rest of the day.

That night, she trudged upstairs, followed by Zeus.

Damn. He didn't think she'd actually go. The burst of grief-fueled anger had fizzled, leaving only regret. Paralyzed by pride, he refused to grovel and apologize.

Men did not grovel. Men did not cry.

Riley spent the night alone.

Chilly March gave way to fragrant hints of springtime. Frosty the Snowman melted away. Savannah mourned his loss but Riley knew she mourned far more than the snowman.

Winter fled from Graystone Heights.

The steel tunnel from the back door to the stables came down. Horses who spent the winter inside were released into the lush green pastures.

Savannah worked with Bitsy every day, leading the blue-eyed Christmas miracle around the arena, teaching the petite filly basic voice commands and behavior. Bitsy loved the attention. While Riley rode other horses, Bitsy learned to walk obediently beside Savannah while under halter; without charging rambunctiously ahead. Her eager responses earned jubilant praise and loving pats. The now-healthy miracle baby glowed. Delicate legs pranced. She loved Savannah. She'd do anything to make that woman happy.

He watched. He never said a word.

At night after dinner, Riley always stayed downstairs while Savannah and Zeus locked themselves away. Since they couldn't discuss Ryan or the past, they fumbled over rare sporadic conversations that usually ended in awkward silence.

He missed talking about Ryan, hearing stories of his life.

He felt disconnected now.

From Ryan. From Savannah. From his own heart.

Their separation was wrong in so many ways.

He knew it. She knew it.

Neither knew how to fix it.

# *Chapter Eighteen*

April burst forth in verdant shades of green. Wildflowers bloomed; berries blossomed. The mountain had survived winter.

That evening Riley felt night air stirring inside Graystone and went to investigate. A window was open, somewhere upstairs. He felt gentle whispers of life scoot down hallways, curiously investigating every quiet corner.

It was eerie. Cleansing. Like the renewing spirits of springtime were benevolently haunting Graystone, whisking away the ghosts of lost dreams.

It felt like second chances.

The breeze wasn't coming from Savannah's room. He checked there first. The door stood wide open. Peering inside, her spacious attic sanctuary was surprisingly dark and empty; no Zeus and no woman.

He hadn't been up here since their fight.

Plenty of lost dreams in this room.

No second chances.

Maybe she left her bathroom window open. Smacking into an end table he couldn't see in the dark, Riley swore. She'd rearranged the furniture. You couldn't walk straight across the room, but had to weave through strategically placed obstacles. He suspected she moved everything on purpose so she'd have fair warning if he came for a nighttime visit.

Good thing he hadn't tried.

That would have sparked a rip-roaring fight.

Standing on the landing outside her room, he still felt air. Dang it. Determined to find it, he trotted down one level. Checking the second story of Graystone room by room, grumbling about what a mess his life still was when marriage was supposed to fix everything, he finally found her.

In a narrow maintenance hallway that he rarely had reason to walk, air danced down steep stairs designed for chimney cleaning and roof repairs. He peered up the hidden access stairwell and saw stars twinkle. Savannah had opened the big weatherproof doors at the very top of the house.

Climbing up, in the moonlight Riley saw his wife and Zeus lying on a blanket spread upon the slanted roof.

Three stories up.

Cautiously, expecting Savannah to tell him to leave, Riley crept out there with her. Zeus lifted his head, questioning his uninvited appearance. She didn't move. He sat down beside her. Eyes open, one arm tucked beneath her head, she was staring at the stars.

"You sure make lots of noise, Riley Rosemont, tromping through the house grumbling about what a terrible nuisance I am."

"I wasn't," but he had been. "Sorry."

She arched one eyebrow at the genuine apology. She looked peaceful. In the moonlight, he could see that her glossy hair was loose. It fanned out around her like chocolate decadence. She wore one of his flannel shirts that hit her slim body about mid-thigh…and socks. No pants. No shoes. She wasn't wearing a bra, either.

She wore sleep clothes, out here on the roof.

Weird woman.

"Come back inside. You're going to fall."

"The only way I'll fall is if you push me."

"Please, honey." He calmly reasoned, "Come back inside. One slip and you'll fall three stories down."

"I already fell. Zeus grabbed me." She lifted the flannel shirtsleeve, revealing a thick white bandage covering her upper arm. "See? I've already learned my lesson."

"Zeus bit you?! When?"

"Yesterday."

He felt a low protective growl build in his chest.

"Calm down. It was an accident."

"That dog bit you!"

"Well, sure." She glibly quipped, "It isn't like he has arms and hands to catch me with. How else is Zeus supposed to save me from falling on your head while you're standing in the front yard hollering at raccoons to get off your damn roof. Thanks for not firing your rifle, by the way." She mischievously grinned and gave a light-hearted laugh. "We clumsy raccoons really do appreciate that."

"I wouldn't have shot them."

"No, of course not. You're much too humane to hurt innocent animals. But you'd probably enjoy taking a few pop shots at me."

Riley just sat beside her and sighed.

He didn't want to fight. Not tonight.

He missed her. Their separation was killing him.

"We do have raccoons. I've heard them up here for a week."

"No we don't. You heard me and Zeus. Since it warmed up, I've been sleeping out here. I even rearranged my bedroom, so if I heard you banging around, I'd race back inside. Tonight I wasn't fast enough. By the time I heard you stomping around grumbling about life, you were already prowling around looking for an open window."

She did the strangest things. Why would she sneak around? Should he get mad and leave? Is that what she wanted? He decided he missed her too much. Walking away would only make that disconnected feeling worse.

"You could break your fool neck up here."

"Oh whaaa." She sarcastically snickered, "Like you'd cry."

Riley bite back a sharp retort guaranteed to spark another hot-blooded fight. One. Two. Three, he counted, breathing slow and deep.

"Can I ask why are you sleeping on the roof?"

"Lay down and you'll see." Surprised she actually invited him to stay, Riley stretched out beside her. Following her skyward gaze, overhead a stunning onyx blanket glittered with millions of priceless star-diamonds.

"Oh wow." The celestial jewels made him feel small. Lighter. It felt easier to breathe. "Do they always look that close?"

"Even closer when there's no moon."

"Cool." He noted the waning crescent moon in the eastern hemisphere, smiling on the peaceful Montana night. Its silver curve seemed friendly, welcoming. "It's beautiful up here."

"There must be a meteor shower tonight," she declared, "So far, I've counted fifteen shooting stars."

The serene diamond blanket glittering in the magnificent night sky made everything turbulent and frustrated inside become silky smooth. Trouble faded away. The past was a mere memory, no longer controlling his heart.

All that existed was right now.

With Savannah.

A streak of white light shot across north to west.

"Look," he pointed, "there's one." The trail quickly faded. "Wow. I haven't seen a shooting star since we were kids."

"Really? I...uh, used to..." sighing, she refused to finish.

"You used to watch them with Ryan?"

"Yeah." She noisily swallowed a lump of regret. "Sorry."

"It's alright. We can talk about him. I was dumb to say we couldn't." He waited several moments for her to continue, but she didn't volunteer her story. "Tell me about watching shooting stars. Please?"

"Are you sure?"

"Positive."

"You won't get mad?"

"No. I miss hearing about our son."

"Well, in summertime, I always rented a beach house in Cape Cod for a few weeks. It was perched right on the Atlantic shore. We heard the waves perfectly. At night, we'd lie on the rooftop deck in cushioned lounge chairs and watch shooting stars drop into the ocean. I'd cover Ryan with a blanket. We made wishes on the stars. He liked to tell me every wish. He was sure they'd all come true. Eventually he would fall asleep and I'd carry him back inside."

"Sounds peaceful. And hopeful."

"It was."

"Is that where I saw you two clamming and building sandcastles?"

"Yeah." Beside him, she sadly sniffed. "Just watch the stars, Riley. The past is over. Let's just live in this moment. I'm here. You're here. Right now matters."

Regretting he made Savannah unwilling to share her memories; he carefully reached over and laced his fingers through hers. She quickly yanked it away. Scrambling to leave, before she could get up Riley snagged her and rolled. Hooking his arm around her slim waist, he pinned her body back to the blanket.

"Just watch the stars, Savage."

Beneath his weight, she huffed and grunted, trying to escape.

"Please? Stay?"

Glaring at him, she held very still.

They hadn't been this close in a while. The stirrings of something far more interesting than arguing warmed his belly. One slim bare leg had tangled around his thigh, and in her struggles to escape, she slid their hips tight together. He could feel sweet feminine heat through his jeans.

"Why should I stay?" Her husky whisper revealed he wasn't the only one keenly aware of how well they fit together, even if locked in combat.

"Because tonight matters. Yesterday is but a memory." He softly quoted the words to "One Moment" to her. "Tomorrow will always be just a dream. Why do we waste so many good Today's not seeing the beautiful moment God placed right in our hands?"

"Don't use my music against me!" She angrily bucked and squirmed again. "I know what that song means. Do you?"

"It means that if I don't kiss you right now," he purposely flattened her body against the blanket, "and mean it," his lips lovingly brushed over hers, "and take you back inside and make love to you, then tonight will become just another precious moment that I let slip right through my hands. I miss you, Savannah."

Breath coming in tiny panicked puffs, her eyes glistened.

"Or we can lay here under the stars," he wisely offered, "and learn how to be friends again. It would be a shame to miss all those silver diamonds God is tossing down at us."

She took a deep relieved breath.

Riley knew watching stars was probably the better choice.

"Stars," she allowed, "that's all."

"I'd like that. Watching the stars is peaceful. But you need to go inside and put some jeans on. I can't lay here innocently knowing that all you're wearing is my shirt and panties."

She gulped. Then her pretty mouth curved. "And socks."

"On the roof. At night. Your Daddy would spank you."

"True. And you?"

"I like your special weirdness."

Smiling wider, her soft hand slid up his neck and into the back of his hair. Fingers gripped it in gentle fists, letting the short hair trickled through her hand. Oh how he liked when she did that!

"I dressed for sleeping. I wasn't expecting company."

"Do you want company?"

"I haven't decided." But raising her head, Savannah softly kissed him, almost an apology, but more like an official pardon. It made Riley wonder exactly who, over the past few weeks, actually needed forgiveness from whom.

"So? Can I stay? Or would you rather be alone?"

"I'm tired of being alone. Company would be nice." He liked the sexy smolder in her voice, proving she wasn't unaffected by their kiss.

"Then get dressed. Please?"

Releasing her, she scampered up the slanted rooftop and through the access doors. Zeus went too, of course. Wondering if Savannah would actually return. Half-betting she wouldn't reappear, Riley lay there on his back enjoying the night. Hands laced behind his head, he watched a trillion stars shine.

Zip. Another silver streak.

That time, he remembered to make a wish.

Five more falling stars and five heartfelt wishes later, he heard Savannah and Zeus climb the narrow access stairs. Tilting his head, she was inching her way down the roof. He felt relieved to see she was fully dressed now.

She even put on boots.

"That was fast."

"Miss me?"

"Yeah, actually. I did."

She naughtily grinned at him. It was exactly the impish expression she wore when they were kids doing something they probably shouldn't.

"I love you, Savage."

Her left heel slipped. Plop, she landed on her butt. Zeus yelped, throwing his gigantic body in front of hers, stopping her from sliding.

"Oh crap!" Riley spun around. "Are you alright?"

"Why'd you say that? Are you TRYING to make me fall?" She hissed; arms wrapped around her ebony guardian.

"No. Sorry. I do love you, though."

213

She made a funny doubtful sound. "I'm alright, Zeus." She assured, rubbing his worried head. "Good boy. So good. So good." Careful now, she crab-walked the rest of the way to their blanket.

"Sorry Savannah. Really. Are you okay? Did you scrape your hands? I didn't mean to hurt you."

She stared at him for a full stunned minute.

"What?"

"Are YOU okay? Did aliens abduct 'Angry Riley' while I was gone and leave 'Nice Riley' instead?" Her tone questionable, in the pale moonlight, he couldn't tell if she was joking or angry. "Or have all those pretty stars gone to your head?"

"I saw six." As she stretched out beside him, Riley swung his arm around his wife and tucked Savannah against his side. Her head comfortably nestled against his shoulder.

"Six what? Aliens?" She sarcastically jabbered like an excited child. "Were they friendly? Were they green or purple? I'm betting green. Did the aliens threaten you with scary laser guns and promise to turn you into a toad unless you learned to behave like a nice Mountain Man?"

Riley smiled. That simple curve of his mouth felt sublime. "Stars, Savage. Six shooting stars. And six wishes."

"Oh." Her finger pointed skyward as another silver streak traveled across the galaxy. "Seven. It's definitely a meteor shower. Cool huh?"

"Yes, it is. Thanks for sharing." Grateful for this rare moment, he absently rubbed her upper arm with his hand. She winced and hissed. "How bad did Zeus bite you?"

"He saved my idiot neck. Don't worry about it."

"Did you treat it with anything?"

"Yep. I cleaned it with that terrible iodine antiseptic you use on horses; that stings like hellfire, by the way. Poor horses. You should use something kinder. I gave myself a shot of penicillin and a tetanus shot for good measure. I even stitched up the holes, all by myself."

"Holes?! You stitched yourself? How did you stitch your right arm? You are right-handed. If you stitched it crooked, the skin heals crooked."

"Do you really think I care about new scars?"

"No. It's just that it's muscle too and..."

"Stop." A pointy female elbow jabbed him in the ribs. "Can we just watch the stars? Lecture me and play doctor tomorrow. Enjoy the moment, Riley. Now counts. Just lay here on the roof of Graystone and listen to our mountain talking." She gently advised, "Don't let this beautiful night slip through your hands."

She was right, of course.

Now mattered. This moment was very important.

"Alright." He couldn't believe she'd stitched up her own arm. "But tomorrow you're letting me look at it."

"Yes, Doc Rosemont," she contritely quipped. "But can you please spare me the atrocious bedside manner? If my medical handiwork doesn't meet your high standards, just re-stitch it. No lectures."

The sides of his mouth curved. "Can I grumble?"

"To yourself. Silently. I don't want to hear it."

Her contrary stubbornness made him softly laugh.

"You're awfully agreeable tonight."

"It's a nice night." He pointed to an exceptionally bright silver orb streaking across their diamonded sky. "Look. Wow. A big one."

That time he wished for something new.

A wish for someone else.

He'd never thought about using a shooting star to send love and happiness into someone else's life, but doing it felt extremely right. Closing his eyes, he wished with all his heart, praying somewhere up there in the stars someone who granted wishes might make it come true.

Eyes closed, the silence of the night was beautiful. Listening, he quickly realized it wasn't actually silent at all.

Their mountain really was talking.

In the grassy yard, three stories down, crickets happily chirped. Somewhere near the stables, a big fat toad honked nasal broadcasts. The air moved through the treetops, gently whispering of hope, chasing the ghosts of lost dreams away from Graystone.

Further away, near the meadow in the upper pastures, Riley heard several animals trot through the tall grass. Too delicate sounding to be horses. Probably a herd of deer.

"Don't you want to know what I wished for?"

"Wishes," she harshly scoffed, "please. You're just humoring the sappy romantic fool who sleeps on your roof because night air and stars feel like heaven."

He gazed up at the magnificent celestial blanket glittering high above them. Lying up here beside her made every problem feel dumb.

"I love you, Savannah."

She gulped and shivered, but didn't answer.

"You don't believe me anymore, do you?"

"It's hard to believe in love. I want to, but your walls are too strong, Riley. I can't tear them down. One minute you are loving and kind; my best friend. Then you remember you're determined to be angry and we fall apart again."

"Sorry."

Higher on the mountain, a wolf howled. It was eerie and lonely. Then another voice rang out, deeper and stronger. It was the male, running across the ridge toward his mate.

Even wolves needed someone to love.

Riley lay there listening to the trees whisper, and the house beneath them creak, and those wolves talking on the ridge. He decided Savannah deserved to know his wish.

"I wished that God would bless you with music again."

"Why? Music took me away from you."

"Because when He talks to you through that piano, you are really happy. I'm too messed up inside to bring you more than fleeting moments of happiness. So, I thought that maybe God might do it better."

Savannah held very still, barely breathing. She stiffened. Then Riley heard her sadly sniff and knew he'd made her cry.

Somehow, something he said was terribly wrong.

Rubbing her face with her fists, she sat up. "Look, God is NEVER going to speak to me again! Ever!" Her distraught voice echoed off the mountain making even the ghosts of lost dreams hold their dying breath. "The music is gone!" Arms frantically flapped skyward, proving exactly how much she missed hearing God's divine melodies. "Got it? Gone. FOREVER. No more music. I feel nothing. God abandoned me. I'm not worthy! I can't play that piano. I can't even touch it! It's sacred now and I just…"

Riley sat up, scooped her up and turned Savannah so she sat between his outstretched legs with her back pressed against his chest.

"What are you doing? Let go of me!"

"Just breathe, Savage." He ordered, compassionately wrapping the hysterical woman in his arms. "Just sit here on the roof with me. Let's enjoy this beautiful night. Please? Let's not think about how we hurt. Or why. I didn't mean to upset you. My wish was for you to be happy, that's all." Stroking one hand down her sleek hair, she clung to him. "Let's make tonight count for something good. Let's give ourselves one good memory, okay?"

She silently nodded. Riley gratefully held her tighter.

So they sat there three stories up on the shingle roof of Graystone, watching stars streak across the sky, listening to the slight breeze whisper through tall pine trees and animals quietly move around on the mountain.

The ghosts of lost dreams compassionately sighed and moved further up the glacial peaks, so high that Riley couldn't sense their mournful presence anymore.

The wolves were still talking, together now. Their lonely howls had become funny playful yips that seemed almost like wild canine laughter. The toad throatily croaked, making deep long honking sounds. In the front yard, something fast and small scurried noisily through the grass. It squeaked. Riley hoped it was just a mouse and not a pack rat.

Somewhere in the forest, high upon the ridge, an owl hooted. All around the meadow and throughout the darkened hills dozens of joyful crickets riotously rubbed their wings together, composing an oddly discordant plucked-violin-string symphony.

"Thank you." Savannah finally whispered.

"You're welcome."

Riley wasn't quite sure what she thanked him for, for soothing her hysterics, for having the good sense to listen to life instead of talk, or for just for being here. He didn't want to push his luck and ask.

"It's getting late. Should I go back inside so you can sleep?"

Shaking her head, she confessed, "I don't really sleep. I just listen to our mountain and cry."

"I don't sleep either."

"I know. I've heard you prowling around downstairs."

Worried he might say something wrong again, Riley considered his options. His first inclination was to talk about all kinds of unimportant things, but he stifled that evasive habit and focused on what he really needed to say.

It was hard.

It took a while to find the right words.

"You're my best friend, Savannah." He softly proclaimed, making her spine stiffen. "I really miss you. Can I please stay up here with you tonight?"

"On the roof?"

"Wherever you are, honey, that's where I want to be."

She considered his request. He waited while she purposely breathed in and out, real slow, trying to stay calm. "Just for tonight?"

"Well, no." Riley couldn't lie. He wanted much more than just one night. "I like the roof, but maybe, if things go well between us, maybe tomorrow we could sleep by the fireplace in a blanket, just like we did when we were first married."

Those precious perfect honeymoon days were good days, good memories. Maybe they could recreate them and start over.

"I think...I'd like that."

"Good. Me too. Then eventually, if that goes well, maybe we could graduate to sleeping in a bed." Her spine stiffened again. "But if you like sleeping in odd places, that's fine too. Roof, floor, couch; whatever. I'm there."

She giggled at his quick compliance. "In the stable?"

"Sure. You, me, Goliath, and Zeus on a pile of straw. Sounds cozy."

A short laugh burst from her lips. "And Merlin. Don't forget him."

"Nope. I draw the line at sleeping with horses."

"Gee. You're so discriminating. Merlin will have hurt feelings."

"Tough."

Turning slightly, she twisted around in the protective cradle of his body and looked at him. "I've missed you, Riley." Cupping his cheek with her palm, soft lips gently brushed against his. "You're my best friend, too."

217

"I love you, Savannah." As her fingers slid from his cheek to palm his chest, tugging at his shirt to remove it, he knew they'd make music right here, under the stars. "Wherever you are, that's where I want to be." He kissed her deeply, making his beautiful wife shudder and cling to him with need. "Forever isn't long enough for how much I love you."

This time, Riley knew she believed him.

****

"Two more weeks of sun and our mountain will be completely green again." Riley cheerfully commented as they hiked up the ridge behind Graystone Heights. It was warmer today, comfortable sweater weather. Determined to make her leg stronger, Savannah wanted to hike the mountain. Riley and Zeus joined her. Friendly and unusually talkative, she appreciated the protective gesture, but she needed freedom. She wasn't a china doll. Being coddled was annoying.

"It could still storm again."

"Nah." Smiling at the sunny blue sky and waking world, he held her hand. "Spring is here."

"How do you know? Are you a weather forecaster?"

"Maybe it's just wishful thinking."

"Sure. Riley Rosemont, the positive thinker. Right."

He wasn't deterred. "People can change."

Walking under towering ponderosa pines whispering in the morning breeze, the damp earth beneath their boots made slight squishing sounds. Wild birds chattered in the distance. It was a beautiful day.

"Wandering Creek is overflowing with spring runoff water." She commented about the normally polite laughing trickle running down Lookout Canyon, a mile north of Graystone Heights.

"Really? How do you know?"

"I feel it. Can't you hear it roaring?"

Tilting his head, Riley tried to listen. No. He couldn't hear water. Only his feet marching up the hill. A fat gray squirrel chattered above their heads. The familiar soft rustle of pine trees. "Maybe I need my ears checked. I can't hear water."

"Listen with your heart, Riley. Not your ears." He looked at her funny. She stopped walking, turned, placing her hand over his eyes, forcing them closed. "Listen, Mountain Man. Let God's world talk to you."

He listened. Eyes closed, other senses amplified. Savannah's hair smelled like vanilla shampoo. Her hand over his eyes smelled like juniper, as if the aromatic branches had trickled through her fingers. He snagged her waist and found soft lips.

She whimpered, yielded to his embrace, giving.

This was nice. A kiss in the forest.

Not nearly as spectacular as making love on the roof, blanketed by a million stars, making wishes on falling stars, but he'd take it.

When he opened his eyes, she was smiling. "Did you hear anything?"

"No. Maybe I need to practice."

"Want to walk to the creek?"

"Sure." They'd reached to top of the ridge behind Graystone. Sun shone bright upon the open meadow gracing the high crown. Spindly stiff tuffs of grass held streaks of green. "See, I told you spring was here."

That earned him a small approving smile. "It's because this is the first place the morning sun touches when it wakes the world and the last place it kisses as it says goodbye."

"A special place."

"It can be."

"Ryan would have loved it here." With that thought his smile disappeared. For a little while today, he let himself stop mourning Ryan. It felt selfish to smile and appreciate life when his beautiful son lay buried in the cold hard ground. In New York City.

The thought was an evil slap.

Shaken, he sat down on a fallen log.

"I should have buried him here. Right here. On this sunny ridge."

"At the time, you didn't have a choice."

"I know…but still."

"We could move him." She offered, sitting down on their barky chair too. "We could bring Ryan home to Montana."

"Home…" It made his chest ache.

They didn't walk any further. In silence, they sat upon that log, contemplating. He thought about Ryan. He wondered if Ryan would like watching the sunrise and sunset from this mountain ridge.

Finally, Savannah stood, turned and took his hand. Violet eyes gleaming with unshed tears, she promised, "I'm bringing him home."

"It's expensive."

"I'll pay." Her stubborn chin tilted. "I know it's only his body. I know his spirit is safe with God. I don't care. I'm bringing our son home to Montana."

Three days later, she did.

Ryan's small pearly white casket arrived in a luxury hearse limo, escorted by four funeral executives wearing black tuxedos. His new burial ground was solemnly prepared, the earth blessed and consecrated by Pastor Davenport from Harmony Hills. Surrounded by family members, Riley, Paul, Jacob, Papa, and Sam Lawson carried the casket up the hill, to his final resting place upon that beautiful sunlit ridge.

Savannah had ordered a beautiful marble statue of an angel. It towered life-sized with wings spread, overlooking his sacred grave.

At sunset, Ryan's carefully relocated tomb lowered into the earth of Graystone Heights. His home. Forever. Even the forest became reverently silent. After prayers, the men burying it deep, sealing the remains of that loving child in the mountain. When they were finished, the ladies planted living flowers upon the mound, marking his grave.

When night came and stars appeared above Graystone, their mournful family members left them alone. Riley tugged Savannah into his arms.

Together they cried.

It was over.

Ryan had come home.

***

She wanted to hike. She claimed the forest called to her. Riley tagged along, toting his rifle in case bears or wolves decided his wife looked tasty. The untamed wilderness surrounding Graystone Heights deserved respect. After the land became a protected game preserve, wild creatures thrived, fearless of man.

Humans did not walk alone and defenseless.

She sulked, complaining he was too noisy, that she couldn't hear the forest talk when he stomped around in his big boots. He argued the forest didn't talk and if she heard voices in her head, she was officially nuts. She glared and marched ahead, making him traipse behind her for miles.

They continued this odd hiking routine for eight days.

Even since they buried Ryan.

Therapy? Riley could only guess. Although they shared the same bed again and shared beautiful evenings in each other's arms, she was guarded now, extremely protective of her inner thoughts.

Today she slipped away to walk alone. He was riding Mirabelle in the arena when he realized his woodland sprite wife was gone. His gut clenched. Instincts made him hurry, grabbing his already loaded rifle. As always, his bowie knife hid inside his boot.

Damn Savannah for wandering around alone!

Stubborn woman!

She knew the mountain was dangerous. Didn't she care?

Galloping up the hill on Mirabelle, he checked Ryan's monument first. A fresh rose lay at the angel's feet. No Savannah.

Which way?

Following the well-worn trail across lush forested ridges so thick with trees and vegetation the sunlight became mere dappled shade, he finally found her in wild raspberry grove beside Wandering Creek.

From a distance, he watched her lips move. Jabbering away to herself, she picked wild raspberries and popped them into a purple stained mouth. Still talking through dribbling juice, Riley saw his name. A slight frown. Then an offhanded shrug and she ate more berries.

He could only imagine what she said.

220

To herself.

Crazy woman.

A big shadow moved at the edge of the meadow.

Riley's skin instinctively prickled.

A body immerged, twenty yards behind Savannah.

A grizzly! Grumpy from winter and...oh crap! She had a cub, tumbling recklessly through the ferns behind her. Shouldering his rifle, Riley held the beast square in his sites. He hated to kill that bear, but he'd shoot her down if she moved any closer to Savannah.

He'd only get one shot.

If that bear charged, Savannah would meet a bloody death.

The jabbering woodland queen flinched.

She knew that big Momma grizzly was there.

Still bent over, pursing her lips, Riley heard a single-note whistle. Suddenly, Savannah wasn't alone, after all. Zeus rolled like a lumbering ox to his feet. Those ridiculous looking bent branches weren't from a fallen tree; they were blissfully happy dog legs!

Zeus sauntered over offering his mistress a wide slobbery grin. Savannah gratefully rubbed a head so big, it make her hands seem childishly small. Wrapping her arms lovingly around the giant dog's neck, she leaned over and carefully lay astride Zeus. Her belly lay flat along his strong back. Her head near his, her legs dangled down his sides.

Zeus didn't object at all.

In fact, he seemed proud to carry Savannah.

That dog really was half horse.

Walking slowly, not from her weight, but for sheer gentle sense of calm that might bring their safety, Riley could see Savannah's mouth was still running. She couldn't hear her, but she kept talking to Zeus as though the two never sensed danger. With a sigh of relief, he watched the loyal Great Dane carry her out of the meadow, safely away from the bear and her cub.

Damn she scared the hell out of him!

He waited. Several moments later, the pair appeared on the trail, the woman walking now, patting and congratulating her rescuer.

"What the...? Are you following me?" She accused, hands on her hips. "Put down your gun, Riley."

He lowered the rifle. "You deserve a spanking."

She made a rude noise and scoffed.

"You know better than to wander around alone this time of year."

She laughed at his worries. "That bear didn't want a Savannah sandwich for lunch. She only wanted raspberry jam."

"Sure, now you speak grizzly bear?"

"The forest would have warned me if I were in danger."

Frustrated by her mystical nonsense he dismounted off Mirabelle. "Savannah, you talk like a crazy person. The forest isn't alive. It doesn't talk to you. There are no voices in the wind."

"No?" She innocently asked, approaching Mirabelle, stroking the sweet mare's silvery forelock, "Then what made you follow that trail to the creek? Why didn't you look for me in the meadows? Or along the path to Crystal Haven Lake? You know how much I love going there."

"Because…" he didn't know why he chose this particular trail. Logically the others made more sense. "It just felt right."

"See? The forest whispered it to you."

"Whatever." Snagging her lean waist, he hoisted her onto Mirabelle.

She squawked. Violet eyes were wide. Angry and startled, yet oddly pleased. As he swung her through the air she had gripped the saddle horn with both hands, landing with legs curled up in a squat. She was perched upon the saddle, feet planted where her butt should be.

"Cute."

"Damn it, Riley! Why'd you throw me up here?"

"Because. I wanted to. I know you want to ride again. Besides," he tipped his head and observed, "You make a very pretty bird perched upon that shiny silver dancing horse."

The indignant quarrel died on her pert lips. "You're a stubborn, confusing, irritating man."

"Right back at ya', Savage." Determined not to fight he stroked Mirabelle's smooth face, wishing he could tell Savannah how emotionally torn he felt inside, tell her everything he worried about, and trust her to understand.

Pride got in the way.

"Sit down. Carefully."

"If it hurts, you'll help me down?"

"Yes, but try first."

Holding her breath, Savannah gingerly lowered herself into the western saddle so her jean-clad bottom sat where it should and legs wrapped around Mirabelle's sides. It hurt, he could tell, but she didn't cry. Instead, fierce determination lit her face. He loved her raw courage. She hiss-breathed through the initial pain. Relaxing her legs, he knew the instant the pain disappeared. A brilliant smile lit her face.

"I did it."

"Good job. Can you ride alone?"

"No. It hurts to grip her sides with my knees, like I should."

"Just sit there. I'll lead her."

"There's room." She scooted forward in the saddle. "She's strong." Taking that as an invitation, he grabbed the sturdy western saddle horn and swung up behind her, gathered the leather reins, and turned the mare around.

"Where are we going?"

"Crystal Haven Lake. Its sunny today and the mountain peaks will be reflected in the water. Plus, it's the opposite direction from the bear."

She grinned and laced slim fingers into his hand holding her waist. "Thanks Riley. After being housebound all winter, I love being outside."

He hadn't considered that was the reason for this hiking nonsense. He just thought she was escaping to irritate him. He'd been wrong, making him realize how little he understood Savannah's wild heart.

Crystal Haven was a cool crescent of water a mile higher on the mountain, carved into the bedrock by year-round glaciers. During the winter, it was solid ice. In springtime, when the snowline receded a little, it became a glistening watery mirror, reflecting the grandeur of glacier covered majestic white peaks piercing the blue sky.

They spent the afternoon sitting beside the reflective water. They didn't talk much. Silence here seemed sacred; being here felt like a privilege. An eagle soared overhead, riding currents in lazy graceful circles.

The air this high was crisp and ultra-pure. It felt sublime.

Riley let Mirabelle graze. The mare greedily devoured virgin grass and tender clover growing beside the mirrored water. In the reflection, there were two silver mares. Finally, she stepped into the water, sending a million ripples across the crescent lake.

"You can take me home now." Savannah contritely consented. "I'm ready for walls and civilization again."

"Who should we ride when we come back tomorrow?" He nonchalantly asked, letting her know he respected her need for freedom.

"Mirabelle." A joyful smile joyful lit her pretty face.

"And the next day? Anyone else?"

She squealed with delight at the prospect of returning. "Voodoo." Naming his famous leggy reddish-black dancer who had starred in several movies. "That way both fancy ladies can visit the gateway to heaven."

He glanced at the perfect double image of the mighty glacial peaks reflected in the pristine blue lake and agreed; this really was Montana heaven at its finest. Crystal Haven definitely lived up to its name.

"We could ride Merlin too. He's strong enough for two riders."

"I love you, Riley."

He kissed her, trying to prove he loved her too. Her grateful smile was beautiful. That night, she wrapped her arms around him and didn't let go until morning. At dawn when Riley woke with her sleek body nestled in his arms, he knew he couldn't tame Savannah.

But he could love her.

Was loving her enough?

*Leslie D. Stuart*

# Chapter Nineteen

"Why Mirabelle?!' She raged, infuriated Riley suddenly decided to sell the beautiful mare after they had enjoyed a dozen blissful rides in the forest to Crystal Haven Lake. "Sell that rich lady Jinx or Absolute, not Mirabelle!"

Unfazed, Riley continued saddling his favorite dapple-gray dancer. He hated to sell Mirabelle. He had no choice. It put a lump in his throat. Avoiding, he glanced past Savannah at the Montana hillside. April flowers and velvet clover covered verdant pastures where horses grazed in sublime contentment. Free food.

Thank heavens for something that didn't cost his last dime.

"Can't keep them all."

"But I love her! She's special! Sell her to me!"

He turned around, glaring at his obstinate wife. "You can't afford her." He coldly informed. "Mercedez will be here soon. Stop giving me grief. I have business to take care of."

"Mercedez? That's her real name? That's a car."

"Well in California people name their kids whatever they want. Go clean the kitchen and prepare several guest rooms on the second floor. The people transporting Mirabelle to California will stay here tonight. And be civilized. Mercedez is a highbred lady with money. She deserves our respect."

Stomping away, Savannah did as Riley ordered, making Graystone sparkle and shine. She heard a big truck arrive, but ignored it. Then she heard a flirtatious feminine laugh. Business? That didn't sound professional. Stealthily, she crept unnoticed toward the stables.

"Well, well…we meet again," the buxom blonde wearing designer skinny jeans and a bra-revealing flimsy pink blouse walked toward her husband. "Riilley Rosemmont," she seductively enunciated his name, drawing it out with a lusty purr. Strolling toward him like a huntress on the prowl, she lazily trailed manicured fingers down his chest, "it's been a long time. Miss me?"

A dagger of jealousy speared Savannah's soul.

225

The woman was stunning! Curvy as a road race, spoiled to the core, she oozed money. And was purposely giving her husband a generous view of creamy cleavage!

Hell, those weren't breasts!

They were plastic balloons designed for sexual pleasure.

And Riley wasn't immune.

She could practically see his mind screech to a halt.

"Hello there." Savannah nonchalantly stepped around the wall, offering a charming feline smile meant to wither that seductive rich jezebel. "You must be Mercedez."

Without answering the blonde socialite princess cattily assessed her slim ordinary figure from head to toe, deciding the brunette country bumpkin wearing an ordinary pink tee and plain denim jeans wasn't a female threat.

She promptly turned her attention back to the man, ignoring Savannah as if she were beneath her notice. Although Riley wasn't touching her at all with his hands, Mercedez kept her perfect claws planted right on his chest.

Why didn't he shove her away? What was this?

Had he slept with Mercedez? Did he lie about being faithful?

"So, you two know each other." Savannah prodded, eyeing her husband. "How interesting."

Riley didn't like this: not that predator gleam in Savannah's violet eyes or being cornered by Mercedez, who obviously thought the one time he took her to dinner in hopes of getting solid information about buying good broodmares was somehow a romantic interlude.

What he thought would be a simple business transaction had very quickly become an unexpectedly perverse situation. Mercedez sashayed up to him, gleaming of lust and flashing skin before he even realized her intentions.

And he had been caught.

Red-handed. Well, no. His hands awkwardly hung by his sides, but still. This wasn't good. He saw in Savannah's eyes her exact assumption: she thought he lied about being faithful, which made everything between them a lie.

This was bad.

Finally thinking straight, he stepped away from the faux blonde minx with a wallet too fat and morals too thin.

Way away. To the other side of the corridor. His back was against the wall. "Don't be rude, Savi."

"Am I? I'm terribly sorry. It was not my intention." Innocently, she offered a sweet cherubic smile.

His spine bristled. Savannah was madder than he had ever seen. Contained. She wouldn't yell. Oh no, that would be far too kind.

She was going to humiliate him to death.

"I just came out here to see if there was anything else you needed, Riley." She sweetly and subserviently purred, as if satisfying his needs were her highest priority in life. "I see your guest is a personal acquaintance. I hope our humble accommodations at Graystone Heights will meet with the lady's approval. Shall I prepare something special for dinner?"

"She's only here to buy Mirabelle." He gruffly reminded both women, a little too late. "The guest rooms are fine."

"Guest rooms?" Savannah coyly questioned, eyeing the other woman's playgirl figure. "Oh right. For her drivers." She half-laughed as if she'd made a joke and everyone knew whose bed Mercedez would share. "How many men did you bring?" She pretended to count the men obediently waiting by the flashy Cadillac Escalade limo and luxurious horse carrier.

"Four men. Good. I prepared enough rooms. Gee, they look hungry. And thirsty. Bet those men can drink a lot of beer. Looks like Graystone will be a busy place tonight." She chattily observed. "I should drive into town." At a loss for words, he made a noise to object. "But we want your guests to be happy, Riley."

"I don't drink. Neither do you. We don't need beer. Besides, you wouldn't even know what kind to buy."

"I'll ask them."

"Oh my…" Mercedez pursed her lips. Obviously annoyed by the intrusion, she was trying to appear contrite. "Have I inconvenienced you...uh, Savi?"

"Savannah. Riley never properly introduced us."

Eyes a shade too intensely bright blue studied her. Colored contacts. Was anything about that superficial woman real? Mercedez clearly had her nose done. It looked like a child's nose on an adult face. Makeup perfect, she smelled like flowered money.

And those breasts!

Holy hell almighty, you could see every lurid detail through a ridiculously sheer blouse that was open about three buttons too many. She wore a lace bra underneath that looked about as useful as cotton candy.

No wonder Riley stared!

Who the hell walked around like that?! In broad daylight! With strangers gaping! Savannah shuddered to imagine what Mercedez might wear around people she intimately knew...gold tassels and a whip maybe? Uugh!

"You know, Savannah, you look like someone quite famous. Arianna Hartwell." Mercedez purred as if the name were decadent gold. "I swear you could be her sister." Her over-whitened smile beamed as if the comparison to the famous composer was a tremendous compliment to a plain-Jane nobody from northern Montana.

"Really."

"Oh, sure."

"What do you know about her?"

"I watched Arianna perform. Several times. Such a fabulous pianist. I have every song she's ever written. It's amazing how much you look like her."

Mercedez gushed in false flattery. "That thick glossy brown hair, that's what it is. Arianna's hair is just extensions, but look at you..." she reached out to touch it. Savannah slithered away, avoiding the hand. "Yours is like chocolate silk."

"Arianna's hair is real." She defended.

"Oh, you've heard of her! You really think her hair is real? Hmm. Maybe. She was just stunning on stage. So passionate. Her music brought tears to my eyes." Mercedez merrily recalled, not noticing Savannah's fists had balled up in cold rage.

Last year I flew to New York City to see her. At Carnegie Hall, she performed with this adorable little boy. He played the violin. So cute! But poor Arianna was in a terrible car accident. She was in intensive care for weeks. Then she mysteriously disappeared." Mercedez leaned forward as if sharing a dark secret, "Suffered a mental breakdown. A real tragedy. Her music was so marvelous."

"His name was Ryan."

"Was?"

Violet eyes glistening, Savannah whirled around. She ran all the way back to the house. Riley heard the front door slam.

Then another door slammed, somewhere inside.

"What a peculiar woman. She likes you, Riley. But then, who wouldn't?" Before he could react Mercedez strut forward, effectively corning him against a paddock door to resume their bizarre liaison. "Who was that? Your estate manager? Your housekeeper?"

Watching her pert sculpted face reflect not a single ounce of compassion for the tears even a fool would have seen in Savannah's eyes, Riley wondered how anyone could be so self-involved. And just plain dumb.

"Arianna Hartwell. My beautiful talented wife."

Riley almost enjoyed her stricken gasp and truly horrified expression. She stumbled away from him. Good thing, too. He was tempted to shove her back. Hard. Except that required touching a body that had been around the world more times than the space shuttle, and he would rather not contaminate himself.

"But...you called her Savi."

"Arianna was her stage name," he proudly proclaimed, knowing nothing he originally planned for today was going to turn out right. Solutions to problems had somehow spawned even bigger problems.

"Her real name is Savannah Graystone-Rosemont. My wife. She grew up here. Graystone Heights belonged to her father."

"She's your...seriously? Arianna lives here?"

"Yes. Savannah does live here. With me. Married people do that." He enforced. "Ryan was my son. Our son. Our son died in that accident." Riley solemnly informed her. "Savannah didn't have a breakdown. She just came home."

All the blood drained from the golden harlot's face. A manicured fist clutched dramatically at her heart.

"Oh…my…god. I should apologize."

They both heard Savannah's jeep engine roar. "Too late."

Through the open stable doors Riley watched her tires spin, throwing gravel all over creation, pelting the bizarre SUV limo and extravagant horse carrier. Thunk! Whap! The rock storm her spinning tires flung across the yard made the hired hands run for cover.

"But Riley," she pouted, looking thoroughly deceived. "I thought you were single. I thought offering to sell me Mirabelle was just an excuse to see me. I thought you wanted…"

He sadly shook his head at her presumptuous notions.

"But when we met you weren't wearing a ring."

"I am now." He held up his left hand, but knew that wide gold band meant absolutely nothing to her. The only thing that deterred Mercedez from her visceral full-frontal sexual assault on a man too dim-witted to see trouble coming was the great musical icon, Arianna Hartwell.

"Isn't this awkward." She giggled as if the incident were simply a humorous byline to tell her country club friends.

Riley wasn't smiling.

She pouted like an arrogant movie star. "You seriously have a wife? And a son?"

"I did." He scowled, wondering where Savannah was going. Definitely not to buy beer. Bow and arrows maybe, so she could sit in the hills and torture him with a slow and painful death. Or a hatchet to drive into his thick skull. Or bullets for her pistol.

She'd left Zeus. He sat in the driveway staring forlornly down the road, which meant she would eventually return.

Damn dog would probably sit there waiting until she did.

"Don't worry about it. My complicated life isn't your problem. Let's introduce you to Mirabelle. The *only* reason I called."

"Uh, well…actually, I think I should go." She was already backing away. "Arianna Hartwell. My god. In Montana. Here. Of all places. I love her music, Riley. I've always wanted to meet her, but she's so private. She never attends celebrity receptions. She's a legend. And what do I do the minute we meet? I insulted her. And worse! I planned to sleep with her husband."

He was too shocked to respond properly. "What about Mirabelle?"

"I wanted you." She offhandedly shrugged. "If fifty-thousand dollars for a dancing Spanish Andalusian was the price I had to pay, then so be it."

Riley was aghast, choking on her filthy truth. "You flew into Montana, hired those men to drive Mirabelle all the way back to Los Angeles, and you were willing to pay fifty grand just so you could sleep with me?"

It was the sleaziest thing he'd ever heard.

Hands planted on curvy hips, she didn't apologize. "I knew it wouldn't last," she nervously clarified. A low disapproving rumble escaped Riley's burning chest, "I just figured we could fool around and have some fun."

"So you waltzed in here and turned on the charm, expecting I'd throw you down in the hay and oblige this little fantasy?"

"I was hoping for a big bed, actually." She tartly replied, glancing at Graystone's towering presence. "And a fireplace. But hay might be interesting. Besides, men don't refuse me." Perfectly groomed fingers tapped her hips, waiting for him to comply. "Not even you."

That haughty smirk on her face made him furious.

"Get out!"

"Hey, that's not fair. Until Aria…Savannah disturbed us; you were red-hot and rearing to go. I saw it in your eyes. You just couldn't decide which part of me you wanted first!"

"Then you read me wrong, lady! You've confused attraction with shock and disgust. You need to leave Graystone. Now!"

Obviously, no one insulted her, either.

Perfect face screwed into an ugly pout. "I want my horse!"

"Mirabelle isn't for sale." Grabbing her upper arm, Riley firmly escorted Mercedez out of his stables. "And neither am I."

Leaving that spoiled blonde spluttering obscenities no lady would ever utter and her men scrambling to remove themselves from his property, Riley turned on his heel, walked back into the stables, and firmly closed the doors.

Good lord…what just happened?

He thought he was simply selling a horse.

Things went upside-down fast.

Was his wife going to say? Or worse…do?

\*\*\*

Savannah was back. Riley heard the front door angrily slam. The heels of her boots tap-tapped across oak floors. Working in his office, he tried to ignore her, but it was hard.

She was a noisy little thing.

For nearly an hour, he listened to boots stomp as she scoured the house for her belongings. Muttering like a crazy person unhinged, Savannah marched upstairs. A few minutes later, boots trotted down oak treads again. Her leg was strong now, not a hint of hesitation in those indignant footsteps. Back and forth, she made noisy trips to her jeep, just daring him to say a word.

Must be moving day.

Listening to it made him furious.

Now here she was, marching into his office like hell's fury.

"What's this?" Riley barked as Savannah vehemently slapped a thick black briefcase onto his desk. "Too small to be a suitcase."

"Payment for services rendered, you mule-headed jackass!" Popping open the leather lid, she held it up and swiveled more cash under his stunned nose than he'd ever seen. "Now we're even."

Riley's mind stumbled. "Even? For?"

Disgusted by her husband's obvious mental deficiencies, she spitefully flopped the open briefcase onto the mahogany desktop. It dropped with a thud. Several thick stacks of twenties tumbled out. She snagged them and shook the fat bundle in his face. "Seven month's rent on lodging at Graystone Heights at current New York luxury penthouse rates equals thirty-five thousand dollars."

"But that's…"

"I'm not finished." Savannah grabbed another handful of money and rudely smacked it down on the desk. "Food, escort services, and compensation for your valuable time and obvious suffering: another forty grand."

Smack went the stack of money.

Thud went his heart.

"Gratuity for saving my wretched life," she furiously waved another bundle in the air, "fifty thousand dollars; the same amount I receive for one lousy piano performance."

Smack.

"Fifty thousand?" He tried to sound cool and calm. "For a few hours at the piano?" Did he sound cool? Not really. Lowering his voice, Riley struggled to keep from sounding utterly thunderstruck. "Seriously?"

"Sometimes more. Music pays big bucks."

"Obviously."

Leaning closer, she resumed her vindictive tirade. "Hospital fees for being my reluctant attending physician and payment for my physical therapy sessions with your horses: another sixty-five thousand. Although I docked you a bit for your atrocious bedside manner."

Raging like Medusa scorned, she upended the entire briefcase onto his desk. "The rest is for Zeus. Maybe ten grand seems a bit much for a dog, but money can't buy love and that dog loves me, so he's mine! There. Two hundred thousand dollars. Cash."

She straightened and glared, waiting for a fight. Hands on her wonderfully curvy hips, Savannah looked nothing at all like the cheap vixen he'd recently tossed out of here. She looked like a proud queen handing down her final verdict.

He was a more than a little in awe.

"Nothing to say, Mountain Man?"

"Nope."

"Good! Now, I'm taking my one lousy friend in this world and we're leaving this god-forsaken place! Goodbye, Riley!"

He didn't know if he should laugh or cry. She looked so frightening and beautiful. His heart ached. He was losing her. Forever, this time.

She deserved to know the truth about Crystal.

231

Savannah deserved to know the truth about so many things.

He didn't know where to begin.

Nothing ever went right between them.

"I won't take your last penny, Savage." He gently declared.

"Pfft. It isn't." Violet eyes sarcastically rolled. "I'm loaded. Residual sales alone keep my bank accounts very happy. 'Second Chances' was recorded in five languages and commissioned by some pop star princess I'm sure you've never heard of. Her sappy romantic version became the theme song for 'Some Angels Fall'. You know: that tragically hip happily-ever-after blockbuster love story that broke hearts and Hollywood ticket sales. It only made about a gazillion dollars. Of which, I get a fat percentage."

Trying to keep his eyes from falling out of his empty skull, Riley casually leaned back, lacing his hands behind his head as though he couldn't care less. The old leather executive chair's metal wheels squeaked.

"Then don't toss me your chump change and expect that we're square. You want to leave me? Then become my business partner, Lady Big-Bucks. I need another new barn for all the pregnant mares Merlin seduced over Christmas. I'm expecting eighteen colts. Training them will require more time and energy than I've got. I need an investment partner. Two hundred thousand sounds about right to seal that partnership. In two years, I'll buy you out again. We'll get the marriage annulled all nice and quiet. Then...you can leave."

"Two more years? Are you out of your mind?" She raged, stomping her foot. "Walk downstairs by yourself," she imitated his low voice, "then you can leave Graystone." The dark rendition of his prior demands was accurate, and not very kind.

"Play the piano, Savage. Then you can leave. I promise." Flinging her hands in frustration she glowered, "I can't play music! It's gone!"

Marching around the solid oak desk separating them, Savannah grabbed the arms of his rolling chair and shoved it with such force he almost fell on the floor. "Live, Savannah! Walk, Savannah! Play the piano! Maaarrrry me! Oh wait," she tipped her head and cheekily added, "marriage didn't make you happy either. I can't please you!" Leaning over him, just inches away, she snarled. "Become your business partner. Is that all I have to do, Riley?"

"Pretty much."

"You break my heart."

"Likewise."

"Did you sleep with Mercedez?"

"No."

"Liar!"

"Believe what you want. Partner," he gruffly added, clarifying the boundaries of their business relationship. "Now take your stinky giant dog and make yourself useful. You know what needs to be done around here. Pick a job to do. Make a difference instead of constantly making me sorry. I'll have my attorney draw up the papers."

Her bottom lip puckered. Releasing his chair, she stepped back. For a second, Riley knew she wanted to plop on the floor and cry. But her chin stubbornly tightened. Eyes gleamed. Shoulders squared in defiance.

"I want to live at Graystone. The top floor is mine. All mine! You can't come up there. Ever!"

"Fine. Then you'll never be late for work."

As she stomped out, slamming his office door with all of her might, Riley finally decided how to react to Savannah's vehement tirade. She's meant to cut deep and rip their lives apart forever, but it only made him more grateful for her and had inadvertently bound them tighter together.

He would cry.

Reopening the ledger book he just spent three hours stressing over, wondering how he was possibly going to pay all those outstanding bills, he stared at the red numbers in the accounts payable column and the money strung recklessly across the desk, eyes stinging. Two hundred thousand dollars. Fingering a thick stack of twenties, for a several aching heartbeats he just couldn't breathe.

He owed the feed store at least nine thousand, probably more. The grocery kept a running tab, so did his dad's store. He paid whenever he could, which wasn't nearly often enough. Shaky didn't even begin to describe his finances. Bankrupt was more like it. Mortgaged to the hilt so he could remodel the stables and buy more horses, his utilities bills habitually ran a month past due. The Avalanche needed new tires and a suspension overhaul.

He wasn't kidding about needing the new barn. He'd need it built before next winter. Thanks to Merlin's friendliness over Christmas, his herd was going to double and he needed to keep those valuable horses safe from the cold. Eventually those sweet young foals would grow into rough and rowdy yearlings, needing a space of their own away from Momma.

Now, he could pay for it all.

She was his miracle.

And his curse.

*Leslie D. Stuart*

# *Chapter Twenty*

"I just came to say goodbye, Sam." Savannah sadly announced to the gray retired cowboy who was comfortably lounging on his front porch, sipping iced tea and watching the evening sun begin its final decent across the sky.

"You're leaving?" He stood and ambled down the porch steps. "But honey, Montana is your home."

"Not anymore." What drew her to the Lawson ranch? Saying goodbye was sentimental silliness. She should driving away from here, leaving Montana forever.

"What about Riley?"

"We're splitting the sheets. Riley found someone else a whole lot prettier and sophisticated to tickle his fancy."

"That rich California blonde that bought Mirabelle?"

Her jaw dropped. "You know Mercedez?"

"We've met." Sam scowled with distaste, "Don't tell me Riley was dumb enough to actually buy what that wanton woman was selling."

"He was, uh…window shopping."

The man who by his heart and deeds was Savannah's real father, rocked back on his heels and naughtily grinned. "So what did Riley do? Grab a handful of that plastic cleavage Mercedez flaunts to every man with eyes and melt like a fool when she purred sexual favors in his ear?"

"Good grief, Sam! Were you hiding in the stables this morning? Riley hadn't done anything. Yet. But he couldn't keep his eyes in his head."

"Oh. Well. It happens," he sagely established, slinging one arm around her shoulders. "Men are real slime of the earth, you know. 'Specially when some immoral hussy offered ya' a free lunch."

She reluctantly grinned. "You're vulgar."

"Nah. Just calling it how I see it. Met that woman few years back, when Riley was buying his first good broodmares. We'd all gone to this big horse show filled with rich folks and fancy pedigree horses. Mercedez was there trottin' around, showin' off her assets."

"She has big round assets."

Sam made as face, proving he wasn't impressed.

"God didn't make those. Man did. Mercedes got one look'a Riley and decided he was the stud she wanted to tame. Waltzed up to him all cutsy-like, offerin' information on good bloodlines and horses she knew were for sale. She acted all helpful and sweet, you know, trying to make everyone like her. But I saw her eyein' Riley like he was dessert. And earlier Millie saw her kissin' on a man older than me. Dirty woman," he fairly spat in disgust, "No self-respecting man wants candy like that."

"I interrupted before Riley could decide."

Releasing her shoulders, he stepped over to the porch and grabbed his gray sweat-stained Stetson that had seen better days. Mulling over their situation, Sam put the cowboy hat on his head. "So...sounds to me like you got a little jealous and Riley got caught with his pants still up, but his morals way down."

"Pretty much."

"Is that worth splittin' up over?"

Savannah shrugged and looked away.

Anyone could see there were deeper issues at work here, but Sam didn't push. "Well, ya' gotta at least stay one night with us, honey. My sweet Melinda would pitch a fit if she got home from town and missed seeing you." Without asking if she wanted to, they began to walk toward the stables. "Feeding time." Sam offhandedly commented. "Wanna help?"

"Sure." Quietly following along, Savannah found herself offering two dozen hungry horses extra handfuls of grain, rubbing grateful nickering foreheads, and admiring the fine stock of Spanish Andalusians' housed in Sam's stables.

"Are all these horses Riley's?"

"Yep. Yours too, I reckon."

"Mine?!" She was tempted to throw the grain bucket clear across the stables. "Is Riley gloating already? Dang! I just dumped that money on his desk no more than an hour ago."

"Money?" Sam looked confused. "For what?"

"To make us even. But what does he do? He turned it all around on me. I thought we'd be finished forever, but he coldly took that two hundred thousand dollars without a bit of guilt. Then that confusing man made me his business partner! The nerve of that man!"

"Business partner?" Tilting back his cowboy hat, Sam arched a brow and scratched his graying head. "Hell honey, you stayed away from these mountains too long."

"What's that supposed to mean?"

"By my way of thinking, the moment you married that man you became his partner. In life. In money. And in everything else God tosses your way."

"Oh. Gee." The bucket dropped from her hand. It made a loud plop and didn't tip over, but the sudden fall sent a golden spray of grain bursting like tiny fireworks that landed on the clean cement floor. "I did, didn't I?"

"Yep. Sounds to me like Riley just accepted what was already half-his and redefined the rules a little."

"He did." Embarrassed by her vengeful thoughts and actions, Savannah cuffed the spilled grain with her toe. "Boy, I feel dumb."

"Did you know Riley was hurting for cash?"

"No." Her stomach hurt.

"He's mortgaged to the hilt, Savi."

"Why? Graystone Heights was paid for."

"He had to refinance and use Graystone as collateral just to renovate the stables and the arena. Your daddy left a pile o' debt behind. Riley paid it all by sellin' the ski equipment, turned Graystone into a game preserve so he got those federal grants. He took care o' the past, but his financial future is mighty shaky. Now Riley can't sell anymore colts until they get properly trained, but he's got more bills to pay than one man can handle."

"That's why he sold Mirabelle," she reluctantly realized. "He needed to stay afloat for a while longer."

"Yep. You know Riley didn't want to. That dancing mare is his favorite. Probably did it just prayin' God might send somethin' his way to make things right."

"Oh, Sam." A stinging stunned breath whoosh-whooshed through her guilty lungs. "God sent me!"

"Appears so."

"I made a mess."

"Sounds like ya' tossed that money at him all mean-like, expecting Riley had too much pride to actually take it. When your husband did take that money and actually swallowed his stubborn pride, you decided to walk away, no goodbye or explanation. Just one last big fight with a bunch of shouting and slamming doors."

Ashamed to the core, she looked at her feet and didn't answer.

Sam knew them both too well.

"Riley never yelled. Only me."

"Whatch'a gonna do about this mess?"

"I don't know. Maybe I need to swallow my pride too."

Letting Savannah stew for a while, the old man finished feeding horses. Zeus and the contrite woman followed him. The sun was setting. The Montana sky had turned a luscious coral pink that highlighted the mountains.

"Two hundred thousand ain't nothing to you, is it honey?"

"Not really. I made a fortune with my music."

"And here your poor worried husband is struggling just to keep a roof over your heads," Sam gently chastised in a fatherly tone, "living off last year's savings and too damn proud to tell you the truth. He gives up being a Doc 'cuz death tears him up inside. But raising those horses is expensive and paydays are few and far between. Aren't you two a ridiculous pair? Pushing and tuggin' at life instead of embracin' it."

"When was the last time Riley sold a horse?"

"Let's see…" he rubbed his stubbly chin, "last June he sold two mares. But they weren't good dancers like Mirabelle; just regular show horses. Didn't sell for as much."

"Dang. Almost a year? That's a long time."

"Yup. You could'a just offered that money real nice, honey." She nodded, knowing it was true. "He would'a been eternally grateful."

"I didn't know he needed it. He seems fine. I never realized Riley doesn't have any income. We don't discuss money. I never even considered Riley might need my help." She kicked the dirt again. "I was just being hateful because of stupid Mercedez."

"He didn't touch her, did he?" It was a fact, not an actual question.

"Not while I was there."

"And I'd bet my ranch Riley didn't touch her afterward, neither."

"What about before I came back to Montana?" She questioned, trusting her godfather's reply. "Did he sleep with her?"

"Hell no. Riley ain't never touched anyone but you, darlin'. He may be struggling to let go of the past, but that man loves you, through and through."

She believed him. Hugging her stomach, she felt nauseatingly flu-ish with guilt. "I'm a terrible wife. It was ugly, Sam. I made a big scene. I acted like a spoiled rotten child. This is bad. Oh, gee. I royally screwed up."

"Sounds like you both have. If he'd trusted you with his truth, none of this would'a happened. Pride. That's the problem. Pride kicks us in the ass, every damn time."

At that moment, a truly sinister squeal of fury rang out, followed by angry smashing of metal. Thump, thump, whack! It kicked so hard it shook the entire enclosure.

"Good Lord, what's wrong with that horse?"

"That's Hitler."

"What an awful name."

"He's earned it. Some creatures are just born hateful."

Walking closer to peer through the steel slats, Savannah saw a beautiful silver-white Andalusian stallion attacking the high walls of his circular prison. Well, not quite white; he was grubby from neglect and streaked with dirt. His thick mane and long tail were a hopeless thicket of tangles. Taller than most, even taller than Merlin, his withers were probably nineteen hands high. Wow. A six-foot-four horse. His back was taller than Riley! Hitler's broad chest and muscular sides were mottled with small scars that on a white horse, always turned into a tell-tale line of black. In the evening light, he truly looked silver. And slightly evil.

"What's he mad about?"

"Everything. Born white as an angel, with a soul black as sin. Riley did his best to gentle him as a colt, but Hitler bit a chunk out'a Riley's hide one too many times. He finally gave up tryin'. Now he doesn't really know what to do with him. Hitler's too ornery to tame and too special to put down, so we keep him caged. But if Hitler ever gets out, he'll kill anything that crosses his path."

"Besides being gorgeous and utterly insane, why is he special, Sam?"

"He's Diablo's last son. His Momma was Starlight."

"Ohhh." An electric quiver of higher awareness fluttered through her. A divine answer; the reason she felt inexplicably drawn here to say goodbye to Sam. "Between Diablo and Starlight, Hitler is pureblood Andalusian royalty." A true Spaniard, tracing back a hundred years. "He's so silvery-white, even filthy he still shines."

An idea sparked.

The ache of regret cramping her belly eased.

"God, Sam..." she single-mindedly breathed, already making plans. "Colts from Hitler would sell for three times what the others do. Merlin's foals are pretty and sweet as angels, but people worship those pure white ones."

"Yep. The white ones look like magic doing those fancy dance steps in the show ring. It's a waste, really. All that muscle and beauty and..."

Standing high upon a ladder, leaning over Hitler's impermeable steel fence, Sam stopped tossing clean straw into the stable and looked down at her. Savannah just grinned and rubbed her hands together in anticipation.

"Oh, no you don't!"

Hustling back down the ladder with the agility of a far younger man, Sam shook his finger in her face and scolded. "I see that look in your eye. You stay away from Hitler!"

"Ahh, Sam. He's just a horse."

"I mean it! This isn't Diablo! That beast loves no one; not even himself! Riley would kill me if something happened to you!"

"Nah. He would rejoice."

"Stay away. That horse is evil."

"I have to try." Divine guidance had spoken, showing her a way through stormy shadows and into light. "Will you help me? Please?"

"I will not!" Her honorary cowboy father puffed his chest and looked deeply offended she dare ask for his assistance on a suicide mission.

"Fine. I'll do it all by myself."

"Savannah! Damn it!" She just softly laughed while Sam fumed. "You are not too big for me to bend over my knee and paddle."

"I'm only watching him," she sweetly justified, "That's all. There's no crime in watching, is there?"

239

Peering through those narrow-slatted steel bars again, she watched Hitler ruthlessly toss around the hay Sam had dumped inside the stable. Powerful front legs pawed, flinging pieces into the air. He angrily slung the hay round as if it wasn't fit to eat.

Savannah grinned.

She just found an excuse to stay.

And maybe a way to make things right.

\*\*\*

"Hey, Doc?" a familiar gravely cowboy's voice on Riley's cell phone demanded, "you need to get over here. We've got trouble brewin' with Hitler."

"Geezus Sam, what the hell has that evil stallion done now?"

Riley grabbed his truck keys, striding out the front door, almost grateful for something to do besides wonder if he'd ever see Savannah again. "I knew he was bad blood, not worth keeping. Whatever he's done, I'll pay for it."

"Ain't done nothing. Yet. The two of them," Sam muttered, chuckling softly under his breath, "like a pair of sleeping scoundrels."

"What? You sound drunk, Sam."

"Nah, but I am dawg-tired. Dawg…ha-ha." The old man chuckled, finding that funny too. "Just get your ass over here before all hell breaks loose. I won't be held responsible for whatever that insane beast does when he wakes up, and I'm not riskin' my neck to save your stubborn business partner."

Gunning the Avalanche's big engine, Riley roared down the dirt road linking his ranch with Sam's, throwing rocks and gravel everywhere. "My partner?" He questioned, looking at the cellphone in his hand, wondering if he heard Sam right. "I don't have a…" he suddenly felt incredibly stupid. Somehow, Sam knew about their fight. "What the hell has Savannah done?"

"Well gee, Son, if I tell you, it'll ruin the surprise."

"Is she there?"

"Hell Riley, can't you keep track of your own wife?"

Damn if that old codger didn't laugh.

Riley snapped his cellphone shut.

So that's where she went. Savannah was at Sam's all this time, leaving Riley to worry and prowl the house. Alone. Five days she had been gone. He thought she had left his life forever. She packed everything she owned inside that jeep.

She even took Zeus.

Ten thousand dollars for a worthless mutt. Insane.

Swearing and driving like a maniac, twenty minutes later Riley roared into Sam Lawson's quiet stables in a blaze of raging dust. The old man sat in a rocking chair on the sprawling front porch of his brick ranch house, sipping coffee, grinning like a sleepy scraggly-faced Cheshire.

"Mornin' Doc. Looks like you're racin' to put out a fire."

"Where's my wife?" He barked, in no mood for games.

"Out yonder." Sam jauntily flipped a weathered hand in a vague direction of the stables. "Been here hauntin' my ranch for days. Your half-horse giant dog too. Actually," the cowboy rubbed his scruffy gray chin, "Zeus is her dog, now. Isn't he?"

"I guess so."

Sam looked like he hadn't slept in days. Or shaved. His clothes were clean, but judging by the dusty smudges on his weathered face, Riley wasn't so sure about the cleanliness of the man wearing them.

"I kept telling her to leave that damn thing alone." Sam dryly commented, ambling down the front steps. "But day and night, she just stood there, talking away as if it actually understood. That stubborn woman never listens." He softly laughed, far too amused with life for Riley's taste. "But then, you know that, don't ya' Doc?"

"I do. What has she done, Sam?"

"She's just sleepin'." He grinned as they walked, shaking his head at Riley's highly agitated state. "Pretty as a picture. A miracle, really."

"Savannah is performing miracles?"

"Yep. Just like old times."

Following the bowlegged horseman toward an oversized circular arena that stood a safe distance away from all the others, its twelve-foot tall steel barred fence was maliciously bowed in odd places, as if the enclosure walls struggled to cage one of Satan's most ferocious minions.

"Now be real quiet, or you'll get us all killed."

Peering through the narrow slats of reinforced steel fence, expecting to see bloody horseflesh scattered all over the arena or an insane monster waiting to take a chunk out of his hide, Riley's heart stopped cold.

There, curled up inside the oversized paddock was Savannah.

Her long glossy dark chocolate colored hair tumbled across the yellow straw like silken sheet. And she slept nestled atop the biggest, meanest, most untouchable silver-white stallion that ever galloped the earth.

Once, she had probably draped comfortably over his back, but she'd slid forward and to the side. Now she mostly covered his ribs. Hitler was flopped over quite undignified on his side, letting the side of his body be Savannah's mattress. The deadly hooves of that formidable horse were inches away from her legs.

If he stood, Hitler would crush her.

But they were both breathing deep and slow; utterly content, sleeping together like exhausted children. Her delicate hands twined possessively into his thick mane. Her peaceful face rested against his powerful neck.

Heart racing, Riley suddenly realized the brown eyes of that fearsome horse were open, staring right at him, with truly evil intent.

But Hitler didn't move a muscle. He just blinked.

"Savannah," he whispered.

The horse issued a warning "Pfffft."

"Mmm," she murmured, "what is it, boy?"

Her legs slid bonelessly off the stallion's back and into the straw. She crumpled into a heap beside a horse so mean no one could touch him. Yawning as if awakening from the first sleep she had enjoyed in forever, Savannah rubbed her eyes with dirty fists and leaned lazily against Hitler's broad chest.

Sleepy violet eyes slowly opened.

Hitler still hadn't moved.

"Oh. It's you. Go away, Riley."

He silently urged her closer with one wagging finger.

"Why? So we can fight? No thanks." She slowly stood anyway. Testing her leg gingerly and finding it good, she brushed pieces of straw out of tangled hair and then stretched tight muscles in her back. Her face was dusty, clothes filthy, but pink cheeks were streaked with the tracks of heartbroken tears.

Freed from his grubby nighttime companion, Hitler the Supreme Commander of the Third Reich and Slayer of all Things Unworthy lifted his regal silver-white head and snorted another warning at Riley.

Savannah casually reached down and rubbed his forehead. The mighty horse sighed and dangerous legs stayed folded up in the straw.

In the corner, another shadow grumpily moved. Zeus. Noisily shaking his black coat clean, the giant dog sauntered right over to Hitler and licked the Furor's white muzzle. The damn thing softly nickered at Zeus; as if they were old trusted friends.

"What the…?"

Seeing Riley peering through the fence, Zeus wagged his tail and offered a wide slobbery grin, but didn't leave Savannah.

Traitor.

Watching Riley's stunned face, the lazily stretching loyal dog, and the devil horse that was sure to explode into action and slaughter them all, Savannah grinned. "Meet my official guardians. Bet that makes you mad too."

Reaching out toward Hitler, her small fist clenched a handful of wavy silver mane. She clucked her tongue and swift as an antelope she was perched on his back. Up she went, moving as one with a glorious wild stallion who now defiantly stood. Snorting and shaking his head at Riley, the evil towering horse dared him to make a move.

"Look. I'm riding. All. By. Myself. Happy?"

"Not really. Couldn't you have picked a nicer horse?"

"He picked me."

Bouncing a little, Hitler impatiently pawed deep chop marks into the ground, throwing straw several feet behind them. Savannah impishly grinned at her husband's displeased scowl. Pursing her lips, she made two little kiss sounds. Just like that, the triumphant stallion proudly tucked his chin into his chest and obediently pranced into the sunlit arena.

"Good God…"

Perched upon his powerful back, Savannah truly looked like a grubby little savage. In stark comparison, Hitler was clean and silvery-sleek, as if she spent days brushing him. The stallion arrogantly danced around the arena, muscles flexed in a militant show of intimidating force. She clucked and softly cooed, patting his proudly arching neck with loving hands.

"So good," she softly mewed. "So good."

Sliding back so she could lie flat along his withers, the crazy woman draped herself over Hitler's back. Burying her face in his silky white mane, she wrapped her arms around his neck in an affectionate hug.

"Such a good boy. So good."

The horse pawed the ground and danced sideways in apparent agreement.

Savannah sat up again and laughed. "You like dancing, don't you? So good." There was no saddle or bridle to control and break his spirit; but that willful beast acted as if he just understood her wishes.

It really was a miracle.

They made three full prancing circles of the big arena. Riley watched in awe. On the third round, he finally noticed she was directing Hitler by shifting her knees and giving corresponding little pats upon his withers.

If she pat on the right side and shifted that knee, he pranced right. Left side movements, and the Furor immediately moved at her command. It was subtle and extremely impressive. They turned circles and danced in a beautiful figure eight. She brought him to a halt several times, just by saying, "STOP." Savannah backed him up, "BACK," and everything that beast did right; she rewarded him with that dusky murmur of approval, "So good, so good."

Hitler didn't hesitate or resist her will. He just did it.

In fact, as Riley watched the stallion's ears flick and muscles flex in response to her voice, he realized Hitler eagerly wanted to please that grubby woman perched upon his silvery back.

She was in total control.

His wild heart had joined with Savannah's.

"Open the gate," she sharply commanded. "We're going home."

Reluctantly, Riley obeyed. He wasn't overly surprised when the deceptively docile monster snapped white teeth in warning as he slowly sauntered past, flaunting his glorious wild-hearted rider, but behaving for Savannah as tame as a worn out old mare.

Following at a safe distance, with defensive admiration, deep fear, and unreasonable fury all churning inside, Riley cringed as the stallion started prancing again. Hitler was a bomb burning to detonate.

Risking a good beating and a painful death, he stayed close, hoping he might save Savannah if that feral beast changed his mind about playing nice.

That horse hadn't tasted freedom since he was a yearling tearing apart stables, smashing everything within reach with snapping teeth and deadly

hooves. Riley didn't have the heart to put him down or sell him. He was
Diablo's last son. That still meant something. Not knowing what else to do with
Hitler, he caged the white devil-demon inside his own concentration camp.

Which only made The Furor more furious.

"How'd you do it, Savi?"

"Love. Remember love, Riley?"

With that, the wild horse flipped its silver-streaked tail in defiance. Rearing
straight up, Hitler pawed the air like a lightning-bolt warrior. Undaunted by the
terrifying display, Savannah sat upon his back like a statue, glaring icy-violet
tears at her husband. Hitler came down to earth again with thud. Shaking his
head, snorting like a white freight train, he looked eager to plow Riley down.

"Easy, boy." She softly soothed, rubbing that thick arching neck. Riding
with natural grace that would have made her Native American ancestors proud,
she was completely unshaken by the jerky threatening movements of her
prancing ride. Her leg was healed, strong now. Seeing it made Riley proud.
"Easy. We're fine. Riley isn't mad at you, Big Boy. Only me."

Great. Now she was telling Hitler their personal problems.

"Wanna run?" She asked the pawing stallion as he crow-hopped around in
small circles, reveling in his first day of freedom. But he was still restrained,
clearly waiting for permission. Oddly obedient, those thick-corded muscles were
bunched so tight with pent up energy he looked ready to explode.

"Okay, Champ. Let's burn off that anger."

Fists tightly clenching his silvery mane, she made that tiny kiss noise again.
Hitler sparked into action. Savannah's legs stayed glued to his sides. In a burst
of white-hot fervor, they galloped away. Hitler victoriously pounded the
Montana soil with thundering hooves. A wild woman rode his unadorned back
and a big black dog loped behind.

"Whoo-ee." Sam whistled in admiration. "She's a miracle, Doc."

"No. A curse." But as Riley watched them go, he didn't see a grubby
woman, feral white stallion, and lumbering black dog. He saw a dazzling
celestial archangel with gleaming brown hair riding a luminous shooting star.
And they were being chased by a trustworthy ebony guardian warrior.

He really was losing his mind.

"Ya' married her."

"I was stupid."

"You're wrong. Dead wrong." The man who'd practically raised Savannah
staunchly defended. "You two, you're each other's destiny. Always have been.
You can fight it Riley, but you're bein' a mule-headed fool. Go ahead; stay
angry she stole your son. Find reasons to push that loving woman away. But
pretending to blame Savannah for the sorrows of life is just lyin' to yourself. I
saw you watching her bouncing around on that horse. If that stallion made one
false move, you'd have taken him down with nothing more than your own bare
fists and possessive nature. Hitler didn't have a prayer."

244

"It's true."

"Admit it, son," Sam gently chastised, "even after all these years, all the heartache, and all the mistakes, she still holds your heart in the palm o'her pretty little hand."

"You know Sam, I think I was born loving and hating that woman."

"Eh, love and hate are always intertwined." Sam shrugged, "Just gotta decide which one to hold on to." Watching Savannah race away, he sighed. "She's so beautiful." The old man gazed fondly at the horizon where the white stallion galloped triumphantly across the ridge. Savannah's hair streamed like a banner behind them.

"It's just like when she was a teeny little girl and roamed these mountains on Diablo. No one worried. She was protected. Like some god-touched supernatural phenomenon."

"Wonderful. I'm married to Medusa." But Sam grinned and affectionately slapped his back, knowing Riley didn't mean it. "So, she told you our problems."

Sheepishly uncomfortable, Sam toed the dirt with his worn-out boot. "Didn't mean to jump in your business, Riley. And don't go thinking Savannah betrayed your trust, because she didn't," he staunchly defended. "But when a headstrong woman decides to spend five days and nights jabbering away to a beast that would rather kill her than listen, the man holding the rifle aimed at that demon's head can't help but listen too."

"Five days? And nights?"

"Yep. The first day I yelled at her to leave Hitler alone. Threatened to paddle her stubborn little butt. Kept shooing her away. Savannah stood outside that cage, talking like that horse actually understood. He charged her down a couple'a times, kickin' and hollerin' at that steel fence like something possessed. I swore I'd put a bullet in Hitler's head. But she begged me not to and just kept on talking. About everything. You, mostly. And your son. Heard all about her regrets, Riley."

"Sorry you had to listen."

"Nah, 'twas no hardship. Most the time I knew Savannah wasn't really talking to anyone at all. She was just tryin' to sort out the rights and wrongs of her life. She carries a powerful ache inside; misses Ryan something awful. Misses him every damn day. Even talked about how she wishes God would'a taken her instead of your beautiful son. But she's here, still livin' and God doesn't seem to want her. Even you saved her life."

"I had to. She came here to die, Sam."

"I heard. But she know giving up wasn't right either. She thinks God abandoned her, that He's making her pay for keeping Ryan a secret. She even lost her music. She feels empty inside. Now all she wants is your love. There are moments when she's real happy, but bitterness creeps back inside o' your heart and the past steals everything good from what you two have now. She thinks you blame her. She doesn't know how to fix it. It hurts to be so unforgiven. Regret is a powerful weight to carry, Riley, and she's tired of being punished. But she loves you somethin' fierce and can't let you go."

"I know. Me neither. I do love her, Sam. We're just all tangled up in each other. But we're tangled up inside too."

"Talkin' helps." The levelheaded horseman respectfully advised. "It's one thing Savannah's good at: talking."

"Not to me. She talks to Zeus and tells her life story to a demon horse."

Sam kindly smiled as he leaned back against the fence, watching Savannah disappear into the trees. "Me n' Melinda was like that too, in the beginning. Millie would gossip all hotheaded to your Momma instead a' working things out with me. But eventually, I learned to recognize the signs that something 'tween us was wrong. Instead'a gittin' mad, I'd make Millie take a walk with me. Before long, we were talking. Then those dumb little things stopped becoming such great big messes. Millie likes to talk when we walk. Something about puttin' one foot in front of the other gets everything else straight inside."

"Not Savannah. She likes to listen to the mountain."

"Does she? Her Daddy was like that. Said God whispered truth in the wind. Takes a smart woman to tune out herself and hear the pure flow of life instead. You should respect that. It's a gift. You can learn to hear God's whispers too," his friend wisely advised. "The hard part about listening to truth is to stop being mad. Doesn't help anyone. 'Specially the one being bitter."

"I hate feeling this way. I really do."

"Can't keep walls, Riley. It's breakin' her heart. Gotta let go of pride. Let go of the past. She's here, now, and she needs your love."

"I know. I guess you heard about Mercedez, too."

Chuckling, Sam mischievously grinned. "Sounded like you got yourself cornered by a hungry she-lion."

"I did. Didn't see it coming." Feeling dumb, Riley kicked a rock with his toe. "We were already fighting over selling Mirabelle. Savannah caught Mercedez turning on the charm...hell, I'm lucky she didn't grab my rifle and shoot me."

"Did ya' touch that woman?"

"Hell no! Except to grab her arm and escort her out of my stables! I didn't sell Mirabelle. I made Mercedez leave. But I never got a chance to tell Savannah. She was too busy packing and throwing money at me."

Envisioning it, Sam peered at him beneath the brim of a sweat-stained Stetson. "Are you mad about Savannah and Hitler?"

"A little." But the trusted cowboy-godfather wryly snickered, forcing Riley to admit the truth. "Okay. I'm furious. I have two stables full of perfectly tame horses. If she wanted excitement, Merlin is a big dopy dog compared to Hitler. But we get into a stupid fight and she comes running over here. I spent days worried sick about her. Just to spite me, Savannah picks the worst horse of the bunch and tames him! Rides him without even a saddle or a bridle. It's defiance. That's what this feels like. Proving me wrong, just because she could."

"Nah. Savannah's not spiteful. You know better than that."

Fuming, Riley didn't answer.

"Seems to me," Sam quietly drawled, "Those two were drawn together. Who knows why? By God's hand, probably. Keep thinking this was something personal against you, and you'll have war."

"Worse than we've already had?"

"Big enough to destroy everything good. You should be proud of your wife. She did everything right. The very first day, Savannah took away Hitler's food and water. Then she kept that damned hateful creature awake for five days straight. I never left her side, Riley. Neither did Zeus. We would'a taken that evil horse down. Hitler knew it too. He kept a close eye on me sitting a'top that fence with my rifle aimed at his angry white head. When Savannah opened that gate and walked in there, Zeus went too; stalking around that horse like a prison warden, all bristly and protective. She never asked that giant dog for help, but if Hitler got feisty, Zeus snapped at him. Not nicely nipping his heels to keep him in line; oh no, Zeus went for his neck, growling and snarlin' like some big black demon-dog."

"Good hell. This could have been a bloody massacre."

"Nah. Zeus was just lettin' Hitler know he wasn't in control anymore. Millie brought us food and drinks, fussing around like a worried mother hen; but Savannah kept talking, refusing to leave Hitler's cage. At night, after I couldn't convince her to leave, I turned on the big floodlights. We kept going. When she ran out'a words, she sang. Dumb things, mostly. Patriotic songs, kids tunes, and Christmas songs. Every silly thing that rolled through her head. That stallion fussed and stomped around; angry she made such irritating racket. But curiosity is a powerful thing. Hitler found that crazy woman interesting as all hell," Sam proudly grinned, "and just downright annoying."

Riley grudgingly half-smiled. "I'll bet."

"Hitler was spellbound. Couldn't ignore her. Couldn't get rid of her. And couldn't stop watching her. For five long days, the only thing he ate or drank came right out'a Savannah's hand. When he got sassy, she sang at the top of her lungs. Not pretty sounds. She sang all loud and obnoxious, like a punishment." Remembering, Sam rubbed a scruffy chin that desperately needed shaved. "Hitler quickly decided he'd rather nibble apples instead'a fingers, and screaming at that irritating noisy woman wasn't getting him anywhere. By the second night, her hands were all over him, rubbin' that beast down 'til he glittered. For another whole day, she loved on him, getting Hitler used to her touch, pickin' up his feet and walking around teaching him ground signals and voice commands."

"He just let her?"

"Yup. Damn horse caught on quick. This was a new game. He seemed determined to learn the rules. Savannah kept telling Hitler how good he was. As if saying it made it true." Sam scoffed in disbelief. "But it worked. When she stopped to eat or because she was talking about something that made her cry, he followed her around the arena, nudging her with his nose, beggin' for more love. She'd hug his neck and cry her heart out. Hitler let her cry, as if he knew she needed someone strong to love. Last night, she coaxed him over to the fence and climbed right on top'a him. Scared me half to death."

A little misty around the eyes, Sam stopped and discreetly wiped his face with his sleeve. Riley could imagine how hard it had been, sitting there rifle in hand, guarding a stubborn woman that Sam loved as much as his own flesh and blood. Just imagining the "what-ifs" of Savannah's adventure made Riley's insides kink into an awful knot.

"Hitler could have killed her."

"Maybe. But by then," Sam continued, "they had this little private language goin' on. Hitler was frantic, tossing his head, threatening to buck her off. She was smart. She just laid her belly along his back, like you saw her do this morning, and wrapped her arms around his neck, all non-threatening-like. She never stopped letting that wild stallion hear her voice, so calm and loving. It was just how a Momma would talk to a frightened child. They walked round all night while he relaxed and learned how to behave. Not even a rope around his nose. Damnedest thing I ever saw! At least with Diablo she used a saddle and bridle. Not Hitler. Only thing controlin' that horse was her voice."

"And his heart." Riley conceded.

"It's true. That stallion loves her. She used every trick you ever taught her, about gentling them down and earning their trust. 'Cept she did it in five scary days instead of two years like you're supposed to. Just before dawn, Savannah fell asleep, hanging all limp and exhausted over Hitler's back. I watched that silver demon stand there real quiet, decidin' what to do. If he would of flinched wrong, I still would have shot him. To hell with Savannah's tears. Finally, Hitler walked into the paddock and lay down in the straw, as careful as if she were a fragile china doll. Savannah woke for a minute and told Hitler how good he was; then they all fell asleep. She had worn him down and cried herself out. That's when I decided you should see what she did."

"Think he's safe?"

"As safe as any man in love. Hitler fell hard, Riley. She owns his wild heart. That's why he was mad at you. Hitler might not fully understand her words, but he sure as hell sensed the tension. I'd tread lightly, if I were you. Might wanna let Hitler know your Savannah's friend, not her enemy."

"Good idea. I don't feel like being trampled."

This changed things. In big ways.

"Well, guess that means I'm re-claiming my stallion. Thanks for watching over her, Sam. Sorry our problems became yours." Sam offhandedly shrugged as if his role were no big deal. "Get some sleep. You've earned it."

Riley sulked away and got in his truck, knowing Savannah would probably beat him home. Now he would be dealing with a giant black dog who loved her senselessly, a sulky cat who purred like a fool every time she appeared, and a merciless white stallion who'd obviously given his untouchable heart.

Why couldn't he?

He didn't have an answer.

***

A big lump of shimmering snow glittered against green grass, smack in the middle of his front yard. But it wasn't snow. It was Hitler, more relaxed than he'd ever been in his life, getting warm and toasty soaking in the springtime sun.

Riley couldn't decide if The Furor was guarding the place or simply collapsed. Parking in the driveway, he slammed his truck door a little louder than necessary, just to get the damn thing's attention. Hitler lifted his head and glared.

Guarding.

Savannah must be inside.

The only way into the house was around Hitler. Well actually, he could sneak in through the back door, but that wouldn't resolve anything.

"Well sir," Riley casually declared, folding his arms over his chest. He leaned against the red truck, not moving one step closer to walking through Graystone's formidable iron gates, "aren't you a big ornery watchdog."

The horse didn't rise, but shook his wavy mane in warning.

"Okay. I get it. You have a purpose now. Something to do besides rage around like hell unleashed."

Hitler huffed, making rumble noises deep in his chest, as if he agreed.

Riley grinned. Crazy horse.

"Looks like you're taking that job seriously, too. But that's my house and my wife you're guarding, Furor, and I'd really like to go inside and talk to her."

Walking at a safe lazy strolling pace, Riley began whistling a little tune. Wandering casually around the yard and into the stables, he left Hitler with perked up ears and a confused expression. He returned with an armload of hay and a bucket of molasses-soaked grain.

The horse still lay in the grass, watching. Listening. Still whistling to himself, Riley continued right through the gates of Graystone.

Snorting a noisy freight-train complaint, Hitler defensively stood. Neck arched, he pawed the earth, ready to strike.

"Oh good. You're still here. Want some breakfast?" Inching closer, he shook the bucket making that sugary scent waft across the yard. The horse smelled it. His mouth started working in anticipation. He was definitely hungry.

"You know, Hitler," Riley commented as coolly as if they were two men having a casual chat, "it's probably a good thing you've decided to help me take care of Savannah. She's a wild thing, you know. A woman like that just can't be tamed. But a man sure can love her. And you know what? She'll love you right back with all her wild heart."

They were a dozen feet apart now. Hitler looked murderous, muscles bulging like a warrior, but his eyes remained riveted on the hay in Riley's hands and that sweet-smelling bucket of molasses soaked grain.

"Your big daddy Diablo loved Savannah too. I guess you think you're man enough to take his place."

Squatting down on his heels, making his tall body a minor threat, Riley tossed the hay halfway between them. Nostrils flared, brown eyes widened. Hitler took a deep green whiff of fresh alfalfa. He hadn't eaten in days, except right out of Savannah's hand. The stallion was starving. He'd already chomped big bites from the yard grass.

"I can't protect her all the time. She'd feel smothered. Savannah needs freedom. You understand that, don't you? Freedom?"

Hitler sidestepped in frustration, torn between attacking the soft-spoken man and devouring the food that he'd enjoyed only a scarce few handfuls over the past five days.

"Seems to me a woman like that needs a guardian. Someone big and strong and smart." As he talked Hitler inched closer, wary of Riley knelt in the grass, but his mouth smacked noisily, eager to steal a few wisps of hay.

There. A quick reach. The first hesitant bite.

Hitler quickly backed away. Chomping the mouthful greedily, the horse arched his neck and seemed to laugh. Snorting, he puffed his chest, making funny grunting noises.

"Yeah, yeah. You're tough. I'm scared." But Riley smiled. This was working. "Go ahead, big guy. Have some more. A man needs to keep his strength up, you know. Can't have some wimpy-ass pretty-boy being bodyguard to my beautiful wife."

Considering Riley for a moment, Hitler cocked his head to the side. Taking him up on the offer of food, he snatched another piece. Chomp, chomp. The white stallion puffed his chest and strut around the yard, chewing that hay like he'd won a major victory.

Swallowing the bite, he came back for more. This time, after he snatched a bite, he didn't back away. "Bet you're thirsty too." Brown intelligent eyes focused on Riley as he chewed, Hitler grunted in reply.

Damn. Did the stallion really understand?

"Let's get you some water."

Standing slowly, leaving the hay on the grass, the big horse kept crunching. Forgetting all about trampling the bad man, Hitler dove right into his generously offered breakfast. Taking the bucket of sweet grain with him, Riley walked in a slow circle, giving the stallion a wide berth as he casually made his way to the front corner of the house.

Once, Hitler snickered a half-hearted warning, but a shake of the syrupy-grains put his mind at ease. Turning on the faucet, Riley squatted down again, rinsing an old steel washtub Savannah used to bathe Zeus. Cleaned of dog hair, Riley carried it closer to Hitler. Using the hose, he filled it to the brim with water. Hitler angled his body so he could eat and watch Riley at the same time.

He could smell that water too. Nostrils flared as he took deep breaths, inhaling that pure liquid scent. He wanted it bad.

"Well? What are you waiting for?" He half laughed, "Are you so civilized now that you need an invitation?"

Hay still sticking crudely out of chomping teeth, Hitler obviously decided Riley wasn't worth killing. Marching straight over to the tub, he stuck his nose in deep, sucking up water in big noisy gulps. Still kneeling down, only separated by that old-fashioned washtub, Riley carefully reached out and rubbed Hitler's luminous forehead.

"Ah, that's better." The horse flinched and watched him warily with big brown eyes, but kept drinking and didn't shy away. "You were thirsty. Don't drink too much. You'll swell up like a battleship and end up sleeping all day." Riley gently stroked his smooth white face. "Then again, maybe today is a good nap day. For all of us."

Suddenly, Hitler's eyes and ears focused on a noisy woman charging out of the house and down the front steps. Shadows of caution in those intelligent brown eyes immediately became brilliant glimmers of welcome and great joy.

Oh yeah, The Furor was in love.

Raising his head to watch Savannah, water dribbled out of Hitler's whiskery chin and into the tub, rudely splattering Riley with fat wet droplets.

"Uh, are you two okay?" She tentatively asked from somewhere behind him. Riley couldn't see her, but Hitler could.

"So far."

"What are you doing, Riley?"

"Feeding your horse."

"Oh. I could have done it, after I finished showering."

"I didn't mind."

"Well, thanks. But Hitler isn't mine. I just tamed him for you. You said to find a job and make myself useful," she repentantly explained. "So, I did."

"Yes, honey. You certainly did. Thank you."

Hitler was keyed up, muscles tensed, keenly listening to the casual tone of their purposefully mild conversation. Riley carefully stood. The big mane-tossing white stallion glared at him and shuffled several steps away.

"He's yours now. But he can't live in the stables, Savannah. He's tasted freedom now and it's made him happy. Caging him again would be cruel. He can live in the far north pasture this summer. But by winter, he needs to be tame, so he can come inside with the rest of the horses. You need to teach him that being inside isn't a punishment. It keeps him safe. Riding him today was special, but you can't always count on him to listen. Today he was grateful and obedient, but some days he'll feel sassy. You need to teach Hitler to accept a saddle and bridle so you have control. And he can't attack the other horses. He needs to mind his manners if he's going to be rewarded with freedom."

"Okay. I can do that. Gee, Riley…aren't you mad?"

"I was. I decided that was dumb."

Stepping away from the water-tub, Riley invitingly shook the bucket of sweetened grain at the horse. The anxiously prancing hooves tearing up the front yard halted. Hitler's rapt attention focused on that sugary scent again.

Like a curious child, his interest was easily swayed.

Scooping up a fistful, the sweet grains trickled through his fingers. Hitler came closer. Inching toward the oats in Riley's hand, those pert white ears swiveled, listening carefully, deciding if he should trust this or explode.

"I don't like fighting with you, Savage. I love you."

He heard her suck in breath and knew she wanted to cry. "I'm sorry I threw all that money at you." She softly apologized. "There's plenty more, Riley. What's mine is yours. It always should have been. We're just fine, financially. We can build as many barns as you need. I didn't mean to be selfish. We never talked about money. I didn't realize what a sacrifice running Graystone is. I should have seen it, but I didn't."

"Well, now you know. I'm broke."

Riley stopped himself. Bitterness wasn't the answer. Bitterness tore them apart. Remembering Sam's quiet wisdom, he sighed. *Love and hate are always intertwined. Just gotta decide which one to hold on to.*

*Love. I want to hold on to love.*

"That's the reason I tried to sell Mirabelle." He mildly explained, relieved at how good it felt to just love Savannah and not lash out. "I needed to pay bills. She's still here. I didn't sell her."

"But…I saw that transport truck leave. I was parked beside the road…uh, crying. Didn't Mercedez like Mirabelle?"

"Pfft, that spoiled woman had some damn twisted ideas. She came here for me, not Mirabelle. Turns out, she was only willing to buy Mirabelle so she could sleep with me. Guess in her world, that's how things work. Not in mine."

"You should be flattered." But she sounded disgusted.

"I'm not. We met once, when I was buying broodmares. We had a business dinner. Once. Sam and Millie were there too. I always took them with me to buy horses. I trust Sam's opinion. I never touched Mercedez. I promise I didn't. But since then, she's sent me emails with pictures of good colts that her wealthy friends had for sale and invitations to exclusive dressage events so I could get first pick of good bloodlines. I really thought everything was just business. So, when I needed the money so bad, I offered her Mirabelle. She took it as an invitation for something else."

"When I saw her pawing you, I wanted to kill her."

"Honey, even if we weren't married, I still wouldn't have touched her. To be perfectly honest Mercedez reminds me of your Mom. No self-respect or real charisma, just flaunting what few assets she thinks she has, believing if a man likes her body, then that attention makes her worth something. She's wrong. And you're wrong if you think I was interested in sampling used goods."

Behind him, Riley heard her relieved half-laugh. "Sam said you were too smart to buy what she was selling."

"Hell, she thought *I* was for sale. It was sleazy."

Kneeling down again in the grass, not overly surprised Sam set the record straight; Riley knew he needed to set the record straight too. "After you stormed out of here, I told Mercedez you are actually Arianna Hartwell and that Ryan was our son. I told her we were married. Then I threw her out."

"Oh. Wow. You did? Really?"

Listening to Savannah behind him, he casually offered another handful of grain to the suspicious stallion. If Hitler thought they were fighting, he'd be trampled in a heartbeat. He prayed that wouldn't happen.

"She was humiliated."

"Good. Thanks for doing that." Hitler was listening, eyeing that grain. "But I still didn't like you window shopping, Riley."

"Sorry. Guess I was too shocked to react right."

"Um…are you still selling Mirabelle?"

"No. She's yours. There's two hundred thousand sitting on my desk to pay the bills. I know if I would have confided in you, we never would have spent weeks with me being worried and mean. You would have shared. My pride hurt us. I'm sorry."

"It's okay. I acted childish and mean."

"And jealous."

She half-laughed. "Yeah. I did. Big-time."

"Just promise to ride Mirabelle in our mountains, not Mr. Unpredictable. Promise you'll ride Hitler in the arena while I'm watching, so I can help if you need it. We need to teach him to behave like a civilized man. Okay?"

"I promise. He'll learn. Thank you, Riley. Thank you so much!"

Hitler's velvety muzzle sniffed the grain cautiously. Opening his palm nice and flat, minimizing the chances those big teeth might grab one of his fingers; Riley cringed. A show of force was inevitable, especially with Savannah watching.

"Sam told me how you've spent the past five days. You did everything right. You earned Hitler's trust."

"It wasn't easy. He's a stubborn man."

"Most Montana men are."

She giggled, agreeing.

Miraculously, that wet horse mouth just nuzzled the grain, slurping up every sticky kernel out of Riley's hand without even a warning pinch. Like a happy white dog, a big pink tongue gratefully licked his palm.

Grateful too that he still had five fingers, Riley offered Hitler some more. "You have no idea what taming this stud will do for our ranch, Savage. It's a godsend."

"Our ranch?" Her quivery voice behind him asked. If he turned, he knew he'd see big tears. But Riley couldn't look. He had somehow managed to pin himself quite defenselessly between a natural born slayer and his new mistress.

"Graystone Heights is ours, not mine."

"But Riley," her trembling voice caught on a forlorn whimper, "I don't want to be your business partner."

"Will you still be my wife?"

"Do you really love me?"

"With all my heart. You always say this moment matters. I've been stuck in the past. Now does matter. It's all we have."

He could hear her moving and knew exactly where she was by the possessive gleam in Hitler's brown eyes. She shuffled across the grass as though her shoes were too big. It was a funny sound. Offering more grain to Hitler, he fed the horse and waited. If Riley stood right now, that stallion would feel threatened and pound him.

Finally standing beside him, Savannah stopped. A soft hand lovingly caressed his copper-bronze hair.

Glancing up, Riley smiled. She was still dripping from her shower. Wearing nothing but that fuzzy pink bathrobe with crazy red hearts Ryan gave her, she had hastily slid wet bare feet into a pair of his boots.

It was the sexiest thing he'd ever seen. Honestly. No made-up millionaire madam could compare to his Savage.

"You look ridiculously beautiful."

"Oh." Wet cocoa hair glistened in the sun. Her bottom lip pouted. "Ridiculous? That's not very nice."

"You're wearing my boots, babe."

"I am?" She glanced down and giggled like a little girl, apparently just now noticing her small feet and slender legs slopped around in a worn pair of men's size eleven Justin's instead of her fancy turquoise Lucchese ladies boots.

"I was hurrying. They were by the door. I do look ridiculous!"

"Beautiful. Don't forget that part."

Grinning, Savannah's fingers still stroked his hair. Slowly. Just how she did when they were making love. It was unintentionally provocative. Gripping his hair in gentle fists, she let the short strands trickle between her fingers before gently gripping it again. Those affectionate movements made Riley want to close his eyes and revel in her touch.

"My pride hurt us. From the beginning, I've clung to pride, creating walls. I avoid issues and I avoid talking about feelings. I find reasons to get mad instead of telling you the truth. I've been wrong. I'm not proud of my behavior at all. I'd rather be a good husband. I'd rather just love you, Savannah." She still stroked his hair. It felt so good. He glanced at her bathrobe and grinned, "What I'd really like to do right now is help you finish your shower and reconcile a few differences. Maybe later we could make a little music together and take a nap."

She laughed. A sweet husky sound. "I'd like that."

Watching them with disapproval, Hitler tossed his head and grumbled, showering them both in sticky half-eaten grain. "Think you can call off your Supreme Commander?" Riley asked, shielding his face with one arm from being pelted by the mushy rain.

"Hitler!" She firmly commanded. "BE-HAVE!" Almost two words, all drawn out, then snapped short at the end, there was no mistaking the disapproval in her voice.

The stallion stopped fussing and stared at her. Eyes wide, he tucked his chin to his chest as if embarrassed for being so rude.

"That wasn't nice," she sternly said. "Be nice."

The big horse huffed in resignation.

It made Riley want to laugh.

If ferocious white stallions could pout, Hitler was.

"Now listen," she softly purred as if speaking to an unruly child, "Riley is our friend. He's letting you run free. So you need to be a gentleman and behave." Reaching out, she offered her fingers to the wary horse.

Hitler eagerly nickered.

"So good." She soothed in a tantalizing dusky voice that turned even the most unconquerable man all buttery inside. "So good." Hitler nuzzled her skin as though it were precious silk. Riley knew exactly how that big horse felt. Loving Savannah was addictively irresistible. "Stand up, Riley. Real slow."

He carefully complied.

"Now give him some more grain."

That went well too.

"See? Riley won't hurt you. And you'd better not ever hurt him."

255

# Chapter Twenty-One

There are a precious few instances in a woman's life where time stands perfectly still in very good ways and every word, every single touch, even the subtle scent of that memory stays forever preserved in the archives of her mind.

This was one.

They crept inside, leaving Hitler mowing the front yard with eager teeth, but Riley didn't waste time with finishing her shower or discussing financial records; he jumped straight into making music.

"I need you." He huskily demanded, eagerly pinning her body against the foyer wall. That first kiss was stunning, leaving Savannah gasping.

"I need my wife."

Hands fervently roved, sparking all the right fires, demonstrating his ardent sincerity. Yanking aside the neck of her robe, Riley's warm mouth feasted on her firm breast, quickly revved her astonished body up to speed.

"I need you in my bed, Savage." Gold-green eyes were luminous. Like a wild cougar. "And in my life. Forever."

All she could do was grip Riley's shoulders and whimper. Nuzzling her naked body until her knees grew weak; a starving man sinfully chuckled and resolutely held her up with his hands. "No more leaving. We're married. We're staying married. If we fight, no one leaves. We stay here and talk it out. Got it?"

"Yeah. Okay. I got it." She panted, hoping Riley wasn't through with her yet. "No leaving. Leaving is for quitters. And I'm no quitter."

"Damn straight, you're not. You're my lunatic wife who talked a homicidal horse into loving her. Good job, by the way. Very impressive."

She laughed. Smiling felt so good.

Lifting Savannah right out of his sloppy boots, never giving her a chance to think or even breathe through his decisively seductive kisses; that determined man carried her right through the house and into their bedroom.

Good god, he wasn't kidding!

He needed her desperately! Now!

Riley was taking. And giving. Having his wicked way with her. It was so hot and deliciously honest she felt euphoric.

"Hungry, Rosemont?" She curled her fingers into auburn hair.

"Famished. And the more you touch me like that, the hungrier I get." Riley's knowledgeable hands were provocatively everywhere, sliding off her robe, feverishly removing his clothes at the same time.

"I love you, Savage." He earnestly murmured through another searing kiss. "Don't ever leave me again! I need you. I just want to love you. I've always loved you."

They were both naked. It was wonderful.

Adamant and wildly uninhibited, strong hands clasped beneath her bare thighs as Riley hoisted her up to cling to his middle. Knees locked around his waist, he tortured her with a passionately feral tangling of lips and tongue and teeth.

She needed this.

She needed his love.

Surrendering completely to Riley, her unspoken permission to take whatever he needed created a low impatient growl rumble in his chest. With one sublimely fluid motion, he lowered them both to the bed and plunged deep, all at the same time.

Savannah saw stars.

"Oh!" Towering over her, letting the initial shocking sensations ease, he slowly rocked. Gentle, almost sorry he had taken her so fast. But Savannah's fired-up body was already playing a thunderous crescendo. For the first time in forever, piano notes chimed in her head.

At first, she wasn't sure it was real.

But as they moved together, the music grew.

"More!" She raspily begged. Grabbing his hips, she arched her body into their union and groaned. "Please!"

He grinned. "You've missed me."

"I love you! I obsess over you!" She wailed, hearing golden trumpets inside her soul blare triumphantly. "I cry like a baby when we fight. I need you, Riley!"

"Mmm, I sure like hearing that."

Then their frantic reconciling desperation became something even better. Sweeter. Like one magnificently orchestrated symphony, Riley moved with purpose, guiding Savannah with his body and hands and mouth, note by eloquent note through that first gasping pinnacle of musical splendor.

And then another.

Oh, he knew her body so well!

"Look at me," he ordered, gently holding her face in his hands. Sight blurred by spectacular pianoforte crashing sounds resonating inside her soul; she obeyed.

Riley. So manly and dusky-auburn.

Those gold-green eyes gleamed.

Riley. With his wonderful strong body making hers quiver and sing.

Riley. His everlasting love made her spirit burn with passion so bright, pianos and violins and flutes all combined their voices into one magnificent heavenly celebration.

"Forever isn't long enough," he huskily whispered, "not for how much I love you." And then, as tears of joy filled her eyes, Riley softly kissed her.

Suddenly the music clamoring inside Savannah seemed everywhere, all around them, uniting her with Riley. She could hear it. Feel it! Alive! A bright golden blanket of music enveloped them. So real! The music was breathing and smiling and sweating. Loving. Two hearts, together. As one.

It was a new song. A great triumphant song!

And Savannah captured it inside her soul.

A gift from Riley.

The music had returned!

***

Much, much later, after the crashing cymbals, jazzy saxophones, and laughing harps in her mind became a serene melody of two pianos whispering contentment on a lazy spring afternoon, Savannah felt deliciously loose and limber and all liquid-gold inside.

Free. And loved.

Really truly loved.

Lying beside her on his stomach, Riley wore a sly expression of absolute male satisfaction on his handsome face. She had been happily napping. His gold-green eyes were open. He was awake, just watching her.

"So…we're rich?" He softly questioned.

"In money or love?" She smiled, lacing her fingers into his. "In love, I'd say we're billionaires. If you're still worried about money, we're moderately wealthy, but not obscenely rich."

His mouth lazily curved. "That's good. I'd hate to be obscene. Again." His other hand stroked across her bare stomach. "Unless you want to, of course."

Savannah laughed. Oh how she loved this man!

*Thank you! Thank you, God for giving me a second chance! Thank you for Riley! And for love! And for music!*

"I'm gonna make you even richer, Riley Rosemont." Sitting up, she saw his shirt carelessly tossed over the bedpost and put it on, buttoning a few as she walked.

"Where are you going?"

"Just wait. You'll see."

Grinning, she padded semi-naked through their quiet house.

In the pristine parlor, her courage stumbled when she saw that white grand piano. But soft sunlight filtered through the big semi-circle of windows, giving the serene sunny room that same liquid-gold luminosity she felt magically shimmering inside.

For the first time in years, she walked across that sacred floor.

It felt like stepping into God's cathedral.

*I'm worthy.*

Glinting atop the glistening glacial peaks that towered above their house, Savannah imagined that she saw the archangel Gabriel hovering on glorious wings of fire, holding his golden trumpet, waiting to herald in a heavenly miracle.

She sat down.

It was time.

The wooden piano bench felt cool beneath her bare thighs. Fingers reaching, Savannah simply closed her eyes. Letting go of everything else, focusing only on this divine moment, she took a deep breath.

Music! Not trapped inside her head anymore!

The triumphant song Riley embedded inside her soul was shivering, singing. Gloriously alive and resplendently free, it echoed though their house.

She didn't hear the man charging across wooden floors and skid to a stop at the parlor doorway. Savannah only heard two hearts; her right hand and her left, asking and answering; talking to each other. High notes warbled. Low notes thundered.

Becoming one.

Stronger together. Growing together.

Happier together.

She played and played, not seeing written notes at all. She felt each chord powerfully vibrate through her hands as she perfectly reproduced the original version they created while making love. Each note exuberantly proclaimed that forever really wasn't long enough.

As that piano joyously sang, she kept her eyes closed and let pure inspiration flow. In Savannah's mind a bright light shone upon her. Not a spotlight, but something magnificent and pure, cast straight down from heaven's pearly gate. She envisioned that light touching her and the white piano, then encompassing their house and the grassy yard.

Sound from her fingertips intensified.

Luminous as diamonds, that perfectly pure music-light changed everything shadowy to glistening white. It enveloped that silvery horse sleeping in the grass, making Hitler perk up his ears and happily sigh.

But it couldn't be contained.

Divine light touched everything.

From the mighty peaks above them to the amiable streets of Harmony Hills far below, her music cast a brilliant ethereal glow upon their Montana world. In her mind as that heavenly melody swelled, even the mountain trembled. She could feel its mighty shockwave of eternal reverence.

The gates of heaven had opened.

Savannah's music was a gift from God.

It always had been.

She didn't create it. It would be pompous and sanctimonious to take credit. Those harmonious sounds were too timeless for one woman to invent.

God whispered it to her.

Later, Savannah knew as her sightlessly fingers continued their instinctive dance across those ivory keys, angels would write the words. Perfect words. They'd come to her heart as soft as a dove when she was sleeping. She would wake with clarity, already knowing every poetic nuance.

But the music always came first.

Opening her eyes, hearing the last elated echoes of love from those unforgettable piano notes die away, tears had soaked her cheeks. Savannah was breathing like she just ran a mile, but felt so buoyant inside she wanted to shout for joy.

There he was.

Standing in the parlor doorway as if stepping any closer into that room would be treading upon sacred ground, Riley's hair gleamed with bronze-red embers of afternoon sunlight. Utterly awestruck, half-wrapped in the white sheet he hastily yanked off their bed and clutched at his waist with one hand; his face wasn't dry either. Her handsome thunderstruck husband looked like he just witnessed a miracle.

"It's back," he huskily breathed. "God touched you again."

"He did. I felt His hand upon my heart. I just had to play that song for you. I couldn't wait. It felt too good to keep it locked inside."

"You just wrote that? Just now?"

"We did. You and I. We did it together."

"Together," he repeated, but no sound came out at all. Tucking the sheet around him so it would stay, he walked toward her. "Will you remember it again?" His voice wasn't steady, but the arms drawing her off that bench, hugging her tight against his bare chest were strong and sure. "Do you need help writing it down? I'll help you. I don't want you to lose it."

"I won't," she grinned, "I have it memorized."

"Just like that?"

"Just like that."

He'd never been there to witness her moment of creation. Always before, inspiration would hit and Savannah would play the first time all alone, showing it to Riley later.

"God's gifts are never forgotten, not in my mind."

"It was perfect, Savannah; like you had practiced that song for years."

"Maybe I have." Twining her fingers through love-ruffled auburn hair, she pulled his dampened face closer. "It's called Riley's Heart."

"For me? God touched you...through me?"

She had never seen a man become truly choked up with emotion, but her beautiful music destroyed Riley's tough steel walls. Right now, with golden sunlight illuminating every emotional shimmer, there was no hiding the honesty in his face.

Riley loved her with all his heart.

And was so proud of her it spilled down his cheeks.

This moment too, Savannah would hold forever inside. It was rare and very precious. That's what life was, she decided: a collection of beautiful moments. Savannah vowed to cherish every single one. In the end, your collection of moments was all you took with you. And the love. But that's what made good memories, wasn't it? Love.

"You have another song. 'Second Chances.' Have you heard it?"

"Yeah," he huskily managed. "I have."

But this song was different. So triumphant. Every time "Riley's Heart" was played, the memory of their powerful love would shine again, captured not just for Savannah alone to remember and treasure, but for Riley too.

For everyone!

This song belonged to more than them. That heavenly light Savannah envisioned growing from this music was meant to reach far beyond their world. It would speak of love and truth, inspiring people she'd never meet, but she would touch through this song.

"Oh! I need to call Marcus! 'Riley's Heart' belongs to the world!" She gushed, "Just wait! People everywhere will hear your song! It'll be in another movie! I just know it! It's the best song I've ever played! Do you think it needs words? It might not. It's so powerful all by itself. Words might make it less spectacular. What do you think?"

Riley wasn't answering. He just watched her with glossy eyes. He breathed slow and deep, as if that were all he capable of doing. She knew his thoughts. Today he finally gained forever, but he also lost her again to the world beyond Montana.

"I won't leave you, Riley." She sternly reaffirmed. "We'll design a sound studio. Here. We'll produce new recordings right here at Graystone Heights. This is my home. With you. And I won't be Arianna Hartwell anymore. The world can know our truth. We'll tell them about Ryan. People will know that we've loved each other our whole lives. I'll do interviews and tell everyone how you fixed me when I was so broken; how you made me strong again. They'll understand why 'Riley's Heart' is special. The world will agree I'm damn lucky to be Savannah Rosemont."

Speechless pride glistened in his luminous green eyes.

"You look ridiculously handsome, Riley Phillip."

"Stop." He gruffly begged as she lovingly wiped his damp cheeks with compassionate fingers. "Men aren't supposed to cry."

"Only men with very good hearts." Standing on her toes, she softly kissed him. "And I love you with all my noisy musical soul."

"A miracle. That's what you are." Holding her tight, Riley appreciatively buried his wet face in her hair. "Play it again," he quietly requested. "Play it so I can memorize it too. Please. I've missed hearing you play."

She did play. Over and over.

Savannah played that glorious love song while Riley sat behind her on the piano bench. Long legs on either side of hers, wrapped in his loving arms, the powerful music coming from her hands vibrated through her body and into his chest.

Right into Riley's heart.

Like one. Forever.

As golden afternoon sunlight faded into a starry blanket glittering like laughing diamonds over their Montana mountains, it seemed to Savannah that their room still glowed. Perhaps it was just moonlight. Or magic.

But Riley saw it too.

He said it was God's divine love.

*Leslie D. Stuart*

# Chapter Twenty-Two

Riley was pleased with Hitler's progress. Two weeks ago, he'd been untouchable. Now, thanks to Savannah's loving attention, the glistening white stallion even allowed Riley to ride him. Well, he bucked a little, now and then, just to remind the man on his back the Furor wasn't entirely civilized.

Savannah played the piano every evening. Riley sat listening to her play, feeling honored to be privy to her private performances.

She smiled constantly.

They talked about money. They discussed letting go of the past. They embraced right now. He told Savannah exactly how he felt about everything, holding nothing back. She rewarded him a hundred-fold for having the courage to demolish his emotional walls.

He had cheated himself out of happiness.

No more.

The strutting stallion suddenly jerked his head toward the open arena doors. Ears perked, hearing something, he whinnied in earnest and nearly shot out from under Riley. "Hey, easy big guy. The metal gates are down. Unless you can fly, you aren't going anywhere."

Hitler reared, pawing the air, fighting the bridle and bit that were reining him in. Riley's butt stayed in the saddle, but they landed with a thud of hooves pawing the earth. "What the hell has gotten into you?"

Then, he heard it.

Savannah screamed.

Hitler bolted toward the gates, screaming too.

"Wait!" Another deep voice commanded, making Riley tug so hard on the reins the stallion sat back on his haunches.

"You'll need this."

Beside Hitler stood a proud fearless man. A man who condemned himself to be a voice in the wind after his mortal life went to hell.

John Graystone held out his hands, offering Riley's rifle.

"Don't hesitate, son." That familiar dusky voice ordered. "Save my daughter. It isn't her time. That beast is pure evil. Protect the innocent. They are precious to me."

Well hell. Now he was seeing ghosts.

Offering guns and warnings about monsters and death.

A pit formed inside his heart.

"Thanks." Snatching the rifle from John, he swung Hitler around, kicked the gate latch open with his boot heel and let the stallion run free.

Hooves pounded the earth. Wild. Frantic. Searching.

Glancing back, John Graystone had disappeared.

Maybe he'd never even been there.

Shifting the rifle in his fist, Riley couldn't question it now. He had no idea where Hitler was going. Savannah had left hours ago, riding Mirabelle in the hills. But she needed him! Now! He heard it. That big charging stallion wove between trees, taking them straight up the mountain.

Riley let him go.

"Find her, buddy."

He only prayed they'd get there in time.

***

With it roaring over her, Savannah knew her life was over. God finally decided to call her name and his voice was the roar of a crazed grizzly bear. A killer. She could see it in his eyes. This monster didn't kill for food, but for the pure sadistic pleasure of tasting destruction.

She had ridden to Crystal Haven Lake, letting Mirabelle enjoy the beautiful spring day. The sun shone upon the pristine water, reflecting mountains and sky.

Everything went horribly wrong.

She never heard him coming.

The mountain didn't warn her.

It never even whispered.

That grizzly loped out from beneath the trees, side-swiping Mirabelle with razor sharp claws. The mare screamed in agony. Flanks were shredded. Blood dripped on the ground. Savannah clung to her back as silver-gray horse instinctively twisted toward the bear, hind legs kicked out, striking the beast in the face.

Bones crunched. It was a sickening sound.

The bear's face looked distorted. It grunted, stumbled blindly for a moment, then stood on hind legs and roared.

A black shadow leapt. It snarled, biting hard, drawing blood.

The bear stood firm, towering, swatting with razor sharp claws. The black shadow yelped. Flying through the air, Zeus landing in a heap on the ground.

The grizzly charged toward them again.

Mirabelle jumped and spun, kicking out hard. Fighting for her life, she came down and reared, shielding the woman on her back from deadly claws.

Savannah slid. She fell, rolling away. She watched in horror as teeth tore into silver-gray flesh.

"Nooooo!!"

The mare fell, kicking in a frantic tangle of legs, teeth, and blood. The bear pummeled her, over and over, enjoying every squeal of pain.

"Leave her alone!"

The beast spied a new target.

Savannah.

It stood, roaring, towering ten feet high.

Covered in blood she screamed in defiance at the massive beast, unwilling to exit this world without a fight. As Savannah stood there screaming like a banshee, suddenly a single shot rang out. That giant grizzly's head exploded into flying bloody-brain soaked pieces.

For one awful second, the towering headless corpse shuddered. Fearsome paws helplessly clawed the air. Then the monster started to fall. Right toward her! Damn it all, she was going to be crushed beneath a thousand pounds of dead grizzly bear.

Paralyzed in fear, she couldn't move.

But a strong hand snatched her waist, wrenching her away from that spot.

The bear fell with a thunderous sound, right where Savannah had stood.

A few feet away Mirabelle lay on her side. Throat torn open, chest a shredded mass of horseflesh; her strong back and muscular sides were slashed bone deep. One hind leg was broken, crumbled beneath her body like a grotesquely twisted vine. Mutilated, the beautiful dappled gray mare lay drowning in her own puddle of blood.

She needed help!

But Savannah was still being tugged away.

"No! Stop!" Yanking out of Riley's firm grasp, she scrambled closer, slipping and sliding on red-stained rocks, becoming as covered in blood as her dying horse.

"Oh God! No!" She sobbed, wrapping her arms around Mirabelle's face, lifting her nose out of the spreading pool of crimson rapidly staining the mountainside. Wheezing, her breath was pained. Brown eyes begged for mercy.

"Step away from her, Savannah." Riley commanded. Over her shoulder, she saw the barrel of his rifle pointed the mare's head.

"No Riley!" she shouted, shielding Mirabelle's body with her own. "You can save her! It's not too late! You can save her! Please!"

"I can't." He flatly declared.

"Please! You have to try."

"If you love your friend, you won't make her suffer. Mirabelle gave her life for you. She fought that bear, keeping you alive. Look at her. She hurts deeper than any soul should endure."

267

It was true. Her beautiful gray flesh in mutilated tatters, every remaining muscle quivered with pain. But she didn't thrash about how most horses would. Mirabelle lay very still, valiantly waiting for her command.

For final release from her duties.

"Goodbye," Savannah whispered; sobbing so hard her tears ran gruesome rivers through the blood smeared across her cheeks. Mirabelle's blood. Lovingly, she caressed the mare's bloody wheezing face one final time.

"So good. Such a beautiful girl. You flew with real wings, Mirabelle. You saved me. You were so brave. You kicked so hard. Such courage." She gently soothed the listening mare. "But this life is but a twinkle, honey. Don't be afraid to leave it. What lies beyond is so much better. I just know it." She explained as if the dying horse truly understood.

"You loved, Mirabelle. Deeply. With all your magnificent heart. And you were loved in return. And that's the best anyone can hope for in this life."

Carefully, Savannah slid her hands over brown frightened eyes, closing them for the last time. The valiant horse shuddered and visibly relaxed, accepting her fate.

"Now take that love with you and be free. Fly among the stars, Mirabelle. You've earned your wings. We'll meet again, my beautiful dancing friend."

Then she stood and solemnly walked away.

A single shot rang out; a sound that echoed through the mountain like thunder and ended with a woman's heartbroken scream so fierce and frightened and furious, Riley knew that dreadful sound would settle deep inside his soul and in his worst nightmares, Savannah's voice would haunt him.

But her sobbing heartfelt eulogy and parting words to a horse that sacrificed herself so that deeply loved woman might live a bit longer would haunt him even more.

***

It took Sam exactly twenty minutes to drive the back-roads from his ranch to Graystone. Every second they bounced along the dirt road, he steeled himself inside for the mayhem he waiting just around the bend.

"Melinda, you have to promise not to get all hysterical. Savi don't need no cryin' and fussin' around. She needs someone strong."

"Samuel Lawson, don't you dare treat me like a fluttery mother hen." His wife of forty plus years snapped. Braiding her long white hair, she twisted it into a tight bun. "I know how life works. I just fuss at you cuz' you like the attention."

Rounding the last bumpy curve, Sam was grateful Millie insisted on coming with him. From what Riley described on the phone, Savannah would need a strong mountain Momma to love on her before this day was through. Rumbling into the Graystone driveway, he quickly realized it was every bit as bloody as he envisioned.

268

Standing like a valiant soldier in the front yard, Hitler gleamed in the sunlight, but his body and face bore crimson handprints.

The damn thing actually wore a saddle and bridle.

The reins hung loose, tied at the ends, the leather straps draped around his neck. On his back, lying slumped over the saddle horn, a bloody woman buried her face in his white mane. Her long dark hair streamed like a sheet of death down his mottled side and chest.

Savannah looked like something from a horror movie.

"Stay there, Millie. Just for now." He ordered his wide-eyed and very silent wife. Climbing out of the truck, Sam slowly walked toward Hitler. The big horse didn't move. "Savi? Honey? Are you alright?"

"Go away, Sam." She murmured, making Hitler flick his ears from the man to the woman, then back again.

"Is that your blood?"

"Noooo," she made a long sad wailing mournful sound that to Sam sounded like it came from the bottom of a deep well. "Mirabelle!" She cried, fisting Hitler's white mane tighter into her bloody hands. "That bear!"

"I know. Riley called me. He's up there on that mountain, just as upset as you are. He hated shooting her, Savannah. You know he did. Don't go blamin' your husband for doin' what he had to do. Mirabelle was suffering. Now Riley hurts. He could barely talk. Forgive him, Savannah. You know what death does to him."

"I know."

A few feet away, Sam stopped walking. He was afraid Hitler might pound him. The towering white horse staunchly stood his ground, looking like an Indian warhorse painted in handprints of the enemy's blood. He was guarding Savannah. Sam saw worry in that stallion's eyes and knew Hitler wouldn't hurt him.

"Look at me, Savi. Please, honey. Let me see your face."

Lifting a face gruesomely covered in blood, streaked with rivers of tears, she just blinked at him. "I'm not hurt."

"Inside you are."

She nodded.

More trucks were rumbling up the long rough driveway. Jacob's white jeep and Paul's black Dodge, both loaded with men.

Hitler's ears dangerously flicked and Sam saw him shiver.

"That big horse is real damn scared, Savannah." He gently advised, "He's feelin' your pain and it's a real frightening thing. But he loves you. Hitler's tryin' real hard to be brave about it, but too many people come millin' around, he's liable to stomp a few."

Fists clenched into his wavy white mane, she buried her face again and sadly whimpered. "I need Riley."

269

Without any signal that Sam could see, beyond the wishes of Savannah's tattered soul, that big stallion turned and slowly walked straight toward the Graystone iron gates. He walked as if his load were incredibly fragile and precious. Hitler walked right past his truck. Then Paul's and then Jacob's truck too.

Everyone silently watched. Hitler kept walking.

His gait lengthened, but the walk remained smooth. He didn't bounce Savannah at all. Then Sam saw why the horse sped up.

Riley emerged from the trees.

His rifle slung over one shoulder, big Natchez Bowie knife still clutched in one fist, his arms and chest were drenched in blood.

Sam knew what happened.

Riley had cut out that grizzly's evil heart.

Seeing the white stallion obediently walk toward him with his precious cargo, the ache inside Riley's own heart eased a little. Leaning his rifle against a pine, he wiped the bloody knife across his pant leg and returning the weapon to its protective leather sheath inside his boot.

"Hey, buddy." He stood, softly greeting Hitler. "You did real good, big man. Real good." The woman draped over his back looked dead. The stallion sighed with relief as Riley rubbed his white face and powerful neck.

"Savage?" He cautiously touched her arm.

"I...love...you, Riley!" She cried through body-shaking sobs, scrambling off that horse so fast he barely had time to catch her. Arms and legs frantically wrapped around him. Overwhelmingly grateful; he caught her and together they slowly slumped to kneel on the ground. "I was so scared!"

"I know." He held her tight.

Beside them, Hitler hung his head so his nose could touch her shoulder, as if he needed that reassuring contact with Savannah.

"Zeus?" She whimpered. "Where's Zeus?"

"He's still up there. He'll be okay. His front leg is broken." She clung to him tighter and shuddered. "We'll carry him down the mountain and I'll fix it, okay? I can fix Zeus; I promise I can. I'm so sorry that I couldn't fix Mirabelle."

"She was suffering."

"Aren't you mad at me?"

"No. Letting her go in peace was right."

Men were coming. His family. Sam, his Dad, Paul, and Jacob. Some of the toughest men Montana ever knew, but they looked wary, almost fearful of the bloody couple and their hellfire demon horse. Still kneeling on the ground, holding Savannah's face close to his neck so they couldn't see her tears, Riley grimly nodded at his older brother.

"It happened near Crystal Haven Lake."

"Sam said he was big."

"Huge. A Kodiak; the biggest one I've ever seen. He busted Zeus up too. He was lying quiet when I left him, but if Zeus snaps at you, just wait and I'll carry him down."

"Just take care of Savannah, Riley. We'll handle the rest." Paul ordered. Picking up Riley's rifle, he checked it for bullets. Only two were fired. One for the bear. And one for Mirabelle. Pulling hollow tip shells from his pocket, he reloaded the missing two. He cocked the gun with a noisy click-click.

"That big bastard got a mate?"

"Maybe. I saw a big female last month. She had a cub."

"Another Kodiak?"

"Probably. She was big. I didn't consider it at the time."

"We'll need to track her down." Jacob stated, standing a cautious distance away from Hitler. The white stallion had earned quite a reputation. "If Kodiaks are wandering this far south looking for food, then game and fish need to relocate them. This land being a wildlife preserve, we can't just go gunning her down."

"Oh, hell." Riley swore. "I forgot." He'd shot an animal on a game preserve, a crime punishable by serious jail time.

"Self-defense." The shivering woman in his arms declared.

"That's right. It was." Sam knelt, brushing hair away from her face until she cautiously peeked at him. "Got lots'a witnesses. 'Sides, if that big Momma tromps on over to my land, I got no problem shootin' her down."

"The cub too, Sam." She urged. "Bad blood. Real bad blood."

"You saw it in his eyes, didn't you honey? You looked right into that murderin' devil's dark soul."

She nodded and tucked her face against Riley's neck again.

"You cut out his heart." His Dad proudly observed of Riley, carrying his own rifle and two shovels. "Just like Big John would have done."

"I did."

"We'll get rid of him, son. We'll find his mate too. There won't be nothing left of that bear to haunt these hills."

"Thanks." Standing, Riley lifted Savannah onto Hitler's back and saw the horror in their faces at her macabre appearance. "She's okay. It's Mirabelle's blood." Grabbing the saddle horn with one hand, Riley swung up behind her. "Let's go home, Hitler."

The stallion had never carried both of them before, but as Riley gathered up the reins that big horse arched his neck and proudly strutted military style all the way to Graystone's front steps.

Millie waited, solemn and steely. After Riley slid Savannah off Hitler, Millie wrapped her in a blanket.

"Get her warm and clean, Melinda. And thanks for coming. Brew some chamomile tea and put a few drops of valerian root extract in it. It'll calm her

271

nerves. There's chicken soup in the 'fridge if she gets hungry. Call if you need me. I have my phone."

"We'll be fine." Motherly, she tipped Savannah's red-stained face up, checking her patient. Shivering now, she was in shock. Her eyes were glassy, skin pale. "Quite a morning you've had, honey. Must'a had an angel watching over you." Arm around her shoulders, Millie steered her into the house.

They only went a few steps. Savannah turned around.

"Riley? How did you know that I needed you? We were too far away for you to hear me screaming."

"I heard in my heart. I heard your voice scream in the wind long before you were actually in trouble. Your horse heard it too." He mounted Hitler again, who was a renewed man, eager for action without his fragile passenger. "Then your Daddy appeared, handing me my rifle, and ordering me to protect the innocent." He told her, bouncing a little with Hitler's eager steps. "I figured I should probably listen."

"My dad?"

"Yep. Without my rifle, I couldn't have killed that bear. You really did have an angel watching over you today. I hope saving you helped him earn his wings. John loves you, Savannah. He said you were precious to him."

"He did?"

"Yes. Protect the innocent. They are precious to me."

"Oh wow."

Unable to hold back the prancing stallion, Riley released the tight hold on the reins and galloped away, burning off fear and anger in both their hearts, replacing it with courage.

Up through the trees they ran, pounding like a white freight train over the meadow. Right up the face of the ridge, Hitler raced. At the top, near Ryan's angel monument, Riley turned and saw Savannah still standing on the front steps, watching them.

She waved.

Riley heard it again.

This time the wind whispered that she loved him. Riley felt it on his face, as if her hand caressed his skin. That eternal warmth trickled into his bones. Her heart would ache for a while, but he hadn't lost her; not to that Kodiak Grizzly, and not to hate for shooting her horse.

Everything would be all right.

Eventually.

\*\*\*

"We should honor that mare, Riley." Jacob reverently advised. By now, they all knew how John Graystone appeared, saving his daughter. No one doubted Riley's sanity. In fact, they accepted the bizarre incident with profound gratitude. "She gave her life for Savannah. We should bury Mirabelle at Crystal

Haven Lake and gather the family together for prayers. We should give thanks. That's what John would have done."

They were all watching him; Paul, Sam, his Dad, and Jacob; men who understood the old ways. Blackfoot Indian ways. Graystone chieftain ways, traditions and respectful beliefs of men who held this mountain in their iron-fists for many generations.

Men who lived and died here.

"Alright," he agreed. "Let's prepare a ceremonial bonfire, but not at Crystal Haven Lake. It's too far to walk after dark and we still have a Kodiak Momma roaming these hills. Until Game and Fish catch her, no one walks the mountain. Let's hold prayers on Ryan's Hill, near Graystone." Everyone nodded, consenting to his decision. "Call Mom?" He asked his Dad, knowing his whole family would come. "We'll light the fire with Savannah. She needs to hear our prayers."

Just before sunset, it was ready. At Crystal Haven Lake, they carefully buried Mirabelle on a grassy knoll, letting her body become part of the mountain. On Ryan's Hill, in clear sight of Graystone, they dug a fire pit; filling it with rich smelling cedar and pine for the bonfire.

Ryan's Hill became a meeting place, under the stars.

Every time he looked at their house nestled in the valley below, Riley saw his wife sitting on Graystone's front steps, her long hair glistening in the sun.

It helped to see her there. Alive.

Leaving Zeus resting in a soft blanket bed in the stables, Riley treated his wounds, set his leg, and gave him enough painkillers to make him comfortable.

The grateful dog fell asleep.

There she was. Still waiting for him.

While he cared for Zeus, Hitler had raced ahead to find her. Happy now, the Supreme Commander nuzzled Savannah's hand, grunting with satisfaction when she hugged his neck. "Good boy," she murmured, loving on the stallion until he sighed. "So brave. So good."

Riley wanted to hold his wife, to assure himself she was fine, but he was still coated in red death and she was clean.

"Are you taking me back up there, Riley?"

It was simple question, but the love and courage in her violet eyes made his answer stick in his throat. "For Mirabelle." He managed. "To honor her."

"Shower. Then I'll walk up with you. I made you some dinner. And I packed those." She nodded toward the heavily loaded leather satchels waiting on the porch that Hitler would carry up the hill for them.

"There's food, water, and warm tea for everyone. And a couple of blankets. Oh, and a bottle of that expensive brandy we found in the wine cellar. We'll each take a drink for tribute and toss the rest into the fire."

"You knew what we were doing?"

"It's pretty hard to miss those pieces of bear carcass being trucked away in black plastic bags and I watched you men pile wood on Ryan's Hill all afternoon. I don't know how it's supposed to work, but I recognize a sacred ceremonial fire when I see one."

"We disposed of the bear in that sawmill incinerator. That thing gets hot enough to burn him straight to hell. I didn't want him buried on our land."

"Good. Me neither."

"We buried Mirabelle beside the lake." He quietly revealed and watched her eyes glitter. "Tonight we'll honor her with prayers, as a family."

"Like Dad would have done?" He nodded. Expression perplexed she asked, "You really saw him?"

"Either that or I left Hitler charging around the arena hollering for you," he reasoned, "ran into the house, grabbed my rifle from the locked gun safe, loaded it, and then jumped back on Hitler without ever realizing I'd left the saddle."

She smirked. "I highly doubt that." Despite him being disgustingly dirty, she inched up to his chest. She smelled like strawberry lotion. Damn he wanted to kiss her. And more. "You look pretty rugged and scary, Mountain Man."

"Uh, where's Millie?"

"Pretending to be asleep."

"Oh." Smiling felt weird. "Then shower with me, Savage. I need to touch you."

"I planned on it."

*** 

So much gratitude. Savannah was overwhelmed with the thankfulness pouring from every heart as they gathered around the bonfire. Papa prayed, blessing Mirabelle's passage from this life, making her cry. Paul praised the mare's courage, her beauty and grace. Sam thanked the heavens for the time Mirabelle danced upon the earth. Even Jacob prayed, solemn and amazingly eloquent. When Riley stepped forward, offering the depths of his thankfulness, she thought her heart would burst.

"Forever isn't long enough," he proclaimed to God and their family, pulling her right into his arms. Heads bowed together as a couple, she clung to him as he prayed. "Not for how much I love you, Savannah." He prayed for Mirabelle. Then expressed his gratitude for Zeus, asking that his body quickly heal. Then he prayed in earnest for God to bring peace to his wife's heart, to protect her, to watch over her always.

In all their years together, she had never heard Riley pray. Judging by the natural ease that he expressed himself, this was not the first conversation he'd sent skyward. In fact, she felt certain her husband acknowledged God daily.

It made her love him even more.

His spiritual strength was beautiful, awe-inspiring.

Afterward, they shared the bottle of brandy, with each person having one small glass to toast to Mirabelle. It made her cry. Savannah flung the remaining brandy into the fire making orange-hot flames leap toward the sky. Watching sparks mingle with stars, she knew the beautiful dancing mare's spirit was in peace.

Would hers ever be?

# *Chapter Twenty-Three*

"Riley." She startled him.

He was deeply engrossed in trying to befriend the fancy laptop she bought for him on their recent trip to Kalispell for supplies. The complicated thing contained too much technology for his simple needs, but he was determined to figure it out and show Savannah he appreciated having it.

She looked quite alarming standing in his office doorway brandishing that big pair of scissors like a weapon.

"Will you help me?"

"Maybe." It had been three weeks since the bear attacked. She had been quiet; eerie quiet sometimes, but he respected her needs and didn't push. Yesterday the forest rangers finally trapped the female Kodiak and her cub. The mountains were safe again.

"Will you please put those scissors down?"

"Oh." She glanced at the eight inch silver blades as if suddenly realizing they were gleaming in her hand. "These are for you."

"That's nice, my love." He said with an amused but patronizing smile. "At least you gave me fair warning before cutting out my heart."

"No, you dope. They are for you to use on me."

"But I like you, Savage. Really I do."

"Riley! Dang it! Don't tease me!"

Marching away, grumbling something unintelligible, curiosity made Riley follow her. On the kitchen table lay a pristine white cotton cloth and red satin ribbons.

And the scissors.

That she handed to him, nicely.

Then abruptly turned her back toward him.

"Cut it!"

It took him a whole minute to realize Savannah meant her hair.

"No. Absolutely not." The scissors went back on the table. "I'll do anything for you. But I won't cut your hair."

277

"But I need to feel…" tears welled in her eyes.

He pulled out a chair, sat down, and pulled her onto his lap. "Talk to me." He urged, "We're good now. You can tell me anything."

"I just can't seem to shake this. I see that bear, everywhere." She shuddered. "I see Mirabelle…" she started to cry, but sucked back the sob and tipped her chin instead. "I thought since we gave Mirabelle a ceremony, honoring her life, I should do something to cleanse this awful ache I carry inside."

"Like what?"

She seemed shocked he was actually listening. "Well, maybe if I left something sacred from me up there on the mountain, I might feel better. I could pray. I got this white cotton cloth to bind it in and…I've never ever cut my hair. It's pure. That's a sacred offering, isn't it?"

"I guess so."

"Well it's all that I have."

"Maybe we should take a walk. You, me, Zeus, and Hitler." He suggested, hoping to deter her from this bizarre personal sacrifice.

"No, listen to me! I need to get past this. I need to feel like Savannah again. I hate feeling guilty that I'm alive while other people I love are gone! I feel sick. I can't eat. Nothing tastes right. Everything smells funny. I'm all messed up."

"How much?"

Her brow furrowed in confusion. "How much do I feel sick? Bunches." Hands clutched at her stomach and she made a nauseated face.

"No, honey." He gently smiled at her antics. "How much of your hair are you going to sacrifice?"

"Oh." She nervously chewed on her bottom lip. "I hadn't decided." Thinking, she pulled a long three foot strand over her shoulder and studied it. "Half," she abruptly decided. "It should be cut in half. Mirabelle deserves that much."

"Half is more than eighteen inches."

Riley stood her up and turned her around. Measuring with his hand, he ran his finger in a line across the middle of her back, three inches below her bra.

"We'd cut here. Right now your hair goes all the way down here." He stroked another line across the lower curve of her butt. "That would be half, if we measure from the top of your head."

Facing him again, she asked, "Are you actually considering helping me? Or are you just patronizing your fruitcake wife?"

Riley stood, gathered her close, lay her head on his chest, smoothing his hand down that long sheet of virgin hair. "I'll help you."

"You mean it?"

"I do." He kissed the top of her head. "If you want to make a traditional sacrifice like your grandfathers did, we need to bundle it with herbs like lavender, maybe some roses. Then we can bury it on Ryan's Hill."

"You'll stay with me?"

"I'll never leave you."

It took Riley nearly an hour of careful trimming. One strand at a time he measured and snipped, making sure none of Savannah's precious pure hair fell on the floor. Then he placed it in the white cloth, lined up exactly how it was on her head.

With that very first small cut, she shuddered. He immediately set the scissors down. "Let's think of a different sacrifice."

"No. I'm fine. This is the right one. Go ahead. Cut it. We'll only do this once," she decided. "If the line you cut isn't straight, oh well. No trims. After this, my hair will just grow again."

When he finished, the bundle of glossy brown hair was big around as his fist. They didn't talk much. Cutting her hair was a huge personal sacrifice. It wasn't vanity; her long hair was part of her identity. She'd worn it long her whole life. For Savannah, it was like cutting off her arm or a foot, just less painful. But she stood firm and determined, patiently letting him carefully cut away those silken strands.

Riley was proud of her for wanting to heal. But he didn't say it. Hearing praise might make her cry and weaken her resolve. She asked for help. He gave it. Despite his own unspoken misgivings, he cut Savannah's beautiful hair. He saw immense gratitude in her violet eyes.

That light was worth keeping his mouth shut.

Just going through the preparations, he watched her negative feelings fade. Her small smiles were deeply reverent and hopeful.

Maybe this was the right thing to do.

As they walked through the meadow to pick wild lavender for the bundle, she leaned over and that shortened sheet flipped past her shoulder.

"Oh! It's so short!"

"Nah. It's still longer than most women have." For a heartbeat, Riley thought she was going to sit down in the grass and bawl like a baby, but her chin bravely tipped. He admired her courage.

"It looks thicker. Glossier." She bravely blinked back tears and sternly studied the neatly snipped ends that still hung to the middle of her back. "You did a good job, Riley. Thanks for helping me."

"Hell Savage, I figured I had to. If I didn't help, you would have hacked it off yourself, making a big mess of it. Your hair is so damn thick, now we'll have to buy new scissors."

She grinned at his gruff comment. "I like that."

"What? Your hair? Or buying new scissors?"

"You're not treating me like I'm broken. You never do."

"It's all just part of my atrocious bedside manner."

Laughing, she took his hand as they continued to walk. "I love you, Riley. I married my best friend."

Those words were payment enough.

Returning to the kitchen, they preparing the bundle, adding generous handfuls of lavender, six Don Juan roses, wild sweet-grass from the meadow, juniper berries, and sage. Folding the white cotton cloth over each end, sealing in the contents, Riley helped her roll the big bundle and wrap red ribbon around her precious offering.

"Ready to walk up Ryan's Hill?"

"Sure." Holding the bundle up to her nose, she sniffed it. "It smells good. Clean." She made a disappointed face. 'Nothing smells good anymore. Food smells gross. Even your aftershave; that I usually love, smells weird. I really hope making this sacrifice fixes my broken sense of smell."

That stuck him as odd.

His next thought made his heart gallop.

"Come with me." Snatching up her hand, he declared, "We'll bury your offering later." Towing her with him, he rushed toward the stables.

"Where are we going?" Savannah felt confused by Riley's wide grin and bemused chuckle. Hazel eyes gleamed. So handsome. Such a good man. She hurried to keep up with his leggy strides.

"I want to check something."

"You have a cure?"

He laughed. It was optimistic and deeply pleased. "It may take several months," he snickered again, "but yes, I think there is a cure for your upset tummy and over-sensitive sense of smell."

"That's good. I hate being sick." Feeling the lighter weight of her hair swing at mid-back as she half-ran to keep up with her excited husband, she pouted. "You could have told me there was a cure before I chopped off my hair."

"It'll grow."

She didn't understand why he found that hilarious.

She felt even more baffled when their race stopped in the medical supply room and her husband stuck his silver veterinary stethoscope in his ears.

Riley recently invested in the high-powered Littman electronic scope because it blocked ambient noises and could detect foal heart flutters on the thick bodies of horses that most devices missed. Plus, it digitally recorded sounds he could then transfer onto his laptop, helping him keep accurate health records.

Unceremoniously, he knelt down and yanked up her shirt.

"What are you..." he pressed the cold chest piece against her restless belly. Low. Below her belly button. "Ooh, cold. Riley, my heart is up..." he pressed one finger to her lips.

"Shhh."

Savannah sighed. "I think you're losing it, Doc."

It made him grin. Riley's heart felt eight times too big for his chest. Savannah had been so preoccupied by life, she had overlooked the obvious transitions within her own body. Just as he suspected, her once flat stomach had a slight bulge in the lower region, as if she'd eaten a huge meal. Her sleek flesh felt surprisingly firm beneath his hand. How had he missed this? He listened. At first, all he heard were amplified rustling sounds, body gurgles that were pure Savannah. Moving the bell lower, near the cradle of her left hip, he nearly laughed aloud.

"What are you listening to?" She griped.

"Music."

"In my rumbly stomach?"

"Yep. It's the most beautiful sound in the world."

Her brow furrowed.

"You're pregnant."

"What? No. I can't..." spluttering, her face blanched. "Oh. God. So much has been going on. I didn't think about...but I'm on the pill. Shoot." He watched her mind race. "I haven't had that time of month in...wow. Early April, maybe?"

Measuring with his hand, feeling the hard outline of her growing womb, he grinned. "I'd say you're about nine or ten weeks along."

"I am?" Her knees half-buckled, but he caught her with his hands. Violet eyes were wide and a little misty.

"Are you alright?"

"I'm shocked." She stood firm again. "I just thought I'd finally gained a little weight. I was kind'a proud, actually. I didn't even consider a baby. Are you mad?"

"Honey, I'm thrilled. You going to have my child."

She finally smiled. "Can I listen?"

"Sure." Placing the ends in her ears, he held the telltale silver disk over the magical spot. At first, she frowned, doubtful. Then she squealed.

"There!" *Swish-a-Tic-a-swish-a-tic-a.* The sound was so fast, strong, and healthy Savannah wanted to cry. "A heartbeat!"

"Told you."

"Ooh! This is cool!"

For timeless magical moments, she listened in awe to their unborn child's rapidly beating heart. Her own aching heart felt free, buoyant. Music! Inside! God had blessed her! A gift! The baby moved, creating a strange double-time duet fluttering in her ears.

"Dang. It moved. I'm hearing an echo."

"Let me try." Taking the stethoscope from her ears, he listened again. *Tic-a-tic-a* "There. It's clear now. Just one." He started to return the earpiece to Savannah so she could hear their child, but beneath that area and to the right, he detected another distinct racing patter. He slid the bell, following the echo.

Maybe he heard it wrong. Checking the first spot, then the other, Riley dropped to his knees.

"Twins…?"

She nervously laughed. "A duet? Are you sure?"

"Positive." But he checked again, for good measure. Yes. Two. "You're having…" his voice caught, "my twins?"

"No you goofy man, I'm having Albert Einstein's babies."

"Well. Dang. How the hell did that happen?"

"Gee Doc; do you need an anatomy lesson?"

"I mean twins, Savage. Twins don't run in our families."

"Maybe God decided to whisper to my body twice."

"Twins." He repeated, astounded. "Your dad knew."

"Protect the innocent?"

"Yes. He said they were precious."

She thought about that for a second. "Maybe it happened the night we were watching shooting stars and made love on the roof."

Remembering that beautiful night made him smile. "Then wishes really do come true." Riley proudly proclaimed. "I love you, Savannah. This is a blessing. Those two heartbeats are more than music, they are our miracle."

***

Standing here in the sun-soaked wildflower meadow, surveying the world he loved, listening to Allegra and Donovan clamor to each other in their joyful four-year-old private twin language of constant jabber and curious exploration, Riley knew his life had come full circle.

Once, as an innocent young man infatuated with a pretty girl who was as untamable as these mountains and trickling streams, he trusted his heart and believed in love. He embraced love with all his soul. Then, when trouble came, he let sorrow and pride steal away his ability to love.

Now, he was submerged in love.

Sleeping against his chest, curled up in the soft denim baby-carrier that kept eight month old Amelia positioned against his heart. She looked just like her Momma. The cocoa-haired girl stuck her tiny fist into her rosebud shaped mouth and happily sighed. Beautiful. They'd been married for five years and Savannah made him a father three times.

Four, actually.

Ryan would live forever inside their hearts.

Music drifted from Graystone. The parking lot overflowed with parked cars. People from across the nation had come to hear her play. Piano rang out, triumphant and clear.

She was practicing one last time.

Soon, she would lock herself inside the soundproof recording studio on the second floor, surrounded by men and women whose job it was to preserve every note perfectly right, and Savannah Rosemont would give the world glorious new melodies.

Songs of love.

"Daddy?" a small girl's hand slid into his, "is that your song?"

"Sure is." He smiled down at the slightly dirty face with rosy pink cheeks and a pouty mouth currently stained purple from wild raspberries.

The twins weren't identical.

Different faces and bodies. Different character.

Allegra was buoyant, petite, and sweetly feminine with his moss-green eyes, but Donovan was tall for his age, already strong, but had deep violet-blue eyes that quietly studied life.

They both had his bronze-red hair.

"Momma wrote that song when you and Donovan were still angels living in heaven. Today she is finally giving 'Riley's Heart' to the world."

"But I like it." Small lips indignantly pursed. "Can't we keep it?"

Riley laughed at her innocence. "Always. We have Momma to play us her beautiful songs, whenever we want. But now other people can hear it too. When you have something beautiful, Allegra, you should share it. Momma's music makes other people happy too." Scanning the grassy knoll and missing someone, he asked, "Where's your brother?"

"O'ber 'dare." She pointed to a smattering of boulders near the tree line where a little boy was perched. Eyes closed, his head tossed back to gather sunlight on his face, he was listening. So thoughtful, he'd always been sensitive to the flow of life. At five, Donovan already played the piano, the flute, and of course the violin.

Allegra, on the other hand, loved to sing.

"Don'van says I talks too much." His twin complained, "He can't hear nothin' but my big mouth."

"It's because right now he's listening to the world, learning from the things he feels inside, and he doesn't want to miss this moment."

"Oh. Should I lis'n?"

"Yes. But listen with your heart, Allegra. Like Momma taught you." Closing green eyes, his sweet daughter tipped her head back and sighed. Watching them, Donovan quietly walked over and silently took his sister's hand.

So much love.

There would never be another right now.

Riley learned that from Savannah. There is only each moment, one at a time. We can embrace now or let those precious grains of time slip unappreciated through our hands until all we have left is a handful of regret.

Once, he was so fearful of getting hurt, he lost many years to stubborn aloneness. He pushed love away, too afraid to hold on. Yet equally afraid to let go.

But he made peace with the world.

Thanks to Savannah.

Riley knew one day he might lose his precious wife, but he accepted that fact too. This life wasn't the end or the beginning. This life was simply a small part of a glorious existence that he knew deep in his soul, went on forever. Ryan was still with them, yet he was also part of that forever. When Donovan and Allegra were born, the instant he saw their angelic faces, Riley finally understood God's lesson.

All we bring into this world is a soul yearning for love and the love we gathered along the way is the only thing we take with us in the end.

Love lasts forever. Love never dies.

So he loved. Fiercely, protectively, yet with an open hand instead of clinging tight with clenched fists that crushed the sweetness out of every moment without ever tasting one drop.

If God called Savannah's name, he would bury her body on Ryan's Hill where the first rays of morning kissed the earth with kindness and the last pink shimmers of fading Montana sunlight danced the longest.

She would do the same for him.

Every day he woke grateful. Life on the mountain was hard. But Riley knew he and Savannah would never be sad voices in the wind or ghosts with lost dreams. Their loving spirits would flourish. Even on hard days, he could just look at her and know forever wasn't long enough. Not for the great love he kept burning inside.

He told her, honestly. Every day.

So each moment became precious, not by counting seconds until the end, but by building upon something bit by bit until heaven's gate opened and let you in with a whole treasure chest of priceless life-diamond memories.

Gazing across the meadow, he saw Savannah standing on the top balcony, a silver-gray video recorder in her hand. She was filming them. Her family.

For there are no ordinary moments.

There are only precious feelings and memories we piece together one by one. We call it a lifetime.

One day, someone might need to see them standing there. They might need to remember this day, to heal or to maybe simply understand. Someday, someone Riley loved might need an ordinary moment to feel special; to glimpse a time that might have passed them by.

He raised his hand to his wife and slowly waved.

He couldn't see her face, not clearly, but he felt Savannah's bright smile kiss his cheeks, warming his heart as her love enlightened his soul.

"I hear music." Donovan quietly revealed, watching his mother disappeared inside the house again. "It's in the air and on the mou'tin. Hear it?"

But Savannah's music had stopped.

Piano notes no longer drifted on the breeze.

But Riley did hear the music. It was the sound of silence and forever. The music spoke of perfection bound for all time in the tops of the trees. It trickled like laughter down small streams making twittering soft melodies of hope and joy.

"I hear it. Do you like listening to our world, Donovan?"

"Yes. Listening makes me feel strong inside."

"You are strong. We all are. Because we love each moment."

Across green grass, her fingertips brushing against wild lavender, his private piece of heaven was walking toward her family. Her glossy chocolate colored hair was long again. It gleamed, drifting loose in the morning breeze. "Look. There's your Momma." A big shadow trotted beside her. "And Zeus."

The twins scrambled to meet her, jabbering both at once about music and their mountain and visiting Papa Rosemont tonight and a butterfly Allegra managed to watch for a whole five minutes without making a noise.

By the time she reached him, her face was flushed from laughing with her children. "I brought you something." Savannah held a sheet of paper in her hand. "I think it's perfect."

Holding the heavy photo stock paper she just printed, Riley smiled. There they were. Riley, Allegra, and Donovan; all holding hands with baby Amelia strapped to his broad chest. All stood with their eyes closed, the sun shining on their faces, lighting their bonze-red hair. All were smiling.

"I want that to be my CD cover."

"You want to use us? But we look so ordinary."

"No Riley, you look like you've opened your big Mountain Man heart and embraced something special. You look amazing." Tears glistened in her eyes. "I love it."

He looked at it again, finally seeing what Savannah did.

At first, he only saw his faded jeans with the worn spot in one knee, a baby's limp sleepy body dangling from the carrier strapped to his chest, and two dirty-faced mountain sprites holding hands.

But that wasn't what she captured.

She captured a proud father teaching his children to appreciate life. Donovan and Allegra looked like sweet angels. Their faces were serene and accepting, unafraid of embracing the moment, loving the simplicity of being together. A family. The great peaks of the mountains rose behind them like resilient blue guardians.

"But it's missing two people."

"Two?" She looked genuinely puzzled. "Who?"

"You." He leaned closer, sticking his nose beside her neck and inhaling that sweet familiar smell. Twice before he had savored that scent. This time he wouldn't miss a single minute. "And you're carrying my baby." He whispered. "Again."

"Oh!" She squealed. "Are you sure? Really?!"

"Positive. You only smell like wild strawberries when you're pregnant."

"But...it can't be more than..."

"Three days. You woke three days ago smelling like heaven."

"But I don't feel any different."

"You will."

"It's so soon. Amelia isn't even a year yet."

He did the math in his head. "They'll be about twenty months apart. This is the last one, Savage. Or ones." She giggled at his reference to the curious listening twins. "After this, we'll watch them all grow from babies to children, then into young men and women who make a difference in their corner of the world. You and I will grow old together, and walk these hills until God decides to take us. We'll have a houseful of noisy grandchildren. Someday, today will seem very special."

She beamed.

He'd come so far from the bitter man she'd married.

"If you're wrong, we should try anyway."

"I'm not wrong. But we can keep practicing."

She laughed and hugged him tight. She kissed each one of her children on their sweet faces and danced around, overflowing with joy.

She was his life. And his music. Savannah was his miracle.

Forever wasn't long enough.

But he would take it!

## About the Author

Leslie currently lives in Tucson, Arizona with her wonderful loving husband, her son who makes her extremely proud, three spoiled cats, and a bird who likes to watch TV. She also has a step-son and step-daughter who live nearby and their family was recently blessed with a beautiful smiling granddaughter.

Leslie moved frequently as a child and saw amazing places. She has lived in beautiful Oregon, wild Montana, chilly Minnesota, and several locations in Arizona. While married, she also lived in heavenly Monterey, California. Many of her books are fictional twists of real places she has visited.

She loves roses. Their house is surrounded by a hundred rose bushes; all highly fragrant and thriving, in colors ranging from buttery yellow, delicate pink, vibrant orange, rare purple, and of course deep red.

When she isn't writing the Destiny Whispers Collection, Leslie enjoys hiking in the mountains, exploring new places, and walking beside the sea. Her favorite beach is Silver Strand on Coronado Island, California. Her favorite mountain is Mt. Hood in Oregon, and her favorite city is Boston.

Leslie believes in the power of love. Love changes lives. People are not perfect. We make mistakes, choose unwisely, and we suffer the consequences. But real love picks us up when we are down, dusts us off, and set us on the right path again.

"I am grateful to be married to a wonderful man; my best friend. We do everything together. We love to travel and explore new places together. We share so many beautiful memories. Yet, even ordinary days feel special when spent with someone who knows you by heart. After 13+ years of marriage, we are closer now than I ever dreamed possible. Love is a gift that I truly cherish."

Leslie began writing the Destiny Whispers Collection of romantic adventures after developing the autoimmune disease, Lupus. Fortunately she is in remission now and lives a fairly normal life.

"Your health is a gift we often taken for granted. Every day I take handfuls of vitamins, faithfully take my prescriptions, and focus on staying positive and strong. Lupus was awful, so painful, mentally and physically debilitating. But as I gained control over the symptoms, I gained emotional clarity. I saw life differently. Lupus changed me as a person. I am a better woman today, because it made me stop and re-evaluate life. I discovered how strong my spirit can be. I learned humility and gratitude, appreciation for little joys, and learned that my attitude makes all the difference. I can make today beautiful, or awful. I choose to make this moment beautiful."

Join Leslie on facebook at www.Facebook.com/Destiny.Whispers
www.DestinyWhispers.com
www.RosesInWinter.com

Made in the USA
Charleston, SC
15 October 2011